T0196922

The SLY FOX of Penrith

The SLY FOX OF Penrith

Book 2 of the Penrith Series

J. A. Sperduti

iUniverse

THE SLY FOX OF PENRITH
BOOK 2 OF THE PENRITH SERIES

Certain characters in this work are historical figures, and certain events portrayed did take place. However, this is a work of fiction. All of the other characters, names, and events as well as all places, incidents, organizations, and dialogue in this novel are either the products of the author's imagination or are used fictitiously.

Author Credits: Joseph A. Sperduti

iUniverse books may be ordered through booksellers or by contacting:

iUniverse
1663 Liberty Drive
Bloomington, IN 47403
www.iuniverse.com
1-800-Authors (1-800-288-4677)

Because of the dynamic nature of the Internet, any web addresses or links contained in this book may have changed since publication and may no longer be valid. The views expressed in this work are solely those of the author and do not necessarily reflect the views of the publisher, and the publisher hereby disclaims any responsibility for them.

ISBN: 978-1-5320-8731-8 (sc)
ISBN: 978-1-5320-8730-1 (e)

Library of Congress Control Number: 2020910804

Print information available on the last page.

iUniverse rev. date: 06/09/2020

This work of fiction is dedicated to my beloved spouse, Soni.

My dear nephew John Peter for challenging the
author to write this work of fiction.

Robyn Trowbridge for her enthusiasm and wisdom.

Angela Deluca for her guidance and artistry.

About the Author

Born in Cornwall, New York in the early thirties, Joseph was the youngest of a brood of six. The family resided in a valley in The Forest of Dean by the Hudson River. The family relocated to Connecticut in the mid-thirties.

In his teens, he often sat listening to his brothers reminiscing of their days of happiness in the old homestead.

After serving in the military during the Korean War, he married. A bit later he, his bride and brothers revisited their beloved valley to find a Dam had been built across the valley creating a lake. Thus, the valley is at present under water and exists only in memory.

The many adventures experienced by his siblings in that enchanted valley were denied the author. Subsequently it remains one of many disappointments he has harbored over the years. He now lives out those adventures through Leland Thomas and the other characters in the town of Penrith.

Shall we continue following in the footsteps of Leland Thomas and will be present in Penrith as Princess Ashley becomes proficient with the bow 'neath the tutoring of the archer.

A grievous error results in a rift between Prince Frederick and the Princess Ashley creating much tribulation for Leland.

Lady Juliana's mischievous behavior becomes a concern for Princess Rebecca.

The relationship between Sir Cartwith and Whitney moves forward and becomes much more.

When traveling to Dumfries with the King and Prince Frederick for a fox hunt, prior to leaving Gretna Tom pleads with Bridget to relocate to Penrith.

Having grown up a commoner on the outskirts of the castle walls, Leland Thomas learned from this father to become an expert archer to feed the hungry villagers. Despite the king's warning that poaching carried a severe penalty, Leland continued in his quest for the hunt.

Because of his ability to avoid detection while in the king's forest, the villagers came to refer to him as The Sly Fox.

Leland's skill with the bow not only won him the king's tournament and thus the right to legally hunt in the king's forest., he also fell in love with a winsome lass who, unbeknownst to him, was the Princess Ashley.

Contents

About the Author vii
Prologue xv

Chapter 1 1
Chapter 2 8
Chapter 3 12
Chapter 4 15
Chapter 5 18
Chapter 6 21
Chapter 7 24
Chapter 8 29
Chapter 9 33
Chapter 10 36
Chapter 11 39
Chapter 12 42
Chapter 13 45
Chapter 14 48
Chapter 15 51
Chapter 16 54
Chapter 17 58
Chapter 18 62

Chapter 19 65

Chapter 20 70

Chapter 21 74

Chapter 22 80

Chapter 23 84

Chapter 24 88

Chapter 25 91

Chapter 26 94

Chapter 27 97

Chapter 28 101

Chapter 29 109

Chapter 30 113

Chapter 31 117

Chapter 32 120

Chapter 33 128

Chapter 34 132

Chapter 35 136

Chapter 36 140

Chapter 37 143

Chapter 38 148

Chapter 39 151

Chapter 40 155

Chapter 41 160

Chapter 42 166

Chapter 43 170

Chapter 44 175

Chapter 45 178

Chapter 46 182

Chapter 47 186

Chapter 48 191

Chapter 49 197

Chapter 50 201

Chapter 51 205

Chapter 52 209

Chapter 53 213

Chapter 54 216

Chapter 55 220
Chapter 56.. 224
Chapter 57 229
Chapter 58 233
Chapter 59 238
Chapter 60 244
Chapter 61 247
Chapter 62 251
Chapter 63 254
Chapter 64 258
Chapter 65 262
Chapter 66.. 266
Chapter 67 270
Chapter 68.. 273
Chapter 69 276
Chapter 70 279
Chapter 71 285
Chapter 72 288
Chapter 73 292
Chapter 74 295
Chapter 75 301
Chapter 76 310
Chapter 77 314
Chapter 78 318
Chapter 79 323
Chapter 80 327
Chapter 81 331
Chapter 82 339
Chapter 83 344
Chapter 84 348
Chapter 85 351
Chapter 86..355

Prologue

Prince Frederick, an avid hunter, when in the forest came upon two bucks battling over a doe. Slaying the younger, the other charged him. A village poacher, concealed on a stand he had built in a willow, let fly an arrow slaying the charging buck, sparing the prince from certain death.

King Frederick, upon hearing of his son's encounter with the stag, wished to reward the mysterious archer. The many attempts made to identify the archer failed. Two clues were found linked to him. The arrow, which had slain the charging buck, and another found at the site at the edge of the forest where, after capturing a horse thief, the archer had left him bound to a birch. Both arrows bore feathers plucked from ravens. Aware raven feathers were rarely used for fletchings, the king planned a tournament inviting archers throughout the realm to participate; hoping the mysterious archer would compete. Sir Milford with his page Bryce, were to man the targets watching for arrows launched by the bowmen bearing raven fletchings. The plan succeeded. The man they sought had been identified and went on to win the tournament.

Sir Milford left his post at the targets and went to escort the handsome bowman to kneel before the king. When the king asked his name and where he laid his head, the archer replied, "Your Majesty, be named Leland. Reside 'neath the stars; the forest floor be me bed."

The king extended his hand holding the purse of gold to the archer for emerging victorious.

The archer spoke, "Your Highness, hath no need of gold. Request permission to hunt the King's forest in' it's stead."

The king was puzzled by the response yet did not hesitate to afford the archer the freedom of the woodland.

At dinner that evening, a discussion ensued as to what was known of the archer at that moment. Other than the man's name, skill with the bow and his willingness to intervene in a moment of crisis, his history and character remained a mystery yet to be brought to light.

Determined to learn more of this man, the prince dressed as a peasant hunting the forest wishing to encounter the archer with the intention of engaging him in conversation and eventually establishing a relationship. Aware of Leland's ability to avoid detection, he purposely failed at every opportunity presented him to make a kill; praying the archer was present to observe his ineptness at the hunt.

From his stand in the willow, Leland had laid eyes on the man he deemed to be a poacher and thought to afford him a word of caution. The next morning Leland stood on the deer run, with bow at the ready, waiting for the poacher to appear.

When the prince, ambling along the path, came upon the archer, he stood startled; unable to speak. Leland greeted him kindly, and so began their relationship. However, neither revealed much of themselves to the other.

In the days to follow, as they hunted together, Leland afforded the prince a bit of tutoring.

At dinner, on the days they hunted together, the prince would speak of the archer. The day of the tournament, Princess Ashley had briefly laid eyes on the archer from high above the courtyard and felt an odd stirring within. Upon hearing the prince speak glowingly of the archer, she felt a return of that feeling. The more she heard, the greater her desire grew to meet this handsome man of mystery.

Weeks passed; finally, she vented her frustrations to the queen. Her Mother advised her to be patient for one day the opportunity would present itself.

Sometime later, Earl William of Dumfries with his wife Countess Sarah and daughter Rebecca, when on a trek to brother Oliver's manor in Leeds, sought shelter at the castle of King Frederick in Penrith. Prince Frederick, laying eyes upon the maiden, immediately became mesmerized by her beauty.

The earl planned to remain in Penrith for a short stay then continue with his party on his journey, expecting to return to the palace in two weeks.

In a conversation with the king, the earl stated he intended to exile his brother to the Americas for his treachery and expected resistance.

The king, aware Earl William had come accompanied by Sir Cadwalter and only six cavalrymen, expressed concern. Might Oliver be prepared to engage the earl in a battle, and the number of men in service to Oliver be not known, the Earl might be outnumbered and fail in his mission. Thus, the king volunteered Sir Cartwith and six of his own cavalrymen to accompany the Earl and the Countess and suggested his commander, Sir Milford, be consulted for a plan of strategy which would insure a favorable outcome.

Speaking with the earl, Sir Milford recommended upon nearing Leeds that Countess Sarah be left to wait out of harm's way in a nearby village.

Princess Ashley and cousin Lady Victoria, aware of the attraction the prince had for Lady Rebecca, pleaded with the earl to permit his daughter to remain at the palace and await his return. The earl agreed. In the absence of the earl and countess, the prince and Lady Rebecca became smitten with each other.

Having succeeded in exiling brother Oliver to the Americas, Earl William needed a few days to address matters relating to ensuring the estate would be maintained; what was to be done with it was yet in question.

Meanwhile, the countess waited for a report on the outcome of the mission. Had it been a success, she would then join her husband. Sir Cartwith volunteered to perform the task. He would then return to Penrith and report to Sir Milford the outcome of the mission. Riding with a horse in tow to expedite his trek to Penrith, Sir Cartwith arrived at the lodging of the countess and passed the entire morning engaged in conversation with her resulting in a friendly relationship.

Continuing on his ride until late-afternoon, he stopped at a pub for a tankard of ale. Sitting at a table outdoors the knight noticed a woman watching a group of children frolicking beside the pub.

The door to the pub opened, the proprietor stepped out and shouted for the children to disperse. The knight told the man to leave them be and instructed him to prepare a platter of fish and tea for the tots. The woman, a bit surprised, came to his table, greeted him, and thanked him for his intervention and generosity. He invited her to join him in a pint. She graciously accepted and as they spoke, he learned one of the children was her daughter, Tiffany, and she to be Whitney; widowed two years past and residing in the hamlet Skeeby nearby. They chatted until the light began to fade, the children finished their meal and Tiffany came to the table. The knight then volunteered to escort them home stating he was riding in their direction. She accepted.

Sir Cartwith aided Whitney onto the spare horse then took Tiffany in his arms and mounted the other. Riding along, Whitney spoke of being a seamstress and with the population of Skeeby being sparse, she could barely sustain herself and the child at her craft. The knight suggested her relocating and offered to speak with Eleanor of a position for her at the millinery in Penrith. He pledged to return to Skeeby for her decision.

The return of Earl William, Countess Sarah and the cavalry without incident was a joyful moment for Lady Rebecca. She was then saddened, aware they would be leaving Penrith; thus, perhaps the end of her relationship with the prince.

Arriving in Dumfries, Lady Rebecca shared her concern and her feelings for the prince with her mother who spoke sympathetically.

"Rebecca, must ye not despair, might the prince share thy feelings wilt he not forsake thee."

For weeks, other than the hours he passed with Leland at the hunt, the prince went about beneath a cloud of darkness; discontented and ill-tempered. The reason for his melancholia became obvious to the queen. Summoning the prince to her chambers, she handed him a jade ring and advised him to follow his heart. Upon the prince leaving, the queen instructed Lady Winfried, her lady-in-waiting, to fetch the princess.

At the celebration held in honor of Earl William and the countess upon their arrival, she had danced and engaged in conversation with the Marquess of Edenhall. Her ladyship would one day rue her involvement with his lordship. The marquess, a womanizer, had been courting the princess attempting to win her hand. She afforded the lout no encouragement, yet he persisted.

Upon speaking with Princess Ashley, the queen informed her of the prince's intention to visit Lady Rebecca; affording her the opportunity to acquaint herself with Leland. Leaving the room, the princess hurried to seek the counsel of Lady Victoria. Knowing the archer not to be a fool, they deemed it wise not to attempt a meeting with him as a princess. Aware of the debt owed the king for his leniency when dealing with Jarin, the widow Tate's son, they decided the best approach was for the princess, escorted by Sir Milford, to ride to the Tate cottage and request the loan of Jarin's sister Arabella's garments, then go to the forest garbed as a village maiden.

At the dinner table that evening, the prince requested permission of his father to ride to Dumfries at sunrise. The king granted his approval then ordered Sir Milford to assign four cavalrymen to escort him. At meal's end, the prince hurried to his chambers in the tower and called to Tom. From his room above the man servant came scrambling down the stone steps, bowed and stood waiting for instructions. The prince informed him he was to accompany him to Scotland and to prepare for the journey.

Well before sunrise, Tom dressed and went about setting out garments for the prince to wear. His clamoring awakened his master. The prince instructed him to go to the kitchen and have his mother, the cook, prepare a bit of breakfast for them. Tom bowed, left the room, and went to do his bidding.

Mildred was alone in the kitchen filling the caldrons over the fire with water when Tom entered. He greeted her, then asked her to prepare a bite for the prince and himself. She replied: "Good morn. Thomas, heed well, must ye be on thy best behavior when with the prince; lest ye be an embarrassment to him."

"Mother, be not concerned; hath been well tutored at me task. Christy be not yet about? Shalt she be missed."

"Aye, Tom; be she yet a 'bed."

The sentry at the castle gate, seeing the cavalrymen waiting at the palace entrance with their mounts, lowered the drawbridge.

Having finished breakfast, the prince and Tom stood from the table. Tom went to kiss his mother and bade her farewell. She curtsied to the prince and wished them a safe journey as they left the kitchen to join the cavalrymen in the courtyard. The group mounted their steeds, rode over the drawbridge, down the hillside and took the road north.

Riding into Gretna in late afternoon, they came upon a small inn. The prince, thinking to call it a day, entered to seek lodging for the night. The proprietor greeted him. Upon seeing six in his party, he apologized, stating there were only two vacant rooms above. However, might they be acceptable, there was a bed in a small room over the stables and a cot in the tack room. The Prince told the gent the accommodations were acceptable. The prince thanked him then returned to the men waiting in the courtyard. The prince instructed the men to stable the horses and two of the cavalrymen were to stow their gear in the room above the dining hall, the other two were to make their bed in the room above the stables. Tom was to occupy the tack room.

That evening, the men sat at a table together to dine. A comely young maiden came to serve them, introducing herself as Bridget. Over the course of the meal, the men noticed her displaying an interest in Tom. Subsequently, he became the target of their foppery.

After eating and drinking their fill, the men thought to retire. Tom followed the prince to his room to aid in preparing him for bed. Leaving the prince, Tom took the stairs to the floor below, walked through the dining hall and out of the inn. He found Bridget standing in the courtyard. As he approached, she asked his name and what he intended to do for the remainder of the evening. He introduced himself and asked what she had in mind. Taking his hand, and at a run, she led him out of the courtyard, over a rutted road down into a glen where a host of villagers were singing and dancing to music being played by an old gent on bagpipes. Much later, returning to the inn, he bade her a good night in the courtyard. Chuckling, she followed him into the tack room.

Meanwhile at the palace, after dinner, Princess Ashley spoke with Sir Milford of her intentions to enter the forest in an attempt to meet the archer. She then requested he accompany her to the Tate's cottage, then to the forest early the next morning. The knight assured her he would make himself available to her.

After breakfast, the next morning in Gretna, the men went to saddle the horses, led them into the courtyard and stood waiting for the prince to compensate the proprietor. He then joined them in the courtyard. They mounted and rode off. Bridget stood in the doorway of the inn, waving as they turned their steeds north.

The melancholy mood Lady Rebecca had been in since leaving Penrith vanished with the arrival of the prince. Soon after, Lord Gaelan, brother to the earl, arrived with his three children. He had come to address matters of the estate with Earl William; thus, would stay the night. The eldest of the children, Lady Juliana, the same in age as Lady Rebecca, was known to be spirited and brazen.

Later that evening, Lady Rebecca took the prince aside to alert him of cousin's promiscuity and not to be surprised if she entered his chambers in the dead of night for a bit of foppery. The prince, fearing an unforgiving incident, remained silent for several minutes. He related the ruse he had in mind to Lady Rebecca.

Donald, one of his men with similar physical characteristics as himself, would be asked to pass the night in the room of the prince and the prince would sleep with his men. Might Lady Juliana dare enter the darkened room, she would not be aware she was getting in bed with one of the cavalrymen.

Back in Penrith, early the next morning, the Princess and Sir Milford rode to the Tate's. The princess requested the loan of Arabella's garments. Arabella, pleased to be of service, aided the princess with her change of clothing.

Leaving the cottage, they then took the road to Clifton, tethered the horses, and entered the forest. Finding a berry bush beside the deer run, she began gathering berries into her apron. Sir Milford took a position behind a huge oak, well within sight of the princess.

Leland, sitting on the stand in the willow, heard the rustle in the brushes and descended from his perch onto the forest floor. Bow at the ready and treading gingerly, the archer followed the sound around a bend on the deer run to find a young maiden plucking berries. Speaking harshly, he reprimanded her for entering the forest alone and with no weapon for protection. Unaccustomed to being spoken to in such a manner, the princess turned on her heels and scrambled out of the forest. Sir Milford waited for Leland to walk out of sight before following her.

Returning to the palace, she related the incident to her mother. Attempting to console her, the queen told her not to despair for the archer's words were uttered out of concern for her safety, which spoke well of his character. Fortified by her mother's words, she resolved to attempt another meeting with the archer. She expressed a desire to be at the Tate's at sunrise the next morning and in the forest before Leland.

Hints of sunrise penetrated the woodland the next morning as she and the knight rode to the Tate's then to the forest. They followed the deer run to a stand of pine; unbeknown to her, to be from where the stag had sprung to charge brother Frederick. She stood hidden behind the pine, patiently in wait of Leland. Sir Milford was concealed, well in sight of the princess.

Leland, entering the forest from the hillside, walked along the deer run. He was about to trudge through the underbrush to the willow when movement caught his eye. Raising his bow, he prepared to launch his arrow. The princess ran out from behind the stand of pine pleading with him to be merciful. Leland lowered his bow and spoke to her in anger.

"Woman, must ye be a bit demented! Be ye not aware there be rascals and bandits about these woodlands to lay hands upon thee and leave thee severely injured?"

Tears fell to her cheeks. Moved by her tears, he repentantly continued speaking.

"Must ye persist in placing thyself in harm's way, best ye be prepared to defend thyself. Might it please thee shalt begin tutoring thee a bit in the use of the bow."

And so, began the relationship between Princess Ashley and Leland which in time was to become something more.

Prior to leaving Dumfries, the prince presented Lady Rebecca the ring given him by the queen. The significance of the presentation alerted the earl and countess of the feelings the prince bore for their daughter. In a conversation, they strategized on how they were to proceed.

Annually, in the autumn, the earl held a fox hunt; a gala affair lasting for days. It offered a perfect opportunity to extend an invitation to His Majesty and the prince.

Upon their trek to Penrith, the prince and escorts once again sought lodging in Gretna at the inn to the delight of Tom and Bridget.

The travelers arrived at the palace late in the afternoon the next day. At dinner, the prince recounted the highlights of his visit to the others at the table. Princess Ashley informed the prince of her meeting Leland and her being tutored in the use of the bow. The prince expressed delight at the prospect of them one day hunting together.

Sir Cartwith had not been to visit Whitney and Tiffany for more than a week. Whitney wondered perhaps he had lost interest in them or that some ill might had befallen the knight.

Chapter 1

At sunset King Frederick, Prince Frederick, Sir Cartwith, Tom, and their escort had returned to the castle in Penrith from a fox hunt in Scotland. Although quite entertaining, it was not the highlight of the visit, as prior to leaving Dumfries, the King and Earl William had arranged for the prince and Lady Rebecca to be wed.

Arriving in Penrith with the news of the prince soon to marry Lady Rebecca, was indeed a reason for the royal family to celebrate.

The return of the prince created a problem for Princess Ashley. She was being tutored by Leland, the archer who had spared the prince from certain demise by a charging stag.

Recalling Princess Ashley's reluctance to even lay eyes upon the handsome gent, the day of the archery tournament and only a for a few minutes at her brother's insistence, one would never expect the princess to be so eager to be with Leland.

Yet after the prince had befriend the man and heard the prince speak highly of the archer. Leland became a person of interest to the princess.

Driven by curiosity, she then plotted to seemingly encounter Leland by accident in the forest. Not as a princess but dressed as a village maiden. To that end, prior to entering the forest, accompanied by Sir Milford, the commander of her father's forces, she rode to the Tate's cottage and change into the maiden Arabella's garments.

Thus, the princess, thinking the prince might want to hunt with Leland the day after returning to Penrith, planned to leave the palace before breakfast the next morning, escorted by Sir Milford. As with every other meeting with Leland, she would ride to the Tate's cottage for a change of garments to those of a peasant. She would, then ride with Sir Milford to the forest to be given lessons in archery by Leland, who thought her to be a village maiden.

The prince, entering the dining hall for breakfast the next morning, noted the absence of the princess and Sir Milford. He inquired of his mother where they might be.

The queen replied, "Frederick, in thyne absence, Ashley befriended Leland, and hath been preparing to be tutored by the archer in the use of the bow."

The queen's reply gave the prince cause to chuckle, recalling the day of the archery tournament when he had to plead with the princess to accompany him to a viewing point above the palace entrance to lay eyes upon the archer.

After breakfast, the prince thought to stroll about the courtyard. As he stepped out of the palace, Sir Cartwith, upon his steed with another in tow, greeted him.

He said, "Good morn, Prince Frederick."

"G' day, Sir Cartwith where be ye bound?" asked the prince.

The knight replied, "Be off to the village upon an errand."

He waved to the prince as he passed and rode out of the castle grounds.

More than a week had passed since Sir Cartwith had gone to the village for the boots he had commissioned the cobbler to make for Whitney and Tiffany. He had been quite busy these past days.

It was a beautiful Sunday morning. Sir Cartwith thought to take Whitney and Tiffany for a ride to Clifton. Fetching Sweet Sorrow and a gentle mare for Whitney from the stables, he fastened the boots to his saddle and set out for the village. He first stopped at the smithy's to fetch the pony he had gotten for Tiffany. She knew nothing yet of the pony in wait of her in the smithy's stable.

Sir Cartwith found Howard sitting in front of his shop whittling on a piece of wood. Seeing the knight approach, he set his whittling aside, and rose to greet him.

"G' day, Sir Cartwith, what be ye about this fine Sabbath morn?" Howard asked.

Sir Cartwith replied, "Good morn, Howard. Come by to fetch the wee horse for the little one. Thought to take the lady and the child for a ride."

Sir Cartwith tethered the two horses to the hitching post in front of the smithy's shop; then they walked to the stables for the pony. Howard saddled the pony then led it across the road, tethering it to the hitching post in front of the millinery. The knight followed with the two steeds.

Howard then spoke to the knight saying, "Me thinks the lass shall be quite surprised on seeing the beast. Upon returning, need but tether the wee horse to me hitching post, it will be stabled for thee. Hath ye all a good romp this day. Farewell, Sir Cartwith."

Sir Cartwith took the stairs at the rear of the millinery to the flat above. His tapping on the door was answered by Eleanor. She greeted the knight then bade him enter. Tiffany, standing in the kitchen, ran to leap into his arms. Eleanor stood grinning at the tot's reaction.

Eleanor then addressed the knight saying, "Sir Cartwith, thought haps we hath been forgotten. Hath it been neer a fortnight since last ye come to visit."

He replied, "G' day Eleanor. Good morn, dear Tiffany. Be ye missed. Thought we might romp about a horse this fine day."

Whitney was busy tidying up her room when the knight entered. Hearing his voice, she came to the kitchen. She stood with her arms entwined across her breasts. By the look on her face, he was certain she was not pleased with him at the moment. He would have to choose his words well to appease her.

Whitney said, "Good morn, Sir Knight; hath been concerned by thy absence. No word be heard of thee these days past; thought haps ye hath been ailing."

He replied, "G' day Whitney, nay be in good stead. Haps be ye a bit ired with me at the moment, and for good reason. 'Tis not for lack of interest hath me not been about. Hath been a bit occupied of late; beg thy forgiveness. Hath come to make amends. Might a romp to Clifton for a bite at the pub, then a time beside the River Lowther, aid in thy appeasement?"

Sir Cartwith crossed the kitchen to the lady, stood silent for a moment looking at her and smiled, then whispered, "Whitney, ye must not be cross with me. Know I love thee as no other. Come, hath fetched the wee horse from the stables for Tiffany. Be he tethered below with Sweet Sorrow, and a mare for thee."

The knight stepped away from the lady. Tears fell to her cheeks. She uncrossed her arms from her breasts, pulled the knight to her, and kissed him. Eleanor and the tot clapped in approval.

Whitney took a moment to compose herself then said, "Tiffany, accompany Sir Cartwith to the road below. Must don me garments for the ride. Shall me be a bit."

A few minutes passed. Tiffany came running into the flat all excited. She ran through the kitchen shouting, "Eleanor, Mother, come see out the portal. Sir Cartwith hath procured a wee horse and boots for me, and boots for Mother as well. Ye must make haste, Mother, for Sir Cartwith doth await."

Eleanor chuckled, and said, "Patience little one, hath me fashioned a comely attire for thee. Mother hath fashioned the like for herself. Must shed thy frock then don the new garments."

Tiffany turned from the window wondering what was wrong with the dress she was wearing. She looked to see if she had unknowingly soiled her clothes.

She asked, "Eleanor, why must me shed me frock for another? These hath donned but this morn, be they not begrimed."

"'Tis so, however when ye hath lain eyes upon thy wee steed, hath ye not noted the saddle upon the beast be for a lad? Art ye to ride about with undergarments in full view? 'Tis unbecoming a lady. Go ye now, Mother awaits," Eleanor replied.

Tiffany went to her mother's room carrying the two pair of boots Sir Cartwith had given her. Laid out on the bed were two blouses, and riding breeches fashioned the same as those fabricated for the princess, and the two ladies. In her excitement, she emitted a screech so loud it was heard by the knight waiting at the hitching post. He chuckled, knowing quite well what was taking place in the flat above.

Some minutes passed. Whitney and Tiffany came from behind the millinery into sight of the knight.

Sir Cartwith stood mesmerized by the beauty of the lady, and the child walking beside her in their new riding attire.

Sir Cartwith first lifted Tiffany onto her pony leaving it tethered to the hitching post, then helped Whitney mount the mare. Loosening the pony, then Sweet Sorrow, he mounted his steed, holding the reins to his, and those of the pony firmly in his hand.

Sir Cartwith said, "Hold fast to thy saddle, little one. Would not do for thee to be thrown. Until thy steed hath become familiar with thee, and ye with thy mount, shall guide thee."

Eleanor waved from the open window of the flat above the millinery as the three rode off at a leisurely pace toward Clifton. Tiffany rode proudly on her new mount, yet a bit unsteady.

Whitney thought to distract the child with a question.

She asked, "Tiffany, thy mount is to be given a name. 'Tis for thee to do so. What might ye deem a proper title for the wee steed?"

"Mother, hath not yet given it a thought. Shall me ponder on it a bit for must it be a title befitting the wee horse," the child replied.

They rode along for quite a while, Whitney enjoying the beauty of the surroundings, and discussing it with Sir Cartwith. As they rode, he pointing out places of interest to her.

Tiffany, oblivious of her surroundings, was deep in thought.

Whitney and the knight looked at the pensive child then at each other, smiling.

Tiffany finally spoke. She said, "Shall he be dubbed Cupid for this day hath he launched an arrow into Sir Cartwith's heart; affording him the courage to declare his love for thee. Another into thyne, Mother, for hath ye expressed thy love for him with a kiss. Hath Cupid launched yet another into mine, for hath come to love Sir Cartwith dearly, for this reason. 'Twas by his counsel came we to Penrith, leaving the drudgery of the hamlet Skeeby behind. Hold him dear for that, and for his kindness. Indeed, shall me steed bear the name Cupid. 'Tis fitting!"

"Well done, Tiffany. Cupid doth be a proper title for the beast. 'Tis certain Sir Cartwith will agree," said her mother.

They stopped for a bite at a pub beside Emont Bridge before continuing to the River Lowther.

At the river, the knight lifted Tiffany from Cupid, then helped Whitney off the mare. He tethered Sweet Sorrow and the mare to a birch beside the river; then handed the reins of the pony to the child telling her to lead him to the river for a drink of water, then to walk him about, pausing to permit him to graze a bit.

The child went off with the pony. The knight sat with Whitney beside the river chatting. Whitney removed her boots, put her feet into the cool flowing water.

Whitney said, "Richard, this day past, the prince came to the millinery. Know ye, he hath been on holiday to Scotland. When at the estate of the earl, the prince stated the countess requested the pattern for the riding attire. How come she to know of thee, me, and Tiffany as well?"

He replied "Oh, Countess Sarah, know her well. Hath me met Lady Rebecca, daughter to the countess. Be she one of the ladies come to the millinery with the princess. Lady Rebecca must hath worn the attire on a ride in Dumfries. Admired by the countess; she desired the like for herself. Be we known to the countess for spoke with the lady when upon me trek to Leeds."

She said, "By this ye say, would seem the prince intends to return to Dumfries, and for what purpose? Surely not solely to deliver the pattern to the countess. Something be a 'foot."

Whitney paused a moment then said, "Upon another matter. When Tiffany spoke of the reason for naming the wee steed Cupid, the child's words opened me eyes. 'Twas then come to discover the depth of me love for thee. Be ye the most kind, gentle, and caring gent known to me. Hath ye rescued me, and the little one from a life of poverty, in a wee hamlet, to be fetched to the beautiful village of Penrith."

Sir Cartwith remained silent for a minute, mustering his courage. He, then said; "Whitney, me time in service to the king shall expire in but a year. Hath thought to then return to Lancaster for Father will soon be in need of aid about the estate. The manor rests upon a goody portion of land; a most delightful place of residence. Might it please thee, shall pen a note to Father of me intentions to visit him with thee and the child in early spring, and of wedding thee. Might he desire for the ceremony to be performed at the estate in Lancaster, with me kin in presence. What say ye, Whitney; will ye grant me thy hand in marriage?"

"Richard, ye honor me, would me wed no other, yet be a bit concerned. Might not thy sire frown upon a union 'tween thee and a widowed woman with a wee one? Wish not to be the cause of discontentment within thy family," she replied.

"Fret ye not, for upon knowing thee, me sire will embrace thee. As to Tiffany, Father and Mother will find her to be a true delight," said the knight.

Whitney reached for him, hugged, then kissed him. In jest she then whispered, "Sir Knight, am I to wait unto then for thee to bed me?"

"Woman beware, should ye continue to tempt me with thy words, might me ravage thee this very moment," he replied.

They both began to laugh. Tiffany came, still holding the reins of her pony. She asked what they had found so amusing.

The child's question caused them to laugh all the harder. Tiffany, not getting a reply, shook her head without speaking, and walked away.

Chapter 2

Sunday passed. Tom had not yet been given a reply to asking his mother to speak with Lady Verna on Bridget's behalf. He prayed the cavalrymen had not spoken of his tryst with the maiden to their peers. He feared, should it reach Mildred's ears she might not be pleased with him.

The night before, he had laid out the garments the prince was to wear that morning. He waited for the prince to leave his quarters before going to tidy up the chambers. He completed his chores, then thought to stroll about the courtyard. Had his nights in Gretna with Bridget been revealed by the cavalrymen, he would surely hear of it.

Tom took the three flights of stone stairs to the main floor of the palace. Passing the kitchen, his mother called, then came out to him and said, "Thomas, hath ye not eaten? Shall fetch thee a bite. Oh, Martin wishes a word with thee. Come ye now to the kitchen. Eat, then go speak with the man," said his mother.

It was apparent to Tom his mother had not yet heard of his brief affair with Bridget. Might she had known she would not have spoken so kindly to him.

He replied, "Mother be ye at present occupied preparing the morning meal. The kitchen be in turmoil. Will go speak with Martin, then return for a bite."

Tom left his mother and walked over to the butchery. Martin was standing at a chopping block, cutting into a hind quarter of beef. Seeing Tom enter, he set his cleaver aside, went to wash his hands in a basin of water, and dried them with his apron before speaking.

The butcher said, "G' day Thomas; come set, we will speak. Thy mother hath revealed to me the events of this Saturday morn past; 'twas not our intent for our involvement to be discovered by thee in such a manner. For this me beg thy forgiveness. Yet assure thee me intentions toward the lady be quite honorable. Be thee in any manner opposed to our courtship, ye must now speak of it."

Tom replied, "Martin, hath known thee for many years. Nary an ill word hath heard of thee. Mother hath labored hard since me sire's passing, rearing Christy, and me; 'tis certain 'twas not with ease. Be she deserving of a bit of happiness."

Martin said, "Hath been alone since the passing of me mate many years as well. Thy mother hath aided in relieving me loneliness. Thus Thomas, by thy words art me to expect hath ye no objection to me asking for thy mother's hand in marriage?"

"Nay sir, and with me blessing," replied Tom.

The two came to their feet, Martin extended his hand, taking Tom's in his, and then hugged the lad. They bade each other farewell. Tom left to stroll a bit in the courtyard. Not hearing any derogatory remarks from anyone of his involvement with Bridget, he returned to the kitchen for a bit of breakfast.

Mildred, not wanting to share the family's business with the kitchen help, kissed him on the forehead, then whispered; "Thomas, would seem all went well with Martin. We will speak of thy visit with the gent a bit later this night. Come ye, set for a bite."

Learning of Martin's intentions to wed his mother could not have come at a better time, for it presented an unexpected opportunity. Yes, Tom was sincerely happy for his mother, knowing she would have a caring companion in her remaining years. Yet there was a selfish reason for Tom to be elated at the news. Should he succeed in securing a position for Bridget on the palace staff, his mother's bed would be available. Bridget could then share the room with Christy. Might Mildred not wish to speak to Lady Verna on the matter, Tom would then need to speak to Prince Frederick.

Tom waited for the evening chores in the kitchen to be completed before going to speak with his mother. There were still a few stragglers puttering about when he entered. He sat silent at the table waiting for them to leave.

Mildred also waited for the kitchen to be vacated before making two cups of tea, then sat with her son.

Tom was the first to speak. He said, "Mother, hath gone to visit Martin earlier. Be he quite sincere, addressed me as one would a man. Spoke of his intentions to request thy hand in marriage. He then expressed concern for haps might me be harboring some opposition to thy union; requesting me to voice any objection might bear me in mind."

She replied, "Thomas, hath me like concerns as well. Martin may never be more than a butcher. Yet find him a comfort to me. However, 'tis not me intent to cast thee and Christy aside for the want of a man. Hath ye voiced a valid objection to Martin for this union not to proceed, shall reject the man's proposal."

"Mother, ye hath sacrificed much in these years past to rear we children. Be ye deserving of a bit of joy. To Martin's disclosure of his intent to request thy hand, hath given the gent me blessing. We shall speak to Christy together come morn. Be she in her early years yet will be made to understand thy desire to wed. 'Tis certain will she be happy for thee as well," said Tom.

Continuing, he said, "On another matter Mother, me request for thee to speak to Lady Verna on the maiden Bridget's behalf. Hath ye given the matter some thought?"

His mother replied, "Aye Thomas, shall speak with the lady by week's end then render to thee her reply. Thy interest in the lass be a bit of concern too, however. Bear in mind, be ye in a position to one day be manservant to a king. Know not the reason for thee to desire the lass near to thee. Ere it be, honorable or no, ye must tread lightly. If thy actions with the lass be of a sordid nature, ye might place thy position with Prince Frederick in danger."

"'Tis understood, Mother. Bridget and her proficiency in service be known to the prince. He hath met and been served by the lass when in

Gretna at the inn. Upon receiving Lady Verna's reply, shall me speak to the prince of this to be certain he will not object to it," he said.

Mildred replied, "Ye hath pondered well on this matter, Thomas. Pray be ye mindful as well upon thy behavior with the lass should she be fetched to Penrith. Go ye now lad, 'tis certain hath ye many chores yet to be done."

Chapter 3

That same morning King Frederick, the queen, and Prince Frederick sat at the table in the dining hall for breakfast. The prince asked why the princess and Sir Milford were absent.

The queen said, "Frederick, early this morn Ashley, escorted by Milford, went to the forest to be tutored by the archer. Other than her attraction for the man, would seem she be quite intent upon mastering the use of the bow. The other day, I entered Ashley's chambers to find her smiting a basin of water with her hands. What might that be about?"

"Mother, 'tis an exercise used to lend strength to the arms and shoulders. 'Tis needed to launch an arrow with force. Must say, Leland hath the patience of Job; foregoing the hunt to pass his days tutoring a village maiden," the prince replied.

The queen said, "Would seem the man be as a gem bearing many facets. Need they but to be properly revealed to be of great value. Haps too, Ashley may hath become a lady of interest to the archer. One be left to wonder what is to become of all of this."

The king said, "Margaret, tend to agree. The man be endowed with many fine qualities, some yet to be discovered. Haps he be not well read, yet a man to be admired. Hath proven his worth upon more than one occasion."

He paused, then continued saying, "These many hours being tutored by Leland may well be a benefit to Ashley. Milford hath spoken little of it. Yet from what he hath observed, he stated the experience will add a bit of grit to the lass as well as a bit of humility. Be she in need of a bit of both for be no longer a child to be pampered."

The prince said, "Father, hath found Leland to be quite severe in his tutoring. Must grant Ashley credit for enduring Leland's stern tutoring these past few days. Should she persevere, 'tis certain she will be the better for it."

Meanwhile, in the forest, the princess was still at her exercise, and Leland sitting with his back to the oak, whittled on a piece of wood. The princess stopped for a few minutes to rest.

She turned to him, and said, "Mercy Leland, must me pass the entire day with thee in this mundane activity? Might me not in the least be tutored a bit in the use of the bow?"

"Patience Ashley, 'tis not for naught be ye subjected to this exercise. Come, leave me lay hands upon thy palms," he replied.

The princess scrambled to her feet and went to sit cross legged before the archer. Leland took her hands in his for a moment then let her loose; asking her to bend her elbow and make a fist.

He felt her muscle, and said, "Hath ye done well, Ashley. Suspect ye hath performed this exercise when not in me presence for be ye not in need of much more. Might ye heed me words, there will soon be ye a time at the river, and a time at the proper use of the bow."

The princess, elated, had all she could do to restrain herself from throwing her arms around the archer. She stood a 'right, then returned to the river, hitting the water with more vigor than before. Leland shook his head smiling; a bit surprised at how much he had pleased her with but a bit of encouragement.

Sir Milford, standing behind the large oak, could not hear the conversation between the two, yet seeing the jubilance expressed by the princess, smiled knowingly.

Later, upon returning to the palace, the princess went directly to speak with her mother. She tapped on her mother's chamber door, then entered without waiting for permission to enter. The queen was startled by the hasty entrance of her daughter.

She said, "Mercy Ashley, such haste! Hath something gone awry?"

"Nay Mother. Moments past, hath returned from the forest. Be told by Leland, two days hence he shall begin tutoring me in the proper use of the bow," replied the princess.

The queen said, "Ashley, me think before ye hath mastered the weaponry, Leland will hath taught ye much more than but the use of the bow. Must say, thy perseverance in this activity is to be commended. Go ye now, thy garments be completely disheveled; thy hands, thy cheeks be mudded. Be ye in dire need of a bath."

The princess ran from the room. The queen stood in the center of her room, chuckling to herself.

Chapter 4

During the Wednesday morning breakfast, Prince Frederick asked the princess if she was going to the forest that morning.

The princess replied, "Aye Frederick, am to begin me tutoring with the bow. For what reason hath ye imposed this question upon me?"

"Be a bit curious as to thy progress; haps shall come see for meself how far ye hath progressed in these days past," said the prince.

She replied, "Dare ye not, Frederick!

Mother, it must not be permitted!"

"Calm thyself, Ashley; know ye well the joy thy brother finds in tormenting thee," said the prince, in jest.

She replied, "Frederick, be on thy guard, for haps one day ye shall pay dearly for the pleasure ye reap from thy foppery at me expense."

The princess asked, "Sir Milford, might we be on our way? Hath endured enough of this teasing for one day by this mindless twit."

"As ye wish, Your Highness. Shall go fetch the steeds from the stables, then await thee in the courtyard," replied the knight.

The princess bade her father, mother, and Lady Victoria farewell; ignoring her brother, she left the dining hall to change into her riding garments. Sir Milford, smiling, bowed then left for the stables.

When the princess was out of hearing range, the king began to laugh, and said, "Frederick, would seem Ashley becomes quite annoyed when ye make light of her tutoring with the archer. Beware, for haps when she becomes proficient with the bow, she may well unleash a shaft into thy bottom."

Everyone at the table broke out in laughter at the king's quip, including the prince.

Meanwhile, Leland was in the forest hunting before the princess was to arrive. He had flushed, and downed two grouse early on, and had seen a buck, but too far away for a good shot. He was tracking the deer when he heard the sound of water being splashed. He knew it was the maiden at her exercise. Nearing the large oak, he saw her laying on the riverbank. The archer felt a stirring within as he stood silent watching. He waited until she had paused to rest before speaking.

He said, "Good morn, Ashley; hath stood watching thee for a bit at thy task. Be ye in wait of me for a time?"

The princess had not heard Leland approaching, and was surprised by the archer's greeting. She came quickly to her feet, ran to the archer, and said, "Mercy, hath startled me Leland! Good morn, hath ye been a while; thought to be forgotten. See ye hath already downed two grouse. Ye must hath come early to the forest."

"Aye, lay restless in me bed most the night, thus thought to come to hunt a bit while in wait of thee. Come leave us set together 'neath the oak. At the outset ye art to be familiar with the bow itself," said Leland.

Leland began by pointing out the different configurations in the bow, and their functions. The archer then took a few arrows from his quiver, pointing out the notch, the fletching, the different types of arrowheads, and the reason for each arrow's configuration. He then handed Ashley the longbow, and said, "Look to the drawstring. Along its length will see a bit of color. Upon the grip there be a wee score."

"Aye Leland, the two be found; yet what purpose be served by these markings?" she asked.

Leland replied, "The notch in the arrow be set upon the marking on the drawstring, and the shaft of the arrow be set beside the scoring upon the grip. Be this the proper setting for the arrow to be launched. When next we meet, need ye no longer smite the waters. Shall ye gain strength by drawing back the bowstring. Go ye now, 'tis enough tutoring to be absorbed for one day. Must return to the hunt, for me larder and those of others art to be replenished."

"Leland, might me not remain for a bit to observe? Yea too, who might these others be to deprive me of thy tutoring?" she asked.

"Lass, our movements here about hath driven the game away, thus must venture further into the woodland. Ye hath not the skill yet to tread quietly. As to who the others might be, it will one day be revealed to thee," he replied.

The princess was not happy with Leland for the brief lesson she had been given yet dared not complain further knowing it would only anger the bowman. She bade him farewell, and took the deer run toward Sir Milford. Leland stood watching her walk away with that same stirring within.

Leland had not been truthful with the princess. His did not intend to walk the forest floor, but hunt from the stand in the willow. The presence of the maiden would not have permitted him to do so.

Chapter 5

Early Friday morning the prince thought to get a little hunting in before lunch. He washed, dressed, and then reached for his bow and quiver. The quiver was there; the bow was missing. Quite upset, he called to Tom. The manservant was fast asleep. He called out again. Tom came running down the stone steps, barefoot, and still in his nightshirt.

"Damnation, Tom! What hath become of me bow?" asked the prince.

"Me Prince, know naught of it. Come to do me chores this morn past; be not then hung upon the wall," Tom replied.

The prince a bit upset said, "At this hour, Sir Milford and Sir Cartwith be yet asleep; much too early to request another bow from either. No matter; hath lost me taste for the hunt. Look to it a bit later. Hath no further need of thee; do as ye will."

Tom returned to his cot. The prince took the stairs out to the courtyard. The sentries were at their posts. Seeing the prince, they bowed, exchanged greetings, then they stood chatting in the dimly lit courtyard. The door to the butchery opened, and a shadowy figure was seen running to the side entrance of the kitchen.

Minutes later, light from a lantern cast golden rays through the portals in the kitchen out onto the courtyard. The prince left Robert, the sentry at the gate, to investigate. Entering the kitchen, he found Mildred setting flame to the kindling beneath the caldrons hanging in the hearth.

He greeted her saying, "Good morn, Mildred. What be ye about at this early hour?

Someone be seen leaving the butchery and entering the kitchen, but minutes past. Know ye who it might hath been?"

Mildred curtsied to the prince, then stood a moment with a sheepish look on her face, and replied, "G' day me Prince, shant attempt to deceive thee; must confess, hath been to visit Martin."

He said, "Assume the man be ailing, thus in need of a gentle hand. There be no need to speak of it further, Mildred. Might ye brew a bit of tea? Shall await thee upon the terrace."

"Me thank thee, me Prince. Will see to it; might it be a bit," Mildred replied.

The prince left the kitchen to sit alone out in the morning air. A bit of light could be seen above the garden wall. He watched the shadow of the wall creep across the garden, slowly bathing the garden in sunlight.

Breakfast would not be served for at least an hour. He thought to finish his tea, then occupy himself writing a letter to Lady Rebecca, to be delivered with the king's reply to Earl William.

Later at the breakfast table, the prince asked the king if he had drafted a response to Earl William.

A bit irritated by his son's impatience, the king said, "Frederick, there be no need for haste, the earl hath stated in his note the fox hunt is to be in autumn. 'Tis yet weeks away."

"Father, hath not thought to press thee. Hath scribed a note to Lady Rebecca; wish me letter to be sent with thyne," said the prince.

The queen said, "Frederick, these weeks will pass slowly, lest ye occupy thyself. Go pass a bit of time with the archer. Ye hath not been to the forest in days."

"Mother, thought to go this morn. Washed, donned me garments, went to fetch me bow to find it gone. Know not what hath become of it," he replied.

The princess sheepishly said, "Forgive me, Frederick; came to fetch it two nights past. Forgot to speak of it to thee."

Scornfully, the prince said, "Ashley, might ye hath requested permission before 'twas taken. What need hath thee of me bow? Know ye naught of the hunt yet."

"Be told by Leland to lend strength to me arms, must draw the bowstring unto be weary," she replied.

"Ashley, thy eagerness to please the archer hath led me to believe Leland be no longer just thy tutor, but thy master as well," said the prince.

The princess stood, leered at the prince for a moment, then stomped out of the dining hall.

Chapter 6

Late Saturday afternoon, Princess Ashley sat on the terrace with Lady Victoria. Sir Milford was on the stone bench by the pond playing the flute. The two ladies were discussing the remark made by the prince at the table the night before.

Lady Victoria said, "Dear Princess, wish not to offend thee; thus, request permission to speak freely. Shall impose a question upon thee. Be advised, however, should permission be granted, ye must pledge to reply truthfully."

"Lady Victoria, there be no secrets 'tween we two nor be thee in need of permission to speak freely to me. Pray tell what might ye wish to inquire of me?" the princess replied.

Lady Victoria said, "Princess, hath observed when ye ere be teased by the prince or he speaks unkindly of thy involvement with the archer, become ye quite defensive. Now then, might it be ye hath become smitten with the archer?"

The princess replied, "Lady Victoria, be uncertain. Know when with Leland I feel quite secure, but with a touch be left a 'tremble."

Lady Victoria looked squarely at the princess for a moment smiling knowingly, and said, "There ye be then, me Princess; be no shame in it. Leland hath been deemed to be a gentle, righteous man; yea too, a handsome one, might add."

"Yet Lady Victoria, the man hath expressed no interest in me as a woman. Be left to wonder haps upon becoming proficient with the bow, might me be abandoned," Princess Ashley replied.

"Be patient, Princess. Soon this will be made known to thee; one way or t' other. Yet should the man bear no interest in thee, why would the archer devote hisself these many hours to thy tutoring?" asked the lady.

Godfrey came to the terrace, interrupting the conversation. He bowed, then handed the princess a sealed note. The princess dismissed the butler, then opened and read the message. It was from the marquess. The princess displayed an expression of disgust.

She said, "'Tis writ by the marquess. Damnation! This man will be the death of me. Despite me affording him no encouragement, the rascal doth yet persevere in his pursuit of me. How might me be rid of this twit?"

Lady Victoria said, "Be consoled Princess, matters not the many times come he to visit; 'tis an effort with no reward. Know ye, should Edward or the duke come with a proposal of marriage, the king with a few chosen words will hold them at bay unto they hath wearied of asking."

Lady Victoria continued, saying, "Will it be but an hour, haps two of discomfort. Thy sire would expect thee to be pleasant, yet distant. Dare the imp not lay hands upon thee; fearing the wrath of thy sire, should he be so brazen to do so. When hath he thought to visit?"

The Princess said, "On the morrow, past midday. Lady Victoria must ye not leave me side for a moment when be with the wretched beast."

Prince Frederick came out onto the terrace. Lady Victoria came to her feet to curtsy. The princess looked away from him, then said, "Lady Victoria, moments past hath felt a chill, yet here we be in the warming sun. Haps be made to suffer from some unknown malady."

The prince said, "Ashley, once more be ye cross with me. Recall, 'twas thee hath fetched me bow without seeking permission."

She replied, "Oh, 'tis thee, Frederick. Thought me hath heard a voice, yet he who spoke be not seen. Aye, the bow be taken without permission. However, might ye recall, be ye told hath forgotten to speak of it with thee. Ye, too, be plagued with the loss of memory.

Hath ye found it convenient to forget, 'twas with Lady Victoria hath devised a plan to keep Lady Rebecca in Penrith for the fortnight. We two hath aided thee in winning the ladies heart, as well. Yet when in me attempt to enhance me relations with one speak ye of as a friend, make ye light of it. 'Tis apparent, ye hath placed more value upon a bow than upon a friend, and thy sibling."

The princess visibly upset, ran from the terrace without another word. Lady Victoria excused herself, then followed the princess up to her chamber, leaving the prince alone on the terrace. Sir Milford, seeing the ladies leaving, stopped playing his flute and went to join the prince on the terrace.

The prince asked, "Sir Milford, hath ye heard the rebuke given me by the princess? Be not deserving of it nor shall it be tolerated! Ye must agree."

"Me Prince, forgive me; 'tis not me place to voice an opinion as to who hath been wronged in this exchange of words; nor in a position to side with one or t' other," replied the knight.

"Haps not, Sir Milford; yet ye should speak thy mind. Might it aid in resolving this dispute 'tween me and Ashley," said the prince.

Sir Milford said, "Well then, shall solely relate what hath seen. The princess hath been pampered since birth by those who be loved, and too those she be served. Yet, these days past, in the forest hath stood concealed in awe of what she hath been subjected to and endured 'neath the tutoring of the archer. Me Prince, hath seen the princess lie prone upon the bank of the river smiting it's waters for hours on end. Be she not taught solely the use of the bow by Leland, but humility as well, 'tis to be encouraged."

The prince could believe his ears. He stood silent, as the knight continued.

The knight said, "Me prince, might me suggest Monday morn, unbeknown to the princess, come to the forest by way of the path at the bend in the road. Silently take the path. Will find me concealed behind a great oak. Stand with me to view for thyself what the princess hath permitted herself to be submitted to attempting to please the archer. Beg thee, me Lord, speak naught of this, for were Princess Ashley to learn she be seen by thee in such a demeaning position, shall me never be forgiven."

The prince replied, "Sir Milford, pledge to thee, shall not betray thy confidence. Haps hath wronged the princess; if so, will make amends. We shall meet in the forest Monday morn then.

Chapter 7

Sunday passed uneventfully. Princess Ashley avoided the prince as much possible. The princess became more irritated by the visit of the marquess in the afternoon, which she thought to be a complete waste of her time.

The queen had noticed at breakfast and again at lunch that the two had avoided speaking to each other but was not about to mention it fearing they would begin squabbling at the table, upsetting the king.

Monday morning the queen thought to have a chat with the princess when she returned from her visit with Leland.

The prince awoke that morning, washed, dressed then stood in the tower window waiting to see Sir Milford leave the courtyard with the princess. He then went to the stables to wait for Gavin to saddle Silvermane. Mounting the steed, he rode to the entrance of the castle. He waited for the princess and the knight to leave the Tate cottage and ride beyond the bend on the flats.

Spurring his steed to a gallop, the prince rode to tether Silvermane beside the other two horses at the forest path, then quietly walked and found Sir Milford standing behind the oak.

The knight raised a finger to his lips signaling the prince to be silent, and then motioned him to approach. The knight pointed in the direction of the princess.

The prince, seeing the princess prone on the riverbank hitting the water with open hands, was astounded.

He whispered, "Sir Milford, hath it not been seen with me own eyes would it never been believed. Hath me erred grievously in taunting Ashley. Must ponder upon a proper gesture to display repentance for me stupidity. Need not see more, Sir Milford, thus shall leave thee."

The prince left the forest, retrieved Silvermane, and rode toward the palace at a walk quite displeased with himself. Suddenly a thought came to mind. He spurred his horse toward the village. Many of the shops were not open. The prince rode through the village to the cobblers and tethered the steed in front of the shop.

He found the shop closed as well. Through the window he saw the cobbler sitting at his workbench, sipping his morning tea. He tapped on the door and waited.

The man stood and came to the window. Seeing the prince, he opened the door.

He bowed, and said, "Good morn, me Prince. Be closed for 'tis the Sabbath. However, shall not turn thee away. Come, enter. How might me be of aid to thee? Hath fine boots, pouches, and saddles."

The prince said, "Sir, be in need of a bowyer to fashion a fine bow, and quivers, haps yet another bow of lesser quality. Be they for a lady. Know ye of a bowyer in the village?"

"Me Lord, hath skill in the crafting of quivers, yet none constructing bows. Hath kin who fashion them, then be brought to me to vend. Hold, shall fetch a few of each for thee to view."

The man disappeared behind a partition, was heard rummaging about for a bit then reappeared with arms full of bows. He laid them out on the workbench for the prince to choose from. The prince chose one he would have liked to own, then another a villager might be seen with at the hunt. He then chose two quivers from the cobbler's shelves to match the bows.

The man said, "Hath ye chosen well, me Prince. One be of the finest quality fabricated by me kin. Might the lady be not pleased; she may return it to choose one of her liking."

The prince paid the cobbler, thanked him for his assistance then left in a much better mood than he had been upon entering the shop.

Arriving at the palace, a stable boy came running to relieve the prince of Silvermane. With the bows and quivers in hand, the prince went directly to his chambers. He placed them on his bed and covered them with his cloak.

In the dining hall at lunch, the prince sat with the king, queen, and Lady Victoria.

The king said, "Of late would seem Ashley be more in the forest than with her kin. What be she about these many hours with the archer?"

"Husband, leave her be. What ere passes 'tween Ashley and the archer in the forest be known to Sir Milford. The knight must not be placed in a position to be forced to betray Ashley's confidence. However, should he speak of it, 'tis certain will it be but for a proper reason," the queen responded.

Sir Milford entered the dining hall, bowed, greeted those at the table then went to take his seat beside the prince before speaking.

He said, "Princess Ashley will be joining us soon. Hath she a bit of grime upon her person in need of attention."

"Sir Milford, be there any progress in Ashley's tutoring with the bow?" asked the queen.

The knight replied, "Me Queen, bear in mind, the princess hath never been expected to perform tasks requiring strength. This must be developed before wielding a bow. However, the princess be an avid student, determined to succeed. Haps within a fortnight shall she be launching arrows, but with little success. Skill is to be developed o'er time."

The princess entered the dining hall with a lilt in her step, bearing a smile. Certainly, in a much better mood than the day before.

She said, "Forgive me, be a bit late. Be famished for hath labored hard with Leland this morn. He spoke of thee Frederick, not by name, only of tutoring a young gent.

Leland stated he be quite pleased with thee. Yet a bit concerned for hath ye not been about of late."

The prince replied, "Indeed! Ashley. Then there be a need for me to render the man a proper excuse for me absence.

Might ye stop by me chambers a bit later? There be a matter wish to discuss with thee."

After lunch, the prince asked to be excused. With permission, he left the dining hall and went to his chambers to wait for his sister.

As the group left the dining hall, the queen turned to her daughter and spoke.

She said, "Ashley, speak with Frederick then join me in me chambers."

"Very well, Mother," replied the princess.

The princess then turned to Lady Victoria asking her to wait for her on the terrace. She would join her after speaking with the prince and her mother. She then took the three flights of stairs to her brother's room.

On entering, the prince hugged her and said, "Ashley, hath thought long upon our bickering. Hath oft spoken to thee in an improper manner. Pray ye forgive me. As a token of me sincerity, wish to present thee with a gift. Look ye 'neath me cloak lying upon me bed."

Princess Ashley reluctantly walked over to the bed, suspicious of the prince. Throwing back the cloak, she saw the two bows and quiver and, emitting a screech, she ran to throw her arms around the prince.

She said excitedly, "Frederick, ye would not hath pleased me more hath it been a cask of gold. Thy apology be truly sincere, thus accepted. Hath forgiven thee. As a gesture of sincerity shall disclose something known solely to Lady Victoria.

Hath feelings for Leland yet not quite understood. Frederick, must ye thus pledge not to interfere in me attempt to fully understand these feelings."

"Ashley, 'tis given. Might ye be in need of aid in this endeavor, need but make it known to me. Shall be a willing participant," said the prince.

She said, "Me thank thee, Frederick. Must flee for mother awaits. Shall return thy bow and fetch me gifts a bit later."

She left and took the stairs to her mother's chambers. Entering, she found the queen writing a letter. The princess waited for her to turn from her writing table.

She, then asked; "Mother, wish to speak with me?"

"Aye Ashley, be a bit concerned for hath noted of late be ye at odds with brother Frederick. Granted, at times his choice of words to thee be a bit repugnant. Yet be ye quick to take offense.

Know ye well, oft his words be said in jest. Ye must but smile, giving him no satisfaction in knowing he hath riled thee," said the queen.

The princess said, "Mother, forgive me for the interruption. There be no need for thee to be concerned. But minutes past, Frederick hath pleaded forgiveness for his improper behavior, granting me gifts in reconciliation. All hath been forgiven."

The queen replied, "Indeed! Be left to wonder what hath come to pass for him to make such a gesture. Whatever it be, 'tis a welcomed turn of events. Go ye then, be happy."

The princess hugged her mother then left the room to join Lady Victoria on the terrace. By the mood of the princess stepping out onto the terrace, there was no need for Lady Victoria to ask her of her chat with her mother, and the prince.

Princess Ashley could hardly wait to tell Lady Victoria she had reconciled with the prince, and he had given her gifts as a token of his repentance.

She said, "Victoria, the prince be made aware of me feelings for Leland. He hath expressed a desire to render aid in this endeavor. He hath also presented me with gifts in repentance."

"Indeed! Princess, better for the prince to be an ally than a foe in this matter."

Chapter 8

Princess Ashley awoke early the next morning anxious to get to the forest. She was about to leave her room when Sir Milford came tapping on the door. Opening the door, the knight bowed then spoke.

He said, "Good morn me Princess, hath rained this night past; 'tis not a good day for the hunt. Be certain Leland will not be about this morn."

"G' day, Sir Milford, come enter. Curses! Hath thought to pass the morn with Leland. Well then haps will pass the morn in the garden with the bow," the princess replied.

"Me Princess, Prince Frederick hath voiced displeasure for the use of his bow lest permission be granted. Might it please thee, I shall fetch one from me quarters," said the knight.

"No need, Sir Milford, come look ye, hath two of me own given to me by the prince. Might ye tutor me a bit in the garden this morn?"

"With pleasure. Shall join thee in the garden after the morning meal," Sir Milford replied.

The knight bowed, and left the room intending to go to his quarters. In the courtyard, Sir Cartwith approached him.

He asked, "G 'day Sir Milford, will ye be accompanying the princess to the forest this morn?"

The commander replied, "Good morn, Sir Cartwith. Nay, the forest be mudded by this past night's rain. Why hath ye inquired?"

"Sir, hath ye no need of me this day, thought to fetch Tiffany from the village for a wee ride to Clifton," Sir Cartwith replied.

"Go ye then, Sir Cartwith, much of me day is to be passed with the princess in the garden. Me best to the lady," said Sir Milford.

Sir Milford continued on to his quarters; Sir Cartwith went to the stables for his mount.

Sir Cartwith arrived at the village to find the millinery not yet opened. He took the stairs at the rear of the shop to the flat above, tapping on the door. Eleanor came to open the door.

She said, "G' day Sir Knight, come enter, set ye. Might me fetch thee a bit of tea, haps a bite?"

He replied, "Good morn, Eleanor. Me thank thee, hath eaten; yet could do with a bit of tea."

Whitney and Tiffany were at the table eating breakfast. Sir Cartwith went to Whitney, kissed her on the cheek. He, then picked Tiffany out of her seat. He sat, putting the child in his lap.

He said, "Good morn, Whitney, little one! Hath come, for thought Tiffany might wish to ride with me this morn."

Excitedly the child asked, "Mother, might it be permitted?"

Whitney said, "Good morn Richard.

Tiffany, ye must finish breakfast then ye may don thy riding garments. Must ye pledge to not be a bother to Richard."

Whitney continued saying, "Sir Knight, Prince Frederick came by requesting a pattern for the riding attire. Be he told when complete would be given to thee for delivery to him. Shall ope the shop in a bit. The pattern be in the shop. Come fetch it in passing."

They chatted until after breakfast then Tiffany went to change.

Eleanor left the flat to open the millinery. Tiffany returned to the kitchen in her riding garments. The knight told her to go ask Howard to saddle the pony for her then wait by the hitching post at the front of the millinery.

Whitney waited for Tiffany to leave before speaking.

She said, "Richard, it hath been a time since be we alone. Might we not pass a day together by the water at Eamont Bridge?"

He replied, "Me Lady, yearn to be alone with thee. Come the Sabbath, I shall fetch thee and Tiffany. The lass will be left to pass the day at the palace with Christy. We shall then pause for a bite in Eamont then ride to the river."

Sir Cartwith rose from the table to leave. Whitney came to her feet, went to him, and pulled him to her, kissing him. They stood together for a moment then he left her to meet with Tiffany, stopping in the shop for the pattern.

Tiffany was by the hitching post waiting for him to help her onto Cupid. Howard was standing across the road smiling.

He shouted to Sir Cartwith, "Good day, Sir Knight, the lass requested haste. Be she all a 'flutter. And what of the lady Whitney?"

"G' day Howard, the lady will be occupied with her chores in the millinery this morn. Stay well, me friend," Sir Cartwith replied.

The knight and Tiffany rode off to the castle. He wanted to deliver the pattern to the prince before riding off to Clifton. At the palace Sir Cartwith dismounted, lifted Tiffany off the pony, then the two entered the kitchen.

Breakfast had already been served; the servants were tidying up the kitchen. Sir Cartwith went to ask Godfrey where the prince might be. He then asked Tiffany to wait in the kitchen while he went off on his errand. Tiffany went to speak with Mildred.

Tiffany asked, "Good morn, Mildred. Christy be about?"

Mildred responded, "G' day Tiffany. My, art ye the winsome lady in thy riding garments this morn! Christy will be by in a moment. Where be ye off to?"

The child said, "Be invited to ride with Sir Cartwith to Clifton. We shall pause for a bite at the pub then set by the river for a time."

Minutes later Christy came skipping into the kitchen. Seeing Tiffany, she stopped then ran to hug her friend before saying, "Tiffany, be ye alone? Hath ye come to visit?"

Tiffany answered, "Nay Christy, be with Sir Cartwith. Me mum be occupied at the millinery. Come ye, there be something to be seen."

Tiffany took Christy's hand, and led her out into the courtyard. The two stood together, Christy admiring the pony.

"Tiffany, 'tis a beauty. Be thyne own? How come ye by the wee steed? Where be off ye with Sir Cartwith this morn?" asked Christy.

"Christy, Cupid be a gift presented to me by Sir Cartwith. Shall accompany him to Clifton."

Sir Cartwith stood at the entrance to the palace, beckoning to the two children.

Tiffany asked Christy to wait while she spoke to the knight.

She then went to Sir Cartwith and whispered, "Sir Knight, might we be accompanied by Christy on our ride this morn?"

"Should it please thee, Tiffany; aye. Yet she must be given permission to do so. Go ye fetch the lass, we shall speak to Christy's mum," he replied.

The three stood in the doorway to the kitchen, the knight signaling to Mildred to come join them. Christy spoke.

"Mother, Sir Cartwith and Tiffany hath invited me to accompany them on their ride. Me chores be completed. Might it be permitted?"

Mildred replied, "Well now, 'tis a fine gesture made by Sir Cartwith. Be ye deserving of a bit of pleasure. Must ye not go off bearing those soiled garments. Be forewarned, ye must not be bothersome."

Christy promised to behave, thanked her mother, and then she ran off with Tiffany to her room to change her clothes. Sir Cartwith addressed Mildred.

"Mildred, shall fetch a gentle mare from the stables for the lass. Inform the children shall await them in the courtyard," said the knight.

Minutes later the three rode down the hill toward Clifton, the girls chatting together merrily. Sir Cartwith enjoyed the display of friendship between them.

Chapter 9

Wednesday morning, Princess Ashley was determined not to pass another day without being with Leland. Sir Milford stepped out of his quarters to find her standing by the hitching post with Titus and Goldentrot, saddled and ready to ride.

Sir Milford greeted her. "G' morn, me Princess; hath ye slept this night past to be in wait of me at first light?"

The princess replied, "G' day Milford, a bit. Hath it not been for thy tutoring in the garden, this day past would hath been a waste. Come, leave us make haste."

The drawbridge had not yet been lowered, forcing them to lead the horses through one of the guarded gates. Outside the castle walls they mounted their steeds and rode down the hill to the Tate cottage for the princess to change into Arabella's garments.

Many minutes later in the forest, Sir Milford took his position behind a large oak. The princess continued on to sit at the river, tossing pebbles into the water. Leland arrived carrying two bows; his, and another, similar to the one used by the prince.

She said, "G' day, Leland; ye hath come with two bows and quivers. Shall me be launching arrows this morn?"

Leland replied, "G' day Ashley. Nay, not for a time. Yet, on leaving, ye shall shoulder the quiver and tote the bow in hand. Should there be a ruffian about, he will not dare attempt to accost thee, fearing haps be ye a skilled archer."

"Leland, be in awe of thy concern for me wellbeing. Now then, how art we to pass this morn?" asked the princess.

He said, "Come; grasp the wee bow and stand before me. Will stand behind, guiding thee to the proper position of thy hands upon the bow. Now then, draw back the bowstring, then rest. Continue to do as instructed. Shall leave thee for a bit to hunt. Fear not, for never be ye out of me sight."

The archer let loose her hands, picked up the longbow, and walked off leaving the princess to her task.

Half an hour later, the archer returned, and stood a moment watching, then spoke.

Harshly, he said; "Woman, be ye told to draw the bowstring, then rest. Ye hath drawn then let loose. Look ye there, hath ye bloodied thy hands and arm."

The princess, not accustomed to being spoken to in anger, dropped the bow and turned to Leland with tears falling to her cheeks.

Leland remorsefully looked at her bleeding hands and shook his head. She looked up at the archer for a moment, reached up, pulled him to her, then kissed him.

Leland stood for a bit with his arms at his side. The kiss was not expected. He, then took her in his arms and returned the kiss.

Sir Milford, standing behind the oak, saw the two in each other's arms. He smiled in approval.

The princess then spoke to Leland. Sir Milford could not hear what was said.

Whispering, she said, "Leland, hath longed for thee to hold me thus. Thought for a time hath ye no interest in me as a woman."

He replied, "Ashley, and I, thee; yet feared should me be so bold as to approach thee, would ye flee never to return."

Much later, leaving the forest, Sir Milford stopped on the path and spoke to the princess.

He said, "Me Princess, be thee well protected by the archer. There be no need for me to be near. Henceforth, shall escort thee to the forest, then return to the Tate's to await thy return."

She said," Sir Milford, then be left to expect ye approve of this thou hath seen, and will ye not speak of it at the palace?"

"Princess, no word of it shall pass me lips," the knight replied.

Chapter 10

That night, in the dining hall, the princess' attempt to conceal her injured hands was noticed by the queen.

The queen asked, "Ashley, how come thy hands to be bloodied? These injuries ye hath sustained be caused by the tutoring of the archer?"

She replied, "Nay, Mother; failed to adhere to Leland's instructions. Be told by the archer to draw the bowstring, then rest. I drew back the bowstring, then let loose. Sir Milford, is it not so?"

Sir Milford said, "Me Queen, 'twas as the princess hath stated. The archer reprimanded the princess severely for her disobedience."

The king, being surprised, said, "Me word, Milford; and Ashley failed to retaliate for the verbal abuse?

Ashley, but weeks past would ye hath demanded the bloke be flogged."

The princess responded, "Father, 'twas befitting and just, yet quite humbling."

Addressing the king, the prince said, "Father, Sir Cartwith come by this morn with the pattern for the riding attire requested by Countess Sarah."

The king replied, "Good, Frederick. It shall be sent with the letter of reply to that of Earl William's, along with thyne and Mother's."

He, then addressed Sir Milford, saying, "Milford, one of the cavalrymen is to be dispatched upon the 'morrow to Dumfries."

"Will see to it, Your Majesty. Your Highness, hath the steed given thee by the earl been named?" the knight asked.

The king replied, "Aye, Milford; 'twas given to Lady Verna by the comely dancing maiden. The lass thought the beast to be fierce as a lion, thus suggested the name Abas. Thought it to be fitting."

At supper, Lady Victoria had noticed the princess was extremely pleased with herself. Something was in the wind.

After supper, on leaving the dining hall, the princess took Lady Victoria's hand and lead her out to the bench at the far end of the garden, then spoke excitedly.

She said, "Lady Victoria, must confess to thee; not all that hath come to pass this morn in the forest be revealed at the table.

Leland's outburst drove me to tears. Went to stand before him and looked to him. In the archer's eyes, found a sign of sadness. Placed me arms about him then kissed him. For a moment he stood bewildered, then took me in his arms. Never hath felt such joy."

"Me word, 'twas quite bold of thee. Sir Milford witnessed this display of affection yet said naught?" asked Lady Victoria.

The princess replied, "Aye, Cousin; at that moment bore no fear of rejection. Milford later stated there be no need for him to stand watch. Henceforth, shall he escort me to the forest then leave me be. He hath deemed the archer trustworthy, and quite able to protect me from harm."

"Ye hath become quite fond of the archer. Haps 'tis best to seek the counsel of thy mother before proceeding further in thy involvement with the bowman," said Lady Victoria.

The princess replied, "Well thought, Victoria."

Meanwhile in chambers, the king and queen sat chatting. King Frederick brought up the subject of his daughter and Leland.

He said, "Margaret, hath ye heard Ashley's account of the incident in the forest? Could not believe me ears; be she scolded for her disobedience yet sought no vengeance. What hath become of the lass of late? Must state, however, hath she been in need of a bit of taming."

The queen replied, "Frederick, Ashley be no longer a child. She harbors feelings within not yet understood. Me thinks the lass be smitten with the archer. She will do well 'neath his tutoring. Be he gentle yet firm. He will not tolerate the whining of a pampered maiden."

"Margaret, for this Leland must be commended. He stands firm, unyielding to anyone, much the like of Milford. Oh! But for me to lead a force of such men!" said the king.

"Come to bed, Frederick, a 'fore ye be tempted to don thy armor then go stomping about the courtyard bellowing commands to the wind," the queen replied.

Chapter 11

Leland had been in the forest with Prince Frederick since midafternoon that Friday, attempting to down a few birds while waiting for deer to be on the move around sunset. They had managed to slay two grouse and a pheasant, then decided to sit by the oak beside the river and wait for the deer to come for water.

The prince asked the archer how he had managed to poach in the king's forest without being caught. Leland was not about to tell his hunting companion of his stand in the willow. For, although he was now free to hunt without fear of being caught, it was still a good vantage point from which to launch his arrows at game on the deer run, and the clearing beyond the river. Were the prince to know of the stand, he might be tempted to use it as his own.

Leland replied, "Frederick, 'twas not with ease. Since be a lad, hath roamed about these trees and brushes. Be they well known to me. Yet, must confess, with a bit of good fortune as well.

Two days past hath been with the maiden Ashley, tutoring. She failed to heed me words, thus sustained injuries to her hands and arm. I became ired, then spoke harshly. The damsel commenced to weep. I hath been remorseful since."

The prince said, "Leland, upon recalling the event, surely the lass will come to understand be she deserving of thy ire. Haps not, then shall it be known to thee by her absence. Be left to wonder, hath ye feelings for this maiden?"

Leland did not reply to the man's question.

The sun had fallen below the tree line. The forest was in shadows. Leland heard some movement in the underbrush from beyond the clearing across the river. He motioned for the prince to be silent.

They came quietly to their feet, set arrows to their bows then stood to wait. A six-point buck broke into the clearing then stood looking about. Leland held out his hand signaling the prince to wait. The buck ambled to the riverbank then lowered his head to drink. Leland raised his bow and took aim as did the prince. They both let fly their arrows striking the deer. The buck stepped back from the river, staggered a bit then fell to the ground.

Leland, pleased with the prince's performance said, "Well done, Frederick; ye hath been an attentive student. Hath learned thy lessons well. Shall ye not hunger for a time."

The prince replied, "Indeed Leland. 'Tis a fine animal, yet too much for me and me sire to consume. Shall be content with the three birds. Come, shall we dress the beast."

Leland unsheathed his blade and cut open the deer. They removed the innards, tossed them into the river then washed the blood from their hands. They tied the stag's hooves together, retrieved a sturdy length of wood to tote it with, then lifted the beast to their shoulders.

The prince offered to help the archer carry the buck to his hut.

Leland was not about to reveal his living quarters to one not yet well known to him.

Thus, in response, he said; "We shall tote the beast to the forest entrance, Frederick. No need for thee to go further for hath a chum with a cart to render aid. Shall come fetch the beast in the dark of night, thus will we not be seen."

The prince's offer to help the archer carry the deer home was not entirely an act of kindness. He had hoped to learn of Leland's place of residence. He had thought to catch the archer off guard. The prince had not succeeded. At that moment, he came to realize that Leland was much more cleaver than one would expect.

The prince then thought back to the day of the tournament. Since then, when the king had spoken with the archer, Leland avoided divulging anything of a personal nature.

He said, "Very well then, Leland. One day shall ye enable me to repay thee for thy kindly tutoring. Haps one-night will ye agree to come sup at me table with me sire."

Leland gave no reply.

At the edge of the forest they set the stag down. The sun had already set. In the waning light, they bade each other a good night, and went their separate ways. Later Leland returned with Howard and his cart to retrieve the deer.

Seeing the two arrows imbedded in the deer, Howard said; "Leland, the beast hath been struck twice. One shaft be not thyne."

"Aye Howard, be with a young lad hath met some weeks past in the forest. A most inquisitive gent."

Chapter 12

Sunday morning Lady Verna instructed the servants to set up a canopy in the garden with seating for seven. After lunch King Frederick, Queen Margaret, and Prince Frederick sat watching the princess with Sir Milford, opposing Lady Victoria and Sir Cartwith, in a game of Quoits.

The princess and Sir Milford were at a disadvantage. For although the hand of the princess had not yet completely healed, she insisted on participating. The king commented on his daughter's eagerness to play despite her discomfort.

The king said, "Must say, Ashley hath acquired a bit of grit these weeks past 'neath the tutoring of the archer. 'Tis a welcomed trait."

He then turned to the queen, and said, "Margaret thought the lass to become a pawn in the hands of a noble attempting to enhance his position at court. Haps there yet be hope for the child."

The queen replied, "Husband, look ye to Ashley as a young maiden schooled in the arts, literature, and social graces. Should she become skilled with the bow, she will then gain confidence, thus becoming a woman to be reckoned with. Will she, then never bend a knee nor agree to be led about by that pompous twit, the marquess, with the hands a 'kin to those of a damsel."

"Margaret, there be no fear of it. For will never bestow me blessings upon a union 'tween Ashley and that viper," said the king.

He then addressed his son saying, "Frederick, this day past, me response to the earl hath been dispatched to Dumfries with thyne, thy mother's, and the pattern for the countess."

The prince asked, "Father, dare me inquire as to what the letter to the earl might bear? Hath ye accepted the invitation of the earl?"

"Aye Frederick, hath proposed a week in September for the fox hunt. 'Tis certain the earl will agree. Earl William will be pleased to see me arriving at the estate upon the steed, Abas," replied the king.

The queen speaking said, "Husband, detect a bit of excitement in thy words. Would seem ye find the thought of this journey quite pleasing to thee."

"And why not Margaret? It hath been years since hath met with me comrades in arms from Dumfries. There be adventures to be recounted, many tall tales to be told. Too, the Scottish brew be quite pleasing to the gullet, adding fabrication to these tales," replied the king.

The prince said, "Father, recall Countess Sara requesting Sir Cartwith be included in the party going to Dumfries? For reasons wish not to reveal, request the cavalryman, Donald, be one of the escorts in the party as well."

The king replied, "Frederick, suspect a bit of mischief be involved in thy request. Yet shall not press thee. So, shall it be."

Godfrey came out to the garden with servants toting refreshments. The butler bowed, the servants curtsied, then set the trays on the table before retreating into the palace.

With the game being played to the end, the participants came to sit beneath the canopy.

The queen asked, "Well now, Milford, who be the victors, and who the defeated?"

The knight replied, "Your Majesty, the outcome be preordained by the injuries sustained by the princess. Yet Princess Ashley must be commended for her eagerness to participate."

"Indeed, Milford! Oh, hath decided, come September shall be riding to visit Earl William. The presence of Sir Cartwith hath been requested in Dumfries by Countess Sarah. Thus, shall he command the escort.

The day prior to departure a cavalryman is to be sent to an inn, midway 'tween Penrith and Dumfries, to procure lodging for the night."

"As ye wish, Your Majesty," replied Sir Milford.

The prince said, "Father, suggest the inn at Gretna. 'Twas there found we shelter for the night in passing."

The king replied, "So be it."

Addressing Sir Milford, the king said; "For some reason, Frederick hath requested one of the men in escort be the cavalrymen Donald."

The knight replied, "Shall see to it, Your Highness."

The remainder of the afternoon was spent by the group in idle conversation.

Chapter 13

Monday morning Sir Milford escorted the princess to the Tate cottage, then to the forest. At the oak tree where he normally stood concealed, the knight spoke to her saying, "Me Princess, shant stand in wait of thy return. Take the path to the river. Shall remain unto the archer comes to join thee. Will be in wait of thee at the Tate's. Upon completing thy lessons, come to the cottage. Shall escort thee to the palace."

The princess thanked the knight for his trust in her, and in Leland. She bade him farewell, then with the bow Leland had given her in hand, and the quiver over her shoulder, she took the path to the oak by the river and sat to wait for Leland. He arrived some minutes later.

The princess greeted him, and he came to sit beside her.

He said, "Good morn, Ashley. Hath ye no need of the bow this morn. The injuries sustained this week past hath as yet not mended. Shall ye, for haps two days be tutored in the stalking of thy prey. A 'fore we begin, however, must plead thy forgiveness for speaking harshly to thee t' other morn."

She replied, "Leland, there be no need. Hath disobeyed thee. Thus, well deserving of thy wrath. Shall we not speak of it further."

The princess kissed the archer on the cheek.

Leland smiled, then said, "Woman, hath ye come this morn for haps a bit of foppery or to be tutored?

Come stand; leave us begin. Tread lightly lest ye be heard. Follow me lead. Upon seeing a patch of bush, walk before me. Might there be birds within they will take flight."

The princess followed the archer, mimicking his every step. Approaching a stand of bushes, she took the lead. This went on for the better part of half an hour.

Passing a patch of bushes, a grouse took flight, startling her. Leland let loose an arrow, downing the bird. She jumped up and down in delight. Leland could not help but laugh at her exuberance.

He said, "There ye be lass, as this be it done."

Meanwhile at the Tate cottage, Sir Milford sat in conversation over a cup of tea with Mother Tate.

The woman Tate said, "Sir Milford, Jarin hath been incarcerated since mid-spring. When first he returned upon the Sabbath to tend to chores, spake of being in a dungeon, yet the door be not secured. Might ye not deem this a bit strange? What manner of incarceration might this be?"

Sir Milford replied, "Madam, 'tis a means to determine the lad's character. Should Jarin attempt to flee, will he be apprehended then punished severely. Should he adhere to the terms set forth for his incarceration, shall it bode well for the lad.

Gavin, the stable master, be a stern taskmaster who will afford the lad a bit of discipline. Shall I soon speak to the ole gent. Might he deem the lad obedient and worthy; will I then speak to the king on the lad's behalf. Should all go well, Jarin may be returned to thee near autumn's end."

Mother Tate said, "Sir Knight, thy intervention in the plight of me daughter Arabella, and thy involvement in the infraction committed by Jarin, hath left me to trust in thy judgment. Be in thy debt."

Sir Milford came a 'right to the sound of hoof beats approaching the cottage. He went to the doorway to see the princess riding toward the cottage. He turned to speak to the two at the table.

He said, "Mother Tate, Arabella, 'tis the princess. Shall wait without for her ladyship to change her garments.

Bade thee farewell."

Sir Milford waited for the princess to reined in Goldentrot, then went to help her off her mount.

The princess entered the cottage. The knight waited beside the horses for her to change her clothes, then escorted her back to the palace.

Entering the courtyard of the palace, a stable boy came running to relieve the riders of their steeds.

Sir Milford returned to his quarters. The princess went to her chambers to wash and change.

Thinking of taking the advice Lady Victoria's had given her of speaking to the queen regarding her relationship with Leland, the princess left her chambers to her mother.

Chapter 14

Princess Ashley walked to her mother's chambers to find the door open. Lady Winfred was setting the rooms in order. She greeted the lady-in-waiting, then asked her where the queen might be.

The lady replied, "Me Princess, but minutes past, the queen departed with bible in hand. Would assume hath she gone to the chapel."

The princess thanked her, then took the stairs to the chapel.

Queen Margaret was sitting alone in the first pew, reading. The princess went quietly to sit beside her.

The princess sat silent waiting for her mother to speak. The queen finished the passage she had been reading and set the bible by her side.

Turning to her daughter she said, "Good morn, Ashley. Be ye missed at the table this morn. Hath ye been at the forest with the archer?"

The princess replied, "Aye, Mother. Leland voiced concern for me injuries, saying hath they not healed as yet. Thus, thought to forego me tutoring with the bow. Be taught to stalk prey in its stead.

Mother, hath not come to speak with thee of me tutoring, but of another matter concerning the archer."

The princess paused, then continued saying, "Spoke with Lady Victoria this night past of me relations with Leland. She suggested me seek thy counsel.

Were me friendship with the archer to become something more and were Father to learn of it, what might he say? Might he forbid me to visit with the archer?"

The queen said, "Ashley, leave me begin by assuring thee Father shall not barter thee off as he might a herd of sheep or for a parcel of land. Nor will ye be forced to pass thy days in misery with the likes of the Marquess of Edenhall.

Should ye choose a man of honor who will cherish and protect thee, thy sire will grant thee his blessings.

Must be ye patient, however, in thy choosing. Be not swayed by idle words a man might say. For there be men with tongues well tutored in the art of seduction. Look to that be found within the man's heart, for therein lie the truth of his feelings.

At the present thy sire speaks highly of the archer. Might he deem the archer a proper suitor for thee be yet not known."

"Mother, hath come to thee for counsel with no haste to wed. Yet dare me not wait unto Leland hath become dear to me, then to hear Father voice objection to our union," the princess replied.

The queen said, "Lest laying eyes on this man at the tournament and that horrid night he entered the dining hall with Frederick and enraged, fled. The little known to me of this archer hath heard from Milford, Frederick, and thee. Yet from that be heard, be left to believe the man bears qualities oft not found in a villager, nor 'mongst the nobles as well. Were it me in thy position, would pursue this friendship with the archer, yet with caution, following me heart not solely me desires."

The princess replied, "Mother, hath done well to heed Lady Victoria's suggestion to speak of this matter with thee. Thy wise counsel hath dispelled many of me concerns. These days in the forest hath left me to wonder why we ladies pass our days reading, chatting, embroidering and at mundane games. While the men be about with chums, enjoying the passion of the hunt, riding off in search of adventure, and on quests of their choosing. Much of that they do find pleasing to me as well."

The queen said, "And to me, Ashley. When yet in me early years thought to participate in these activities. Alas, 'twas not to be, for thy grandfather be quite steadfast in his beliefs. He thought a proper lady was to bear children and tend to the needs of her husband.

When first be wed, would accompany thy sire to the forest, but to set and wait. For thy sire thought me to be much too fragile to be stomping about the trees and underbrush in me cumbersome garments.

Child, might ye find pleasure in the forest, at the hunt? A man the likes of Leland will suit thee well. Go ye now, Ashley, for desire a bit more time at me scriptures."

The princess left the chapel intending to look for Lady Victoria in the garden. In the hall, she ran into Lady Winfred.

Lady Winfred said, "Me Princess, a servant came with a message from the marquess. Be told his Lordship thought to come by in two days hence to visit."

Princess Ashley thanked the lady-in-waiting then stomped off, cursing the marquess under her breath.

Chapter 15

Wednesday morning, Leland and the princess sat by the oak at the river. Her hands had not completely healed. Leland thought to give her a lesson in the proper stalking of deer.

He said, "Ashley, when stalking, ye must be patient, move slowly, keeping thyne eyes upon the forest floor for signs of scoring by hooves. The markings will reveal from whence the animal came, and the direction it hath gone. Follow silently unto the beast be in sight. Attempt to remain concealed. For the sight of thee or a movement will cause the deer to flee."

The archer had been so intent on delivering his presentation, he had not noticed his student had nearly fallen asleep.

He shook her and said, "Ashley! Hath ye come to set beside me but to slumber? Hath me words fallen upon deaf ears, thus hath spoken to the wind?"

Startled, she said, "Forgive me, Leland, 'tis quite peaceful in the forest. Hath been lulled by the gentle breezes through the trees, the water's flow, and the singing of the birds, in the comfort of thy presence."

Leland reached into his pouch. He withdrew a three fingered glove from it and put it on her hand. From the pouch he then fetched a patch of leather and two strips of hide and fasten the patch on her forearm.

He said, "This ye must do prior to the hunt, Ashley. Thus, will ye not sustain an injury when drawing and releasing the bowstring."

The princess thanked the bowman, then kissed him. They sat chatting for a while longer before the archer sent her on her way. Leland stood watching her walk the path until she was out of sight, then began to hunt.

The princess rode to the Tate cottage to change. She and Sir Milford, then rode to the palace.

The marquess was waiting on the steps at the palace entrance when the two rode into the courtyard. The riders dismounted. Sir Milford took Goldentrot's reins from the princess, then returned the horses to the stables. Princess Ashley climbed the steps to greet her guest.

She said, "Good morn, Edward, hath thought ye to arrive later in the day. Hath been to the forest for lessons with the bow."

The marquess replied, "Come early, thought to ride with thee to Newton Regney for a bite, then on to the River Petteril for a time."

She replied, "Mercy, Edward, hath been away much of the morn. There be much to do past noon. Might ye join us at the midday meal? We shall then chat a bit on the terrace."

He said, "Very well then, me Princess. Be ye tutored by Sir Milford? Haps so. Why not upon the palace grounds?"

"Nay, Sir Milford be but me escort. Be tutored by a skilled archer from a village nearby. The bowman be known to thee. Might ye recall, 'twas he who bested the lot in the tournament held here at the palace," replied the princess.

The marquess asked, "Me Princess, be he not the fool refusing the king's purse for permission to freely hunt in the forest?"

"Me Lord, aye 'tis he, yet the man for some reason unbeknown to thee haps deemed the freedom of the forest of more value to him than a few crown.

Come, Edward, shall escort thee to the garden. Be a bit soiled. Must change me garments then join thee there."

Sir Milford was not about to leave the princess alone with the marquess. After returning the two steeds to the stables, he entered the palace. Princess Ashley was about to take the stairs to her chambers when the knight entered.

With the flick of her hand, she motioned him to her.

She whispered, "Sir Milford, the marquess awaits in the garden. Might ye engage him in conversation? Shall join thee there. Will we escort him to the dining hall for the midday meal. Shall devise a ruse to politely send the twit upon his way."

After lunch, Princess Ashley asked the marquess if he wished to join her and the ladies-in-waiting, for a reading of essays. The marquess politely refused and took his leave.

Chapter 16

At the breakfast table Saturday morning, Prince Frederick asked Sir Milford to accompany him to the village.

The prince said, "Sir Milford, hath commissioned the cobbler to fashion balls for the game of stick and ball. Might we see what he hath accomplished thus far? Hath he succeeded; will then request he fabricate sticks with which to play."

"Me Prince, this game ye speak of be not known to me, nor hath me seen it played. How come ye by this game?" asked the knight.

The prince replied, "Upon returning from Dumfries, we took shelter in Gretna. 'Twas there the game be seen played by a Scot upon the hillside. The game be then explained to me by Bridget, a servant at the inn."

After breakfast, Sir Milford went to fetch the two steeds from the stables and led them to the entrance of the palace where the prince stood waiting for him. They mounted and rode out of the courtyard taking the road to the village.

Tiffany was playing in front of the millinery when the prince and Sir Milford rode by. She curtsied to the riders. The men waved to the child then continued on to the cobbler's shop.

Upon entering, they were greeted by the cobbler.

The man said, "G 'day your Lordship, Sir Knight. Come ye for the spheres hath requested? Of the many woods, hath come to deem the apple the better. Hold, shall fetch them for thee."

Moments later, the cobbler returned with four well rounded wooden balls. The prince took one from the cobbler then forcefully bounced it off the wooden floor several times expecting it to shatter. To his delight the ball bounced back stinging his hand.

The prince excitedly said "Gad Zeus! Hath ye succeeded. When struck with a stick, the ball will surely take flight.

Now then, must ye fashion a stick. Might ye fetch a quill, and bit of parchment, will scribe a rendering of it for thee."

The man went off, and soon returned with a quill, and paper. The prince sat with quill in hand to sketch a shaft tapered top to bottom with a flat faced head. The cobbler looked intently at the rendering then paused to think awhile before speaking.

He said, "Me Prince, would seem the shaft must flex a bit, and the head be durable. Haps a shaft of hickory with a head of apple or that of persimmon.

Shall do me best to please thee, me Lord. Might ye grant me a week at the task? Be in need of a carpenter to complete the chore properly."

The prince replied, "Sir, there be no need for haste. Must it be constructed properly. Upon completion, might ye fetch it to the palace? Shall we then put the stick to a test. Should it be acceptable, will there be a need for four. Shall ye be well compensated for thy efforts."

The cobbler thanked the prince for permitting him time to produce a functional club and promised to bring it to the palace.

They exchanged farewells, and Prince Frederick and Sir Milford mounted their steeds to return to the palace.

On the road, the prince asked Sir Milford when he expected the cavalryman to return from Dumfries with a reply to the king's letter.

The knight replied, "Me Prince, hath thought the messenger to return this day past. Be uncertain as to the reason for the delay. Surely the man will arrive by day's end.

Be aware of thy concern, yet 'tis certain will ye find Earl William's response quite favorable. When in discussion with thy sire of thy holiday to Dumfries, his Majesty stated ye hath requested Sir Cartwith command the escort. This be understood for 'twas the wish of the countess. Yet might me inquire why the cavalryman Donald must be included as well?"

The prince laughed then related to Sir Milford the ruse he and Lady Rebecca had played on Lady Juliana. The knight joined the prince in laughter.

The prince said, "Sir Milford, hath spoken with Donald of his night with the lady. The man revealed it to be a night of many delights. Thus, thought to afford the gent another opportunity with the winsome maiden.

Be told by Lady Rebecca, should she become me bride, Lady Juliana would come with her to Penrith as her lady-in-waiting.

Lady Rebecca hath expressed a desire for the lass to be tamed of her mischievous behavior. Donald may well be just the man for the task."

The knight replied, "Me Prince, haps so, haps not. Yet 'tis likely the man will find much enjoyment in the attempt."

The prince said, "In me letter to Lady Rebecca, be she told, haps Donald would be one of the cavalry escorting me sire to Dumfries. 'Tis likely she will inform Lady Juliana of this."

Continuing, the prince asked, "Sir Milford, will ye be joining us at the table for the midday meal?"

"Aye, me Prince. Shall stable the steeds, then return to me quarters to tidy up prior to coming to the dining hall," replied the knight.

Arriving at the palace, the two men dismounted their steeds. Sir Milford took the reins of the prince's steed from him and led the horses to the stables.

At the dining table, the prince told the group that he and Sir Milford had gone to the cobbler's in the village to instruct the craftsman of what was needed to play the game of ball and stick. The king, a bit puzzled, asked the prince where he had come by this game.

The prince replied, "Father, 'twas seen being played upon a hillside in Gretna. Be told the men in Scotland pass much of their time at the sport. Found it of interest, thus thought to acquaint it to me mates in Penrith."

Godfrey entered the dining hall. The butler bowed to the royalty, then went to whisper to the king.

He said, "Your Majesty, a messenger but minutes past arrived with three letters from Dumfries. Might there be a reply?"

The king took the letters from the butler, told him to have the messenger wait, then dismissed him.

The king passed one of the letters to the queen, and the other to the prince. He, then broke the seal on the third. He read the message, then took a minute in thought before speaking.

The king Said, "Well Frederick, would seem shall we be going to Dumfries on holiday in early September."

The queen said, "Husband, the countess hath suggested me accompany thee. Alas, must decline for someone must attend to thy affairs.

Frederick, what say the Lady Rebecca?"

The prince smiled and said, "Mother, words writ herein art from me lady's heart. Be meant for me eyes alone."

Chapter 17

Princess Ashley had been in the forest with Leland for the past two days. Wednesday, he had commented on how well her hands had healed and had developed a bit of strength in her arms. The archer decided she was ready to attempt launching a few arrows.

He took her hand and led her over the fallen tree to cross the river to the clearing beyond. The stake the prince had driven into the ground days before was still standing. Leland took his cap and set it on the stake.

He said, "Ashley, set an arrow to thy bow, draw a breath, and hold. Sight the arrow to the cap and let the arrow fly."

The princess followed the archer's instructions. The arrow flew high over the cap. It came to rest in a patch of briars at the far end of the clearing. Leland was pleased with the distance the arrow had flown.

The princess asked, "Leland, hath ye seen where me arrow hath come to rest? Hath lost sight of it."

Leland laughing said, "Ashley, ere it hath struck, 'tis certain shall ye not be dining upon it this night. Be pleased with thy strength. Ye need but to improve thy skill. Come ye to me. Will stand behind thee to guide thy hands."

The princess came and pressed firmly back against the archer. She set an arrow to her bow, raised it, took a deep breath, and held it. Leland placed his hands over hers. The two drew back on the bowstring, aimed, and let the arrow fly. The arrow missed it's mark by but a little.

Elated, the princess dropped her bow and turned to hug the archer.

Leland told her to continue launching arrows at the cap until she grew weary.

Intermittently he asked her to wait while he retrieved the spent arrows, returning them to her.

The princess, still a bit awkward, was improving her aim with every attempt, much to the bowman's delight.

Many minutes had passed when Leland called to her.

He said, "Ashley, hath ye labored enough for the day. 'Tis certain be ye weary. Come shall we set 'neath the oak to chat a bit a 'fore ye take thy leave."

Leland, then went to retrieve his cap and the arrows scattered about the clearing. Returning, he took Ashley's hand to guide her over the fallen tree to the oak. They sat together, their backs to the large oak. Leland turned to the princess and saw a look of concern on her face.

Leland frowning said, "Ashley, would seem be ye a bit troubled. Should ye be pleased with thyself for hath ye done well this morn. Yet set ye beside me, discontented. Should something be a 'miss? Speak of it lass; might me be of aid."

The princess replied, "Leland, these many days hath we been together hath ye looked to me as but a lass in need of tutoring. Haps ye find me loathsome."

Leland asked, "What reason hath given thee to ponder in such a manner? Quite the contrary dear lady, hath bewitched me since first set eyes upon thee. Hath longed to hold thee yet dare me not for might ye be courted by another or haps wed. Be me not the sort to lay hands upon another man's woman."

The princess said, "Hogwash! Hath ye thought me to be spoken for by another when hath bestowed a kiss upon thee t' other day in the clearing? Must ye hath thought me to be but a harlot!"

Leland replied, "Nay lass, deemed it to be but an act of elation, yet must confess to thee, thought it to be quite pleasing."

"Leland, there be no husband. Yet upon one point be ye correct. 'Tis so, be courted by a shameless ogre. Would rather pass me days in a nunnery than to be burdened with that barbarous oaf."

Princess Ashley came to her feet. She stood before the archer for a minute then reached out to take his hand, pulling him to her.

She whispered, "Leland, know ye not to be a coward; be me a person of interest to thee; must ye make it known."

Leland took the princess in his arms, looked into her eyes for a moment, then slowly bent to kiss her passionately. She lay her head on his chest and held him to her not saying a word. At that moment, the princess was certain she wanted Leland in her life.

Stepping away from her he said, "Go ye now lass a 'fore we begin upon a path might we one day regret."

The princess reached up to kiss him on the cheek then turned to walk the deer run. Leland stood watching as she walked out of sight, wondering if he had at last found his mate.

At the forest opening the princess mounted Goldentrot and rode to the Tate cottage to change her garments. Then with Sir Milford she rode back to the palace.

In the courtyard, they dismounted their steeds. Sir Milford took the reins from the princess and led the two horses to the stables. Princess Ashley went to her chambers to tidy up a bit before lunch.

Returning to the main floor of the palace, the princess asked Godfrey to have the servants set up a target at the far end of the garden. She then went to the dining hall to join the family for lunch.

Princess Ashley entered the dining hall to sit beside her mother. The queen asked her how her morning had been with the archer.

She replied, "Mother, Leland hath found me fit to begin tutoring me in the use of the bow.

Some weeks past Frederick hath set a rod of wood in a clearing in the forest. The stake doth yet be in place. Leland set his cap upon it for me to use as a target. Needless to say, me arrows oft failed to run true. Yet Leland be pleased with the distance of the arrows flight. Am to but hone me skill."

The queen said, "Ashley, at the outset thy reason for ye to go to the forest hath been to befriend the archer. Would seem of late the use of the bow hath become a passion for thee as well."

Replying, the princess said, "Mother, Leland be a tutor with a desire for his students to excel. Fear would me be dismissed might me not display an eagerness to learn. Hath instructed Godfrey to set a target at the far end of the garden. This midafternoon shall practice."

The prince said, "Splendid Ashley, will join thee. Haps Father may wish to participate lest he fears being bested by his children."

The king chuckled, and said, "Indeed, Frederick! Could do with a bit of exercise. Margaret, remain upon the terrace, shall ye see thy husband put these children to shame."

Chapter 18

Every afternoon, for the remainder of the week, Princess Ashley could be found in the garden, practicing with her bow. Lady Victoria often sat on the terrace watching and cheering when the arrow launched by the princess hit the target. Sir Milford came by now and then to give the princess a little direction. Christy was charged with retrieving the arrows.

Sunday afternoon, King Frederick and the prince joined the princess with their bows. Queen Margaret sat with Lady Victoria watching, a bit impressed.

She said, "Victoria, hath not seen Ashley with her bow unto this day. The archer hath tutored her well. Should she continue with her lessons, shall she soon be an archer to be reckoned with."

The sun disappeared behind a bank of clouds. Suddenly it began to rain. Everyone in the garden ran for shelter beneath the terrace. Christy made a hasty retreat to the kitchen. Princess Ashley expressed displeasure with the rainfall.

She said, "Curses! Hath thought to join Leland in the forest come morn. 'Tis certain will he not wish to trudge about the mudded forest floor. Mercy! Must the 'morrow be spent in mundane activities?"

The prince asked, "Ashley, Lady Victoria, what might ye say to requesting Sir Milford's company for a ride to Stockbridge upon the 'morrow? 'Tis but a league away. Shall we pause for a bite at the inn then return a 'fore sunset."

"A splendid idea, Frederick! Recall when last we rode to Skelton; farmers were planting strawberries. Hath the season not passed, haps we may pause to fetch a few to be prepared by Mildred for our evening meal," replied the princess.

The prince said, "So it shall be then, Ashley. Thus, shall leave thee for must speak to Sir Milford of our plan."

After speaking with the prince, Sir Milford went to the stables with instructions to have four horses brought around to the hitching post at the palace entrance after breakfast in the morning.

In the kitchen, Mother Mildred and Tom were talking by the side door when Christy entered. Christy could see Tom was a bit upset.

As she drew near she heard her mother speak sharply to him saying, "Thomas, must ye not press me in this. Lady Verna hath many chores in need of attention other than to pass her time hearing the pleadings of a cook seeking a position for a lass from Gretna not known to her. Pray tell, Thomas, what interest hath ye in this young maiden to bother me so oft upon her behalf?"

Tom was about to reply to his Mother when Christy came to stand beside them. He did not want his sister to be part of the conversation. He spoke curtly to her.

"Christy, take thyne ears elsewhere. These words I speak with Mother art not to be heard by a wee twit with a wagging tongue."

In a huff, she replied, "Fret ye not brother, shall me not linger, hath much more of interest to be about than to heed the braying of a demented mule."

Christy skipped off into the courtyard leaving her mother and Tom to continue their conversation.

Tom then continued, saying, "Mother, upon riding with the prince on holiday to Dumfries, we passed the night in Gretna at an inn. Be invited by Bridget, a servant at the inn, to the glen where the villagers gathered at night to sing and dance. Assure thee, 'twas a night shall me not soon forget.

Upon returning from Dumfries, once more found we shelter at the inn. Upon arriving, Bridget ran to greet me. Me thinks the lass be smitten with me. Never will me be certain lest she be near.

Soon the king and Prince Frederick shall journey to Scotland to visit with Earl William. 'Tis certain the prince will be in need of me. Might Lady Verna grant Bridget a position upon the palace staff, will speak of it to the maiden in passing. Might she accept, shall she return with me to Penrith."

His mother said, "Thomas, would seem hath ye feelings for the lass. Very well then, shall speak to Lady Verna at an opportune time."

Chapter 19

The next morning Lady Victoria came awake early. In the privy, she washed, donned her riding attire for the ride to Skelton, then left her room to tap on the door to the chambers of the princess. Receiving no response, she entered the room. The princess was still in her bed asleep.

Lady Victoria spoke, saying, "Mercy, Princess, be ye yet a 'bed! 'Tis near time for the morning meal. Hath ye forgotten we art to ride with Frederick and Sir Milford this morn? Come, make haste, for thy sire and mother await. Were ye to meet with the archer, would ye hath already been groomed and clothed."

The princess, rubbing the sleep from her eyes replied, "Leave me be! At times, Cousin, be ye quite annoying. A ride to Skelton will never compare with a morn with Leland."

Lady Victoria, a bit annoyed said, "Indeed! Very well then, shall leave thee alone with thy fantasies. Must ye insist upon lingering will ye then be left behind."

Lady Victoria stomped from the room to join the others at the breakfast table. Entering the dining hall, she curtsied to the king and queen, extended morning greetings to everyone, then took her seat.

The queen said, "Good morn, Victoria, be ye a bit tardy, and what hath become of Ashley? Pray be she in good stead."

Still a bit annoyed, Lady Victoria replied, "Me Queen, me thinks at times, the princess be deserving of a good thrashing. Went by to fetch the lass, be she yet a 'bed pouting for the loss of the morn with the archer. Advised the lady, might she linger, will she pass this day alone."

Godfrey entered the room with servants carrying breakfast trays. The room fell silent until everyone was served.

The butler and servants were about to leave when Princess Ashley came running into the dining hall. The servants followed her to her seat, served her, then left.

The king looked at her and exclaimed, "By the beard of Neptune, Ashley, thy garments be in complete disarray, and be ye tardy as well. Surely 'tis not thy intent to be seen about the countryside the likes of a ragamuffin!"

The princess replied, "Forgive me, Father, for me tardiness; awoke a wee late this morn. Assure thee, shall adjust me attire prior to leaving the palace. Lady Victoria became a bit ired with me upon coming to find me yet a 'bed."

The king said, "Must say Ashley, at times thy behavior doth leave me fit to spit! Both of ye hath thy horns on full display this morn. Leave us be civil lest words be said with regret."

The prince chuckling said, "Sir Milford, leave us unsheathe our swords, haps the two ladies might wish to engage in battle."

Everyone at the table began to laugh hysterically at the remark, including the prince himself.

Lady Victoria then apologized to the princess, and they all settled down to their breakfast.

Leaving the dining hall, the princess returned to her chambers with Lady Victoria to tidy up a bit.

The prince and Sir Milford went to wait for the ladies beside the horses tethered to the hitching post at the foot of palace steps.

The two ladies exited the palace wearing their crested jackets and breeches. Sir Milford commented on their comely appearance. The ladies thanked him, then without assistance, mounted their steeds. Sir Milford and the prince followed suit, and they rode the horses out of the courtyard.

They proceeded at a walk, for the rain of the day before had muddied the road leading down the hillside to the flats, making it a bit slippery. At the flats, they spurred their steeds to a gallop.

The rain had cleansed the air. The foliage glistened in the early morning sun. Farmers taking their produce to the villages, and peddlers in carts, nodded respectfully as they passed the riders.

Midway to Skelton they came upon a field of strawberries. A middle-aged man and two children were in the field picking the berries and putting them gently into little baskets.

Prince Frederick called to the farmer, summoning him. The gent came to them holding a half-full basket in his hand. He bowed to the royalty then spoke.

He said, "Good morn, me Lord. How might me be of aid to thee? Hath ye an interest in me luscious fruit? As ye see, be they plucked fresh as we speak. Might ye wish to sample a few out me basket?"

The farmer walked around to a breach in the dry-stone wall surrounding the field, then lifted the basket to the riders. They each took a few to taste.

Princess Ashley addressed the man.

She said, "Kind Sir, be they quite pleasing to the taste. We be riding to Skelton. We shall be passing by upon returning. Might ye set several of the wee baskets into a large one for toting? We shall fetch them a bit past midday."

The farmer replied, "Indeed, me Lady, shall tend to it. Me mate will see to their cleansing. Thus, they will be properly prepared for consumption."

Princess Ashley thanked the farmer.

They bade him farewell then continued their ride to Skelton.

Arriving at the hamlet a bit before noon. They dismounted by a huge maple near the pub. The prince and Sir Milford tethered the horses to the tree.

Removing their capes, they spread them out in the shade for the ladies to sit upon.

Two young boys were playing nearby. Sir Milford called to them.

He shouted, "Ye Lads, might ye fetch water for the steeds? Go ye, speak to the taverner at the pub, will he loan thee a bucket."

The two boys stopped playing. They ran into the pub to do the knight's bidding.

Minutes later, two seedy men in their early twenties came walking toward the group. Seeing the four sitting under the tree they both stopped a short distance away and began to laugh.

One addressing the other said, "Look ye there, mate; four gents. Nay, hold, for hath erred. Two be ladies in breeches! Might ye ere hath seen such a sight?"

The two men stood laughing hysterically. Sir Milford came to his feet, drew his knife from its sheath.

He said, "Ye two ill-mannered rascals be gone lest me lay ye low with me blade. Dare ye not linger lest ye stir me ire!"

Sir Milford feigned an attack on the men. The four broke out in laughter when the annoying men ran off like frightened rabbits being pursued by a pack of hounds.

At that same moment, the two boys who had gone to fetch water for the horses stepped out of the pub. Seeing the knight brandishing a long blade they stopped dead in their tracks, set the buckets down, and stood motionless.

Sir Milford said, "Rest at ease, ye lads, fear not. No harm shall befall thee. Me blade be not meant for thee. Come water the steeds."

The two boys looked at each other, retrieved the buckets, then advanced toward the horses with caution.

When the horses had their fill, Prince Frederick reached into his purse for two coins and tossed them to the boys. They thanked the prince, bowed, then returned to their playing.

The proprietor had seen the rowdy men frightened away by the knight through the window of the pub. He came to the riders with a ewer of ale, and four tankards. Bowing, he spoke as he poured each of them the ale to drink.

The man said, "Sir, hath ye done well to confront those two louts with thy blade. They be a plague upon the hamlet with their unruly behavior. One day they may rile a man of ill spirit. Will it then be the end of them."

He paused, then continuing, said; "Me kitchen shall soon be oped. Might ye wish to enter me pub for a bite? Me fish and chips will surely please thy palates."

Prince Frederick took a long pull from his tankard of ale, and emitted a gratifying belch, then addressed the others.

He asked, "What say ye, mates? Shall we partake of the Tavernier's suggestion? The ale hath wet me appetite. Could me do with a bite."

The others thought the fish and chips to be a fine choice for lunch. Princess Ashley added a request for the Tavernier.

She said, "Good man, 'tis quite pleasant in the shade. When our meal hath been prepared, might we partake of it out here in the summer's air? Aye too, a bit more ale shall be required. Might ye fetch a bite for the children at play as well?"

The gent replied, "Your Ladyship, 'tis an honor to do thy bidding. Shall speak to me mate, then return with another ewer of ale in a moment."

The Tavernier hurried away leaving the four to chat and enjoy their ale.

Many minutes later the proprietor came carrying two heaping trays of fish and chips, followed by the proprietor's mate with two small baskets for the children. The two boys howled with delight.

Having eaten and drunk their fill, the group prepared to leave. Sir Milford entered the pub to settle with the proprietor. He thanked the man for the hearty meal, then bade him farewell.

The proprietor said, "Sir, pray ye hath found the food to thy liking. Me mate be quite proud of her cooking. Safe journey to thee."

Sir Milford left the pub. As the group mounted their steeds, the children ran to thank him for his generosity. Bowing, they bade them farewell.

Passing the farm, they found a large basket filled with small containers they had requested sitting on the stone wall.

There was no one in sight. Sir Milford dismounted Titus and walked through the break in the wall to the farmer's house. A tap on the door was answered by a woman he assumed to be the farmer's wife. The knight addressed the woman.

He said, "G 'day, the basket of strawberries hath requested of thy husband be left with no one in attendance. Ye art to be compensated."

She replied, "Good day, Sir; there be no need."

Sir Milford reached into his purse, counted out what he thought to be a generous sum, and handed the coins to the woman. The woman thanked the knight and bid him farewell.

Sir Milford retrieved the basket in passing, mounted Titus, and the group rode on.

Chapter 20

The group arrived in the courtyard of the palace in the afternoon. The stable master with a stable boy came running to relieve the horses from the riders.

Sir Milford was about to take the large basket of strawberries to Mildred in the kitchen when Princess Ashley approached him.

She said, "Sir Milford, hold, shall relieve thee of one of the wee baskets. Wish to share the berries with Leland on the 'morrow."

Smiling, the knight retrieved one of the small containers and handed it to the princess. He then continued on to the kitchen.

The prince, princess, and Lady Victoria entered the palace going to their chambers to change their clothes and tidy up a bit.

Leaving their chambers, they took the stairs to the floor below. As they passed the kitchen, Godfrey came to speak with the prince. The ladies continued on their way.

Godfrey bowed, then said, "Me Prince, a man come by toting an odd shaped stick, requesting to speak with thee. The man be told be ye not about. He expressed a desire to wait. Be he escorted to the terrace. Shall me fetch him to thee?"

The prince replied, "Nay, shall see to it. Should Sir Milford be yet in the kitchen, advise him the village cobbler hath arrived. Instruct him to join me on the terrace."

Prince Frederick hurried to the terrace anxious to see what the cobbler had accomplished. As he stepped onto the terrace, the cobbler stood, and bowed as he spoke.

He said, "Good day, me Prince, pray this stick hath fashioned will suit thy purpose. Hath taken the liberty of constructing another ball, thus the stick may be tested."

The prince took the club from the cobbler and waved it around awkwardly.

Sir Milford stepping onto the terrace, retreated; attempting to avoid being struck by the club.

The prince addressing the knight said, "Look ye here, Sir Milford. The cobbler hath succeeded in his task. Come, leave us attempt to strike the ball in the garden."

The two men stepped out onto the grass, taking turns trying to hit the ball. Sometimes with success; more often not. Several times the ball landed in the flowerbeds. The men stomped through the flowers carelessly when retrieving the ball.

Needless to say, in no time at all the previously well-groomed lawn was pocked, and the flowerbeds were in a horrible state.

Princess Ashley came a bit later with Lady Victoria to join the prince and Sir Milford on the terrace.

Lady Victoria, seeing what the two men had done to her precious garden, emitted a scream.

"Good Lord, me Prince, Sir Milford, what manner of play might this be to wreak such havoc upon the beauty of me garden?" Lady Victoria asked.

The cobbler, fearing what was to happen next, attempted to slip away unnoticed.

The prince called to him saying, "Good man, hold, art ye to be compensated for thy labor."

Lady Victoria, yet angered, said, "Curses, Prince Frederick! Compensated? The man be deserving of a flogging for affording thee this instrument of destruction."

Laughing, the prince replied, "Calm thyself, Lady Victoria. Pledge to thee, come the morn the beds shall be set a 'right by the gardener and his aides."

The prince went to the cobbler to pay him for the club and balls, then instructed him to produce three more, and a dozen more balls, at his leisure.

The cobbler thanked the prince, bowed, then made a hasty retreat.

Much of the conversation at the dinner table that night centered around the events of the day. Prince Frederick told the king and queen of Sir Milford's encounter with the two scoundrels who had interrupted their conversation.

Princess Ashley spoke of the strawberries they had purchased from the farmer, which were to be the dessert for the evening.

King Frederick asked Lady Victoria if she had anything of interest to add.

She replied, "Your Majesty, at the pub in Skelton we partook our fill of fish and chips, a 'fore returning to the palace.

Thought it to be quite a pleasant day unto a bit later when I, with the princess, stepped out onto the terrace expecting to join Sir Milford and Frederick for a chat. Only to find the two in the garden, smiting the grasses with a strange stick, and trudging about me precious flowerbeds. Alas Uncle, me garden be in complete disarray."

The king turned to the two men, and asked, "Frederick, Milford, what manner of foppery hath ye two been about this day? For what purpose hath ye lain Victoria's treasured domain asunder?"

Grinning, the prince replied, "Father, 'tis the game of ball and stick hath seen played in Gretna. Might ye recall, hath related the playing of the game to thee upon returning from Dumfries.

The village cobbler hath fashioned a stick and a number of balls at me request. Come he by earlier with the stick and balls. The lot must be tested to insure it would endure when in use."

The king asked, "Indeed! Frederick, might this be a game one is to play in a garden?"

"Nay, Father; 'tis best suited for the hillside and the flats. Thus, ye elders may deem it quite wearisome," replied the prince.

The king, grunting, said, "We elders? The devil ye say!"

Addressing the queen, the king said, "Margaret, haps in me absence might ye prepare a place of burial. For upon returning from Dumfries shall we elders challenge these upstarts to a match to determine who is to be the victor, and who is to bury their pride."

The queen replied, "Husband, be ye not at the doors of thy demise nor in thy prime. Haps Frederick hath spoken true. This game may well be for the younger. Traipsing about the hillside might leave thee panting short of breath."

The king looked at the queen, and at the other end of the table with a smirk; thought a moment before replying.

He said, "Dear Lady, haps this very night when in chambers shall we see who be left panting in the darkness."

The king's unexpected reply to the queen, spoken in jest, resulted in a boisterous round of laughter from the diners.

Before leaving the dining hall, the princess spoke to Sir Milford.

She said, "Sir Milford, might we leave for the forest early on the 'morrow? Wish to please Leland with the progress hath made these days past with me bow."

"As ye wish, me Princess. At early light, shall await thee in the courtyard," he replied.

Chapter 21

It had been days since last the princess had been in the forest with the archer. Before sunrise she came awake, went to the privy to wash, then dressed quickly.

Retrieving the little basket of strawberries from the table beside her bed, she hurried to the kitchen.

She emptied the container onto a napkin, then tied the corners together.

Sir Milford was waiting in the courtyard with the reins of the two horses in his hand when the princess exited the palace. Seeing the two walking toward him, Robert bowed and opened the gate for them to exit.

In passing, the princess handed the napkin with the strawberries to the sentry. Outside the gate, the two mounted their steeds. Robert handed the parcel given him by the princess to Sir Milford, and the riders, then rode down the hill to the Tate cottage.

Hearing the riders approach, Arabella ran to open the cottage door. She waved and shouted a greeting as they drew near.

They reined in the horses at the hitching post. The princess dismounted, tethered her horse, and took the parcel from the knight to set it on a step.

Arabella curtsied as the princess entered the cottage to change garments. Sir Milford dismounted, tethered Titus, then addressed Arabella.

He said, "Good morn, lass. Pray find thee and thy mother in good stead."

She replied, "G 'day, Sir Knight, hath thought to see thee this day past. Come enter; we shall chat o'er a cup of tea as we wait for the princess to change.

Mother be a 'bed. Shall she soon be about. Will she be pleased to see thee. Brother Jarin fares well?"

The knight replied, "Aye, oft see him at his chores in passing. Know 'tis a burden upon ye ladies for the lad not to be about. Thus, hath ye a need, must ye speak of it."

Arabella replied, "Sir Knight, hath ye afforded we Tates much more than be deserving. Princess Ashley hath been quite bounteous o'er these weeks past. Hath we fared well by her favors."

The princess came into the kitchen prepared to ride to the forest. She bade Arabella farewell as she left the cottage.

Sir Milford followed her out the door and retrieved her steed for her to mount. He picked up the parcel of strawberries from the step, handed it to her, then stood watching her ride away.

At the entrance to the forest, Princess Ashley dismounted, tethering the horse to a small birch. With the parcel of strawberries in hand, she took the familiar path to the large oak beside the river.

Leland was kneeling at the water's edge, washing his hands. The princess thought to sneak up on the archer. Keeping an eye on the path, avoiding twigs that if stepped on would be heard, she walked gingerly toward the archer.

Without turning from the river, Leland greeted the maiden.

He said, "Good morn, Ashley, be ye a bit early. Must say thy stalking hath improved, yet the scent of thy bath be carried to me by the gentle winds. Thy scent would hath been detected by the beasts of the forest as well. There be a lesson to be learned from this. When at the hunt, the wind must be away from thy prey, toward thee. Thus, will ye remain undetected."

"And a g' day to thee, Leland. Me attempt to come upon thee quietly hath been foiled by thy cleverness. Not only hath thee the ears of a hare, but the nose of a hound as well. 'Tis no wonder hath ye avoided discovery in the king's forest for these many years."

The archer asked, "Ashley, ye come this morn bearing a gift? What might there be concealed within the folds of the parcel hath ye in hand?"

She replied, "Thought to come with a few berries for we to savor together upon completion of me lesson. Might that not please thee? 'Tis wee compensation for thy willingness to assume the role of a tutor."

Leland said, "Little one, at the outset thought to instruct thee for thyne own protection; not to be compensated. Of late hath found it a delight for thee to be near.

Leave us dispense with this conversation for the moment and address the task at hand. Come, shall we traverse the river o'er the fallen tree to the clearing."

The archer took her hand, and she followed, her heart beating rapidly in her chest. Had Leland just given her an indication of his feelings for her? She wished to learn more of this later when they sat chatting together beneath the oak.

In the clearing, Leland handed the princess her bow and quiver, then went to put his cap on the stick set into the ground weeks ago by the prince.

He said, "Now then, Ashley, don thy glove. Shall assist thee in setting the patch of hide upon thyne arm.

Leave us thus, assess the measure of progress ye hath achieved o'er this week past. Be not in haste; sight thy mark with care."

The first few arrows showed strength but were well off the mark. The princess displayed a bit of frustration.

Leland said, "Be patient, Ashley! Draw thy bowstring, draw breath, hold then let fly thy shaft. The swiftness of thy load and launch shall come with time. Now then, continue."

Leland permitted the maiden to launch several arrows without interruption: noting her accuracy improving with each launch. He patiently waited for Ashley to hit her mark; giving her a bit of confidence before permitting her to stop.

Complementing her, he said, "Hath ye done well. Soon will ye be beside me at the hunt. Would seem ye be a bit weary. Shall retrieve the many arrows spent then will we return to set beside the river."

The two sat beneath the oak; neither one speaking for a time. Removing her glove, the princess picked up the parcel she had set beside the oak earlier; and undid the knots in the napkin to reveal the strawberries.

She picked up one of the plumper berries then extended her hand to the archer's lips. Leland took the berry into his mouth, savored it for a moment, then smiled in approval.

A bit of the juices escaped his mouth. The princess licked the juice from his lips. Leland took her in his arms and kissed her passionately. The princess returned his kiss.

The princess asked, "Leland, long hath yearned for thee to embrace me as this. Must inquire of thee, might this hath been but a kiss of lust?"

"Dear Ashley, hath born witness to the consequences of young village maidens submitting to a man's lustful kisses. Then when with child, be they left to fend alone. Aye yearn for thee, yet art we now to continue upon this path, the cost of this bit of pleasure may be quite severe," Leland replied.

She said, "Hath ye spoken with words of wisdom. However, there yet be a need for me to know if within thy heart ye hold me dear."

Leland replied, "Indeed! Ashley, this shall say to thee. Within me heart there be, nor will there be, no other."

Tears of joy fell to her cheeks as she continued clinging to Leland. The two remained silent in each other's arms for some time before Leland spoke.

Forcefully, Leland said, "Heed well this say to thee. Shall not pursue thee lest be me certain their art no others of interest to thee at present nor from times past yet within thy heart. Wish not to court thee but to be played the fool. Art we of a mind in this?"

"Thy words art well noted, Leland. Words fall with ease from many lips; their value must be proven a 'fore a commitment be made."

He then said, "Come, Ashley, leave us partake of these succulent berries. However, must admit, they art not as sweet as thy tender lips."

They stayed by the river eating the berries and chatting for the better part of an hour before Leland decided it was time for the princess to leave.

"Come Ashley, shall walk the path with thee for a bit. There be a matter in dire need of attention. Upon leaving thee, hold thy blade at the ready. Never be known what might be lurking within the forest."

The two walked hand in hand along the deer run for a bit when Leland stopped, raising a finger to his lips, signaling silence.

The princess whispered, "Leland, what hath caused thee alarm?"

He whispered, "The whinny of a steed hath come to me ears from the road beside the forest. Shall accompany thee to the forest entrance. Leave us proceed with caution."

The princess cringed in fear. Were Leland to continue on the path with her he would see Goldentrot tethered to the birch. Would he not be left to wonder who had left the horse unattended, and who the owner might be? Should she insist on proceeding alone, Leland surely would not permit it. The archer was no fool. Upon seeing the horse, he would become suspicious of her insistence. The princess had no recourse but to remain silent and follow Leland's lead.

The horse was in full view of the archer when they came to the end of the path. The princess looked at Leland, bearing an expression of wonderment. The archer stood looking at the horse for a moment before going to stand beside the steed. He looked it over carefully then returned to speak to the princess.

He said, the steed be a breed of quality; it's bridle, and saddle be those of a noble. Hath he entered the forest for reasons yet not known.

Ashley, when come ye this morn, found me at the river washing. Earlier hath slain a buck. The animal hath been dressed, in wait of transport. For this reason, must return to the forest lest it be found by this noble, and taken."

The princess asked, "Leland, no buck be seen upon arriving. Where might it hath been?"

He replied, "It be well hidden. Will retrieve the carcass after sunset. Shall await thee in the morn. Be off ye now in haste. Take the road. Shall stand watch upon thee unto be ye out of sight."

The princess put her arms around the archer, kissed him, whispered farewell, then ran in the direction Leland had indicated; frequently looking back at the archer until she was out of his sight.

She then stopped to catch her breath and waited for Leland to retreat well into the heart of forest before running back to mount Goldentrot. At a gallop she, then ride to the Tate cottage.

In the cottage, Sir Milford sat at the table in the kitchen with Arabella and Mother Tate. The sound of hoof beats coming from the direction of the forest entrance brought him to his feet.

Exiting the cottage, he waited for the princess to rein in Goldentrot at the hitching post, then went to help her dismount. The knight tethered the steed, then followed Princess Ashley into the kitchen.

The two ladies came a 'right to curtsy to the princess. Mother Tate bade the princess a good day. The princess returned the woman's greeting as she passed her on the way to Arabella's bedroom to change her garments.

Bidding the ladies farewell, Sir Milford left the cottage to wait for the princess by the horses.

Minutes later, the princess stepped out of the cottage. He helped her onto Goldentrot, then mounted Titus.

The ladies stood in the doorway waving as the two rode toward the palace.

Riding into the courtyard of the palace, Princess Ashley and the knight recognized the marquess' steed tethered to the hitching post. Disgruntled, the princess spoke.

"Curses, Sir Milford, another day to be tolerated with the shameless oaf. There be no end to this misery."

Chapter 22

Riding the hill Wednesday morning to the flats, then to the Tate's cottage, Princess Ashley related to Sir Milford the discovery of her steed at the entrance to the forest by the archer.

She said, "Sir Milford, thought it to be the end of me pretense as a village maiden. Much more concerned with me safety than who the rider might be. Leland directed me to return to me abode in haste.

Me set upon the road toward Clifton unto be out of sight; remained hidden, waiting for Leland to return to the forest; then quickly ran to mount Goldentrot, and return to the Tate's."

"An excellent maneuver, me Princess. Haps be best upon riding to the forest this morn ye tether thy steed out of sight beyond the entrance to the forest. A 'foot, then set ye upon the path to the river," replied Sir Milford.

She said, "Hath ye given me good counsel, Sir Milford. Thus, should Leland accompany me to the road when leaving the forest, me steed shall not be in view."

Changing into Arabella's garments at the cottage, Princess Ashley rode to the forest following the knight's instructions.

She arrived at the river to find Leland nowhere in sight. Standing with her back to the oak, she drew her blade to wait, wondering perhaps the archer had another matter in need of his attention this morning.

Feeling a bit uncomfortable alone in the woods, she thought to wait a few minutes before leaving.

Suddenly Leland stepped out from behind a stand of pine toting a partridge in one hand and the longbow in the other, startling her.

He said, "Good morn, Ashley! Mercy! Pray be not thy intent to run me through with thy blade."

Laughing, she replied, "G 'day, Leland would ye be deserving of it for coming upon me in such a startling manner. Yet shall not pierce thy heart with me trusted blade, but with a kiss."

The archer came to her, dropped the partridge he had downed earlier and his longbow. He took her in his arms; permitting her to carry out her threat.

She then said, "Leland, this day past spoke ye of me involvement with men; present, and past. Must confess to thee there be one come to court me for some time. In truth, hath given the bloke no encouragement for he be not a righteous man. Nonetheless, he persists."

"Indeed! Ashley, should ye desire to rid thyself of this annoyance, need but to speak of it. Shall confront the fellow upon thy behalf with words certain to sway his resolve," Leland replied.

She said, "No need to be concerned for never be left alone with the man. Cousin Victoria ere be by me side. Yea too, should the rascal dare lay hands upon me, shall he rue the day. 'Tis certain the oaf will soon weary of the chase for from it hath he gained no reward."

Continuing, she said, "Spoke to me sire of the archer who hath tutored me for these many days in the use of the bow. Father hath viewed me progress with much interest. Hath he expressed a desire to acquaint hisself with the man with the patience to instruct his daughter so kindly. Thus, one eve soon must ye come to sup at me sire's table."

Leland replied, "Were me to come then request permission to court thee, would not thy sire inquire as to me ability to provide for thee properly? Be not a man of property. Hath but a wee hut, and garden of me own. Surely shall he reject me as an unworthy suitor."

Smiling, the princess said, "Leland, me sire doth not judge a man by the weight of his purse, but by his true character and his deeds. This too shall thus reveal to thee. Be me in attendance at the archer's tournament held by the king at the palace. Hath seen thee then amusing the children.

Then upon emerging victorious, ye refused the purse presented to thee by the king, requesting permission to hunt the king's forest freely in its stead."

The princess paused, then continued saying, "Many thought thee to be a fool, refusing a purse of gold. Others inquired as to the reason for thy request. Then, from ear to ear, passed the word within thy village be ye held in high regard. Too, be said ye hath desired access to the forest to pursue thy passion for the hunt.

Me sire, aware of the villager's fondness for thee, hath deemed thee a man of worth, and thy skill with the bow a good provider."

He replied, "Ashley, haps at some time shall desire to speak with thy sire, but not as yet.

Come, set thy mind to the task at hand. Might ye display further improvement with thy bow this morn, shall ye hunt at me side this week to come."

After dinner that evening, the princess sat out on the terrace chatting with the prince and Lady Victoria. Lady Victoria asked the princess how her lessons were progressing.

The princess replied, "Victoria, be told by Leland hath progressed so well in me lessons we art to hunt together come Monday morn. Surely will he not expect me shafts to run true at the outset. To date, hath but set sight upon a target mounted upon a stake. Me suspect his intent for me be to experience naught but the feel of the hunt."

The prince said, "Must agree with thee, Ashley. A target in motion doth require much more skill to strike than one set upon a stand. Yet, this too will come to thee with patience."

The princess replied, "Me thank thee, Frederick, for thy encouragement. Haps one day soon will we hunt together."

"Shall look to it, Ashley. Alas, must leave ye ladies, for Father and me chums await. Art we to pass the night at a game of maw. Bade me good fortune," said the prince.

Lady Victoria had hoped the prince would leave them to chat alone. She had many questions to ask the princess which would not be answered in the presence of the prince. She waited for the footsteps of the prince to fade down the hall before she spoke.

She said, "Ashley, enough of this speaking of bows, arrows, and the hunt. Pray tell how hath thy meetings with the archer progressed?"

The princess replied, "Lady Victoria, must ye not speak of this am about to relate to thee for as yet be not certain. T 'other day when launching arrows at a target in the clearing beyond the river, one ran true, striking it's mark. Elated, bestowed a kiss upon the archer. 'Twas returned with passion."

She continued saying, "Recall the strawberries we fetched at the farm t 'other day? Took a wee basket to the forest for Leland. Set we neath the oak beside the river this day past. Chose a plump berry from the lot and put it to Leland's lips. He took it in his mouth, savored it, then rewarded me with a kiss. Thought the moment hath come for me to be deflowered and would hath yielded to him readily. With a few words of restraint from him, the moment of passion passed. Pledge to thee, Lady Victoria, shall yield to no other."

Lady Victoria said, "Princess, by these words ye hath spoken, hath ye professed thy love for the archer, and by his actions hath he for thee. Pray all bodes well for thee in this courtship."

"Lady Victoria, must be patient with Leland. Were he to learn me true identity too soon, might he deem our courtship, but a passing adventure perpetrated by a pampered twit.

Might it be prudent for me to seek Mother's counsel this very night as to how to proceed hence forth," replied the princess.

Chapter 23

Near bedtime the princess went to her Mother's chambers knowing her Father and the prince would be occupied with their game well into the night.

On entering, she found the queen was being tended to by her lady-in-waiting. Lady Winfred curtsied to the princess, greeting her a good evening. The princess returned the greeting then addressed her mother.

She said, "Mother, forgive me for coming at this late hour, requesting a word with thee."

The queen glanced over at her lady-in-waiting. Lady Winfred knowing she was being told to leave, curtsied then quickly left the room, closing the door behind her.

The queen said, "Ashley, come set here beside me. What hath thee in mind to share with me could not wait unto the morn?"

The princess replied, "Mother, hath come to seek counsel in this matter of Leland. Me affinity with the archer hath gone beyond me tutoring. Hath he won me heart with his gentle nature and kindly manner. But to be beside the man doth stir me within."

Concerned, the queen replied, "Ashley, pray hath ye not been so foolish as to engage in activities with the bowman unbefitting thy position."

The princess smiled and said, "Nay Mother; but a token of affection passed 'tween we two. It be Leland at that moment who displayed restraint. Must confess to thee, Mother, hath he not, would hath yielded to him readily."

A bit startled, the queen asked, "And all of this hath come to pass 'neath the watchful eye of Sir Milford? Thought he not to intervene?"

The princess replied, "Mother, Sir Milford hath by then deemed the archer a man of honor. Thus, be he no longer concerned with me wellbeing. Aware of me feelings for the archer, dared he not reveal hisself, knowing it would hath been the end of me affinity with Leland. Must ye not rebuke me, nor Sir Milford, for this am about to reveal.

Well into me tutoring by Leland, 'twas certain the man meant me no harm. In truth, when by his side, felt quite secure. Upon discovering me feelings for the archer became more profound with each passing day.

Pleaded with Sir Milford to accompany me to the Tate's cottage then leave me continue onto the forest alone. Knowing the nature of the archer by his many deeds, Sir Milford yielded to me request."

The queen said, "Ashley, 'tis well known to me the trust thy sire hath in the knight's decisions, and the high regard doth he hold for the archer. Thy sire might yet hath not approved of the course ye chose to follow so soon with the archer."

The queen paused a bit in thought, took the hand of the princess, smiled, then continued speaking.

She said, "Ashley, recall the day of the tournament when stood ye with Frederick upon the ramparts above the courtyard? Frederick directed thyne eyes to the archer sitting with the children below. Much later spoke to me of a feeling within, then yet unknown to thee. This feeling may be made clear to thee in a tale of a maiden in attendance at an event many years ago."

A blush came to the queens face as she said, "Recall, 'twas passed midday 'neath a summer's sky at the estate of a noble. The guests mingled about in idle chatter. Suddenly a maiden set eyes upon a handsome gent, standing alone upon a balcony. As in a dream t 'others about the maiden vanished, but the stately gent remained in sight.

The strange feeling sensed ye within; but weeks past at the tournament, overtook the maiden that moment as well."

The princess said, "Indeed, Mother; a strange tale must say. Pray tell, might the lady in time hath learned what the feeling signified?"

The queen smiled, and said, "Aye, Ashley; the feeling within be but an ember waiting to be nurtured.

She might hath turned away, permitting the feeling to pass. Yet she wished to learn more of this man who hath touched her. As a brazen peasant maiden might hath responded, she went to engage the man in conversation."

The princess wondered where this tale was going.

She asked, "Mother, the maiden and the gent of whom ye speak be a myth? What is to be learned from this tale ye hath spun?"

The queen replied, "Ashley, 'tis not a tale. The event hath related to thee be true. The lady acted in a manner certain to arouse the ire of her sire. Yet despite this, she cast aside her fears, seized the moment, and followed her heart.

The man may hath thought the lady a bit demented, the lady to approach him without escort in sight of all in attendance. For 'twas not proper for a lady to be so bold.

Might the gent hath turned away, would it hath been an embarrassment long to be forgiven by her sire.

Ashley, as the maiden long ago, ye too placed thyself at peril, setting aside the fear of thy sire's wrath for thy disobedience by entering the forest without escort. With good fortune, no harm befell thee. What is to become of thy folly is yet to be revealed."

The queen continued, saying, "The handsome gent standing upon the balcony that summer's day be well known to thee. For be thy sire."

The princess, awed of her mother's disclosure,.

She said, "A bold gesture indeed, Mother. Yet thy courtship with Father began with an emotion. I, in turn, approached Leland with a deception; garbed as a village maiden. Thus, the purpose of coming to thee for counsel.

Never thought to become so enamored with the archer. Thus, the ruse would bear no consequence. However, with these feelings hath for Leland, might he learn of me deception, he may not be forgiving, and lost to me. How am I to proceed?"

The queen, understood her daughter's concern.

She replied, "Ashley, must we set upon a path to follow with caution, and with much thought. One misstep may cause a disaster. Would be prudent to ponder a bit upon a proper course a 'fore proceeding.

Go ye now, for the hour hath gotten late. Soon thy sire will come seeking the comfort of his bed. Rest easy this night. We shall continue this conversation upon the 'morrow."

The princess bade her mother a good night, then left the room knowing in spite of her mother's assurances, it was to be a sleepless night.

Chapter 24

After breakfast the next morning, the group retired to the garden. King Frederick sat on the terrace with the prince and Sir Milford, discussing plans for the trip to Dumfries.

Queen Margaret strolled in the garden chatting with the princess and Lady Victoria.

The princess was anxious to continue the conversation she had held with her mother the previous night.

Sensing her daughter's impatience, the queen directed a question to Lady Victoria.

She asked, "Victoria, hath Ashley confided in thee, of her encounters with the archer?"

Lady Victoria replied, "Yea, me Queen, the princess hath shared much of what hath come to pass with the bowman; certain her words would not be spoken to another."

The queen said, "As hath expected; well then, we shall speak freely."

Meanwhile, Godfrey stepped onto the terrace, bowed, then went to whisper in the ear of the prince.

Prince Frederick sprang to his feet and ran into the palace. Godfrey bowed, and followed.

King Frederick and Sir Milford looked at each other, wondering what had riled the prince.

Minutes later, the prince was heard shouting for his father and Sir Milford to come quickly.

They ran from the terrace expecting some sort of altercation. Solely to see the prince standing beside the cobbler holding three clubs in his hand.

The prince shouted to Sir Milford. "Look ye here! The cobbler hath completed his task. Quickly, fetch Sir Cartwith. Hath we a game to play this morn."

Must retrieve the balls, and t' other stick from me quarters. Shall join thee in the courtyard."

Sheepishly, the prince turned to the king and said, "Father, might ye compensate the cobbler for his labor?

Sir Milford, and the prince, then ran off, leaving the king to pay the cobbler, thanked the man and then sent him on his way.

The clubs and balls the cobble had come to the palace with, had been left on the palace steps.

The king picked up one of the clubs and stood in the courtyard, swinging it in the air aimlessly.

The guards at the gates looked on in wonderment.

Minutes later, the prince returned with the balls and the fourth club and stood beside the king in wait of Sir Milford, and Sir Cartwith who came running from the barracks.

The prince waited for the two men to join them, then spoke.

He said, "Leave us play the hillside beyond the castle walls to the flats. Dare we not invade Lady Victoria's garden once more."

The men walked over the drawbridge to the hillside, each with a ball and club in hand. Dropping the balls to the ground, they began swatting at them wildly, running to, and fro on the hill, howling at a strike, cursing at a miss.

The bedlam drew many of the palace occupants to the ramparts including the queen, princess, and Lady Victoria.

The spectators laughing hysterically at the scene below.

Finally, the king called a halt to the play.

He said, "Gad Zeus, lads; would seem hath we become the laughingstock of the palace. There must be some rule of play and a bit of order to this game. In the least a goal must be set to be achieved.

Leave us ponder upon this a 'fore continuing. At the outset, must impose a question upon thee Frederick.

Might it not be so? This game is meant to be played by the young, and the elders as well?"

The prince replied, "In our previous conversation, in this regard, thought to deceive thee in jest.

Yea Father. The game be for all to play. This be related to me by the lass at the inn in Gretna. Spoke she too of a destination to be achieved; agreed upon by all in play."

The king replied, "As I hath suspected. Must ye lads agree the young be a bit more fleet a 'foot than the elders; thus, granting the young be at an advantage. There must be some rule to compensate we elders for this.

Shall we set a goal. The first to achieve it shall be the victor."

The prince said, "Look ye there to the breech in the wall of stone beyond the road in the flats. The first ball to be struck through the breech by one of we men at play shall be deemed victorious. In fairness, must we each smite our ball, in turn."

"Very well, Frederick, in this manner will we proceed. Yet when in Dumfries, shall request of Earl William a proper set of rules of play," said the king.

The four men ineptly resumed their game beneath the sweltering autumn sun.

Queen Margaret watched for a bit then sent for the butler. Godfrey came and bowed, asking for instructions.

The queen said, "Godfrey, quickly, send servants with ewers of grog to the men at play lest they soon expire from the heat.

Hath wearied of this madness. Come ladies, leave us retire to the shade of the terrace. Shall we set to ponder upon a solution to the plight of Ashley with the archer."

Chapter 25

Friday after lunch, the queen, Princess Ashley, and Lady Victoria met in the sitting room adjacent to the chapel to continue the conversation of the previous day. Many of Thursday's idle hours had been passed attempting to devise a plan as to how the true identity of the princess was to disclose to Leland.

After much bantering among the ladies, they determined it was to be revealed to the archer in bits and pieces.

The princess then spoke of her conversation with Leland Wednesday past, wherein she told the archer of her father's desire to meet the man who had been tutoring his daughter in the use of the bow, and how the archer had put her off, fearing rejection.

Hearing this, they sat without speaking for a time, deep in thought. Finally, the queen broke the silence.

She said, "Ashley, would seem the archer hath deemed hisself unworthy of thee. Haps he is to be convinced to the contrary."

Lady Victoria responded, "Well thought, me Queen, a splendid idea. Haps we might enlist the prince in this endeavor.

Ashley, the archer hath oft spoken freely of thee with the prince. Be it not so? Yea too, might not Leland soon find it odd o'er these many weeks that Frederick and Ashley hath not been in the forest upon the same day?

Haps 'tis time for them to do so as a chance encounter. Then, as strangers, Ashley might speak of the archer's victory at the tournament, revealing her admiration for the bowman.

At some point in the future when Frederick be alone with Leland in the forest, he must attempt to learn the depth of the archer's affection for Ashley.

The victory achieved by Leland at the tournament may be used to blandish the archer into accompanying Ashley to her abode, and sup with her sire."

The queen said, "Would it indeed be a beginning, Victoria. However, Ashley is to give Leland some indication beforehand that she be more than but a village maiden. Thus, preparing the archer for the discovery of her identity"

The queen paused a moment, deep in thought before continuing.

She then went on to say, "Ashley, shall we quickly set this in motion. Victoria, might ye fetch the prince? Must he be instructed as to the part he is to play in this plan."

Lady Victoria hurried out of the sitting room down the hall to the kitchen.

The butler was sitting at the table with the servants having a bit of tea. Lady Victoria called to him.

She said, "Godfrey, go ye quickly; find Prince Frederick. Advise him the queen requests his presence in the sitting room."

The butler left the kitchen to do the lady's bidding and Lady Victoria returned to the sitting room to wait with the queen and the princess for the prince.

Princess Ashley said, "Must thank thee Mother, Lady Victoria for thyne efforts on be behalf."

Minutes later, the prince entered the room asking why he had been summoned.

The queen said, "Frederick, be we in need of thy assistance. The means for Leland to learn the identity of Ashley hath been discussed.

At the outset, we thought it prudent for thee to engage Leland in conversation in an attempt to discover the depth of the archer's feelings for Ashley. Should ye succeed in obtaining this information, will we then know better as to how we art to proceed."

The Prince replied, "Mother, shall be a willing participant in this endeavor.

Hath thought to go to the forest a bit past midafternoon. Should Leland be found at the hunt, will proceed as ye hath directed. Must advise thee, however, will it not be a task accomplished with ease for hath found the archer to be quite hesitant in revealing much of hisself."

"Quite so, Frederick; in this respect, Leland hath the tenacity of a beast of burden, less the braying," the queen replied.

The prince then addressed his sister saying, "Well then, Ashley, should me find Leland in the forest, shall attempt to entice the mule to bray.

Must leave ye ladies to prepare for the hunt. Upon returning, will relate to thee all of importance hath passed 'tween me, and the archer."

Prince Frederick left the sitting room and took the three flights of stairs to his chambers to change into his hunting garments. The three ladies, hoping the prince would succeed in his task, continued to discuss the next step in their plan.

Chapter 26

The sun was low in the sky when Prince Frederick entered the forest. Soon the deer would be on the move. Quietly, the prince walked the path toward the large oak by the river where Leland usually hid in wait. The archer was nowhere in sight.

Passing the stand of pine beside the run, the prince hear Leland whisper.

The archer said, "Frederick, tread lightly. Come, stand beside me. Speak in whispers, lest ye be heard.

A bit ago, two rowdy lads entered the forest by way of the road creating a disturbance. Might they hath frightened the game away from the river. Shall we wait for a time, yet me fear hath the lads laid waste to this night."

The two men remained silent until near sunset. Not a sound was heard but the wind rustling the leaves on the trees. Frustrated, Leland uttered a sigh then spoke.

"Alas, me friend; 'tis futile to stand and wait any longer. Shall return at early light upon the 'morrow. Might ye wish to remain, shall leave thee."

The prince replied, "Nay, Leland; shall walk with thee. Hath a matter in need of attention come the 'morrow. Will return Monday morn."

Leland said, "Shall await thee, Frederick. Will ye find me tutoring the village maiden. The lass hath labored hard these weeks past. Hath she come far, yet there be much more for her to learn.

Find it a joy to tutor the lass for, be she quite eager to become proficient with the bow. Monday morn will be the damsel's first attempt at the hunt. Will it indeed be a day of interest."

The prince said, "Leland, speak ye of the maiden with a bit of reverence. Haps ye hath become smitten with the lady."

"Must confess, be she a winsome lass. Indeed, a pleasure for her to be about. Suspect upon becoming proficient with the bow, will she no longer be in need of me, and will it be the end of it," replied Leland.

The men had come to the hillside adjacent to the forest. At a distance, the castle and the village were in view. The sun had fallen below the tree line, and darkness was rapidly approaching.

Prince Frederick did not wish his conversation with Leland to end without extracting a bit more information from the archer as to his feelings for the princess.

The prince asked, "Leland, be ye in haste? Might it yet be early to sup. Come; leave us set to chat a bit longer."

Leland, not about to permit his companion to see the direction he took returning to his hut, willingly accepted the man's invitation.

The two men sat with their backs to a tree talking as one by one the portals in the upper levels of the palace and the windows in the village emitted light from candles, and lanterns being lit within.

Prince Frederick plucked at the grass beside him, tossing the blades into the breeze waiting for Leland to speak. He did not. The prince broke the silence.

He asked "Leland, hath the maiden given thee some reason for thee to assume, with the end of her tutoring, the lass wilt vanish?

Might it be the contrary. Haps the maiden hath persevered but to be beside thee. Hath some sign of affection passed 'tween ye two?"

Still the archer sat silent. The prince refused to be ignored.

He said, "Here set we in the darkness, but me ears wait to hear thy response. Thy failure to do so doth leads me to believe thy silence signifies something of a romantic nature hath occurred."

The archer replied, "Such tenacity, Frederick! Thy inquisitive mind will not be satisfied lest me bear me soul to thee. Thus, shall me reply to thee in truth this once, and no more.

A tender touch, the joining of lips hath passed 'tween us. Yet there will be no courtship. For hath naught of worth to offer the maiden.

A' fore ye be tempted to pursue this matter further, shall bid thee a good eve."

The prince replied, "As ye wish Leland; yet with but these words shall leave thee. Tend to believe ye hath made a decision will ye one day regret. Sleep well this night, me friend."

Leland waited for the prince to fade into the darkness before making his way back to the village, and the solitude of his hut.

Chapter 27

At breakfast the next morning, Sir Milford thought to bring up the matter of the prisoner, Jarin, son of the widow Tate, incarcerated for the theft of Lady Verna's steed.

Sir Milford addressing the king said, "Your Majesty, as to the young lad yet being held in the dungeons. By his performance in the stables, and obedience to the terms of his incarceration, hath deemed him an excellent candidate for the military.

Add to this, Mother Tate, and sibling Arabella's willingness to aid Princess Ashley in her desire to befriend the archer, might ye consider the lad's release?

Hath it been a burden upon the ladies as well to be without a man in their midst."

The king replied, "Milford, 'tis a matter worthy of consideration. Shall it be addressed upon our return from Dumfries. At the present, be occupied with the terms must propose to Earl William for the union 'tween daughter Rebecca, and Frederick."

The queen, a bit upset by the king's statement, said, "Husband, cannot believe me ears! Surely 'tis not thy intent to profit from this union! The earl hath been thy comrade in arms for many years. Will he not frown upon demands set forth by thee for the joining of his daughter to thy first born?"

He sternly replied, "Margaret, oft ye try me patience. 'Tis not a matter for discussion at the present with thee. Solely the counsel of Milford be required.

However, in an attempt to ease thy concern, this shall divulge to thee. No demands shall be made of the earl. The terms to be set forth art of mutual interest to the earl, and meself."

The room was silent for many minutes. The king noticed the queen, princess, and Lady Victoria making eye contact with the prince with inquiring expressions on their faces.

At the outset he thought it to be the result of words passing between the queen and himself. His intuition then led him to believe it was something else.

Suspiciously, the king said, "Me sense a bit of conspiracy at the table this morn. Might someone enlighten me as to what might be in the wind?"

Sir Milford had no idea why the king had imposed such a question on the group. Yet the silence of the others affirmed the king's suspicion.

"Come ye now, Milford; speak," said the king.

"Your Majesty, pledge to thee, know naught of this ye inquire," Sir Milford replied.

A bit irritated, the king asked, "Must I be left to wonder? The silence of ye others bears proof of me suspicions.

Margaret, but moments past spoke ye upon a matter of little concern to thee yet here ye set, thy tongue frozen within."

Yet angry, the queen asked, "Damnation Husband! Art ye to be privy to all be a 'foot in the realm?

Must ye know, Frederick hath been assigned the task of ferreting out as much information as possible of Leland's feelings for Ashley.

This eve past, Frederick met with the archer in the forest. As yet hath he not shared what he hath learned with we ladies.

Hath we been beside ourselves in wonderment."

The king asked, "And for what purpose art the feelings of the archer to be known Margaret?

Ashley, hath ye become smitten with the archer? Why am I to be the last to learn of this?"

The princess said, "Father, in the process of befriending the archer, hath found him to be gentle, kindly, and a man of honor. Unlike the bawdy knights in thy service, and the many pompous nobles who frequent the palace."

The king agreed, saying, "Shall ye receive no argument from me as to the character of the bowman. Nor shall me lend interference to these proceedings. Must however, be kept abreast of this matter for 'tis of much interest to me."

"Father, hath thought would ye lend opposition to thy daughter pursuing a commoner. Be heartened by these words ye hath spoken," said the princess.

Her father replied, "Hath ye woven a fragile web lass to capture the heart of the archer. What is to become of it upon Leland learning he hath been deceived, and in truth be ye a princess?"

"This, Father, we ladies intend to address and correct, given the information obtained by Frederick this eve past," Princess Ashley replied.

Breakfast had ended. The group remained seated, waiting for the king to leave the table before rising to follow. He stayed in place to speak.

He said, "Go ye then about this conspiracy art about to hatch. Yet with care, for Leland be not a bumbling fool.

Milford must ye remain for hath we much to discuss of the terms intend to present to Earl William."

Sir Milford complied to the king's demand. The others retired to the sitting room to hear what Prince Frederick had learned from the archer.

Queen Margaret was the first to speak. She said, "Well Frederick, must ye not keep we ladies in suspense any longer. What hath ye learned on speaking with the archer?"

The prince replied, "Mother, the man be shackled by his humility. With little to offer, and no prospects in the near future, hath deemed hisself unworthy of the maiden in spite of his profound feelings for her. Hath dared not press him further lest he became suspect of me inquiries."

Turning to the princess, he said; "Am to join Leland at the hunt Monday morn. Haps in some manner might he be enticed to set his fears aside then begin to court thee."

The princess quickly replied, "Nay, Frederick! Shall it be me day with the archer. Leland hath pledged to hunt beside me. Wish not to forfeit the opportunity. Surely will me not be forced to remain at the palace."

The queen interrupted, saying; "Ashley, Frederick hath not stated ye art to remain at home. Must ye meet with Leland as expected. Frederick will join Leland and thee. However, Ashley, will ye play the part of a stranger. At some point begin to speak with Frederick of the archer's victory at the tournament. Leland, upon hearing of thy admiration for him, may find the courage to pursue thee."

Lady Victoria spoke saying, "Me Queen, me thinks ye hath stumbled upon a proper course to follow. In this manner art we to proceed. Leave us pray 'tis to bear fruit."

"Victoria, might it not, shall we then set upon another path. Hath we been tossed a gauntlet. Our intend must be to prevail," replied the queen.

Chapter 28

Princess Ashley passed much of Sunday night in bed, concerned about the prince joining her and the archer in the forest the next morning.

Should she or the prince make a misstep in their conversation with Leland, it might well be detrimental to her position with the archer.

Awaking early Monday morning, she washed, dressed, and took the stairs to the main floor of the palace to the courtyard to meet with Sir Milford.

The knight was already waiting for the princess with the reins of Goldentrot and Titus in hand.

They walked to the gate; Sir Milford leading the horses. Robert bowed to the princess. Holding open the gate, he wished them a good morning as they passed through.

Sir Milford helped the princess onto her steed, mounted Titus, then they rode down the hillside to the Tate Cottage.

Arabella opened the door as they approached. She stepped out of the cabin, and curtsied to the princess, greeting them.

"Good morn, Princess Ashley, Sir Knight. Come enter.

Sir Milford, will ye be remaining in wait of her Ladyship's return?"

Princess Ashley went directly into Arabella's bedroom to change.

Sir Milford went to sit at the table in the kitchen while Arabella went about preparing two cups of tea.

Replying to Arabella, Sir Milford said, "Aye, Arabella. Hath news to relate will find of interest to thee and Mother Tate of brother, Jarin."

The arrival of the princess and the knight awakened Arabella's mother.

She quickly left her bed. Went to the privy to wash, dress, then joined her daughter and the knight.

Sir Milford came to his feet when she appeared in the kitchen, greeting her a good morning.

Mother Tate replied, "Good morn, Sir Knight; 'tis a pleasure to find thee in me kitchen. Arabella, hath ye tended to Sir Milford?"

"Indeed Mother; hath we been chatting o'er a spot of tea. Come set, shall fetch thee a cup. Sir Milford hath news of Jarin with we to share," Arabella replied.

Princess Ashley returned from the bedroom prepared to ride to the forest. The ladies rose to curtsy; Sir Milford to bow.

Mother Tate wished the princess a good morning.

The knight opened the door, permitting the princess to exit; then followed her to aid her onto Goldentrot.

He stood waiting for her to ride off before returning to sit with the ladies.

Mother Tate asked, "Sir Knight, pray tell; what news hath ye of me lad?"

He replied, "Dear Lady, hath spoken to the king. Requested Jarin be released and be made a cavalryman in the service.

King Frederick stated it would be considered and will grant me a reply upon returning from Dumfries. Thus, a decision will be soon given me by his Majesty."

The woman said, "Sir Knight, there be no end to the kindness ye hath afforded me family. How art we to repay thee?"

"There be no further need, Madam. Hath we been well compensated by the assistance given the princess these many weeks," replied Sir Milford.

Meanwhile, Prince Frederick prepared to join the archer and the princess in the forest. There was no need to hurry. The princess was to be given ample time with Leland before the prince's arrival.

The movements of the prince awakened Tom in the room above. The manservant quickly dressed, came down to render aid.

Tom said, "Good morn, me Prince; 'tis a bit early for the morning meal. Might ye desire a bit of tea, shall fetch it for thee. Upon returning, might ye permit me a word?"

The prince replied, "G' day Tom. No need for tea.

Be off to the forest this morn. Shall enter the kitchen for a bite in passing. Hath ye a matter upon ye wish to speak, do so."

Tom speaking said, "Your Lordship, there be word about the palace. Will ye soon be accompanying the king on holiday to Dumfries. Might it be so, will ye be in need of me?"

A bit angry, the prince replied, "Ye Gads, Lad! Art the movements of me sire to be known throughout the realm? Aye, 'tis so, and will ye be required to be of service upon this journey."

Tom persisted, saying, "Well then me Prince, might me inquire, upon passing the village Gretna, art we to seek lodging at the inn?"

The prince laughed, realizing why he was being interrogated with such eagerness by his manservant.

"So therein lie the purpose of this conversation! Hath ye become smitten with the servant Bridget at the inn. Hath she displayed a more than passing interest in thee as well. Will ye be greeted warmly by the lass upon thy return," replied the prince.

Tom said, "Me Prince, upon learning of a second journey to Dumfries, spoke to Mother of the maiden.

Requested she speak to Lady Verna of a position for Bridget at the palace. Might her Ladyship be in need of a skilled servant, and grant the lass a position, will then speak to Bridget of it."

Assuring Tom, the prince said, "Tom, the ability of the lass to serve be not in question. Shall lend me voice to Lady Verna upon this matter as well.

Might the king be successful in the purpose of this journey, Lady Verna will be in need of much assistance."

Tom thanked the prince then went about his chores. The prince left the room, stopped in the kitchen for a bit of breakfast, then went to join Leland in the forest.

Entering the forest, the prince intentionally snapped twigs underfoot on the deer run wanting his approach to be heard.

Coming upon the archer and the princess, Leland scolded the prince for his noisy entrance.

He said, "Heavens, Frederick! Be ye not tutored to tread lightly 'mongst the trees? Thought to soon be trampled by a herd of cattle invading the woodland."

The prince replied, "Forgive me, Leland; be a bit tardy. In me haste failed to take care. And who might this winsome maiden be beside thee?"

Leland said, "Frederick, might me acquaint thee with Ashley, a lass from a village nearby. Hath been tutoring the maiden in the use of the bow as well. Hath she been an ardent student."

Pretending not to know the princess, Frederick said, "G' day, lass. Might me inquire how come ye to be tutored by the archer? Haps be ye kin to Leland?"

Keeping up the pretense, the princess replied, "Good morn, kind sir, but weeks past be found by Leland one morn plucking berries upon the deer run. Concerned for me well-being, he proposed to tutor me in the use of the bow as a means to defend meself. Deem it an honor to be tutored by a master bowman."

The prince said, "Be he well skilled; indeed, yet to be deemed a master, would require Leland to excel above all others."

The princess replied, "Haps 'tis not known to thee, sir. Leland participated in a tournament held by King Frederick months past.

A host of archers from far and near be in attendance, competing for a purse. Leland emerged victorious. Then, to the dismay of all in attendance he refused the purse offered him by the king."

Acting surprised, the prince said, "Indeed Leland, never hath ye spoken of it to me. Why hath ye chosen to shun the glory in this deed? Another man would strut about as a peacock. Haps there be other deeds as this hath ye not yet revealed. Be in awe of thee as be the maiden."

Leland replied, "Frederick, 'tis not me way. Enough with the honeyed tongue! Leave us dispense of this idle chatter. Hath not come to the forest this morn seeking praise, but to hunt. Leave us see to it."

The prince asked, "Ashley, art ye to participate in the hunt?"

She replied, "Aye, Frederick; yet must forgive me for 'tis me first attempt. Ye men art to be a bit patient with me at the outset."

The three walked the deer run gingerly; the men permitting the princess to lead the way. Suddenly two partridges took flight out of a patch of underbrush.

Leland downed one, the prince the other. The princess had only time to take sight when the two birds fell to the forest floor. Yet she became quite excited at the kills.

She said, "Good show ye men, never hath me time to prepare. Will me ere achieve the skill ye two hath displayed?"

Leland said, "Patience, lass! Shall it come to thee in time. A bird in flight be much more difficult to down than a hare at rest. Haps by late autumn thy shafts will run true."

She said, "Be heartened by thy words, Frederick. This day haps it may be best to leave ye two at the hunt alone."

Princess Ashley went to Leland, pressed her lips to his cheek, bade the two men a farewell, then took the deer run out of the forest to mount her steed and return to the Tate cottage.

With her praise for Leland, and her show of affection, Princess Ashley had lain the groundwork for brother Frederick to convince the archer to be more aggressive in his relationship with her.

The two men remained silent and watched the princess walk out of sight. Prince Frederick stood shaking his head, then addressed the archer.

The prince said, "Leland, be ye a master of the bow with the eye of a hawk. Yet see ye not that be before thee.

The maiden hath feelings for thee beyond one of gratitude for thy tutoring. Surely this be known to thee."

Leland replied, "Frederick, be not made of stone. The maiden's affection hath not gone without notice. Shall we pretend for a moment.

Leave us presume I hath set about courting the lass. And with good fortune, come to win her heart. Then approach her sire to plead for her hand and win his approval.

Must the lady then be made to pass her days as the spouse of a mere hunter? Me love for the lass be much too profound to subject her to such a dismal existence. Be she deserving of much more."

"Leland, thy position be well known to the maiden. Might she be in pursuit of a man of means, would she pass her days with a village archer?" asked the prince.

Leland responded, "Frederick, hath passed many a night deep in thought upon this matter, to arrive at the like conclusion. 'Tis not to be.

Might ye place any value upon our friendship must ye not torment me any further."

"Very well then, Leland; no more words of this shall ye hear pass me lips. For hath ye the stubbornness of oxen. Leave us resume the hunt in silence," the prince replied.

Prince Frederick left Leland in the late afternoon; certain the archer was not about to be convinced to further his relationship with the princess by word alone. He was determined to devise a plan to bring the two together.

Princess Ashley was certain to be waiting to hear all Leland had to say after she left the two men in the forest.

Prince Frederick had no desire to face the princess with the disheartening news Leland had no intention of courting her, despite caring for her deeply. In an attempt to avoid the princess, he decided, upon returning from the hunt, he would go directly to his quarters in the tower.

On entering his chambers, the prince called out to Tom. The manservant came scrambling down the stone steps to tend to his master.

The prince said, "Tom, will be taking me evening meal in thy room above this night. Must it not be known to Princess Ashley of me presence in the palace. Might she come inquiring of me, must she be told hath ye no knowledge as to where might me hath gone.

There be a need for me to speak to the queen, thus go ye to me mother's chambers and inform her I will not be present in the dining hall this night. However, I requests a word with her in her chambers after the evening meal.

Tom, upon completion of this task, return to me with me mother's reply, and for further instructions."

Tom bowed to the prince, then left the room to deliver his message. The prince went to the privy, washed, changed into his evening garments, then took the stairs to the room above to wait for the manservant to return with the queen's answer.

Tom had gone to tap on the queen's chamber door, then waited for permission to enter. Lady Winfred opened the door, permitting the manservant to enter.

Tom bowed, delivered his message to the queen, then waited for a reply.

The queen thanked him and said, "Thomas, shall await Frederick here in me chambers as he hath requested. Might the prince given thee any indication as to why he would not be present at the evening meal this night?"

Tom replied, "Your Majesty; only to state, should Princess Ashley come to the tower seeking the prince, she was to be told I hath no knowledge of where he might be."

Queen Margaret stood frowning in wonderment at the manservant's reply then dismissed the lad.

Tom bowed and left the room, closing the door behind him to return to the prince with the queen's reply.

The prince said, "Well done, Tom. Go ye now, fetch me a bit of supper from the kitchen. Speak to Godfrey. He is to advise me when Mother leaves the dining hall to return to her chambers."

Prince Frederick lay on Tom's bed waiting for him to return with his supper. His thoughts turned to the Lady Rebecca.

By this time next week, they would be on their way to Dumfries. He could hardly wait to see his beloved again.

With good fortune, the king would then come to an agreement as to when he and Lady Rebecca would be wed. The thought of holding her again excited the prince.

The matter of the princess and Leland then returned to mind. There must be some way, he thought, to resolve this impasse before his departure.

A tapping on the tower door below disrupted his thoughts. The footsteps on the stairway were Tom's returning from his errands.

The prince asked, "Tom, when in the kitchen, spoke ye to Godfrey?"

He replied, "Aye, me Prince, and with me mother as well. There be no need for thee to speak with Lady Verna of the maiden, Bridget.

Mother hath done so with success. Lady Verna stated, should the lass come to Penrith, a position will be made available to her.

Mother also expressed a desire to wed the butcher, Martin. Thus, there will be lodging for the maiden in Mother's room with Christy."

"Be quite pleased to learn thy mother will be wed to the butcher. Be she deserving of a bit of happiness," said the prince.

He then continued saying, "Tom, when in Gretna must ye indeed speak to Bridget. Shall we pray the lass be receptive to thy proposal."

Tom asked, "Me Prince, should the position be of interest to the maiden, might she be permitted to join our party upon our return to Penrith?"

The prince replied, "And why not, Tom? To that end, it might be prudent to request of Gavin the loan of a second steed for the lass to ride might she be joining the party upon our return."

"Thou art most kind, me Prince. Might me inquire as to when this journey is to commence?" asked Tom.

The prince said, "Shall we be leaving Penrith come Monday next. Must ye prepare well for this journey, for 'tis of much importance to me.

Go ye now, fetch me supper. Bear in mind lad, might ye encounter the princess, know ye naught of where me be."

Tom bowed to the prince, then quickly left to go to the kitchen for the food and drink his Mother had prepared for the prince.

He was about to leave the kitchen when he heard Lady Victoria talking to the princess as they came down the stone steps on their way to the dining hall. He waited for their footsteps to fade before returning.

Entering the prince's chamber, Tom called out to the prince in the room above.

He said, "Me Prince, hath seen Princess Ashley and Lady Victoria pass the kitchen walking the hall to the dining hall. Might ye wish to sup here in the room below?"

The prince descended the stairs to his room to sit at a table. Tom set the plate of food and a tankard of ale before him, then stood to wait.

The prince said, "Hath no further need of thee, Tom. Go ye about thy chores. Shall remain in me room."

Tom bowed to the prince and left the room, closing the door behind him. He had no other duties to perform until the prince was ready for bed.

Taking advantage of his free time, Tom went to the stables to speak to Gavin of the steed he wished to borrow for the trip to Dumfries.

Chapter 29

King Frederick and the queen were already in the dining hall when the princess and Lady Victoria entered. The four exchanged greetings; then the ladies took their seats at the table. The king and queen were discussing the upcoming trip to Dumfries.

The king said, "Margaret, be ye certain hath ye no desire to accompany me on holiday to Dumfries? Countess Sarah would surely be pleased for thee to be about."

She replied, "Husband, should accompany thee, there will, then be need for a coach. Will this but slow thy journey.

Yea too, must ye assume all will go well in thy meeting with Earl William. Thus, there will be much to prepare for these weeks to come. Invitations art to be written and prepared for dispatch. Plans art to be made with Lady Verna for the festivities.

The queen paused, then said; "Ashley, Victoria, thy assistance will be needed as well in these preparations."

The king replied, "Very well, Margaret; will not press thee further. What with all for thee to do, will ye be pleased for me not to be under foot."

Godfrey stepped into the dining hall. Seeing the prince was not yet seated, he turned to leave.

The queen called to him.

She said, "Hold, Godfrey; the prince might not yet hath returned from the hunt. Shall we not wait. Ye may proceed."

The butler left the dining hall to return in minutes with servants bearing trays of meat, vegetables, and ewers of wine. The servants set the food and drink on the table.

Godfrey bowed and the servants curtsied once more before retreating to the kitchen.

Lady Victoria, not addressing anyone in particular, and curious as to where the prince might be, spoke.

She asked, "Be it not a rare occasion for the prince to be absent from the table to sup? Where might he be about this night?"

The king said, "Must ye not fret, Victoria. Frederick may hath thought to linger a bit longer in the forest with the archer. Ye ladies haps be a bit impatient to hear what Frederick hath to say of the conversation with the archer. We may well need to wait unto the morn."

The queen suspected the reason for the absence of the prince was that something had been said in his chat with the archer which would not be pleasing to the princess. Thus, she thought it prudent to quickly change the subject.

She asked the king what terms he intended to present the earl.

The king replied, "Margaret, art ye to fret o'er this meeting with the earl, and the terms to be presented?

Permit me relieve thy concern. Shall me not insult the earl with a demand. 'Tis to be a proposal in security. Lord Morley shall accompany me to Dumfries to assume the role of ambassador to the earl. Lord Morley shall remain in Dumfries with one of our cavalry. A trusted representative and a cavalryman of the earl will return with our party to Penrith. Thus, might either we or the earl be confronted by a common foe, the ambassador will quickly dispatch the cavalryman to the other, requesting assistance. Surely must ye bear no opposition to such a proposal."

The queen replied, "Nay, Husband, 'tis a worthy presentation indeed. Beneficial to both parties. Earl William shall be elated and agree wholeheartedly."

With supper at an end, the queen being quite anxious to hear what the prince had to say.

She bade the others a good night and went to her chambers to wait for him.

Godfrey, seeing the queen pass the kitchen, waited a minute before hurrying to inform the prince of the queen's return to her chambers.

Prince Frederick took the stairs to the floor below to tap on the queen's chamber door.

Lady Winfred opened the door, stepped aside, then curtsied to the prince as he entered.

The queen gave a sideward glance at her lady-in-waiting.

Lady Winfred understood and left the chamber, closing the door behind her.

The prince greeted his mother, saying; "Good eve, Mother. Forgive me for me absence at the table this night. 'Twas an attempt to avoid being questioned by ye ladies of me conversation with Leland. Thought it best to speak with thee. For, doth not know how the comments of the archer art to be related to Ashley."

The queen asked, "Mercy Frederick, what might the archer hath stated ye found so discomforting to relate to her? Hath he spoken ill of the lass?"

He replied, "Nay, Mother; to the contrary. Spoke with deep affection for her. Therein doth the problem lie. He hath expressed a deep fondness for Ashley. Yet given his lowly station, he hath no desire to subject her to a mundane existence."

The queen said, "Hath ye done well, Frederick, to seek me consult a 'fore speaking to Ashley.

One must respect the man, for despite his love for Ashley, the wellbeing of the lass be foremost upon his mind. A rare find indeed! The archer be not solely a handsome gent. Be he kindly, bright of mind, doth bear a fine sense of justice and quite humble as well might add."

The queen paused. She thought for a moment, then continued speaking.

She said, "Frederick, hath ye given me much to ponder upon. This situation hath become a bit of a muddle. Much thought must be given as to how to proceed. Shall speak to Ashley in the morn. Must choose me words with care. Would not do for the lass to fall into despair."

The queen sat silent; a frown on her brow, eyes downcast, her hands clenched in her lap. The prince waited for his mother to speak.

She said, "Well, Frederick, there be naught to be done this night. Alas, 'tis certain sleep shall not come with ease. Go ye now, pray for a joyful resolution of this entire affair."

Prince Frederick came to his feet, kissed his mother on the cheek, bade her a good night, then left the room to return to the tower.

Tom, waiting for the prince to return to his chambers, came to his feet when the prince entered the room. He bowed then told him the princess had been by looking for him earlier.

Tom said, "Princess Ashley be told hath ye supped in thy quarters at a late hour then left to knew not where. The princess displayed a bit of ire at thy absence."

"Pay it no mind, Tom. Will she soon recover. Leave me, for be weary. Hath it been an irksome day," the prince replied.

Tom bowed, wished him a good night then took the stairs up to his room.

Chapter 30

Princess Ashley did not sleep well. She lay wondering if the prince had purposely been avoiding her. Waking the next morning, she was torn between confronting him or going to the forest to hunt with Leland. She opted for the latter. Although she was quite eager to hear what the prince had to say of his chat with the archer, she was not about to miss an opportunity to spend the morning with Leland. Perhaps Leland might shed some light on the conversation he had with the prince. She would need to be very careful when speaking to him. Nothing she was to say to the archer should lead him to suspect she had known the prince before meeting him in the forest.

Early the next morning the princess left her bed. She went to the privy to wash, then dressed.

She quickly left her room to join Sir Milford waiting in the courtyard with the two steeds.

Robert opened the gate, bowing to the princess as they passed. The knight helped the princess onto Goldentrot, mounted Titus, then they rode to the Tate cottage.

Sir Milford tethered Titus to the hitching post at the cottage, then waited with the horses while the princess changed into Arabella's garments.

Princess Ashley stepped out of the cottage and mounted Goldentrot.

Sir Milford stood waving to her as she rode off to the forest.

Entering the forest, the princess thought to test her skill at stalking. She chose her steps carefully, avoiding twigs and leaves, which had fallen to the ground.

Leland was sitting beneath the huge oak, whittling on a piece of wood. She drew her blade. Aided by the sound of the river's flow, the princess managed to come up behind the tree opposite of the archer.

Hearing her approach, Leland said, "Good morn, Ashley; hath ye done well to come so near undetected. However, be ye yet a bit lacking for once more thy scent hath revealed thy presence."

She replied, "Ye Gads, Leland, 'tis no wonder hath ye been about the king's forest undetected. Hath ye the nose of a Mastiff to serve thee well at the hunt. What of thy heart, doth it not speak to thee of a maiden ye hold dear? Must it not then serve thee well, for doth it beat but to sustain thee for thy bleak existence through thy days."

Leland was well aware of where this conversation was going and had no desire for it to continue. He feigned to be a bit upset with her in his response.

He replied, "Lass, what be all this chatter of noses and hearts? Hath ye come to the forest this morn as a hunter or as a physician? Haps be ye be afflicted with the like malady as Frederick, the lad of this day past. Questions, questions, so many questions!"

Leland's abrupt reply brought tears to the maiden's cheeks. She stood before him and spoke sobbing.

"Hath thee no love in thy heart but for this forest? Very well then; will not trouble thee any further, shall leave thee be."

The princess turned from him and ran the path toward the road. Leland sprang to his feet, calling after her, to no avail. She was soon out of sight.

The archer had not expected her to react with so much emotion to his trite response. He stood bewildered for a moment before realizing how deeply he had hurt the maiden. Upset with himself, he returned to sit with his back to the oak; his heart heavy, thinking he had seen the last of her.

Princess Ashley, tears still falling to her cheeks, went to mount her steed, and returned to the Tate's cottage.

Remaining on her mount, she called out to Sir Milford.

The knight came running out of the cottage asking the princess if she was not going to change her clothes.

The princess did not reply.

Seeing the princess in tears, he was certain something was amiss. Not questioning the princess any further, he mounted Titus and rode with her to the castle.

Riding into the courtyard of the palace, the princess quickly dismounted her steed, then ran into the palace to her chambers. Leaving the knight to wonder what had happened.

Sir Milford quickly dismounted, returned the two horses to the stables, then went to the kitchen asking where the queen might be.

Godfrey replied to the knight.

"Sir Milford, the royal family be yet in the dining hall at the morning meal."

Without another word the knight ran from the kitchen, down the hallway to the dining hall.

Entering, he bowed, excused himself for interrupting, then went to whisper to the queen.

She quickly came to her feet and without a word, ran to take the stairs to Princess Ashley's chambers.

Entering, the queen found the princess lying on her bed sobbing; still wearing Arabella's garments.

The queen paused in the doorway for a moment, then went to sit beside her daughter.

She asked, "Ashley, hath ye returned from the forest quickly, yet in the garments of a peasant. What hath come to pass to leave thee in such distress?"

The princess replied, "Mother, might the monster be damned! In an attempt to learn a bit of the archer's feelings for me, be spoken to as one might to a mindless twit! Be he told the only love hath he in his heart was for the forest. Frustrated, I fled, leaving the ogre to his beloved woodland."

The door to the chamber opened. Lady Victoria entered. Seeing the queen sitting beside Ashley on the bed, she expressed concern.

She asked, "Ashley, art ye not well? Thought ye to be with Leland this morn in the forest. Why art ye garbed in the trappings of a peasant?"

Lady Victoria received no response from the princess.

The queen said, "Victoria, Ashley and the archer became involved in a bit of a babble this morn. Quite irate, Ashley ran; leaving Leland alone."

The queen addressing her daughter then said, "Ashley, spoke to Frederick this night past of the conversation 'tween him and Leland. There be much ye might be eager to learn. Come, compose thyself. Must ye shed these unsightly garments. Shall wait with Victoria for thee in the sitting room."

Leaving the room, Queen Margaret turned to Lady Victoria, asking her to speak to Godfrey. Instructing him to have Mildred prepare a breakfast plate for the princess and bring it to the sitting room with cups and a pot of tea.

Descending the stairs, the queen continued on to the sitting room. Lady Victoria went to do the queen's bidding then joined the queen in wait of the princess.

In chambers, Princess Ashley went about changing her clothes while thinking she had made a grievous blunder by leaving the archer in such an abrupt manner. She had gotten herself into a mess and had no idea on how to proceed. She had a sinking feeling Leland might well have determined her actions to signify the end of their relationship.

The princess was certain remaining in her room pouting would not solve her problem. She thought perhaps her mother might have some idea as to how she might rectify the situation.

Dressed and composed, the princess left her chambers to join her mother and Lady Victoria in the sitting room.

Chapter 31

After breakfast that same morning, while the ladies were talking in the sitting room, Prince Frederick and Sir Milford sat out on the terrace with Sir Cartwith discussing the upcoming trip to Dumfries. Sir Milford was giving Sir Cartwith the composition of the group making the trip.

He said, "Sir Cartwith, the party shall include his Majesty, Prince Frederick, Tom, Sir Morley, and six cavalrymen.

Ye will be leaving early Monday morn, riding some seven leagues to pass the night in Gretna.

Early the next morn ye will continue onto Dumfries. Sir Morley and one of the cavalry may remain in Dumfries. This hath yet to be determined. Haps so, two of Earl William's trusted men will be returning with thee to Penrith.

Might ye wish to know, Countess Sarah hath expressed a desire for thee to be in command of the party."

Sir Cartwith replied, "Indeed! A most gracious lady. Spoke we in length upon returning from Leeds.

Shall begin to prepare for the journey, Sir Milford."

Sir Milford then turned to the prince and said, "Me Prince, hath ye further instructions for Sir Cartwith?"

The prince replied, "Aye, Sir Milford."

He, then turned to Sir Cartwith and said, "One of the six cavalrymen must be Donald. The reason will be made known to thee when in Dumfries."

Sir Cartwith replied, "Huh! Haps there be a be a bit of jugglery a 'foot!

So be it, me Prince. Hath ye no further need of me, shall take me leave for there be a matter must attend to in the village."

Sir Cartwith bowed to the prince and went to the stables to retrieve Sweet Sorrow for his ride to the village. His hasty retreat prompted the prince to ask Sir Milford the reason for the hurry.

Sir Milford said, "Haps hath gone to the village to visit with the widow, Whitney. Informing her of his absence this week next. Yea too, haps he may arrange a day together a 'fore his departure. Might ye know, be he quite smitten with the lady."

The prince chuckled and said, "Indeed, would seem the village Penrith be awash with romance. Speaking of romance, Sir Milford, hath ye returned with Ashley early this morn. Haps something be a 'miss?"

Sir Milford replied, "Be not certain me Prince. Haps so. The princess returned to the Tate cottage from the forest in a wretched state. Spoke not a word nor made she no effort to enter. She rode with me, swiftly to the palace. Yet bearing Arabella's garments."

"Then surely something hath gone awry. Shall speak to Lady Victoria later; haps she might shed a bit of light upon the incident," said the prince.

The conversation seemingly over, the prince came to his feet intending to leave the terrace when Sir Milford spoke.

"Me Prince, hath ye aroused me curiosity. Minutes past hath ye given Sir Cartwith instructions to select Donald as one of the cavalry accompanying thy sire to Dumfries. By order of the king there art to be six cavalrymen providing escort. Might me inquire why it be imperative for Donald to be one of the six?"

The prince laughed boisterously, then related the entire event of the night Donald had passed with Lady Juliana. Sir Milford then joined the prince in laughter as the two left the terrace together.

Passing the sitting room, the prince saw the three ladies talking.

Sir Milford continued on to his quarters.

The prince took a position a bit beyond the room's entrance to eavesdrop on the conversation within.

Queen Margaret was speaking to the others of the conversation she had held with the prince the previous night.

The queen said, "Ashley, Frederick hath confirmed the archer hath ardent feelings for thee. Due to his humble beginnings, Leland hath thought it prudent not to engage thee in a courtship. Hath deemed thee worthy of a better future than he might afford thee. Must we in some manner convince this man of honor, the lack of wealth nor property be not a concern.

At the outset, however, the error of this morn must be mended. Come morn, go to the forest, and speak humbly to the archer in an attempt to appease him. Leland hath been deemed to be a kindly gent. In the least, will he continue with his tutoring. This will afford thee o'er time, the opportunity to assure the man the lack of coin be not a concern."

Prince Frederick quietly left his position by the sitting room entrance and went to his chambers to think on what he had heard.

Chapter 32

The archer woke the next morning in quite a melancholy mood. Leland had spent much of the previous night thinking, with mixed emotions, on what had happened in the forest earlier that morning. Although he had no intention of doing so, the quippish response he had given the maiden might well have pushed her away. Was that really what he wanted?

His mind said yes. His heart spoke to him in the contrary. He was certain to miss the many happy hours he had passed with the feisty maiden.

Had he years past not pledged himself to help feed the needy in the village? That path he had chosen might well have put him in a position to properly court the lady. Dismissing these thoughts, Leland reluctantly left his bed to prepare for the forest. Although he had no desire to hunt, there was yet an obligation to fulfill.

Having washed, dressed, and eaten a bit of breakfast, Leland left his hut to make the trek to the forest.

Arriving, he sat on the bank tossing pebbles into the river, thinking of the first day he had lain eyes on the maiden plucking berries from a bush on the deer run.

Preoccupied in thought, he did not hear the footsteps approaching until Ashley spoke.

She said, "Good morn, Leland. Be ye in good stead this day?"

Taken by surprise, the archer sprang to his feet, turned to the lady, his heart beating rapidly in his chest. Leland stood a moment regaining composure.

Speaking politely, Leland replied, "G 'day, Ashley. Though not to see thee this morn."

She said, "Pray; forgive me, Leland; for me hasty departure this day past. Must confess, 'twas the doltish act of a mindless twit."

Leland replied, "There be no need for forgiveness, Ashley. Spoke to thee in an unkindly manner. Leave us set this day past aside. Shall we continue with thy tutoring."

Both she and the archer were elated over the mending of their discord. Yet neither displayed any emotion.

The princess said, "Very well, Leland; what hath thee in mind for me this morn? Art we to hunt or engage in some other activity?"

Leland replied, "Art ye to hunt beside me. Now then, set thy bow at the ready. Bear in mind to tread lightly. Must we speak, 'tis to be done in whispers. Sound and rapid movements art to be avoided."

At that moment, the princess realized her mother had been correct in advising her not to press Leland for his feelings toward her. Princess Ashley had learned from the brief encounter yesterday that the archer did not appreciate being subjected to questions of a personal nature.

The archer was to play the tutor and to afford time for her to win Leland over, she was to play the student.

The two began walking the deer run, Ashley constantly shifting her eyes from the forest floor to her surroundings. Leland was quite pleased with her movement. She had learned the method of stalking well.

Some minutes passed. Hearing a movement in the brush, Leland raised his hand signaling her to stop. The princess brought her bow to the ready in the direction of the sound.

Moments later a rabbit hopped out onto a clearing to stop and feed on a clump of grass.

Leland whispered, "Let fly thy shaft, Ashley."

The princess released the bowstring and the arrow ran true, striking its mark. She dropped her bow and began jumping up and down, clapping her hands in jubilation. Leland began laughing at the maiden's expression of elation then thought to praise her for the kill.

He said, "Art ye to be commended, Ashley. It hath been thy first kill, and well done at that. Be ye deserving of a bit of celebration."

He was about to inform the princess that her reaction to her kill had most likely frightened much of the game in the area deep into the forest. He then chose to save that lesson for another day. Permitting her to enjoy her accomplishment.

Leland retrieved the rabbit, removed the arrow, and handed it to the princess. She hesitated, then took the arrow grudgingly between two fingers and returned the blooded shaft to her quill.

The archer fetched a length of hide from a pouch, affixed the rabbit to it by its hind paws, then tied the hide around the maiden's waist.

The princess, a bit squeamish, asked the archer, "Leland, what is to be done with this hare?"

He replied, "Why Ashley, once it's pelt hath been removed, it must be butchered, then stewed. Will ye sup upon it this very night."

Her heart skipped a beat. The princess realized she had just made another mistake. No village maiden would need to ask what was to be done with a slain rabbit. She prayed the archer would not dwell on the error.

For a moment Leland thought it to be a silly question she had presented. He, then dismissed it. Determining it to be but a question of ownership.

Leland said, "Forgive me, Ashley; meant not to imply hath ye no knowledge of how to dress a hare, and how it must be prepared. Me reply to thy question be but an error in interpretation. The kill be thyne to do with as ye please."

Princess Ashley breathed a sigh of relief, then wisely changed the subject. She picked up her bow and slung it over her shoulder before speaking.

She said, "Leland, me show of exuberance upon slaying the hare might well hath frightened much of the game about into retreat. Hath erred. Shall it not be repeated."

Leland was impressed by her being aware she had made an error with her reaction to the kill which might well have frightened the animals deeper into the forest but thought not to make an issue of it.

Leland said, "Being thy first kill, 'twas expected. Hath ye not spoken of the error, would I hath done so with thee at a later date. The game will not return for some time. Come Ashley, leave us return to the river; we shall sit for a bit."

The two sat on the riverbank, talking for quite a while. Leland instructed the princess on the proper stalking of a deer, and when to take the best shot.

Suddenly he sprang to his feet, Leland pulling her up beside him.

The archer whispered, "Hath heard the sound of hoof beats. Riders approach, best we seek concealment unto they pass."

Leland took the hand of the princess, running with her behind a stand of shrub, his bow at the ready.

The riders came into view.

Princess Ashley recognized the two. The man being Sir Cartwith; the lady, the widowed seamstress from the village.

She whispered to the archer, "Leave them be, Leland; art they but two mates seeking a bit of privacy."

They waited for the riders to pass, and the hoof beats to fade before returning to the riverbank to chat a while longer.

A bit later, anxious to return to the palace, and tell her mother of their reconciliation, she bid Leland a good day; walked the path out to mount her steed, then rode to the cottage.

Sir Milford was standing in the doorway when she arrived. He went to help her dismount.

Seeing the slain rabbit still dangling from her waist, Sir Milford began to laugh.

The princess said, "Sir Milford, 'tis no matter for laughter. Be it me first kill for which be quite elated. Mother Tate and Arabella shall surely enjoy the partaking of it."

As usual, Sir Milford waited by the horses while the princess entered the cottage to change.

As they rode back to the palace. Princess Ashley told the knight of seeing Sir Cartwith riding in the forest with the widow Whitney.

The princess said, "Sir Knight, would seem Sir Cartwith be quite taken with the widow. Hath me lain eyes upon the woman when in the millinery with Lady Victoria and Lady Rebecca. A comely lady, indeed."

It was obvious to the knight that Princess Ashley was in a better frame of mind than she had been the morning before. The princess did not volunteer a reason for her discontent of yesterday, and it was not the knight's position to inquire.

Christy was playing with Tiffany when the two riders entered the courtyard of the palace. The children stopped to curtsey to the princess, then resumed their play.

Sir Milford dismounted. As he helped the princess dismount her steed, the knight whispered to her.

He said, "Me Princess, look ye there, the marquess' steed be tethered to the hitching post. Must say, at the least his Lordship is to be commended for his persistence."

Irritated she said, "The gall of this loathsome viper, coming to visit, void of prior notice nor proper invitation. Must he deem hisself to be the desire of all the ladies in the realm; when in truth, be it not for the depth of his purse, would he be but the likes of a wart upon the rump of a toad.

Alas, thought it to be a day of good fortune, but to find this boresome oaf at me door. Pledge to thee, Sir Milford; find it quite bothersome being of royalty for oft be required to sit and pretend to be entertained by a serpent."

Edward's unexpected presence at the palace meant a delay in Princess Ashley's intentions of speaking with her mother and Lady Victoria immediately upon returning from the forest. She was now obliged to entertain the egotistical scoundrel.

Entering the palace, the princess was approached by Godfrey informing her the marquess was with Lady Victoria on the terrace. The princess thanked the butler and instructed him to arrange another setting at the table for lunch.

She, then took the stairs to her chambers to change her clothes before joining her guest.

A lancer was stationed near the terrace entrance when the princess walked down the hallway. In passing, she dismissed the soldier before stepping out onto the terrace.

On seeing the princess, the marquess stood from his seat, bowed then rendered a greeting.

"Good morn, Princess Ashley. Pray fair ye well this day. Lady Victoria hath spoken of thy desire to be schooled in the use of the bow. Wish not to appear boastful yet be quite accomplished in the use of the weaponry. Mighty me be of service? Would please me to be thy tutor."

The princess replied politely, "Good morn, your Lordship. Art ye most gracious to offer thy assistance. However, there be no need for am being tutored for weeks by another."

The marquess said, "Hath heard of thy many days in the forest with Sir Milford. Be he quite an accomplished archer."

She replied, "Nay; Sir Milford be but me escort. Might ye recall the archer to emerge victorious in the tournament held by me sire?"

The princess was interrupted by the butler Godfrey, announcing lunch was ready in the dining hall.

Princess Ashley was relieved by the interruption, wanting not to spend more time in conversation with the marquess than was necessary.

The princess said, "Come ye, your Lordship; Lady Victoria, shall we continue this conversation at the table."

Princess Ashley led them into the dining hall. King Frederick, the queen, and Prince Frederick were already seated.

Edward bowed to the king and queen.

Princess Ashley, and Lady Victoria took their seats as the king addressed the marquess[1].

He said, "G 'day, Edward; bade thee welcome. Come, set ye beside Frederick. How fare thy sire? Pray be he in good stead. All be well in Edenhall?"

The marquess replied, "Good day, your Majesties. Me sire yet be plagued with a bit of the gout. Other than that, a few of the villagers expressed discontent ore a frivolous matter this week past. Deemed it to be of no consequence. Me men dealt with the matter readily."

The king replied, "Indeed, Edward! Oft when a bit of unrest comes to the fore, 'tis wise to be a bit worrisome. For one doth not known what may lie beneath. I find it prudent to learn the reason for the discontent. Will it, then be certain who be the perpetrators, and who the injured."

"The course to follow may be as ye hath stated Your Majesty. Yet be me and me sire of a different mind. A firm hand be needed to maintain order in the village," said the marquess.

---

[1]

The queen could feel the tension escalating between the two men. Fearing her husband was about to lose his temper with the marquess, she thought to quickly change the subject of conversation.

She said, "Frederick, what activities might ye hath planned for this afternoon? With the marquess, haps ye might challenge the ladies in a game of quoits."

The prince replied. "A splendid suggestion, Mother. What say ye Ashley, Victoria; might the marquess agree to participate? Shall we men play the ladies."

"Prince Frederick, be not familiar with this activity, yet given proper instruction, might find it quite pleasurable," said the marquess.

Queen Margaret breathed a sigh of relief. Having succeeded in changing the subject, she was content to sit silent and enjoy her lunch; permitting the prince to explain the rules of play for the game to the marquess.

After lunch, the diners went to the garden. King Frederick and the queen sat on the terrace to watch the others play.

Prince Frederick stood at one stake with Lady Victoria. The princess with the marquess at the other.

It became apparent to the queen early on that the marquess had left much of the physical activities required of him for others to perform. The iron rings tossed by Edward often fell short of the opposing stake. The marquess was visibly embarrassed.

King Frederick, sitting beside the queen, turned to his wife with a mocking expression on his face. The queen, wanting to spare the marquess any further humiliation, shouted to the players.

"Be it not much too sweltering an afternoon to be engaged in such physical activity? Come ye now to the terrace. Should ye wish to continue the game, might ye wait for the sun to cast a shadow upon the garden."

The marquess breathed a sigh of relief. Accepting the queen's suggestion, he left his position and walked quickly toward the terrace. The others looked knowingly at each other and followed.

The group engaged in pleasant conversation, sipping cool apple cider until the castle walls began to cast shadows on the garden.

The marquess, not wanting to be asked to resume the game, decided it was time to leave. He stood to bow to the king and queen, then address the group.

He said, "Your Majesties, Prince Frederick, ladies, hath it been a most pleasant day. Must me not linger. For wish to arrive in Edenhall a 'fore sunset."

Prince Frederick stood to accompany the marquess out to the courtyard, then waited until Edward had mounted his horse and rode out over the moat. Walking down the hallway, the prince heard the sound of laughter coming from the terrace. Princess Ashley was speaking.

Laughingly, she said, "Me word Mother; 'tis a wonder the oaf hath the strength to lace his boots. Woe to the lady to whom one day to the twit be wed. For shall she be made to endure caresses a 'kin to that of a woman."

The queen said, "Ashley, speak kindly; yet rest assured thy Sire will never compel thee to pass thy days with the likes of the marquess.

She continued saying, "Come ladies, shall we retire to the sitting room for 'tis certain Ashley hath much to relate of her morn in the forest with the archer."

Chapter 33

It was Thursday morning in Dumfries and preparations had begun for the visit of king Frederick. Countess Sarah sat writing, and dispatching invitations for the fox hunt, and the festivities to follow Wednesday next.

Earl William held a meeting with the stable master and kennel master, instructing them to organize the hunt. The head gardener and his staff had already begun to groom the grounds of the manor.

Lady Rebecca sat with the butler, instructing him to have the servants scour, and polish the entire manor, prepare sleeping quarters for their guests, and procure provisions for the feast following the fox hunt.

Earl William sat with the countess and Lady Rebecca at lunch. He was well aware of the efficiency of the countess and Lady Rebecca's ability to oversee the staff. Yet he felt a need to emphasize the importance of this visit by the king.

He said, "Sarah, Rebecca, there be a need to impress upon thee the importance of the king's visit. Must the hunt and the festivities proceed from beginning to end without cause for disdain."

The countess replied, "Husband, haps would be wise to make it known to his Majesty that Rebecca hath been the hostess of the festivities. Will it then make a favorable impression upon the king."

He then said, "Well thought, Sarah."

Speaking to his daughter, the earl said. "Rebecca, hath ye been well schooled in the social graces. Must ye behave as a proper lady."

She replied, "Father, there be no need for concern, hath passed a fortnight with the king and queen when in Penrith. There be no need for pretense."

"Forgive me, child; 'tis not me intent to suggest ye be not a proper lady. 'Twas but a word of caution not needed to be spoken," said the earl.

Lady Rebecca replied, "Father, be we all a 'tither o'er the king's visit. Would be best to set it aside for a bit?

Hath thought to ride to Uncle Gaelan's and pass the day with Juliana."

Lady Rebecca rose from the table, kissed her mother and father on the cheek, then went to her chambers to change into riding garments.

The stable master bowed and greeted Lady Rebecca when she approached the stables, then called out to one of the stable boys.

He shouted, "Lad, go ye in haste to fetch Lady Rebecca's steed. The mare must bear a roman saddle for her ladyship desires to ride as the men."

Minutes later, the stable boy came leading her mare. The stable master gave her a hand up, then stood waving as she rode off toward her uncle's estate.

It was a bit more than a mile to the manor. The estate sat on a knoll, overlooking the countryside. Anyone approaching could be seen well before arriving.

A stable boy was waiting at the entrance to the manor when Lady Rebecca rode into the courtyard.

Lady Rebecca dismounted, handed the reins to the stable boy, then ran through the open door of the manor. She stopped a bit beyond the entrance and called out to her cousin. Lady Juliana came running down the stairs from her room above. The ladies hugged each other and exchanged greetings.

Lady Juliana said, "G 'day, Rebecca; thy visit be a pleasant surprise. What hath brought thee here this day? Pray all be well at the manor."

Lady Rebecca replied, "Aye, Juliana; Mother and Father be in good stead. The preparations for the visit of King Frederick hath left me at wit's end."

Her cousin said, "Come, Rebecca; leave us retire to the sitting room to chat. Mother, Father, and the wee ones hath gone to Cargenbridge for the day."

A servant came from the kitchen, curtsied, and asked if the ladies would like a bit of refreshment.

Lady Juliana asked that a ewer of elderberry wine be brought to the sitting room.

Lady Rebecca speaking, said, "Juliana, in a letter from Prince Frederick, 'twas mentioned there will be six cavalrymen accompanying King Frederick to Dumfries. The prince requested one of the cavalry to be a man answering to the name Donald."

"Rebecca, this Donald be not known to me. Hath ye some reason to speak of this man mentioned in the letter. Of what importance be this cavalryman?"

"Juliana, the name may not be familiar to thee yet there be a bond 'tween ye two. Leave me refresh thy memory," replied Lady Rebecca.

Again, the servant entered the sitting room, interrupting the conversation. Lady Juliana gave her a stern look. The servant blushed, curtsied, then quickly left.

Lady Juliana raised her finger to her lips, signaling Lady Rebecca to remain silent. She waited a minute then went to look out into the hall before speaking.

Returning, she said, "Rebecca, the lass be quite curious, and known to bear a wagging tongue. Yet Father favors the twit for her sire be a fierce member of the military. Now then, leave us resume our conversation.

Lady Rebecca said, "Juliana, recall the night thought ye to be pleasured by the prince but to learn in the morn be he another? The man be ye a 'bed with that night be the cavalryman, Donald.

Prince Frederick thought to afford thee an opportunity to once more pass a time with the gent. However, bear in mind might ye choose to engage the man in some activity must ye be discrete."

Lady Juliana replied, "And so shall it be, Rebecca. Be in the prince's debt for his thoughtfulness, lest the gent be an ogre."

Laughing, Lady Rebecca said, "Juliana, as to the nature of the gent be not aware for be known to me solely by sight. Assure thee, be he a handsome bloke indeed. None the less, bear in mind, on laying eyes upon Donald, 'tis for thee to engage or reject the gent."

Her cousin replied, "Lest he be pocked, ill-mannered or bearing the features of a gargoyle, doth matter not in the darkness

Lady Rebecca, shaking her head, said, "Juliana, love thee dearly; yet must state, thy lust for the male gender may one day be thy undoing."

Chapter 34

Prince Frederick sat in his room the next morning attempting to devise a plan to get Leland to the palace. He thought it time for the bowman to learn the maiden he had fallen in love with was actually a princess. Not certain if the archer would be hunting that afternoon, he thought to ask the princess at lunch.

Leaving his quarters, the prince took the stairs to the dining hall. The family was already seated with Lady Victoria and Sir Milford. He took his seat beside the king and waited for the topic of conversation to end, then addressed the princess.

The prince said, "Ashley, when in the forest with Leland this Wednesday past, spoke of the archer being at the hunt this day."

She replied, "Frederick, know ye well lest inhibited by foul weather, Leland be in the forest never every day. For what reason hath ye inquired of this?"

"Thought to join him a bit later," replied the prince.

He then addressed the knight, saying, "Sir Milford, at meals end might ye accompany me to me quarters? Be in need of thy assistance in a task hath in mind."

"As ye desire, me Prince," the knight replied.

After lunch Sir Milford accompanied the prince to his chambers. Tom was tidying up the room.

The prince told Tom to go to the men's barrack's and ask the Sergeant at Arms to go and wait for Sir Milford in the knight's quarters, then return with a ewer of grog.

Tom left the room to do his bidding.

Prince Frederick turned to the knight and said, "Sir Milford, 'tis certain be known to thee of Ashley becoming quite taken with the archer. The time hath come for the bowman to learn the true identity of the village maiden.

For many days hath attempted to lure the archer to the palace, to that end with no success. Thy assistance in the plan hath devised be required."

Sir Milford replied, "Me Prince, 'tis not me place to oppose thee in this endeavor, thus shall assist thee should ye wish to proceed. However, might it not be prudent for thee to consult with Princess Ashley of thy intent prior to proceeding?"

The prince answered, "Sir Milford, the two hath pranced about for weeks, neither with the courage to commit. Thus, thought to spur one or t' other to step forth.

Heed well this plan hath devised. On speaking to thy sergeant, these instructions art to be given. At mid-afternoon shall be with Leland in the forest. The sergeant is to come to the forest near sunset with soldiers. Must they move quietly. For Leland hath the ears of a fox. We art to be apprehended for poaching in the king's forest.

Must me not be identified as the prince, but as a commoner.

Leland will surely state be he at the hunt with the permission of the king. The men art to pay the archer no mind.

We art to be taken to the castle. Instruct the guards at the gates to pretend to be occupied upon our arrival. Thus, shall we pass unnoticed."

Tom entered the room carrying a tray of grog and two goblets. He set it on a table between the men, then told the prince the sergeant was waiting for Sir Milford in the knight's quarters.

Tom bowed and left the room. The prince, then continued relating his plan to Sir Milford.

"Sir Milford, entering the courtyard, must we be taken quickly to thy quarters.

When ye be in the dining hall for the evening meal, the soldiers will come to inform thee of the two poachers found in the forest. One of the hunters claiming to be given permission by the king to do so."

Sir Milford replied, "Me Prince, 'tis a well thought plan haps to succeed. Pray the outcome shall be to thy liking. Shall see to it."

Sir Milford retreated from the room, leaving Prince Frederick to change into his hunting attire.

The prince took his bow and quiver from the hanger on the wall and left the palace for the forest.

He found Leland sitting by the oak waiting for early sunset when the deer would be on the move. Beside him lay two rabbits and a grouse.

The prince said, "G 'day, Leland; hath ye done well thus far. Why art ye not at the hunt? Hath ye retired for the day?"

"Frederick, hath it been a while. Come set in wait of sunset when the deer be on the move. shall we, then resume the hunt," Leland replied.

The two men sat chatting, enjoying each other's company, not paying much attention to their surroundings.

Meanwhile, Sir Milford went to instruct the sergeant as to how the soldiers were to proceed in carrying out the plan.

He said, "Sergeant, must ye and the soldiers take care to tread lightly upon approaching the two; for be ye detected, the archer will flee; and the plan be lain asunder. Dare ye not cause harm to the prince nor the archer."

The sergeant replied, "Will it be as hath ye instructed, Sir Milford. Shall assemble the soldiers then leave for the forest within the hour."

Sir Milford thought the time and place for Princess Ashley to reveal herself to Leland as royalty should have been left for her to decide. He had voiced his concern to the prince. Prince Frederick had chosen to ignore his counsel. It was not his place to oppose the instructions of a member of the royal family. Thus, reluctantly he went to speak with the sentries at the gate with instructions as dictated to him by the prince.

There was nothing left for the knight to do but wait for the drama to unfold.

He walked to the stables for his steed. The knight mounted Titus, then went to wait for the soldiers to assemble in the courtyard.

The knight rode past the foot soldiers to the entrance to the forest and waited for the foot soldiers to arrive. He, then showed them the path leading to where the prince and the archer were likely to be.

Sir Milford waited for the men to enter the forest. He, then spurred Titus in the direction of the Tate's cottage.

Arabella was hoeing in the small garden beside the cottage when Sir Milford arrived. Seeing the knight, she dropped the hoe and ran to greet him.

She said, "Good day, Sir Milford; bade thee welcome. Mother will be pleased to see thee. Come; be she within. Shall set a pot of tea a 'brew."

The knight dismounted and followed the maiden through the open door of the cottage. Widow Tate was sitting by a window, mending. She came to her feet to greet the knight.

The woman said, "G 'day, Sir Knight; 'tis a pleasure for thee to come by. Come set; Arabella shall brew a bit of tea.

Trust Jarin be in good stead. Pray hath he tended to his chores without incident."

Sir Milford replied, "Aye, dear lady, a fine lad indeed. Upon his release hath thought to invite him to join the cavalry in service to the king."

Addressing her daughter, the woman asked, "Arabella, hath ye heard Sir Milford? Thy brother, Jarin is soon to be released. Will he, then be requested to serve in the king's cavalry."

She replied, "Mother, upon the incarceration of Jarin, with no man in our midst, I feared for our future. To hear brother Jarin may serve in the king's cavalry hath gone far to dispel much of me fears."

Mother Tate said to the knight, "Blessings be upon thee, Sir Milford. There be no end to the kindness hath ye afforded me, and me brood."

He replied, "Dear lady, the lad be deserving of an attempt to right an error hath he made in the heat of anger. Yea too, Princess Ashley hath not forgotten thyne aid in these weeks past. Hath she expressed a desire to render aid in the release of thy son. An ally in this be of much worth."

Mother Tate replied, "Sir Knight, deem it an honor to serve the princess. Be of no concern to we Tate's why o'er these weeks past the princess be about the forest bearing Arabella's garments. Am certain the princess be not demented. Must she harbor a valid reason for concealing her identity. Rest assured, Sir Milford; no word of these matters shall ere pass our lips."

Chapter 35

Sir Milford left the Tate cottage a bit before sunset. Riding to the castle, he had a bad feeling in the pit of his stomach; certain it was not caused by the tea he had consumed at the Tate's. He understood the prince's desire for the princess and Leland to commit to each other, yet uncertain the prince's timing was right. It was a wait and see situation, with an unpredictable outcome.

He rode Titus into the courtyard to the stables. Dismounting, he handed the reins to Gavin, then went directly to his quarters to prepare for dinner.

On his way to dinner, the knight stopped to remind the guards at the gate to ignore the group of soldiers escorting the prince and archer to the palace.

Entering the dining hall, Sir Milford bowed to the royalty then took a seat beside Lady Victoria. They all remained silent for a few minutes, then the queen spoke.

She asked, "What hath become of Frederick? Of late hath he in mind naught but the Lady Rebecca. Mercy! 'Tis a wonder the lad remembers the time of day.

Milford, hath ye seen the prince about?"

He replied, "Me Queen, we spoke after the midday meal. The prince then went to the forest to hunt with Leland. Would me not be concerned; shall his Lordship soon be by."

Godfrey entered the dining hall, bowed to the royal family, then went to whisper to the knight.

The butler said, "Sir Milford, a soldier be in wait of thee at the palace entrance with a message. Shall me bade him enter?"

Sir Milford replied, "Nay, Godfrey; will speak with the man in the courtyard.

Forgive me your Majesties, a message of some urgency awaits."

Bowing, Sir Milford excused himself. The butler bowed and returned to the kitchen. Sir Milford went to speak with the soldiers waiting at the palace entrance.

The two men walked out onto the courtyard with Sir Milford, then one of the soldiers spoke.

He said, "Sir Milford, hath we but minutes past returned from the forest. Prince Frederick and the archer await thee in thy quarters.

"Sir Milford replied, "Me thank thee, lads. Prince Frederick shall take command of the situation henceforth. Ye art dismissed."

The soldier hurried off. Sir Milford went to his quarters to fetch the prince and Leland.

Entering Sir Milford said, "Ye men follow me."

The prince and Leland left the commander's quarters following Sir Milford across the courtyard to the palace entrance.

Entering, Leland stopped and stood in awe of what lie within. On either side of the entrance, and at the foot of a staircase leading to rooms above, stood handsomely dressed sentries at attention. He saw a myriad of ornately fashioned lanterns hanging from the walls with beautiful tapestry between them, depicting scenes from yesteryear. In every corner stood knights of armor so highly polished they reflected the light from the lanterns onto the walls and corridors of the palace.

The prince and Sir Milford waited patiently, permitting Leland to absorb the splendor of the palace. They then continued down the corridor toward the dining hall, Sir Milford leading the way. Sir Milford opened, and held the door. Leland and the prince stepped in.

Leland stood in the doorway in disbelief. At the table sat Princess Ashley beside the king and queen. For a minute he stood bewildered, then spoke in anger.

The archer said, "What manner of jugglery might this be? Look ye there, the peasant girl hath come to love, set she beside the queen; prim, and proper in her finery.

Yea too, here beside me stands the archer hath befriended. Be told by thee, Frederick, thy sire hath a position at the castle. Hath ye succeeded in playing me the fool. Well done, me mate! However, care me not to take part in thy foppery."

Not bowing to the king nor the queen, as a sign of contempt, Leland stormed out of the palace

The prince calling out after him to no avail.

Sir Milford gave chase. Robert the gatekeeper attempted to stop the archer in the courtyard. Leland pushed the guard aside. Throwing open the gate, Leland disappeared into the darkness.

In the dining hall, the queen came to her feet. Princess Ashley broke out in tears; stood stamping her foot on the dining hall floor.

Shouting at the prince, she said; "Be damned, Frederick! Hath ye lain waste to all me plans. Leland should not hath been made aware yet that hath he been courting a princess. Pride be one of the many qualities admire in the man. Thy incessant behavior hath caused me love to flee. Be he lost to me forever!"

The princess ran from the room; tears still falling to her cheeks.

The queen angered said, "Gad Zeus! What hath come to pass this night? Husband, whatever it be, 'tis to be resolved!"

In a huff, Queen Margaret hurried out of the dining hall, following Princess Ashley up the stairway to her chambers.

The prince stood bewildered, wondering what he had done to anger the archer, then realized Leland was not prepared for the shocking disclosure that he had been wooing a princess, and his hunting partner was not one of his peers, but the prince.

The worst of it was the prince had no idea at the moment as to how he was to reconcile with his sister nor how to correct the situation.

He was about to follow his mother when his father spoke.

The king said, "Frederick, hold! At the present must ye not approach thy sibling in an attempt to seek forgiveness. For she shall but turn thee a deaf ear.

We must sort this out. Milford and his men will scour the forest in attempt to find the bowman. Should he succeed, will we then atone for this errant course of events.

The king turned to the knight and asked, "Milford, what part might ye hath played in this foppery?"

The prince, wanting to spare Sir Milford of the king's wrath, interrupted and spoke.

He said, "Father, the blame for this grievous mishap lay solely upon me. Sir Milford in his wisdom advised me to first speak with Ashley a 'fore proceeding. In me eagerness to please her, chose to ignore his counsel."

Frustrated with the prince, the king simply shook his head in response.

Turning to the knight, the king saying, "Milford, shall we soon be leaving for Dumfries. In me absence, an attempt is to be made to ferret out the archer. Leland is to be made aware Frederick acted with good intentions. Aye, 'twas a grievous error in judgment. Never expecting Leland to deem Fredrick's actions an attempt to play him the fool."

Sir Milford replied, "Your Majesty, rest assured every effort shall be made to find the archer. Come morn, shall me men scour the forest to that end, and in days to come. Should we not succeed, shall we then inquire in the villages about the forest for where he might be."

"See to it, Milford. Be not certain unto this night of Ashley harboring such strong feelings for the archer. She is to be afforded a time with the bowman to sort out this matter," said the king.

Chapter 36

Leland left the palace and returned to his little hut in the village, furious with himself for allowing a young maiden of less than twenty years to play him the fool.

He lay on his cot, reviewing the events of the day. Suddenly he realized, in his anger he had shown grievous disrespect for the entire royal family. Surely his outburst had not been appreciated, nor would it soon be forgiven. His life was in danger.

The archer spent much of the night attempting to determine what he was to do. Should he simply disappear? Should he attempt to hide, hoping the incident would eventually be forgotten by the king?

Leland was not the sort of man to hole up like a scared rabbit. He determined neither of the two options were acceptable. For what was to become of the widowed and orphans in the village? He then thought to speak of it with the smithy in the morning. Taking a bit of comfort in his decision, he finally fell asleep.

Leland woke the next morning. He went out to the bucket of rainwater beside the hut to wash.

On the road from the castle, Leland saw a group of men marching down the hillside from the palace toward the flats. He could not identify them from where he stood.

As they drew closer he saw they were five foot soldiers, led by a knight, heading towards the forest.

Leland was certain they were going to search the forest, in pursuit of him. Strangely, he felt a bit exited. He had stalked game in that forest since he was in his teens and had learned well the art of concealment. They would need to look long, and hard to succeed in his capture.

After a bit of breakfast, he walked over to the blacksmith shop to speak with Howard.

The smithy was at his anvil, hammering on a horseshoe. The archer waited patiently for the smithy to complete his task before engaging him in conversation.

Leland said, "Howard, g' day! Might we speak? Hath gotten meself into a bit of a pickle. Wish ye not to be involved yet request a boon of thee."

"G' day Leland. What hath ye gotten thyself into of late? Must it be of a serious nature," Howard replied.

Leland went on to say, "Know ye, hath been tutoring a young maiden in the forest. Unbeknown to me, be she the Princess Ashley.

She came to me in the trappings of a village maiden. Never hath she revealed to me from whence she came but to say 'twas beyond the forest.

This day past be at the hunt with Frederick. Be we set upon by soldiers of the king, accused of poaching. Be then taken to the palace under guard, to learn 'twas but a ruse, perpetrated by Frederick hisself.

Alas, Howard; then found the man thought to be me chum, be a prince; kin to Ashley, and she a princess, not a village maiden.

Taken to the palace, entered the dining hall with Frederick, to find the king, queen, and the princess at the table. In anger, offended the lot, then ran off. Soldiers be in the forest as we speak attempting me capture."

The smithy said, "Mercy Leland, 'tis a bit of a fix hath ye gotten thyself into. The princess be known to me. Come to me shop this week past. A winsome lass indeed!

Now then, what need hath thee of me?"

Leland said, "Advise the villagers, should the soldiers come to inquire of me, they art to say they know naught of me whereabouts. Howard, these soldiers be in for a merry chase."

Howard replied, "Leland, must ye take care; would it not bode well for thee to be shackled then imprisoned, nor for the needy who look to thee for food."

"The soldiers will soon grow weary of the search Howard. Will me then resume the hunt, lest be known to me the stand in the willow hath been discovered.

Our wanting villagers shall not hunger. Will remain in me hut for these days next. Pray should the soldiers come inquiring after me, will me not be betrayed," said Leland.

Howard replied, "Rest at ease, me ole friend. For the wrath of the villagers would befall upon anyone with intent to surrender thee to the soldiers. Should one dare, with much pleasure will meself provide the noose to hang the informant in the village for all to see then shall cast the lout into me forge to the revelry of the entire hamlet."

The archer knew full well, though Howard was a giant of a man, he would not do harm to anyone; less provoked. Leland would have laughed at the smithy's remark had he not been in such a melancholy frame of mind.

Leland thanked his friend. He bade him a good day, then returned to his hut.

Sitting on his cot he weighed his options as to how to provide for the needy in the village yet avoid being found in the forest. It would not be safe for him to hunt walking the forest floor. He would need to return to his stand in the willow or watch for the soldiers to return to the castle then hunt at sunset.

Chapter 37

Princess Ashley did not make an appearance the next morning in the dining hall. Nor did the commander.

Sir Milford had assembled his men early to resume the search for the archer.

Godfrey and the servants entered the dining hall with breakfast. Lady Victoria instructed the butler to have the servants serve breakfast for her and the princess in the chambers of the princess.

She then asked to be excused and went to tap on the door to the chambers of the .princess.

Receiving no response, she cracked open the door and requested permission to enter. None was forthcoming.

Quite concerned, she entered the room to see the princess still in her bed. She walked over to sit on the edge of the bed to speak to her.

Shaking the princess, she said; "Princess, come awake. The servants will soon be entering with thy morning meal. Will not do for ye to seen whimpering yet a 'bed."

Rubbing the sleep from her eyes, the princess replied, "Leave me be, Victoria, hath no desire for food in chambers nor to set at the table with me mindless brother. What possessed the twit to bring Leland to the palace?"

Lady Victoria said, "Cousin, Frederick hath thought but to please thee; bore he no malice in mind. Might it hath been prudent for Frederick to speak with Leland a 'fore returning with him to the palace. Leland would surely hath declined the invitation.

Ye, then when in the forest with Leland, thought it to be the proper moment, could hath explain the reasons for the deception to the archer.

Ashley, know thee well the nature of Sir Milford. Will the knight not rest lest hath he completed his mission.

As we speak, the knight be in the forest with his men attempting to ferret out the archer. Shall speak to Sir Milford upon his return, requesting he keep thee abreast of the search."

"Victoria, when in distress 'tis but thee hath come to console me, requesting naught in return for thyself."

"Princess, and when one day hath ye born children, pray ye look to me to be their governess. This alone shall deem to be me reward," said Lady Victoria.

The princess replied, "Alas, Victoria; and where might a man the likes of me beloved Leland be found to these children sire?"

Tapping on the chamber door brought Lady Victoria to her feet. Certain it was the servants with breakfast, she quickly drew the curtains hanging from the canopy around the bed of the princess before giving permission for the servants to enter.

Millicent entered carrying a huge silver tray followed by Christy with the dinner ware.

Lady Victoria said, "Me thank thee, Millicent, Christy. Princess Ashley hath not completed her grooming. Leave the tray. Shall tend to the serving meself. Ye two go about thy chores."

The servants set the trays down on the table, curtsied, and left the room, closing the door behind them.

Lady Victoria drew the curtains open from around the bed, then went to stand in the chamber window overlooking the courtyard while the princess left the bed to use the privy.

Below, Sir Cartwith was leaving the castle grounds mounted on Sweet Sorrow, riding toward the village with a mare in tow.

Lady Victoria turned from the window to begin setting the table for their breakfast.

The princess returned from the privy dressed, and well groomed. The two sat to eat their breakfast.

Lady Victoria mentioned seeing Sir Cartwith leaving with a spare horse in tow, riding off to the village.

The princess spoke, saying, "Victoria, hath heard Sir Cartwith weeks past fetched a widowed woman and daughter from the wee hamlet of Skeeby to aid Eleanor at the millinery. Recall the tot, Tiffany, come with Christy to the terrace some days past? Be she child to the widowed needlewoman."

"Indeed, Ashley; thought her to be well attired. No wonder the wee lass be garbed in such comely garments," replied Lady Victoria.

The princess said, "The ladies of the court hath flocked to the millinery with requests for riding attire liken those made for thee. Eleanor would hath been hard pressed to fashion many garments without aid. The coming of the widow woman to reside in the village be a blessing for the seamstress."

The princess paused, then continued saying; "Sir Cartwith hath been a frequent visitor to the millinery. Haps the knight hath entered into a courtship with the widow."

Lady Victoria replied, "What with the knight being charged with commanding the cavalrymen accompanying thy sire, and the prince to Dumfries, he may wish to pass a day with the lady a 'fore riding off to Scotland."

"Victoria; speak thee of courtship. I be well aware the marquess comes to court me with ill intentions. Hath wearied of his attempts to deceive. When next Edward comes to visit, shall in a kindly manner put this folly to an end," said the princess.

Lady Victoria said, "Princess, must ye take care to choose well thy words lest the marquess be offended when turned away."

Queen Margaret enter the room with a smile. She stood for a moment looking at the two ladies sitting at the table.

She, then said, "Good morn, Ashley, Victoria. Ashley, be ye missed in the dining hall. Be ye lamenting o'er the loss of the archer. Take heart dear one for assure thee, Leland will soon be found then this mishap shall be set a 'right."

The princess responded, "Mother, this ye say will not be accomplished with ease for the forest be well known to Leland. Hath he the ears of a dolphin, eyes of a hawk, and moves about the forest floor as a serpent."

"None the less, Sir Milford will continue the search for a few days. Having no success, will he then turn his attention to the surrounding villages. Someone will come forth with information as to where the archer might be," said the queen.

The princess said, "Bear in mind, Mother; for years Leland hath rendered aid to many of the needy in the hamlet of his birth, thus the villagers hold the archer in high regard. Will the man not be surrendered to the soldiers lest by force.

Mother, no one is to be harmed in this attempt to find the archer."

"Rest at ease, Ashley; will it not be permitted. Come now, must ye not pass the day pouting. Shall expect thee at the midday meal," said the queen.

Meanwhile, Sir Milford had mustered his men early that morning. Before leading them to the forest, he stood before them with instructions.

He said, "Ye men, heed well. The bowman we seek hath committed no crime against the king, nor be he a threat to anyone. Should he be found, no hands art to be lain upon him. His Majesty desires solely to speak with him. Woe to he who fails to follow these instructions."

In the forest, Sir Milford and the soldiers spent much of the day attempting to locate the archer.

One of the men poked his head between the low hanging branches of the giant willow where Leland had built his stand. He looked about but did not think to look up into the branches above.

After a lengthy search, the men had grown weary and frustrated. Sir Milford decided to give up for the day. Leland was either not in the forest or too well concealed to be found. The commander ordered the soldiers to return to the castle.

The next day being the Sabbath, and His Majesty leaving for Dumfries on Monday morning, Sir Milford thought to resume the search after the king's departure.

Leland, standing at a window of his hut, had seen the column of soldiers returning to the castle from the woodlands late in the afternoon.

The archer was certain the animals had been disturbed by the soldiers and had most likely left the area and retreated deeper into the woodlands.

Should the soldiers continue searching the forest, the archer knew, hunting would be an effort in futility.

He would need to wait to see if they returned the next day. Although he rarely hunted on the Sabbath, there was a need for fresh meat in the village.

Should the soldiers not resume the search the next day, the archer would hunt near sunset.

Chapter 38

There was a somber mood at the dinner table that evening. Sir Milford's failure to find the archer lay heavy on everyone present.

Princess Ashley sat pushing the food on her plate around with her fork, avoiding eye contact with her brother.

Prince Frederick was quite displeased with himself for having created a situation that would certainly not be resolved before his leaving for Dumfries.

Sir Milford sat deep in thought as to what course of action was to be taken, should the archer not be found in the forest in the next few days.

Both the queen, and Lady Victoria were frustrated for not having a clue as to what next was to be done.

The silence was broken by the king addressing Sir Milford.

He said, "Milford, might the archer not be found within the days to follow, hath ye some measure of thought on how ye art to proceed?"

The knight did not immediately respond. King Frederick sat patiently, permitting the knight the time to think. Many minutes passed before Sir Milford imposed a question.

He asked, "Your Majesty, shall we pretend for a moment we to be residents of a hamlet. Soldiers come, posting placards in the village square, requesting information as to the whereabouts of a dear friend. What might we be tempted to do?"

The king replied, "Why Milford, upon their departure would me not hesitate to wrench the posting from where it stood then tear it to shreds a 'fore 'twas seen by another.

Be left a bit confused. Pray tell, Milford. How might this aid in finding the archer?"

Sir Milford replied, "Your Highness, should soldiers post a placard in each of the hamlets surrounding the forest one day, then return the next. Might not the placard in the village in which the archer resides no longer be in place?"

The king said, "By George! Milford, 'tis an alternate plan to be considered. Continue with the search of the forest for a bit longer. Might ye well succeed in finding Leland. If not, upon returning from Dumfries shall we set the scribes to task, creating placards to be posted by the cavalry in the villages, haps along the roads about the woodlands as well."

Sir Milford's suggestion, and its acceptance by the king, changed the mood of the diners. Princess Ashley and Lady Victoria clapped their hands in approval. Queen Margaret emitted a chuckle as the two young ladies displayed elation, then addressed the knight.

The queen said, "Milford, oft be left in awe of thy ability to hastily arrive at a likely solution to a seemingly impossible situation. Art we indeed fortunate for thee to be in service to me husband. Would it not bode well for the realm for thee to be in opposition to the king."

Sir Milford replied, "Be thee a most gracious lady, me Queen; be not deserving of thy praise for be me in thy debt. Your Majesties, o'er these many years hath afforded me much more than an orphaned child could imagine."

The king lent agreement to the queen's statement.

He said, "Here, here, Margaret; and well deserving, Milford."

The king paused, then continuing he said, "Might ye ladies hath eaten thy fill, go ye about what activities might pleasure thee. We men shall remain to discuss matters of no interest to thee."

Prince Frederick and Sir Milford stood to wait for the ladies to leave the dining hall before returning to their seats.

The king waited for their footsteps to fade. He, then cleared his throat then posed a question to the prince.

He asked, "Frederick, be left to wonder, why the urgency for the cavalryman Donald to be included in the party riding to Dumfries?"

The prince replied, "Father, hath ye done well to dismiss the ladies for 'tis a lustful tale indeed. A kin to Lady Rebecca whose name need not reveal, bears a hearty appetite for male companionship."

Continuing, the prince said, "Upon arriving in Dumfries, be forewarned by Lady Rebecca the lass might attempt to join me in quarters in the dead of night.

To avoid an embarrassment, instructed the cavalryman Donald to occupy me quarters in me stead.

Come morn, thought the maiden to be ired. Quite the contrary, for she revealed to Lady Rebecca she hath found it to be a most pleasant evening.

The gent with whom she passed the night as yet be not known to her. Thought to introduce the lady to the lad upon our arrival in Dumfries. Should it be of interest to see what might transpire 'tween the two."

King Frederick and Sir Milford broke out into a fit of laughter.

The king regained his composure before saying, "Frederick, hath ye a bit of jugglery within thee. Art ye to be commended for devising a ruse to avoid a situation which might well hath become quite a calamity."

Chapter 39

Before sunrise Sunday morning, Mildred was in the kitchen setting flame to the kindling in the hearth and the ovens. She had not spoken to Christy as yet of her intention to move in with Martin.

With the possibility of Tom returning from Dumfries with Bridget, she thought it time to prepare the child for a new roommate.

Having completed her task, Mildred took the lighted candle from the table and went to her bedroom to sit beside the child yet asleep. She thought for a moment of how she was to explain the change without unsettling the child before waking her.

Mildred then ran a hand through Christy's golden locks until the child opened her eyes.

A bit disoriented, Christy quickly sat a 'right.

She said, "Mother, hath ye startled me. Be it not yet light. Why hath ye awakened me at such an early hour? Something be a 'miss?"

Mildred replied, "Good morn, Christy. Be not alarmed. There be a need for Mother to speak on a matter of importance to thee.

Know ye this day next Tom will be accompanying Prince Frederick on holiday. He may be returning from Scotland with a lass who hath been given a position as a servant here in the palace. Should this come to pass, will she be sharing this room with thee.

Be she ten and eight in years, responding to the name Bridget. Must ye make her welcome and treat her kindly. For hath she no kin nor chums in Penrith."

Christy asked, "And what is to become of thee, Mother? Art we to be abandoned?"

Mildred smiled and said, "Nay, child, shall be quite near. Martin hath expressed a desire for me to share his quarters at the butchery. Be he a kindly man who will care for me in me waning years.

Upon him speaking with Thomas, Martin afforded the lad an opportunity to object to our union. None be given.

Should ye harbor any objections to these words hath spoken, they art to be expressed. Might ye find discomfort in these arrangements, then all shall remain as it be."

The child said, "Mother, hath ye labored long to sustain me, and brother Tom. Be ye deserving of a bit of happiness; thus, no objection be forthcoming.

As to sharing these quarters with the maiden. In truth must confess, hath yearned for there to be a sister in our midst."

Mildred put her arms around Christy holding the child to her; tears falling to her cheeks.

Sounds from the kitchen alerted her the staff was arriving.

Kissing Christy on the forehead she whispered, "Bless thee, child. Come, don thy garments. Will there be much to do this morn. Preparations for the king's holiday art to be addressed."

Mildred wiped the tears from her cheeks as she left the room to return to the kitchen. Servants were busy preparing breakfast when she entered. She went to stand at a table below a window overlooking the courtyard to see Mortimer, the jailor, escorting a young lad to the palace gate.

Mortimer stopped for a moment to speak with Robert. The sentry opened the gate, permitting the lad to pass.

Mortimer stood at the open gate watching the young lad run down the hill toward the flats in the dim morning light. Mildred called out to the jailor.

She shouted, "Mortimer, good morn; be that not the lad rode off with Lady Verna's steed? Hath he been released?"

The jailor replied, "G 'day, Mildred. Aye, 'tis Jarin. Hath he not yet been given his freedom. Sir Milford hath given permission for him to tend to chores at Mother Tate's upon the Sabbath."

Martin, sitting at breakfast in the butchery heard Mildred shouting to the jailor. He rose from his seat and walked into the courtyard to wave to her still standing in the window.

Mildred waved back, then shouted, "Good morn, Martin; might ye wait? Would share a word with thee."

Mortimer turned from the gate to see Mildred leave the window then exit through the side entrance of the kitchen where the butcher was waiting.

The jailor watched Mildred take the butcher's hand and lead him back into the butchery.

The two sentries standing at the gate turned to each other grinning.

Robert, at his post said to the jailor, "Mortimer, might ye not lend credence to this shall relate to thee. Me thinks the palace be haunted for oft hath seen a shadowy figure pass from the side of the kitchen to butchery in the dead of night."

Mortimer replied. "Indeed, Robert. Haps 'tis a woebegone spirit seeking a bit of comfort. G 'day, ole gent, must see to me tasks."

Returning to the dungeons, Mortimer ran into Sir Cartwith standing by the stables. The knight was apparently waiting for one of the stable boys to saddle his mount. The jailor stopped to speak to him.

He said, "G 'day, Sir Cartwith; where might ye be off to this early morn?"

The knight replied, "G' day, Mortimer; upon the 'morrow shall accompany the king to Dumfries.

Be off to the village. Thought to pass the day with a mate a 'fore departing."

"Safe journey, Sir Knight," said the jailor.

Meanwhile, in the butchery, Mildred was telling Martin of the conversation she had with Christy earlier.

She said, "Martin, must me not linger for there be much to be done in the kitchen. Hath spoken to Christy this morn. Be she told Thomas may return from Dumfries with a lass. Might this come to pass, the lass will be in need of a place to reside. Will she be welcomed to share me quarters."

Martin replied, "Woman, will ye find no comfort in a room meant for two yet bedding three. Suspect shall we soon be in need of a priest. Should Thomas return with the lass, arrangements art to be made for we to wed.

The children need not be concerned with this union. Will they not be forsaken. For shall care for them as would be me own."

"Long hath waited for thee to come forth with these words, Martin. Pledge to thee, will ye not rue this day," Mildred replied.

She kissed the butcher, bade him a good day, then ran from the butchery, returning to her chores in the kitchen.

Chapter 40

Monday morning, activity at the castle was at a fever pitch. Horses were being groomed and saddled. Nine of them were led out and tethered outside the barracks.

Gavin and two stable boys stood holding the reins of Abas, Silvermane, and Lord Morley's steed outside the palace entrance.

The six cavalrymen and Tom milled around in the courtyard waiting for orders from Sir Cartwith to mount and fall into formation. One of the cavalry bearing the king's standard led his steed to stand a bit beyond the drawbridge.

Meanwhile, the royal family sat at breakfast in the dining hall with Lady Victoria, Sir Milford, and Lord Morley who had arrived at the palace the previous night.

Godfrey entered the dining hall, bowed. He announced the escorting party was prepared to assemble in the courtyard.

King Frederick thanked and then dismissed the butler.

Sir Milford addressed the king.

He said, "Your Majesty, shall leave thee and instruct Sir Cartwith to assemble the men. Shall they await thy convenience."

Sir Milford went to stand on the palace steps, waving a signal to Sir Cartwith.

Sir Cartwith ordered the men to mount and assemble.

Minutes later the occupants of the dining hall stepped out onto the landing at the palace entrance.

The group exchanged farewells.

King Frederick, Prince Frederick and Lord Morley mounted their steeds. The king and prince took positions at the head of the column while Lord Morley and Sir Cartwith fell in behind; the cavalry and Tom followed two by two.

The column left the courtyard led by the standard bearer and took the road northwest toward Gretna.

Sir Cartwith had instructed the standard bearer to set a pace getting them to Gretna by sunset.

When the column came upon an apple tree, two of the soldiers went to pick some of the fruit and shared it with the others.

Coming upon a stream, the horses were permitted to take water and graze a bit while the men stretched their legs.

Midway between Penrith, and Gretna, on the outskirts of a village. Weary, the column stopped to lunch on a bit of cheese, bread, and grog prepared for the ride by the kitchen staff.

The column rode into the courtyard of the inn at Gretna a bit past sunset. The ride had taken longer than expected.

Sounds of bagpipes could be heard drifting from the glen.

Sir Cartwith, the cavalrymen, and Tom broke ranks; riding to stable their horses as stable boys came running for the horses ridden by the king, Prince Frederick, and Lord Morley.

The proprietor of the inn came to the entrance, bowed, bade the three men to enter, then greeted them as they passed.

He said, "Good eve, your Lordships. Good fortune smiles upon thee this night. Being Monday, the inn be sparsely occupied. How many rooms shall be needed?"

Prince Frederick stepped forward to reply.

Bridget, tidying up the kitchen, heard the familiar voice of the prince. She ran from the kitchen, curtsied to the three men, then stood waiting for the prince and the innkeeper to complete their transaction.

The prince said, "Sir, but four rooms require. The men art to be sheltered and fed as well. Will there be four to sup in the dining hall this night, and at the morning meal."

The proprietor replied, "Me Lord, tables will be set in the courtyard for the men. They will be permitted to sleep in the stables and the shed. Blankets will be provided."

Bridget, then stepped forward and led the three nobles to a table in the dining hall.

She waited for them to sit before asking the prince if Tom had accompanied them to Gretna.

Prince Frederick did not address Bridget's question when he replied.

He said, "Good eve, Bridget; might ye fetch a bit of ale, then go to the stables to speak with Sir Cartwith? The knight is to join the king at the table."

Bridget took the prince's failure to reply to her question as an indication that Tom had not come to Gretna.

She curtsied, then went off to fetch the ale the prince had requested.

Meanwhile, in the courtyard, the men were about to stable their mounts.

Sir Cartwith, knowing Tom had been at the inn before, asked, "Tom, what be that eerie sound coming from the glen?"

Tom replied, "Sir Cartwith, 'tis the sound of bagpipes. Oft at sunset the villagers gather in the glen to sing, dance, and partake of the local brew. Ye will be made welcome might ye wish to participate. Assure thee, will ye pass a most pleasurable evening."

In the dining hall, Bridget returned with a ewer of ale, and tankards for the table. She set them down, curtsied, then went to deliver the prince's message to Sir Cartwith.

Stepping into the dimly lit courtyard, Bridget could barely see the group of men standing with their horses outside the stables. Drawing near she stopped midway to speak.

She said, "Sir Cartwith, the king hath requested thy presence at the table in the dining hall.

To the others, she said, "Ye cavalrymen art to sup at tables to be set in the courtyard and be bedded in the stables."

Bridget turned from the men and began walking toward the inn when a voice spoke out from the group.

He said, "Dear maiden, and what of the manservant to the prince. Might he be expected to fend for hisself?"

Bridget turned to see one of the men break from the group and walk toward her.

As he came into the light, she shouted; "Thomas! Hath thought thee to be left behind."

Tom took her hands in his. The two pranced in circles.

The men standing by the stables were left to wonder what had just happened.

Sir Cartwith passed the two lovers bearing a knowing smile as he made his way into the inn.

Bridget came against the manservant to whisper.

She said, "Thomas, never thought to see thee again. Upon completing me chores might we go to the glen, and pass this night together?"

"Nay, lass; haps a few of the men may wish to join the revelers in the glen. Must we not, for there be a matter of much importance to be discussed.

Go ye now, tend to thy guests in the dining hall. At sups end, come to me in the shed beside the stables."

The maiden kissed Tom, then returned to the inn to serve the diners. Tom had left her wondering what was so important that he would pass on a chance to enjoy the night at the dance with the villagers.

It seemed forever before the diners had finished their supper before Bridget was able to tidy up the dining hall.

With a lantern in hand she, then went to meet with Tom. Through the open door of the tack rom she saw Tom standing by a bench watching three men at a game of cards.

She called to him. He came, took her hand, and led her to one of the tables standing in the courtyard.

She said, "Thomas, hath ye left me in suspense. What might this matter of such importance be to forego an evening at the dance?"

He replied, "Bridget, hath a proposal to present thee. Hath spoken to Mother of a lass in Gretna, skilled as a servant. Requested she speak on thy behalf, seeking a position at the palace in Penrith. A position hath been secured. 'Tis left for thee to accept or reject."

Bridget said, "Mercy, Thomas! A handsome proposal indeed! Yet not expected. Be it not a decision to be made in haste. Much be left to be considered. How might this trek to Penrith be made a 'foot and with no escort? Shall we assume a manner of transport be found. Upon arriving with but a few shillings in me purse, barely enough to sustain meself; where shall me reside?"

Attempting to relieve her concerns, he said, "Bridget, be not concerned with food nor shelter for will they be provided. Shall ye be bedded with me sibling, Christy. Will ye receive a stipend for thy service as well.

As to transport, hath come with a steed in tow to be left here in the stables. Might ye choose to come to Penrith, the mare will be thyne to ride with the column."

She smiled, and said, "Thomas, suspect hath ye become smitten with me. Should me be inclined to accept thy proposal, and journey to Penrith, might ye not in time grow weary of me? Shall me then be abandoned and left to reside 'mongst strangers. A woe some fate indeed!"

Tom replied, "This ye fear will not come to pass. Be at present manservant to the prince. One day shall be manservant to a king. Will ye by then be me mate.

No need for thee to decide this very moment. Ponder on it for a time. Upon returning from Dumfries shall ye then render me a decision.

The hour hath grown late. Where hath ye thought to bed this night?"

Chuckling, she replied, "Silly goose, surely not 'neath the stars."

Bridget stood from the table, took Tom by the hand, pulled him to his feet, then ran with him to the tack room.

Chapter 41

Bridget did not sleep much that night. She lay wondering if the proposal Tom had made was too good to be true. Might he truly care for her, when arriving at the inn would he not quickly had come to her?

Many lads had come to the inn approaching her with a ruse in an attempt to get her into their beds.

Bridget searched her mind for a way to prove Tom was sincere. Finally, it came to her. She had not seen the column enter the courtyard. Earlier, Tom had said he came to Gretna with a spare steed.

She knew the number of guests occupying the inn, and the horses owned by the innkeeper.

A bit before sunrise she picked up her lantern and went to the room above the stables. She counted six men, and Tom for a total of seven.

Bridget then went to count the number of horses in the stables. There was indeed a spare.

Elated, she hurried back into the tack room, startling the lad awake with a kiss.

She whispered to him, "Good morn, Thomas; must leave thee for there be chores to tend to at the inn. Linger a bit then come to the kitchen. Shall prepare breakfast for thee."

Bridget put out the lantern, took it in hand, kissed the lad again, then ran out into the early morning light.

Some minutes later, Tom went to sit in the dining room with Bridget to partake of the breakfast she had prepared.

The innkeeper entered the kitchen. Seeing the two sitting at the table he stopped with his hands on his hips.

Scowling, he said; "Lass, no time for thee to sit about dallying. There be much for thee to do a 'fore our guests come to breakfast. Who be this lackey upon whom ye squander me vittles?"

Bridget replied, "Forgive me, Sir; be he manservant to the prince. Thought for the gent to be fed a 'fore his tending to his Lordship's needs."

Aware he had insulted a member of the king's party, the innkeeper quickly attempted to make amends. His words were kinder when next he spoke.

He said, "Indeed; well then, Lad, might there be something other ye desire, Bridget shall fetch it for thee."

The Innkeeper then made a hasty retreat into the kitchen.

Tom and Bridget still sitting at the table chuckled.

Having finished their breakfast, they stood from the table. Tom kissed then spoke to her.

He said, "Must tend to the prince. Ponder hard upon me proposal. Shall expect a reply upon returning to Gretna. Bear in mind, will ye never be content in servitude to this man. For hath he the tongue of a serpent.

Lady Verna, overseer of the palace staff, would never speak in such an unkindly manner to a servant. Might one be deserving of rebuke; the lass would be spoken to away from the ears of others."

Tearfully, Bridget said, "Farewell, dear Thomas; shall ye be missed. Hath ye been advised as to when ye might be returning?"

He replied, "Be not certain, yet would suspect by weeks end. Farewell, dear Bridget."

Tom left, took the stairs to the floor above, then tapped on the prince's chamber door. Receiving no response, he entered the room, waking the prince.

He addressed the prince, saying, "Your Highness, art we to arrive in Dumfries a' fore sunset, must we make haste. Hath ye no need of me shall awaken Sir Cartwith."

The prince did not reply. He simply raised his hand to wave him away.

Tom left the room to tap on Sir Cartwith's door. Not entering, he called out to the knight.

He said, "Sir Cartwith, 'tis time. Shall go to the stables and stir the men, then advise the stable master to saddle the horses."

Tom went to the stables to awaken the men. Five lay sleeping. He searched the stables and the grounds around the inn for the other with no success. In a panic he returned to the men yet asleep.

He shouted, "Ye lads, come awake! One of thee, hath gone missing! Woe to he not present when Sir Cartwith comes to fetch thee."

The men startled awake, jumped to their feet, and scrambled through the stables looking for the missing cavalryman. They came together looking at each other.

Donald identified the absent man as Quinn, then noticed the man's steed was not in the stall.

Tom concerned, said, "Set at the table in the courtyard with the maiden, Bridget this night past. Donald and two others be seen at a game of maw. Where hath ye others gone?"

Donald replied, "Tom, the others rode to the glen. Haps Quinn took up with one of the maidens and passed the night in the village."

Tom said, "Might it well be, Donald. Shall ride to the village. Haps will come upon his steed.

Donald, ferret out the stable master. The horses art to be saddled and made ready for the ride."

Tom ran to the tack room, retrieved his tack then hurried back to the stables to saddle his horse.

He mounted then spurred the stallion to a gallop through the glen. There was no one in sight. Riding toward the village, Tom heard a maiden singing the pleugh song. Following the sound, he came upon a milkmaid at her task in a barn. Tom dismounted, tethered his horse then went to speak to the maiden. The young girl rose from her stool as he came near.

He addressed her, saying, "Good morn, Lass. Be ye in the glen this night past? Seek a fair-haired English chap in the company of two others."

She replied, "Aye, the three rode to the glen from the inn. Two of the lads returned at an early hour. T 'other took up with Kinzie, the tinker's daughter. She resides a bit beyond the village beside a stand of pine."

Tom thanked the milkmaid, mounted his steed, bade her farewell, then rode off.

At the far end of the hamlet he came upon Quinn's steed tied to a hitching post outside a little cottage. Dismounting he went to tap lightly on the cottage door.

Tom said, "Quinn, be ye within? Make haste for will we soon be departing for Dumfries. Should Sir Cartwith not find thee about the inn will ye be punished severely."

Moments later, Tom could hear someone scrambling about inside the cottage.

The door flew open, and Quinn came running out with boots in one hand, and tunic in the other.

A bit out of breadth, Quinn said, "Tom, be in thy debt. Must we make haste. Mercy, these Scottish maidens be quite insatiable."

When Tom and Quinn rode up from the village, the cavalrymen were sitting at the tables in the courtyard having breakfast. Seeing Quinn in complete disarray, still clutching his boots, they began laughing hysterically.

One of the men shouted out to the rider, saying, "Gad Zeus! Quinn, hath thought ye to be taken prisoner by the Scotts. Would seem hath ye managed to escape, and yet with thy breeches."

Laughing, Quinn replied, "Indeed, ole chum. Good fortune smiled upon me for in the dead of night managed to pierce one of the lot a 'fore fleeing."

Tom rode past the table, dismounted, tethered his steed to the hitching post in front of the inn, then joined the men at the tables.

Quinn continued on into the stables to make himself presentable before returning to the courtyard for his breakfast.

Some minutes later, Sir Cartwith stepped out of the entrance to the inn onto the landing, calling to the men.

They left the tables to gather around the staircase.

The knight spoke, saying; "Ye lads, see to thy belongings, retrieve the horses and prepare for departure."

Sir Cartwith paused, then said; "Tom, the king and prince be in need of assistance. Donald, Lord Morley may be in need of thee."

Prince Frederick had settled his account with the Innkeeper and was talking with Bridget outside the kitchen when Tom and Donald arrived.

Tom went directly to gather the belongings of the king and prince, while Donald went to assist Lord Morley.

The prince was still speaking with the maiden when Tom and Donald left the inn.

The prince addressed the lass saying, "Bridget, Tom spoke of his desire to fetch thee to Penrith. Hath he secured a position for thee at the palace, and a place to reside. Hath found thee to be an able servant, deserving of the position. Rest assured, will ye be more content in Penrith than here in Gretna."

She curtsied, and said, "Me thank thee, your Lordship, for thy kindly words. Thomas hath become quite dear to me. Hath come to Gretna from Rigg in early spring to labor from morn to past sunset 'neath a stern taskmaster. Might it be prudent for me to ponder upon the proposal presented me by Thomas."

King Frederick came to join the prince. The two walked out to the courtyard together to join the waiting column.

Bridget stood on the landing at the entrance to the inn waving to Tom as they left the courtyard.

The column proceeded sixteen miles west at a good pace, led by the standard bearer.

Nearing Ruthwell, the king thought the men would appreciate seeing the seventeen-foot stone cross still standing, dating back to the eighth century. He had seen the cross years past when riding to Dumfries to aid Earl William in a battle against a common foe.

King Frederick called out to the standard bearer.

He shouted, "Lad, direct the column to Ruthwell. Shall we pause to rest, partake of a bit of food and drink. There be a point of interest wish the men to see."

The prince was not pleased with his father for requesting a detour; being anxious to arrive in Dumfries as soon as possible to be with Lady Rebecca.

He was about to suggest the detour be made upon returning from Dumfries when the king stated the cross was less than a mile out of the way.

Arriving in Ruthwell the men dismounted and stood at the base of the cross in awe. The stone had been sculptured on all four sides with figures of Christ standing on two beasts, Mary Magdalene washing the Lord's feet. Carved into the stone were many Gaelic inscriptions.

Many of the men knelt to pray.

The better part of an hour was spent at the site before resuming the twelve remaining miles to Dumfries.

Chapter 42

Earl William, anticipating the king's arrival in the late afternoon, dispatched Sir Cadwalter and one of the cavalry to the road to greet them.

The cavalryman, upon seeing the column approach, was to return and inform the earl that the king was near.

Well before sunset, the cavalryman came riding hard into the courtyard.

Earl William, hearing the hoof beats of the steed, met the man at the entrance to the manor. The rider delivered his message.

He said, "Your Lordship, the column be but half a league to the west. Shall they arrive in the courtyard shortly."

The earl replied, "Go ye then, lad; make haste. Alert the stable master then speak to me steward. The staff is to assemble in the courtyard to greet His Majesty."

Earl William quickly retreated into the manor calling out to Countess Sarah and Lady Rebecca.

He shouted, "Sarah, Rebecca, come join me. The column will soon be in sight. Shall we await His Majesty's arrival upon the steps of the manor entrance."

Countess Sarah with Lady Rebecca came hand in hand down the staircase and went to stand beside the earl.

The servants came to stood abreast on either side of the courtyard beside the steps to the manor.

The stable master with two stable boys stood at the steps ready to take the horses from the king, prince, and Lord Morley.

Lady Rebecca could feel her heart beating rapidly in anticipation.

Some minutes later, King Frederick and his entourage came in sight with Sir Cadwalter leading the column.

Lady Rebecca said excitedly, "Mother, Father, look ye, King Frederick be astride the stallion, Amas. A sight to behold indeed."

Entering the courtyard, the standard bearer, knights, cavalrymen, and Tom broke formation and rode toward the stables.

Servants bowed and curtsied as the king passed.

King Frederick, the prince, and Lord Morley reigned in their horses, dismounted, and handed their reins to the stable boys.

Earl William waited for the horses to be taken away before descending the stairs to greet the king.

He said, "Bade thee welcome, Your Highness, Prince Frederick. Pray thy journey be pleasant, and uneventful."

The king replied, "Indeed, Earl William. Come; leave me acquaint thee with me ambassador, Lord Morley. Hath he accompanied me for a purpose shall we discuss a bit later."

Lady Rebecca stood silent beside the countess although she was longing to embrace the prince. She was aware it would not be proper to display a sign of affection with the servants present.

Having exchanged greetings, Earl William invited them into the manor, and lead them into the sitting room.

The servants returned to the kitchen to fetch refreshments.

The king praised the earl for the well-kept gardens on the estate, then added he had forgotten the beauty of Scotland.

Servants came with refreshments while the king and earl reminisced of the times they had spent together.

Prince Frederick, Lady Rebecca and Countess Sarah sat silent through the king's and the earl's conversation.

Finally, Countess Sarah addressed her daughter.

She said, "Rebecca, there be no need for thee to sit as King Frederick and thy sire spin their tales of yore. Go ye now. Prince Frederick might enjoy a stroll about the orchard."

Her daughter replied, "A splendid suggestion Mother; however, haps the journey hath left Prince Frederick a bit weary."

She, then said; "What say ye, me Prince?"

The prince replied, "Weary or no, Lady Rebecca; how might one refuse an invitation to accompany such a comely maiden? Yea too, there be many events of interest hath come to pass since thy departure from Penrith must relate to thee."

They excused themselves and left the sitting room. They strolled unhurriedly through the gardens to a stand of fruit trees beside the manor.

The moment they were out of sight of the manor, the prince took Lady Rebecca in his arms, kissing her passionately. She pressed herself against the prince and returned his kiss.

She whispered, "Me Prince, long hath yearned for thee to hold me once more as this. However, hath been at wit's end with wonder as to what is to pass 'tween me sire and the king."

Prince Frederick removed his cloak and set it on the ground beneath an apple tree before he replied.

He said, "Come set beside me; shall speak of it. Me sire be not opposed to our union. In truth, doth he look upon it with favor.

But one obstacle presents itself. There be a reason for Lord Morley's presence. Father shall propose to thy Sire, Lord Morley remain in Dumfries as ambassador of the king and a representative of Earl William return with me sire to Penrith."

She thought a bit then replied, "Me Prince, dare not speak for me sire. Yet see no cause for him to refuse such a proposal. Surely would this be beneficial for both the king and me sire."

Smiling, the prince said, "Well then, Rebecca, must we pray thy sire finds no cause for concern in this proposal. Might he not, shall we soon be wed."

"Dear Prince, shall me then please thee in many ways. As to the subject of pleasure, upon thy arrival mine eyes be solely upon thee. Thus, though not to seek Donald amongst the cavalry. Be he there?"

He replied, "Indeed, dear Lady. Me sire inquired as to why hath I requested the man be included in the party. I rendered him but a bit of a reply. Yet stated, might Father remain vigilant, the response to his query would be forthcoming.

Suspecting a bit of foppery, Father laughed bounteously at me reply."

Chuckling, Lady Rebecca said, "Thy sire doth then bear a bit of wit. Dare say me Prince, upon Cousin Juliana's arrival in the morn, shall we afford her an opportunity to share a time alone with the gent, shall me invite them to join us upon a ride about the countryside."

The prince replied, "Well thought, Rebecca. Will we be afforded the like opportunity as well. Shall speak to Sir Cartwith of it."

The prince in a more serious manner said, "Alas, Rebecca, not all be well at the palace. Must confess to thee hath erred grievously in a matter concerning Ashley. Hath yet to be forgiven for the mishap.

Hath she passed many days in the forest being tutored by Leland in the use of the bow. As a result, hath she become quite fond of him.

'Twas not known to the bowman of Ashley's position. For she went to him garbed as a village maiden.

Upon speaking with Leland of Ashley, he professed his love for her, yet deemed hisself unworthy. Thus, would he not engage her in a courtship.

Hath thought to devise a plan to put an end to this pretense. This Friday past, by way of trickery, Leland accompanied me to the palace then to the dining hall where Ashley sat with Mother and Father.

Leland, seeing Ashley at the table, thought it all a ruse to play him the fool.

Leland, in anger, spoke harshly, then fled.

Be me then chastised by Ashley for creating the entire calamity a 'fore she ran from the dining hall in tears.

Mother, enraged, demanded the archer be found, and escorted to the palace in an attempt to amend this horrid mishap."

Lady Rebecca astounded, yet attempting to console the prince, said, "Me Prince, thought ye to please Ashley. Not to cause her discontent. The archer will be found, and all shall be made a 'right. Pray ye attempt to set this aside for the present for these few days together art to be enjoyed, and cherished."

Chapter 43

Prince Frederick was awakened the next morning by Tom tapping on the bedroom door. The manservant asked the prince if he intended to dress for the hunt.

He replied, "Nay, Tom. Shall be riding with Lady Rebecca this morn. Go speak to the steward and request water for me bath, then beckon Sir Cartwith to me chambers."

Tom went off to do his master's bidding.

Prince Frederick donned his robe and stood in the window overlooking the courtyard. Below, servants were bringing breakfast to the cavalrymen housed in the rooms above the stables. Stable boys were grooming and saddling horses for the hunt.

Minutes later, servants came with water for the tub.

The prince was in his bath when Tom returned. The manservant went about laying out the riding attire for the prince while speaking.

Tom said, "Me Prince, Sir Cartwith be yet a 'bed. Shall he come to thee in a bit. Might there be something other ye require?"

"Me quarters art to be tended to. Shall ye then set out me finest attire for the evening's festivities. Might ye then enjoy the day," replied the prince.

The prince had completed his toiletries and was dressing when Sir Cartwith came to his room. The knight stood waiting for the prince to speak.

The prince said, "G 'day, Sir Cartwith. Shall be riding with Lady Rebecca and Lady Juliana a bit later this morn. Will require an escort. Might ye assign Donald to the task?

The knight replied, "Shall alert the cavalryman to await thy beckoning."

The prince asked, "Will ye be taking the morning meal in the dining hall?"

Sir Cartwith replied, "Aye, me Prince. Hath been invited to the table by Countess Sarah."

Sir Cartwith bowed then left the room.

The prince returned to the window, to see guests of the earl trickling into the courtyard.

Earl William stood in the courtyard greeting them as they arrived.

The earl's brother, Lord Gaelan arrived with Lady Juliana.

Lady Rebecca ran out into the courtyard to greet them.

From the courtyard, Lady Rebecca turned and saw the prince standing in the window. She motioned for him to come to her.

The prince left the room and hurried down the stairs. Passing the sitting room, Lady Rebecca called out to him. The two ladies came to their feet to curtsy when he entered the room.

Greeting them, the prince said, "Good morn, Ladies; 'tis a most pleasant day for a ride. Lady Juliana, hath noted thy steed be a 'fixed with a sidesaddle. Haps the earl's stable master might replace it with another.

The Prince. Then asked; "Hath ye partaken of thy morning meal yet?"

Lady Juliana replied, "Aye, your Lordship; awakened early to breakfast with me sire. As to me saddle, for what reason must it be replaced?"

"Ye ladies chat a bit. There be a parcel hath forgotten in me chambers. Shall return in a moment," said the prince.

Prince Frederick left the two ladies wondering what he was up to. He returned to his room to retrieve the riding attire Eleanor had made for Lady Juliana.

Tom was in the room, organizing garments for the evening for the prince.

The prince addressed the manservant.

He said, "Tom, make haste. Go speak with the stable master. Lady Juliana's steed doth bear a sidesaddle. It is to be replaced with a Roman saddle."

Tom stopped what he was doing, bowed, then hurried from the room.

The prince retrieved the riding outfit from the trunk at the foot of the bed, slung it over his arm, then returned to the sitting room.

Entering the sitting room, he said, "Lady Juliana, wish thee not to ride this morn in discomfort. The seamstress in Penrith hath fashioned these garments for thee. Might ye don them as we others set at breakfast?"

Seeing the riding garments, Lady Juliana jumped to her feet, pranced about in jubilation before composing herself.

She thanked the prince for the gift, then hurried off to Lady Rebecca's chambers to change her garments.

The prince and Lady Rebecca went hand in hand to breakfast.

The dining hall was nearly filled to capacity. Everyone was talking at once. The room was in total bedlam.

Servants scrambled about with trays of meats, eggs, breads, and ewers of beverages.

The hounds had been released into the courtyard and were baying in anticipation of the hunt. The stable master and stable boys stood waiting with reins of the many horses to be mounted.

At meal's end, Earl William announced the hunt was to begin. The men went scrambling for their mounts. Only Countess Sarah, Prince Frederick, Lady Rebecca, and Sir Cartwith remained at the table.

Minutes later, hoof beats could be heard leaving the courtyard soon to be followed by the blare of a trumpet accompanied by the howling of the hounds. The hunt was underway.

Those remaining at the table sat silent waiting for the din created by the hounds and riders to fade. The countess then spoke.

She said, "Thank me Lord for the silence.

Sir Cartwith, might we pass the morn together? Hath long waited to hear what hath passed 'tween ye, and the lady from Skeeby.

Come Sir Knight, leave us retire to the sitting room."

The knight replied, "Your Ladyship, there be much to relate. Yet might me be excused for a moment?

Prince Frederick hath requested an escort for the ride. Shall see to it then return to engage with thee in conversation."

Sir Cartwith left the dining hall to tend to his errand. The others went to the sitting room.

Minutes later, Lady Juliana entered, wearing her newly acquired riding garments.

The countess asked, "Juliana, how come ye by these garments? The seamstress here at the millinery be not yet skilled in their fabrication."

She replied, "Your Ladyship, the attire be presented to me this very morn by Prince Frederick. Cannot wait to ride unencumbered by skirts and petticoats."

"For certain, Juliana. Must say, hath been left a bit envious of ye ladies," said the countess.

Then turning to the prince, she said; "Prince Frederick, art ye to be commended for thy thoughtfulness."

The prince replied, "Countess Sarah, be thee not forgotten. When at the millinery in me village, requested of the needlewoman, a pattern for the garments as ye hath requested.

The countess replied, "Well then, haps with the pattern shall engage the needlewoman in the village to fashion a like attire for meself."

Lady Rebecca said, "Mother, never hath ye yet to experience a romp about the countryside as ye will, garbed in these garments."

The countess asked, "Rebecca, where might ye three be bound this morn? Bear in mind, must ye be present for the festivities this night."

"Will not go far, Mother. Might we decide to ride beside the river, or haps to Uncle's estate. Might we hunger, shall we visit the pub in the village," she replied.

Sir Cartwith re-entered the sitting room advising the prince their escort was in the courtyard with the horses, then went to sit beside the countess.

Exchanging farewells with the countess and Sir Cartwith, the riders left the sitting room to step out onto the courtyard.

Donald, the cavalryman, tending the horses, bowed, then waited for each of the riders to mount before handing them their reins.

The cavalryman then mounted his steed, and the four walked the horses out of the courtyard.

Prince Frederick waited for them to be out of sight of the manor before speaking to Lady Juliana.

He said, "Hold a moment. Lady Juliana. Must confess to thee, harbor a bit of a secret hath shared with Lady Rebecca yet not known to thee."

The riders reined in their horses and stood waiting for him to continue.

The prince chose to have Lady Rebecca explain his statement to Lady Juliana.

The prince said, "Lady Rebecca, might ye enlighten the lady?"

Lady Rebecca, bearing a grin, addressing her cousin said; "Juliana, there be a reason for this cavalryman to be chosen as an escort for Prince Frederick this day.

Might me acquaint thee with Donald. The name may not be familiar to thee, yet assure thee, ye two be well acquainted."

Frowning, Lady Juliana replied, "Mercy, Rebecca, must confess this conversation hath left me a bit a 'muddled. What hath this fine gent to do with me?"

Laughing, Lady Rebecca said, "Juliana, thy ways be known well to me. Thus, when Prince Frederick last came to Dumfries we devised a ruse to avoid an embarrassment to the prince."

Lady Juliana asked, "Pray tell, Rebecca, might this gent be the man with whom hath passed the night in the chambers of the prince?"

Lady Rebecca replied, "Indeed cousin, yet not wanting the ruse to be a complete embarrassment to thee we chose a handsome lad to please thee, not an ogre."

Lady Juliana replied, "Rebecca, at the outset thought this day to be of little interest to me. To the contrary, might it prove to be one of many delightful adventures.

Come, Donald; ride beside me. There be much for we to discover of each other. This holiday, Prince Frederick hath afforded thee, shall ye long remember."

Chapter 44

Early that evening, a few of the king's cavalry stood in windows above the stables watching coaches arrive at the manor. On seeing the dignitaries dismounting the coaches wearing kilts, they began to laugh.

Men of the earl's cavalry standing below, offended by the laughter, began shouting obscenities at the men above.

Sir Cadwalter, standing with Sir Cartwith in the hallway of the manor chatting, heard the shouting coming from the stables, ran to investigate the disturbance. Arriving in time to prevent an incident.

Sir Cadwalter ordered his men to return to their quarters while Sir Cartwith took the stairs to the barracks above.

Sir Cartwith stood at the head of the stairs speaking harshly to the men.

He asked, "What might the meaning of this be? What be the cause of this unruly behavior?"

One of the men step forth to reply, "Sir, upon seeing the dignitaries descending from the arriving coaches, we found humor in the men wearing skirts. Earl William's men below, not pleased with our outburst of laughter, voiced their displeasure."

Still a bit angry, Sir Cartwith said, "Ye bumbling twits, be they not skirts but kilts. The pattern signifies the clan to which they belong; as doth His Majesty's coat of arms.

Earl William's forces, and those of thy king, hath fought and shed blood as one bearing these symbols. Might ye deem either a symbol to be mocked? Think not."

He continued saying, "Now then, we art as one to beg forgiveness of these gallant men for this foppery. Follow me."

Sir Cartwith led the men down the stairs of the barracks to stand in formation outside the earl's garrison. He called out to his counterpart.

The knight asked, "Sir Cadwalter, might we speak?"

Sir Cadwalter stepped out of the barracks to see Sir Cartwith's men standing at attention. He called to his men who quickly filed out of their quarters to stand behind their commander.

Sir Cartwith waited a bit, then said, "Sir Cadwalter, me men stand before thee with deep regret for making light of the attire worn by Earl William's royal guests. We beg thy forgiveness.

To atone for this grievous lack of respect, they wish to invite ye Scots to ride with them to the pub in the village as comrades. There to enjoy the night at the expense of King Frederick."

Sir Cadwalter turned to his men and stood looking at them with his hands on his hips for a moment.

He, then said, "Well lads, be ye a bit demented? Haps hath ye taken leave of thy senses? What cause hath ye to stand in wait? Be gone!"

The Scots emitted howls of delight then everyone scrambled to the stables for their mounts. Only Donald remained, walking to the garden to sit, and wait.

Sir Cartwith stood with Sir Cadwalter laughing as the men rode off to the village. He then turned to Sir Cadwalter to speak.

The knight said, "Sir Cadwalter, must say, this minor disturbance hath been a blessing. Haps one day there may be a need for these men to fight as comrades, not as foe."

Sir Cadwalter agreed, and said, "Indeed! Come, Sir Cartwith, shall we return to the festivities."

The knights entered the manor in time to hear the steward announce dinner was being served. They lagged behind, waiting for the others to take their seats before entering the dining hall.

Lady Rebecca, sitting beside her mother noticed her cousin fidgeting at the table. She caught the eye of the prince then redirected her eyes to her cousin.

The prince, following Lady Rebecca's eye direction, grinned knowingly.

At dinner's end, the ladies retired to the music room to be entertained by a harpist.

The men remained in the dining hall smoking, drinking, and recounting the events of the day.

Lady Juliana waited in the hall for the ladies to file into the music room then ran from the manor into the garden where she had arranged to meet with Donald earlier that afternoon.

Chapter 45

At the breakfast table the next morning, Prince Frederick sat anxiously waiting for the king to ask Earl William for a word in private.

The two men, Lord Morley, and Sir Cadwalter were entertaining themselves with the events of yesterday's fox hunt.

Countess Sarah sat conversing with Sir Cartwith. The topic of conversation being the knight's involvement with the widow Whitney.

Lady Rebecca sat beside her mother, bearing an expression of concern, and wondering if her father and the king were ever going to get together and discuss her union with the prince.

Countess Sarah turned to the earl and spoke.

She asked, "William, what form of entertainment hath ye planned for the day?"

He replied, "Sarah, the lads in the village hath been invited to participate in the games of caber toss and putting of the stone to the sounds of bagpipes here at the manor."

The king said, "Earl William, speak ye of games. The cobbler in the village Penrith fashioned sticks and balls at the request of Prince Frederick. Might there be rules of play for the game?"

The earl replied, "Yea, Your Majesty; shall make them available to thee. Hath ye participated in the game yet?"

The king laughed, and said, "Indeed, 'twas naught but bedlam. For hath we no knowledge of the game nor the skill to play.

Margaret stood upon the ramparts of the palace with the ladies-in-waiting laughing boisterously."

The earl replied, "Must confess, Your Highness; 'twas as this when me chums first engaged in thy game of quoits. We men scrambled about in an attempt to avoid injury from the toss of the iron rings."

The countess addressed the earl saying, "Husband, hath ye done well to occupy the men for the day."

Then turning to her daughter, she asked, "Rebecca, what hath thee in mind to entertain Prince Frederick?"

Lady Rebecca replied, "Mother, Juliana will soon arrive with Uncle Gaelan. Thought to ride to Lochfoot Loch.

Hath instructed the kitchen to prepare a basket of food and drink. Shall we set by the water for a day at leisure."

Lady Rebecca turned to the knight and said, "Sir Cartwith, would ye be so kind as to provide escort for Prince Frederick, and we ladies?"

The knight replied, "Lady Rebecca, upon the arrival of Lady Juliana shall tend to it. The cavalryman will be sent to instruct the stable master to saddle the horses ye will require, then wait for thee in the courtyard."

King Frederick had a question in mind which had bothered him since the earl had returned from Oliver's estate in Leeds.

He asked, "Earl William, out of curiosity. Might me inquire as to what ye intend to do with the estate in Leeds? Surely 'tis a burdensome parcel of property, being so far from Dumfries."

The earl replied, "And that it be, Your Majesty. 'Tis well attended to, thus hath no concerns for its being set upon by vandals. Me sole concern be for the soldiers garrisoned so far from their loved ones.

For the present, however, hath thought to wait for a reason to divest meself of it. Hath ye inquired out of interest in the property, Your Highness?"

"Nay, ole friend; inquired solely out of wonderment. Might there one day be a need for me to procure a residence, must it be in close proximity to the palace," said the king.

Prince Frederick, hearing his father speak of acquiring a residence close to the palace, was left wondering what his father had in mind. His thoughts were interrupted by the sound of hoof beats entering the courtyard.

Moments later, Lord Gaelan stepped into the dining hall bowing to the king.

He said, "Good morn; forgive me for interrupting thy morning meal."

He paused, then said, "Rebecca, Juliana chose to wait for thee and the prince in the courtyard."

The earl said, "G 'day, Gaelan, no need for forgiveness. Hath we eaten our fill. Be we but engaged in a bit of conversation. Come set ye at ease. Will it be a bit a 'for the games begin."

The conversation at the table was being dominated by the older men, and of no interest to Countess Sarah.

Standing, she said, "Rebecca, there be no need for thee to remain at the table while the men spin their yarns. Juliana awaits thee."

Continuing, she said, "Hath me thought to visit the village. Prince Frederick hath given me a pattern for the riding attire. With it the needlewoman may be able to fashion a set of riding garments for me."

The countess, then said to the knight, "Sir Cartwith, lest ye hath some other activity in mind, might ye be so kind as to escort me to the millinery?"

He replied, "Your Ladyship, would please me to honor thy request. Might ye wait a bit; shall fetch the horses from the stables."

The servant, Heather entered the dining hall with a pitcher of fresh brewed tea.

Countess Sarah, still standing, summoned the servant to her.

The servant curtsied, then went to the countess.

The countess said, "Heather, upon the table in me chambers will ye see a rendering of a riding garment. Go ye; fetch it then bring it to the sitting room."

The servant went around the table pouring tea into the diner's cups; curtsied, then went to do her mistresses bidding.

The countess then addressed the others, saying, "Shall we take our leave of ye gents. Come, Prince Frederick, Rebecca; will wait for Sir Cartwith in the sitting room."

The prince and Lady Rebecca rose from their seats. Mother and daughter curtsied to the king before walking from the dining hall.

In the sitting room, the countess suggested Rebecca ask Lady Juliana to join them in conversation.

Lady Rebecca replied. "Mother, no need; for shall we be leaving thee in a bit. Yea too, 'tis certain Juliana be quite content where she be at the present."

A few minutes later, Heather entered the room with the pattern in her hand. She curtsied, handed the rendering to the countess then quickly left the sitting room.

Sir Cartwith returned from the stables to join the countess and the others in the sitting room.

The countess said, "Sir Cartwith, hath ye returned. Come shall we be on our way."

Lady Rebecca said, "Mother, will we accompany thee to the village then continue on to the loch and set by the water."

Leaving the sitting room, they joined Lady Juliana and Donald waiting for them in the courtyard.

Mounted their horses, the group rode out of the courtyard toward the village.

Chapter 46

After dinner that evening, King Frederick sat with Earl William in the garden. They reviewed the games of the day. A bit later in the conversation, they turned to more serious matters with the king presenting a proposal to the earl.

He said, "Earl William, might ye wonder why Lord Morley accompanied me to Dumfries.

Hath we come for the fox hunt, yet beyond that, hath me come to discuss other matters as well. At the outset, shall present thee with a proposal upon which might ye wish to ponder. Be we in agreement, Lord Morley shall remain in Dumfries as me ambassador with one of me cavalry.

Someone of thy choosing will represent thee at court in Penrith. He will be accompanied by one of thy cavalry.

In the event of an anticipated attack by one of our foe, the ambassador shall dispatch the cavalryman with a message requesting aid. The message will be trusted, and soldiers will be dispatched forthwith.

What say ye Earl William?"

The earl replied, "Your Majesty, there be no need for me to ponder upon this matter. Deem it a welcomed proposal indeed. Would be a fool to refuse.

Now then, spoke ye of other matters. Might there be something other hath ye in mind upon which ye wish to speak?"

The king replied, "Aye; 'tis apparent an affinity hath progressed to a point 'tween Frederick and Lady Rebecca which must be addressed.

Margaret hath deemed the lass a bright lady with qualities befitting a queen. Thy daughter hath won the hearts of Ashley and Victoria as well. Be thee in agreement, shall we see the two united by autumn's end."

The earl was elated. He replied, "Your Highness, no greater honor could ye bestow upon me family than to request me daughter's hand for Prince Frederick.

We shall leave it to her Majesty and Sarah to commence preparations."

The earl paused a bit, then said, "Your Majesty, but this day past hath ye inquired as to what was to be done with the manor in Leeds.

In reply, hath stated, thought to wait for a proper reason to dispose of the property.

Upon the visit of the prince to Dumfries, Sarah and I suspected that this union 'tween the two might come to pass.

Sarah expressed concern for Rebecca's being so far from home. To appease the countess, pledged to rid meself of the manor in Leeds then procure another midway 'tween Dumfries and Penrith."

The king replied, "A splendid plan Earl William; then might the ladies wish to visit, be they but a mere day's ride away. Would seem, then shall we see thee more oft in years to come."

The earl said, "Ole friend, upon acquiring a property it shall be made available to thee, and thy kin at thy discretion."

The two men, having completed their affairs, decided to gather the parties involved into the garden to inform them of their decisions. Earl William summoned the sentry posted at the garden steps, instructing him to fetch the steward. The guard bowed to the king, and earl, then went to do his master's bidding. Minutes later, the steward entered the garden, bowed, then stood waiting for instructions.

The earl said to the steward, "Addison, a ewer of our finest wine and six goblets. Then summon Prince Frederick, Countess Sarah, Lord Morley, and Lady Rebecca to the garden."

The steward went off to his task while the king, and the earl continued chatting; waiting for the steward to return with the wine.

The earl turned to the king, and said, "Your Majesty, Rebecca spoke of a bowman to whom Princess Ashley hath become attached. Must he be more than one might expect of an archer."

The king replied, "Alas, me friend, there be much in that matter to be sorted out. Be he the archer who let fly the arrow downing the stag about to gore Frederick.

He hath been tutoring Ashley in the use of the bow. Must say hath she become quite proficient in its use. In the process of being tutored, Ashley hath become quite fond of the bowman."

The earl said, "Shall we retire to the terrace, Your Majesty. The servants will soon return with the wine. Would seem the steward hath gone to fetch the others. We will need to continue this conversation another time."

Heather stepped out onto the terrace, set the wine and goblets on the table, curtsied then scurried off.

The sun was low in the sky, casting shadows onto the garden, when Prince Frederick and the others came to join the two men. The king waited for them to be seated before speaking.

He turned to his ambassador, and said, "Lord Morley, Earl William hath agreed with me proposal. Ye shall remain here as me ambassador. One of the cavalry shall remain as well should there be a need for thee to dispatch a message of urgency."

The countess speaking to the earl said, "Husband, the wine, there be a need to celebrate this pact ye hath discussed and agreed upon with his Majesty."

The earl replied, "Aye Sarah, and another matter upon which we hath spoken hath thought to leave for King Frederick to reveal."

The king spoke, saying; "Hath thought long upon this a 'fore arriving at a decision. One day Frederick shall sit the throne with a proper queen at his side.

Thus, the maiden he is to wed must bear the qualities befitting a queen. No better choice in a mate for me son could hath made than that made by Frederick hisself."

The king then turned to Lady Rebecca, and said, "Lass, hath ye won me heart as well as those of all me kin. No more pleasure be given me than to welcome thee into our fold."

The moment Lady Rebecca had hoped for had come. Tears fell to her cheeks as she curtsied to the king.

She went to hug her father and kiss her mother's cheek before approaching King Frederick.

She knelt before the king, took, and kissed his hand.

The king helped her to her feet, then took her in his arms to whisper, "Go ye now Rebecca, 'tis certain the prince desires to bestow upon there a bit of affection as well."

With tears still falling to her cheeks, Lady Rebecca ran to the prince. He took her in his arms and kissed her.

He then whispered, "Rebecca, the moment we hath yearned for hath arrived. Soon we shall be one. Pledge to cherish thee for the remainder of me days."

Also whispering she replied, "And I thee, me beloved."

Everyone present applauded in approval.

The king speaking loudly said, "Earl William, the wine. Surely, 'tis a time for we to celebrate."

Chapter 47

Lady Juliana had not returned to her father's estate the night before, nor was she present at dinner in the dining hall. She had passed the night in the room across the hall from Lady Rebecca's.

Heather came to Lady Rebecca's room with a cup of tea, finding her already dressed. Aware that Lady Juliana had been with Donald the previous night, she instructed the servant to fetch a bit of tea for her cousin as well.

Heather left the room to do her bidding. Lady Rebecca took her tea to her cousin's room.

Lady Juliana was still in her bed.

Lady Rebecca said, "Good morn, Juliana; art ye to pass this day a 'bed? Prince Frederick will be leaving soon. Must we take our morning meal with him and His Majesty in the dining hall then bid them farewell.

Hath ye been missed this night past. Suspect hath ye been a bit occupied with the cavalryman."

Lady Juliana replied, "Leave me be, Rebecca; the night hath left me weary. This morn shall he be gone, and with him his weaponry."

Lady Rebecca scoffing, said, "Me word, hath ye the morals of a strumpet. Make haste Juliana; leave thy bed and I shall reveal a secret to thee which will surely relieve this anguish ye display o'er the loss of this man ye fancy.

Must ye pledge, however, not to divulge it to anyone unto 'tis spoken of by me to another."

Her cousin replied, "Rebecca, shall ye one day be the death of me. What might ye harbor within to hearten me when revealed?"

Heather entered the bedroom with Lady Juliana's tea, interrupting the conversation. The servant set the cup on a table beside the bed, curtsied, then made a quick exit out of the room, closing the door behind her.

Lady Rebecca continued, saying, "In response to thy question Juliana, this night past, Father spoke with King Frederick. Hath they come to a decision.

We all gathered upon the terrace to hear the king announce me betrothal to Prince Frederick. We art to wed at autumn's end."

Lady Juliana jumped from the bed to hug her cousin and express sincere elation for her impending marriage. She then posed a question to her cousin.

She asked, "Rebecca, hath ye been me dearest kin, and friend since be we babes. What is to become of me with thee in Penrith, and me left behind in Dumfries?"

Lady Rebecca smiled, and said, "Juliana, be at ease. Will ye not be abandoned. Shall ye ere be by me side for thou art to be me lady-in-waiting.

Must ye, however, pledge to behave as a proper lady. Must ye be quite discrete in this foppery with the cavalryman."

Her cousin said, "Rebecca, in granting me this position, ye honor me. Thus, shall render thee me solemn oath; will never knowingly be party to an indiscretion which might place thee in a position of discomfort."

"Very well then, Juliana. Come now; quickly, don thy garments, and make thyself presentable, lest we be late at the table this morn," Lady Rebecca replied.

The two ladies entered the dining hall, curtsied to the king, and exchanged morning greetings with the others. Lady Rebecca took a seat beside the prince. Lady Juliana went to sit beside Sir Cadwalter.

Countess Sarah expressed a bit of surprise to see Lady Juliana so early in the morning.

The countess said, "Juliana, 'tis quite thoughtful of thee to come at such an early hour to bade farewell to King Frederick and the prince. Must ye hath risen to the cackling of the rooster."

She replied, "Nay, Aunt Sarah; hath slumbered in the room across the hall from that of Rebecca. Hath not come to dine with thee this night past. For be invited to dine in the village with a chum."

Sometime later, the king's standard bearer entered the dining hall, bowed to the royalty, then went to whisper to Sir Cartwith.

The knight dismissed the man, then spoke.

He said, "Earl William, Countess Sarah, me thank thee for thy impeccable hospitality. Shall bid thee all a fond farewell."

Then addressing the king, he said, "Your Majesty, beg to be excused for must see to the men."

Sir Cartwith stood from his seat, bowed, then left the dining hall. The others at the table came to their feet and chatted as they made their way out of the room.

Lady Rebecca took the hand of the prince, lead him through the entrance to the library and closed the door behind her.

She turned to the prince, pulled him to her and kissed him with passion.

She whispered, "Me Prince, once more art we to part yet take solace in knowing 'tis to be our final farewell. Many days will need to wait unto I hold thee once more, shall seem as an eternity."

The prince replied, "Me dear Rebecca; of all the jewels and baubles within me father's house to one day be mine, upon wedding thee, shall ye be me most precious gem."

The prince kissed her once more, took her hand, and led her out of the library to join the others at the entrance to the manor.

Sir Cartwith and the cavalry had already mounted their horses and were in formation with the standard bearer at the lead. Sir Cadwalter stood chatting with Sir Cartwith. Donald made eye contact with Lady Juliana. He nodded, bearing a smile.

Prince Frederick kissed Lady Rebecca on the cheek, then Countess Sarah. He shook hands with the earl and Lady Juliana, then went to mount Silvermane.

King Frederick stood for a moment talking to Earl William. The king asked when he might expect the earl's ambassador in Penrith.

The earl replied, "Your Majesty, shall dispatch a message to Lord Reeves residing in Newtonairds requesting a visit. Should he accept the position, shall he be dispatched to Penrith. Will ye find Reeves quite knowledgeable in the art of diplomacy."

The king said, "When last in Dumfries, these many years past, thy mother resided with thee. Recall her to then be a feisty woman. How hath she faired of late?"

"Your Highness, hath the grand lady taken residence at the estate of brother Gaelan. For a time, she be plagued with a malady. Hath she of late, however, been in good stead. Might it please the dear lady, shall we invite her to journey with the family at autumn's end for the festivities in Penrith," replied the earl.

The countess, speaking to the king, said; "Your Majesty, upon speaking with Queen Margaret, will ye convey me best regards? Too, inform the queen 'tis me intent to journey to Penrith a bit earlier than William to aid in the preparations for the wedding. Safe journey, Your Highness."

The king replied, "Countess, 'tis certain Margaret shall be pleased for thee to be about. Hath ye two passed little time together. Will it be an opportunity for thee to become better acquainted. Shall bid thee farewell, dear Lady."

King Frederick went to Lady Juliana, took her hand, and asked her if she would be accompanying her father to Penrith.

She replied, "Aye, Your Highness. Am to be the Maid of Honor at the ceremony. Rebecca hath granted me the honor of being her lady-in-waiting as well."

Laughing, the king said, "Indeed! Mercy, what with all ye Scottish ladies coming to Penrith there might well be a need for me to master the jig. Shall bid thee farewell, dear Lass."

Lady Juliana curtsied to the king, bidding him a safe journey.

The king then went to take Lady Rebecca in his arms.

He whispered, "Dear Rebecca, cannot express the joy there be within me in knowing one day will it be thee beside me son upon the throne. I be content with the knowledge the kingdom will pass into able hands upon me demise. Farewell, dear Lass."

Lady Rebecca kissed the king on the cheek, stepped back, curtsied, then bid him farewell.

King Frederick stepped into the courtyard to mount Abas.

The column left the courtyard onto the road leading out of the estate and headed east toward Gretna.

Upon leaving the grounds of the manor, King Frederick, riding abreast with the prince, and Sir Cartwith, turned to the prince and spoke.

He said, "Frederick, the maiden Juliana, when at the table this morn, spoke of dining the preceding night with a companion. Might this person to whom the lass made reference be someone in me service?"

The prince laughed boisterously and replied. "Father, surely ye speak in jest. Am certain ye need not inquire. Ye know well who this companion might be."

King Frederick chuckled.

Chapter 48

The king's column traveled some ten miles before pausing beside a field of grain to rest the horses and to stretch their legs.

On a knoll beyond the field sat a cottage and a barn. A figure was seen coming out of the barn, only to disappear into the stand of grain.

Minutes later, a boy not yet in his teens stepped out into a clearing, several paces from where the men had sat to rest, struggling with a napkin covered bucket he carried with both hands. A ladle fastened with a strip of hide dangled from his neck.

He stopped to look the group over carefully before continuing to where the men were sitting.

The boy said, "Good morn. Me sire thought ye might desire a bit of refreshment. Thus, hath he sent me with this bucket of fresh milk. Might ye men be in need of a bit more, shall gladly fetch it for thee."

The king came to his feet and approached the lad. He removed the ladle from around the boy's neck, and the napkin covering the bucket.

The king dipped the ladle into the bucket of milk, then put it to his lips and drank from it.

The king said, "Be it quite refreshing, Lad. Must ye thank thy sire on me behalf for his kindness."

The boy set the bucket down and invited the others to drink from it.

The prince came first to drink. Sir Cartwith followed. The others, then came to drink their fill.

The boy, speaking to the king, asked, "And who might ye be Sir? From whence hath ye come? Must ye be of some importance to be in the company of so many horsemen."

King Frederick stepped closer to the boy, and whispered, "Well Lad, might ye believe it, should ye be told ye stand before King Frederick from a kingdom many leagues away in England?"

The boy scoffed, and said, "Kind Sir, me thinks 'tis a bit of foppery ye speak."

The king turned from the boy to face his men.

He asked, "Ye men. How art ye to address me?"

In unison the men shouted, "Your Majesty!"

King Frederick turned back to the child to see him standing, wide eyed. His mouth ajar; unable to speak.

The boy fell to his knees visibly shaken.

The king said, "Hath ye naught to fear, Lad. Be ye protected by thy innocence. Stand a 'right; come ye hither to me."

The king reached into his purse, took out a few coins, and handed them to the child. The boy took the coins, bowed, retrieved the bucket, ladle, and napkin, then quickly ran off, disappearing into the field of grain.

King Frederick waited for the boy to reappear on the far side of the stand of grain then mounted Abas.

The others followed suit and fell into formation. The column, then proceeded on toward Gretna.

Children at play in a meadow on the fringe of the village Annan, saw the group of riders on the road.

They ran excitedly into the hamlet to tell the villagers of the column approaching the village.

Townspeople left their homes and shops to stand beside the road, waiting for the column to pass.

One of the elders who had been in Earl William's service when years past, King Frederick came to Scotland to render aid to the earl, recognized the king's banner and shouted to the spectators.

"Gad Zeus! Look ye, 'tis King Frederick of Penrith passing through the village."

Ladies curtsied; men removed their caps and bowed as the king passed them by.

A few of the village maidens threw kisses to the mounted men.

Children ran into the road cheering as they marched behind the cavalry until they came to the farther end of the village.

Prince Frederick was a bit surprised at the admiration the people of Annan had for his father and spoke of it to the king.

The king replied, "And well they should, Frederick. Many of our subjects fought, and a few men laid down their lives for these people. 'Tis heartening to know the sacrifices made by our forces hath not yet been forgotten by these Scots."

The remaining nine miles to Gretna were uneventful.

The column arrived at the inn a bit before sunset.

Prince Frederick entered the inn to secure rooms for himself, his father, and Sir Cartwith.

While the prince waited for the room assignments, King Frederick and the knight went to sit at a table in the dining hall.

The men stabled their horses then went to sit at the tables in the courtyard to wait for their supper.

While Tom waited for the prince, he went to look for Bridget in the dining hall and the kitchen with no success.

The prince completed his transaction, then called out to his manservant.

He shouted, "Tom, fetch me gear, me sire's, and that of Sir Cartwith." The innkeeper shall direct thee to our quarters."

The prince then join his father, and Sir Cartwith.

Tom left the inn to retrieve the saddlebags left hanging by the men over the gates of the stalls in the stables.

On reentering the inn, Tom asked the innkeeper to direct him to the rooms Prince Frederick had procured.

The man led Tom up the flight of stairs, identified the rooms then waited for Tom to relieve himself of his burden.

As they returned to the floor below, Tom asked the innkeeper where Bridget might be.

The proprietor replied, "The lass resigned her position two days past. Will she be missed. However, was timely for with the coming of autumn;

the patronage here at the inn be on the wane. Might it be of interest to thee, the lass resides in a flat at the village."

Tom thanked the innkeeper, then went to speak to Prince Frederick.

He said, "Your Lordship, hath thought to ride to the village. Might ye be in need of me shall wait unto the 'morrow."

The prince replied, "Be not certain, Tom, haps much later. Might ye not be about, shall fend for meself."

The prince paused, then continued, saying; "Be it not the lass Bridget ye seek?"

"Aye, me Prince. Be she no longer in service here at the inn. Pray she hath thought to accept me proposal, and be preparing to accompany me to Penrith," Tom replied.

The prince said, "Go ye then, Tom; see to thy affairs. The lass haps be in wait of thee."

Tom thanked the prince, bowed, then hurried out of the inn to saddle his horse.

The king heard the conversation between the prince and Tom.

Curious, the king inquired; "Frederick, who might this Bridget be and how come Tom to know this maiden?"

The prince replied, "Father, hath she been a servant here at the inn.

When first came we to Gretna, Tom and the maiden became mates.

Upon returning to the palace from Dumfries, Tom pleaded with Mother Mildred to speak to Lady Verna in an attempt to secure a position for the lass at the palace.

Lady Verna agreed to employ the lass as a servant.

Me thinks Tom hath gone to the village to speak with Bridget. Might she accept the position, she will accompany Tom to Penrith."

The king replied, "Indeed! Must say, what with all the festivities to soon take place at the palace Verna will be in need of additional staff."

Minutes later, Tom came riding out of the stables toward the village. He had no idea what flat that of the maiden might be.

Riding up to two men sitting outside the pub drinking their brew, Tom reined in his steed to ask them if they knew the maiden.

The two men looked at each other and shrugging their shoulders. Tom tried asking the men to provide a bit more information.

He said, "Speak of the young maiden with a position at the inn above the glen. Be she fair haired, and a frisky lass."

One of the men replied, "Aye, lad; me thinks she might be the maiden sharing a flat with another lass above the saddler's shop. The stairs to the flat be at the rear of the shop."

Tom thanked the men, then spurred his steed to the rear of the saddler's shop.

Tethering the roan to a rail, he took the stairs to the flat above the shop and tapped on the door.

A young maiden, unfamiliar to Tom, opened the door to greet him.

She said, "Good eve, Sir. What hath brought thee to me abode?"

Tom replied, "Good eve, Lass. Wish not to disturb thee, yet men at the pub directed me to this flat. Thought haps 'twas the residence of the maiden, Bridget."

The maiden replied, "The men hath spoken true. Bridget and I share this flat."

Bridget, heard the familiar voice from her bedroom.

She called out excitedly, "Thomas, hath ye returned! Bade thee enter. Me feared thy proposal might hath been but a ruse. Come; permit me to greet thee properly."

Tom stepped through the entrance to the flat to see Bridget at her bedroom door; her arms outstretched.

Tom crossed through the kitchen to take her in his arms.

They stood holding each other for a time.

Tom, then asked her if she had decided to accept his proposal.

She replied, "Aye, Thomas. With much willingness."

She, then said, "When of age, the lads here about, leave to seek more fertile pastures. Soon, but the elders alone shall remain. Thus, there be naught about this village lending cause for me to remain. Shall cast me lot with thee. Haps one day will be the better for it."

Tom replied, "Pledge to thee, dear Lass; shall ye not rue this decision. The villagers in Penrith be a kindly lot. Yea too, thy mistress, Lady Verna, will find stern of voice yet quite concerned for her charges."

"Hath placed me faith in thee, Thomas. Pray, be not betrayed. Mercy, in the excitement hath failed to acquaint ye two. Rosalyn, this be Thomas, the young gent of whom to thee hath spoken" said Bridget.

Rosalyn asked, "How fare thee, Thomas? Bridget spoke of ye being manservant to a prince. A position to be envied, indeed."

Tom replied, "A pleasure to meet thee, Lass. Aye, find it to be a position of ease for Prince Frederick be not the sort to be pampered. An avid hunter. In weather fair, oft be he in the forest, permitting me much time at leisure."

Bridget addressing Tom, said, "Thomas, be we about to sup. Be ye welcome to partake of our meager fare."

He replied, "Ye tempt me, Lass; yet dare not, for me Prince may be in need of me."

He paused a moment, then continued, saying, "Bridget, art ye to be at the inn at sunrise for our journey. To make haste in the morn, ride with me to the inn then return upon me steed."

Tom bid Rosalyn a farewell. He and Bridget, then rode double to the inn.

At the inn, Tom dismounted; kissed Bridget good night, then stood watching her return to the village.

Chapter 49

The next morning, Tom left his bed above the stables to tend to the prince.

After laying out garments for the prince to wear that morning, he went to the kitchen for a pitcher of tea and returned with it to his master's quarters.

Leaving the prince's quarters, Tom went to the stables.

He saddled Abas and Silvermane, then tether the horses to the hitching post at the entrance to the inn.

Returning to the stable, Tom found his steed in its stall. Its saddle had been removed and set on the earthen floor beside two canvas tote bags. Bridget was nowhere in sight. He went looking for the maiden to find her in the tack room where they had previously lain together.

Tom went to sit beside her and scratched her head to awaken her gently.

Barely awake, Bridget rubbed the sleep from her eyes, kissed him, then spoke.

She said, "Good morn, Thomas; 'tis pleasing to ope me eyes and find thee here beside me."

Tom asked, "Bridget, how come ye to be here at the inn a 'fore sunrise?"

She replied, "Lie a 'bed sleepless this night past. Fearing would awaken late to then be left behind; thought to leave me bed, dress, fetch me belongings, and ride here to the inn."

"Dear lass, must ye not hath been concerned; for hath ye been absent when the column departed, would hath ridden to the village to fetch thee.

Shall leave thee for the moment for must tend to me Prince. At thy leisure, set ye at a table in the courtyard. Shall we take breakfast with the men."

Tom exited the tack room, leaving Bridget to tend to her grooming.

After making herself presentable, she went to wait for Tom. A few of the men were at the tables when she came to sit. Donald asked the maiden why she was not in the dining hall serving breakfast.

Bridget replied, "Sir, hath resigned me position at the inn. Thomas hath procured a position for me as a servant at the palace. Thus, shall be accompanying ye men to Penrith."

Donald replied, "Indeed! Well then, we lads, must watch our tongues upon this journey lest we insult thee, fair Maiden."

Minutes later, Tom came running out of the inn to the stables to saddle the horses he and Bridget were to ride.

He fastened one of Bridget's canvas bags to his saddle and the other to Bridget's, then led both out into the courtyard.

Tom tethered the horses to a support post, then went to sit beside Bridget.

Minutes later Sir Cartwith stepped out of the inn to address the cavalrymen.

The knight said, "Ye lads, go saddle thy mounts and secure thy gear. Must ye be prepared to ride immediately after ye hath eaten."

The men scrambled for the stables, calling out to the others still in the sleeping quarters above.

Tom turned to Bridget, and spoke, "Bridget, come; shall we collect the belongings of King Frederick, and those of the prince, and prepare them for travel.

Might we encounter the king or the prince, curtsy as ye greet them. Other than that, must ye not speak lest ye be spoken to. Must ye address the king as Your Highness. Upon arriving at the palace, shall instruct thee as to how the other nobles art to be addressed."

She said, "Mercy, Thomas, all this need for courtesy hath rattled me brain. Haps 'tis best for me to follow thy lead."

The two left the table. Thomas took Bridget's hand leading her into the inn and up the flight of stairs to the prince's quarters.

They gathered the prince's belongings then went to fetch those of the king before taking the stairs to the floor below.

Passing the dining area, Prince Frederick called out to them.

Tom and Bridget set their burdens on the floor then went to greet the king and prince.

Wishing the king and the prince a good morning, Tom bowed, and Bridget curtsied.

The king and Prince Frederick returned their greetings.

The prince, then said; "Father, this lass with Tom once be a servant here at the inn. Bridget will be returning with Tom to Penrith. Hath she been given a position at the palace, to service 'neath the guidance of Lady Verna."

The king said, "Come near, Lass. Hath ye kin in Gretna?"

She replied, "Nay, Your Highness. Me sire expired early on. Mother hath taken residence with me wedded brother in Milltown. Came to Gretna this year past seeking employment."

The king replied, "Indeed! Will ye be made welcome in Penrith. Need ye but to be attentive to Lady Verna and all will bode well for thee. Go ye two; see to thy tasks."

Tom bowed and Bridget curtsied, then went to retrieve the canvas sacks from the floor and left the inn.

The king turned to speak to the prince.

He said, "Frederick, 'tis no wonder Tom be so intent on procuring a position for the young maiden. Be she a comely lass indeed.

Leave us partake of this food and be on our way. Must confess, Frederick; the comfort of me own bed be missed."

The prince said, "Father, hath been quite concerned as to the measure of success Sir Milford hath achieved in finding Leland. Desire to put an end to this controversy with Ashley.

The events to occur in the weeks to come should be a time for celebration. However, the merriment of the festivities will be gravely diminished were Ashley to yet be in a somber mood."

The king replied, "Frederick, 'tis indeed a reason for concern. Leave us pray this matter will be resolved within the coming fortnight. If not, might it be prudent to send Ashley with Victoria away on holiday unto we hath succeeded in putting this matter to an end.

Would it be better for Ashley to be absent at the celebration than to be about sulking before our guests."

The prince frowned, and said, "Father, would find this quite displeasing as would Mother and Victoria."

"Hath ye a more suitable solution to this matter? Haps not, shall we set it aside for the present, partake of this food the innkeeper hath prepared then be on our way," the king asked.

The group at the tables in the courtyard had also been served. They sat eating breakfast while teasing Bridget

The maiden was not disturbed by the men. She took it all in stride and managed to get in a few quips of her own.

Having finished breakfast, the men retrieved their mounts and rode into formation to wait for the king. Tom and Bridget took their places at the rear of the column.

Prince Frederick settled with the innkeeper, bade him farewell, then with the king left the inn to mount their horses.

The column rode out of the courtyard taking the road south toward Penrith.

Periodically the prince turned to make certain Bridget was not falling behind. After they had ridden a few miles, the prince was certain she could easily maintain any pace set by the standard bearer.

Chapter 50

It was mid-afternoon in Penrith. Princess Ashley sat at a portal at the top tier of the palace as she had every day while Sir Milford and his men were out attempting to locate the archer. She waited for the knight to come into sight. Not seeing Leland among the men, she retired to her chambers to sit alone until dinner.

With nothing positive to report, Sir Milford shied away from the dining hall knowing his presence would result in a discussion of the situation, causing further discomfort to the princess.

The queen was frustrated not knowing what to do to comfort Ashley and was quite concerned watching her fiddle with her food at every meal.

Lady Victoria often visited the princess, sitting silent, reading, or working on her needlepoint.

The marquess had come to visit. The queen instructed Lady Winfred to inform the man the princess was a bit out of sorts and was not visiting with anyone.

The marquess was not pleased to be turned away and attempted to extract an explanation from the lady-in-waiting.

Near dusk, the sentry was at his post on the ramparts caught sight of a column of men on horseback approaching the castle on the road from the north. Uncertain as to who they might be, he waited until they were clearly in sight.

Seeing the king's standard, the sentry shouted for the trumpeter.

The soldier came to sound his trumpet, announcing the arrival of the king.

Sir Milford ran to instruct his men to line the road leading over the drawbridge.

Everyone in the palace dropped what they were doing and ran out onto the ramparts and into the courtyard.

Queen Margaret, Princess Ashley, and Lady Victoria came together to wait for the king on the landing at the entrance to the palace.

Gavin and one of the stable boys came to wait at the palace steps to relieve the king and prince of their horses when they entered the courtyard.

The column could hear the cheering from the castle as they drew near.

Bridget maneuvered her horse closer to Tom to speak.

She said, "Thomas, hath not expected the people at the palace to display so much affection for the king."

He replied, "Bridget, his Majesty be a just and kindly master. Anyone harboring a grievance, be he a noble or a peasant, hath the king's ear."

Approaching the moat, Sir Cartwith signaled the men to halt.

Only the standard bearer, the king, and Prince entered the courtyard.

They dismounted and handed their reins to Gavin and the stable boy.

King Frederick took the stairs to greet and kiss the queen, then to hug the princess. Lady Victoria curtsied to the king, kissing him on the cheek.

Princess Ashley then retreated into the palace while the prince greeted his mother.

The group then went to sit on the terrace. The princess was not present.

The column waiting at the moat entered the courtyard, dismounted, then went to stable their horses.

Tom, after stabling his and Bridget's mount, asked Bridget to wait for him in the courtyard while he stowed away the gear.

Minutes later Tom returned. He took Bridget by the hand and led her into the kitchen.

The kitchen staff was busy preparing dinner. Mildred was standing at a chopping block dicing vegetables when the two entered.

Seeing Tom, she dried her hands with her apron, then quickly went to take him in her arms.

Bridget stood waiting for them to exchange greetings and for an introduction.

Christy came running to take Bridget's hand.

Tom said, "Mother, this winsome lass be Bridget. Bridget, this mischievous child hath ye in hand be me sister, Christy."

Mildred said, "Bade thee welcome to Penrith, Bridget. Forgive me Lass; be a bit occupied at the moment. Will we set to chat a bit later. Thomas and Christy will direct thee to thy quarters."

Bridget replied, "Good day Mother Mildred. 'Tis pleasure to make thy acquaintance. Must thank thee for thyne aid in procuring a position for me at the palace. Pledge to thee, shall give thee no cause for regret."

Meanwhile out on the terrace, King Frederick was relating the events of his holiday in Dumfries to the queen and Lady Victoria.

The prince sat silent.

Queen Margaret was well aware what was troubling him and thought to give him an opportunity to speak of it.

She said, "Frederick, thought ye to be quite jubilant at the prospect of wedding Rebecca. Yet here ye set in a somber mood."

"Mother, surely ye noticed Ashley turned from me upon me arrival. By her actions 't is apparent Sir Milford hath not succeeded in ferreting out the archer. Lest we succeed in finding Leland, shall me never be forgiven by her. There be no joy in being aware one quite dear to thee doth shun thee as the plague," said the prince.

The queen attempting to comfort him said, "Frederick, the archer be of flesh and blood. Be he not a spirit to simply vanish. Lest he hath fled the realm, rest assured will he be found.

The king said, "Frederick, shall speak with Milford in the privacy of his chamber this very night. Will we devise another approach in this endeavor."

The prince replied, "Father, must ye permit me to take part in this renewed effort, for Ashley must be made aware of me concern in this matter."

The queen said, "Frederick, what ere ye desire to do to remedy this anger Ashley harbors for thee shall be thyne to pursue."

The king addressing his wife said, "Margaret, hath nearly forgotten. Countess Sarah shall be arriving a bit earlier than the earl. She hath voiced a desire to assist thee in the preparations of the festivities.

Will she be accompanied by Lady Juliana, niece to the earl, and haps Lord Reeves, the ambassador assigned to Penrith by Earl William. Shall it be an opportunity for ye ladies to become acquainted."

The queen replied, "Husband, 'tis pleasing to me for the countess to express a willingness to render assistance in preparing for the nuptials. What part might Lady Juliana play in these proceedings?"

The king answered, "Why Margaret, Rebecca hath chosen the maiden to stand with her at the wedding and as her lady-in-waiting as well.

Must say, Juliana be a winsome lass indeed."

Chapter 51

Later that night, after dinner, King Frederick and the prince left the dining hall with intentions of speaking with Sir Milford.

The king ordered the sentry at the palace entrance to follow.

At Sir Milford's door, he ordered the soldier not to permit anyone to enter.

In the absence of the king, Sir Milford had not been taking his evening meals in the dining hall but in the soldier's mess, then had gone directly to his quarters.

That night, knowing the king had returned, he expected either to be summoned or be paid a visit by his Majesty. Thus, the tapping on the door was expected.

The king entered followed by the prince.

Sir Milford rose from his seat, bowed, then greeted them.

He said, "Good eve, Your Majesty, Prince Frederick. Pray hath ye a pleasant holiday, and safe journey. Be ye missed."

The king replied, "Good eve, Milford. Hath it been a journey of interest. Unlike we English, many of the games played by the Scots be contests of strength. A hardy lot indeed.

Now then, 'tis apparent Milford, hath ye little success in locating the archer. Shall we then approach this quest by another route.

The 'morrow be the Sabbath, nonetheless the scribers art to be given a task. Placards art to be fashioned offering a reward for information as to the location of the archer. Postings art to be made by the cavalry in the village squares of Penrith, Pategill, Newton Rigg, and upon the roads to Eamont Bridge, Clifton, and Edenhall."

The knight replied, "Shall see to it this very night. Early Monday morn, cavalrymen will be dispatched to post the placards, as instructed. Might we receive no response by Wednesday eve, shall we then pursue another course."

The king replied, "So, it shall be, Milford. Will thus, leave thee for I yearn for the comfort of me bed. Sleep ye well this night."

With the prince, the king stepped out onto the courtyard, relieving the sentry at the door.

In the dimly lit palace grounds, a figure was seen leading a horse toward the castle gate.

The figure, coming near was recognized by the king as being Sir Cartwith.

The king addressing the knight said, "Sir Knight, where be ye bound at this late hour? Surely the ride from Gretna hath left thee weary."

Sir Cartwith replied, "Good eve, Your Majesty, Prince Frederick. Yea, be near spent yet there be a matter in the village must address."

The king said, "Good man; upon speaking to the lady, be certain to extend to her me best regards."

Sir Cartwith continued to the castle exit.

Robert greeted him and opened the gate.

Sir Cartwith passed through, mounted his steed, then rode into the night toward the village.

Leland and Howard were having a conversation outside the blacksmith's shop when the sound of hoof beats was heard approaching the shop. Not knowing who it might be, Leland stepped into the shadows.

Seeing the smithy standing beside the road, Sir Cartwith reigned in Sweet Sorrow, dismounted, and tethered his horse to the hitching post.

Howard said, "Good eve, Sir Knight. Hath ye not been about for a time. Pray be ye in good stead."

Sir Cartwith replied, "Yea, Howard. The king and the prince journeyed to Scotland on holiday. Be assigned to provide escort. But this night returned to the palace. Thought to come visit the lady."

"The child, Tiffany, come by each morn to feed the wee horse, Cupid; then to visit with me mate. Hath she expressed a desire to ride," said the smithy.

The knight replied, "Will speak with the lass. Haps soon will come with Christy to fetch the two for a bit of a jaunt. Tiffany will enjoy Christy's company."

Howard asked, "Sir Cartwith, each morn hath seen the cavalry ride to the forest. Might they be seeking poachers?"

"Nay, Howard. The king hath ordered the men to scour the woodland for an archer. Hath they not succeeded in finding the chap. Suspect the search will likely be abandoned. Sir Milford may next direct his attention to the hamlets surrounding the forest in the hope someone will come forth with information as to where the bowman might hath found refuge," replied Sir Cartwith.

The smithy chuckled, and said, "Mercy, the chap must be sly as a fox to avoid detection for so long by so many soldiers.

Be left to wonder what deed so vile hath the archer committed to warrant such an effort."

Replying, the knight said, "Howard, hath not yet learned of this. Know solely that the man they seek be the archer who hath been tutoring the princess. What might hath occurred 'tween the two be a mystery. This chap be known not to be abusive nor violent. Thus, must he be sought for some other reason.

Might ye hath heard of the bowman who intervened to save the prince. Be he and this man being pursued, one and the same."

Howard acting surprised, responded, "Indeed! Hath heard the tale yet thought it to be but a rumor. Well then Sir Knight, would seem be we left to wait to learn the reason for the pursuit of this archer."

Sir Cartwith said "And so we shall, Howard. Must leave thee for desire to visit with the lady for a time. Farewell."

The smithy, bidding him farewell, said, "Good eve, Sir Knight."

Sir Cartwith walked to the rear of the millinery then took the steps to the flat above.

Leland stepped out of the shadows to stand beside his friend. The conversation he had heard between the knight and Howard revealed only that the soldiers would no longer be looking for him in the forest.

The smithy said, "Well, Leland, hath ye heard? Will ye no longer be hampered by the soldiers in the forest, and in good time. For the larder be in dire need of replenishment."

"Aye, Howard; shall resume the hunt on the 'morrow. Will there be no pleasure in it, for must be on constant alert," replied the archer.

Meanwhile above the millinery, Sir Cartwith stood tapping on the door to the flat. Opening the door, Whitney stepped out and into his arms.

Chapter 52

Sunday morning before breakfast, Sir Milford left his quarters to instruct the palace scribe what was needed for the postings.

The man asked only for the number required, and when they would be needed.

He was told to deliver them the next morning.

Sir Milford left the scribe to get himself a bit of tea from the kitchen.

Upon entering, the knight caught sight of an unfamiliar face speaking with Lady Verna. Curious, he asked Mildred who the girl might be.

She replied, "Good morn, Sir Knight; the lass be Bridget. Come to the palace from Scotland. Hath she taken a servant's position. Will we be seeing much of the lass."

He replied, "Expect so, Mildred."

The knight paused, then asked; "Mildred, might ye prepare a bit of tea and might the maiden serve it to me out on the terrace?"

Mildred replied, "As ye wish, Sir Milford."

Sir Milford left the kitchen to sit out on the terrace.

Retrieving the flute from his belt, he began to play.

Princess Ashley, sitting sullen and alone in her chambers, heard the familiar melody and thought to join the knight on the terrace.

Sir Milford, seeing the princess step out onto the terrace; stopped playing, stood, and bowed.

The knight greeted her saying, "Good morn, me Princess. Pray hath not disturbed thee with me music."

"Good morn, Sir Milford. Nay, to the contrary. Find it soothing to hear thy flute. Shall set beside thee as ye play," replied the princess.

Minutes later, Bridget came carrying a tray with a cup and a pot of tea. She paused, not expecting to see the knight with a lady.

Bridget, unaware of the status of people she was addressing, said, "Good morn; 'tis a bonny tune ye play Sir Knight. Be sent by Mildred with tea.

Forgive me, come to the palace from Scotland but this day past with King Frederick. The residents of the palace be not yet familiar to me. Might ye be Sir Milford?"

Sir Milford replied, "Aye, Lass; spoke to Mildred earlier. Be told ye answer to the name Bridget. Leave me acquaint thee with the Princess Ashley."

Bridget stood silent for a moment; her eyes wide open, staring at the princess. She set the tray on the table then stepped back to curtsy.

Apologizing, she said, "Must ye forgive me, Your Royal Highness. Hath not intended to be disrespectful. Thy sire, nor Prince Frederick, never spoke of thee in me presence."

"Good morn, Bridget; there be no need for apology. Might ye fetch me a cup as well? Desire to set and listen to Sir Milford play," replied the princess.

The new servant curtsied, then ran to fulfill the request of the princess.

The princess and Sir Milford looked at each other grinning.

The princess asked, "Sir Milford, how come this lass to Penrith?"

He replied, "Hear the maiden befriended Tom when Prince Frederick first journeyed to visit Dumfries. Prince Frederick and the others passed the night in Gretna.

Bridget held a servant's position at the inn. Tom then became smitten with the lass."

The princess said, "Alas, Sir Milford; 'tis heartening to hear someone other than Frederick hath found a bit of happiness."

Consoling her, Sir Milford said, "Princess, must ye not despair. Pledge to thee, by one means or t 'other the archer Leland shall be returned to thee. As ye hath longed for the archer, 'tis certain he too doth yearn for thee."

The princess, curious, asked, "Sir Milford, know ye to be a fearless warrior, yet kindly, and quite pleasing to the eye might add. Oft hath wondered. How come there be not a lady of thyne own beside thee."

He replied, "Well, Princess Ashley, hath not found one yet with the willingness to stand second to me king. Be it not for thy sire, know not what me fate might hath been."

Bridget returned with a cup for the princess. She curtsied, set the cup on the table, then turned to leave as the prince stepped out onto the terrace. She curtsied and continued on her way.

Princess Ashley, upon seeing the prince, rose from her seat and left the terrace.

The princess caught up with Bridget in the hallway. She told the lass she would be taking her breakfast in her chambers.

Princess Ashley continued up to her chambers.

Bridget returned to the kitchen.

Out on the terrace, the prince was visibly upset over Princess Ashley's obvious intent to avoid him. He was not angered by it but saddened. He had hoped to mend the riff he had created between himself and his sibling upon returning from Dumfries. At the present it seemed it was not to be.

With a bit of sadness in his voice, the prince said, "Me word, Sir Milford; how long must I be chastised by me sibling? Will she not grant me a moment to beg her forgiveness?"

Sir Milford replied, "Me Prince; despite her actions at present, there be a strong bond 'tween thee and the princess. The ire hath she for thee at present will subside, and the bond 'tween ye shall prevail. However, considering the festivities which art to take place here at the palace in the weeks to come, would not be prudent for ye two to be at odds in the presence of guests. Surely some measure of mending must be achieved. Might ye seek the queen's counsel. Haps Her Highness will intervene with the princess on thy behalf."

The prince said, "Indeed, Sir Milford, suggesting a chat with Mother be worthy of consideration. Shall ponder upon it."

Godfrey came to inform the prince that breakfast was being served. The prince thanked the butler, then the two men left the terrace.

In the corridor, Sir Milford saw Sir Cartwith talking with Mildred at the entrance to the kitchen.

Sir Milford said, "Me Prince, there be Sir Cartwith. Hath a need to speak with him. Beg to leave thee, shall join thee at the table."

Sir Milford went to stand and wait for the knight and the cook to finish their conversation, and for Mildred to walk away, before addressing the knight.

Sir Milford said, "Good morn, Sir Cartwith; hath we a task to complete on the 'morrow. The scribe shall prepare placards offering a reward to anyone with information as to where Leland, the archer, might be. These placards art to be posted in the surrounding villages and along the roads entering Penrith.

I shall oversee a few of the cavalry assigned to carry out the task. I shall ride with a few of the men to the south and east. Ye, with the other men will ride to the north and west.

Shall advise thee as to when we art to begin upon receiving the placards from the scribe."

Sir Cartwith replied, "Very well, Sir Milford. Shall await word from thee in me quarters then assemble the men."

Chapter 53

At sunrise on Monday, Leland left his hut for the forest. He had asked Howard the previous night to come with his cart to the forest entrance on the flats at midday. The archer reminded the smithy to bring a shroud to conceal him; and with good fortune, a stag he might had slain for their return to the village.

Howard agreed to follow the archer's instructions.

Leland had been in the forest an hour when, in the early light, a stag came to the river to drink. He waited for the animal to show his broadside before letting fly his arrow. The arrow ran true, striking the beast in the shoulder. The animal staggered for a bit, then fell to the forest floor. The beast was a young male; easily carried to the riverbank. Leland was about to dress the deer when he heard the hoof beats of many horses coming from the hillside.

He quickly shouldered the animal, carrying it beneath the willow; then stood listening for the direction the riders were heading.

The horses galloped passed the forest to the flats, then broke off in different directions.

Leland returned to the river with the deer, dressed it, lifted it to his shoulders, and carried it to the entrance to the forest to wait for Howard.

The hoof beats Leland had heard were the cavalry leaving the castle on their way to post the placards in the villages and along the roadsides.

Howard was at his forge when a cavalryman rode into the village, dismounted, then hammered a sheet of parchment to a wooden panel mounted on a post in the village square.

Howard feigned indifference to what the soldier was doing. He waited for the man to leave and was out of sight before going to read the posting.

Seeing it was a reward poster seeking information about the archer, he tore it from the panel, returned to his shop, and tossed it in the fire.

Near midday, Howard hitched his horse to his cart then went to the flats.

Leland remained concealed, waiting for Howard to pass and turn the cart before he shouldered the animal and stepped out to load it onto the cart. He then vaulted on board to lay beside the beast and reached for the shroud to pull over himself and the animal.

Howard continued on and reined the horse to a stop at the shed behind his shop.

The animal was taken from the cart, hung from a rafter within the shed, then the two men went about removing the hide. Howard then related to Leland the event of the morning.

He said, "Leland, this morn a soldier came riding to the village; affixed a placard upon the panel in the square. The king hath offered a reward to anyone with knowledge of where ye might be. Waited for the soldier to ride out of sight, then removed the parchment and set it to flame."

The archer seemed unmoved by the smithy's disclosure. He paused for a moment before responding.

He then said; "Well then, Howard; so long as the soldiers hath directed their search to the villages, shall make me bed 'neath the willow in the forest. Might the soldiers come inquiring of me, there will be no need for the villagers to lie."

Leland paused for a moment, then continued saying, "This very night shall fetch me lantern, a blanket, and leave the village. Should be in need of thee, will set flame to the lantern. The forest will provide me with food, and the river with fish and water. Me wee garden will be in need of tending, however. Might ye see to it?"

Howard said, "Aye! Yet 'tis an injustice for thee to be driven from thyne own abode. How long will ye endure this discomfort?"

"Unto hath wearied of it, Howard," replied the archer.

"Leland, haps those feelings the princess hath portrayed for thee may be indeed sincere," said the smithy.

Leland replied, "Nay, Howard; must they not. For might it be as ye say, then why there be a need for the princess and the prince as well, to indulge in such an elaborate masquerade? At some point in being tutored, the lady could hath revealed her title."

"And pray tell, Leland, what might ye hath done with the knowing?" asked the smithy.

Leland replied, "Well, in the least would me not be in this wretched state. Howard, hath wearied of this chatter; shall we no longer speak of it."

"As ye wish, me friend. Yet must say, oft be ye as dense as the forest ye cherish," said the smithy.

Chapter 54

Tom had completed his morning chores in the chambers of the prince and was thinking of giving Bridget an opportunity to become familiar with the village and the surrounding area.

Taking the stairs to the kitchen, he went to speak with Mildred.

He said, "Mother, hath completed me chores. Thought to acquaint Bridget with the village. Might it be permitted?"

His mother replied, "Thomas, know ye well, 'tis not me place to grant thee permission. Must ye speak to Lady Verna. Be she in the dining hall overseeing preparations for the midday meal."

Tom left the kitchen a bit uneasy. He was intimidated by Lady Verna's no-nonsense manner.

Lady Verna was standing, arms crossed, watching the servants clear the breakfast table when Tom entered the dining hall.

He bowed before speaking, then said, "Good morn, Lady Verna. Hath come requesting permission for Bridget to accompany me a 'horse."

She replied, "Thomas, as ye see, the lass be occupied at present. Unto the midday meal hath been served and the table prepared for the evening meal, be in need of the lass. Upon completing her chores, she may go about what ere might please her. Must she, however, be present in time to serve the evening meal."

Tom thanked the lady, bowed, and left the dining hall, then went to the stables to ask Gavin for permission to saddle two of the horses after midday.

Tom was rarely refused a request, for most of the laborers in the king's employ were well aware the lad had the prince's ear and would one day be manservant to the king. It might not bode well to be out of favor with the lad.

After lunch, Tom returned to the kitchen to wait for Bridget to complete her chores. He then called her aside and asked her if she would ride with him.

She replied, "Thomas, naught would please me more. Shall be a bit for must change me garments. Will join thee in the courtyard."

Bridget left the kitchen to change her clothes.

Tom went to saddle the horses, then led them out to the side entrance of the kitchen to wait for Bridget.

The door to the butchery lay open. Tom saw Martin standing at his chopping block at his task.

Tom went to greet him.

He said, "Good day, Martin. Be ye a bit occupied?"

The butcher replied, "Nay, Thomas. How fare ye this fine morn? Hath ye two steeds in tow. Where might ye be bound?"

Tom said, "Thought to ride with the maiden, Bridget. Hath she not yet been to the village."

Martin asked, "When am I to be acquainted with the lass?"

Tom replied, "Will she be by in a moment, Martin."

Bridget stepped out of the side door of the kitchen onto the courtyard and went to stand beside Tom.

Tom said, "Martin, this winsome lass beside me be the maiden, Bridget."

The butcher said, "Good morn to thee, Bridget. Bade thee welcome to Penrith. Ye two enjoy the day. Farewell."

Mounting their horses, the two rode out of the courtyard at a walk down the hill toward the forest.

Leland was sitting on the riverbank fishing when he heard the sound of hoof beats approaching. He quickly gathered his gear, stowed them beneath the willow, then climbed the tree to his stand.

Soon riders, a young lad and a maiden came into view;. They reigned in their horses at the stand of pines from where the stag had come to charge the prince.

Dismounting, they tethered the horses to a birch and disappeared behind the pines.

Leland, sitting on the stand, could clearly hear their conversation. The maiden was asking the young lad a question.

Bridget asked, "Thomas, stood at the portal in the kitchen this day past to see the cavalry led by Sir Milford and Sir Cartwith leave the grounds. Might the movement of the king's troops be a reason for concern?"

Tom replied, "Nay, Bridget; the cavalry be on a quest to find a bowman. For days hath they scoured this forest with no success. Thus, hath they thought to direct their attention to the surrounding villages."

Bridget said, "Surely the archer hath committed some vile deed to be so earnestly pursued."

He replied, "Lass, be not certain. From the little hath heard, 'twas some sort of involvement with the princess and the prince. The two be at odds o'er the matter."

"Ah! Then be that the reason why, when this Sunday past hath gone to the terrace with a cup for the princess, she quickly retreated into the palace upon the arrival of the prince," said Bridget.

The two fell silent.

From their conversation, Leland had learned only that the princess was not happy and was quite displeased with brother Frederick. He took no pleasure in knowing of their quarrel. For despite being duped by the two, he still had strong feelings for the princess.

Many minutes later the young lad and the maiden stepped out from behind the pines, mounted their horses and continued on the path toward the road to the flats.

Leland climbed down the willow and continue fishing.

Tom and Bridget rode to the village. Dismounting, he led the maiden past the shops. Walking by the millinery, Tiffany, sitting beside her mother, came running out to greet them.

Tiffany said, "Good day, Thomas. What be ye about? Hath ye come to Eleanor's shop with the lady?"

He replied, "Nay, lass; thought to acquaint the maiden with the village.

Tiffany, this be Bridget; hath come to Penrith from Scotland. Bridget, this be Christy's mate, Tiffany."

Speaking to the child, Britney said, "G 'day Tiffany. Haps one day when be ye of age to set a steed, shall we ride with thee and Christy."

Tiffany replied, "Hath a wee horse of me own, Bridget. Hath stabled it 'cross the road. Be given to me by Sir Cartwith."

Britany said, "Haps, then shall we soon ride with thee and Christy."

Chapter 55

Days had passed since the postings, with not one coming forward in response to the placards.

At breakfast, the king, a bit frustrated, asked Sir Milford for his input.

Sir Milford said, "Your Highness, shall dispatch a few of the cavalry to ensure the placards hath not been destroyed. Those removed shall be replaced.

Upon returning, the men will relate to me from which locations the postings hath been discarded.

Garbed as a peasant, I shall visit those sites to inquire. When in the midst of the villagers shall play the clod, thus will they speak with loose tongues in me presence."

While the king and Sir Milford were involved in their discussion, Princess Ashley and Lady Victoria held a whispered conversation.

During the meal, Lady Victoria also spoke with the prince. No words passed between the princess and the prince.

The queen took note of it and was becoming quite upset but said nothing.

Having finished their breakfast, Princess Ashley, Lady Victoria, and Sir Milford left to sit on the terrace.

The king went to attend to some affairs of state with the chancellor.

Queen Margaret thought to return to her chambers. Prince Frederick walking with her in the corridor, turned to his mother and spoke.

He said, "Mother, might we speak?"

The queen did not reply but continued down the corridor, taking the stairs to her chambers.

They entered the room to sit facing each other.

Prince Frederick began to speak.

The queen held up her hand signaling he be quiet. She turned to address her lady-in-waiting.

She said, "Lady Winfred, the princess and Lady Victoria be out on the terrace. Might ye go fetch the princess?"

The lady- in-waiting curtsied, then left the room to do the queen's bidding.

The prince and queen sat silent waiting for the princess.

Minutes later, Lady Winfred returned with the princess.

Queen Margaret turned to look at Lady Winfred.

The lady understood. She left the room and closed the door behind her.

The queen, her face drawn, hesitated before speaking.

She said, "Frederick, here, ye set. Through thy veins flows the blood of a brave and righteous king, about to whimper as a babe.

And ye Ashley, a princess, at the age of maturity. Hath ye gone about pouting as a pampered child.

Must ye two Heed me well. Hath wearied of this bickering. Hath we a situation in need of being set a 'right. Ye must set aside this quarrel and play a part in its resolution."

The queen paused, then said, "Aye, Ashley; Frederick hath erred in fetching Leland to the palace when the gent be not properly prepared for what awaited him herein. Yet, 'twas done with good intent, not with malice.

Be ye not without fault in this mishap Ashley; for in all those days ye passed with the archer never hath ye thought to give the man the slightest indication as to thy identity. Hath ye thought to play the village maiden, unto ye hath become a wrinkled ole hag? This trumpery which hath passed 'tween ye two these weeks past must end, and quickly!

Now, leave me."

Neither the prince nor Princess dared say a word. Coming a 'right, they left the room to join Lady Victoria.

Stepping onto the terrace, the princess went to sit beside Lady Victoria.

Prince Frederick continued on into the garden to sit on the bench beside the pool.

It was immediately apparent to Lady Victoria something unpleasant had taken place. She was not about to ask but waited for the princess to begin the conversation.

The princess said, "Victoria, Mother summoned me to her chambers to then speak harshly of me quarrel with Frederick. Never hath she spoken to Frederick and me with such ire."

Lady Victoria replied, "Be ye blessed this morn, for 'twas thy mother to chastise thee. Might it hath been thy sire, would it hath been much more severe."

Prince Frederick came walking past the ladies into the palace without saying a word.

Minutes later, servants came toting a target and setting it at the far end of the garden. The ladies looked at each other, wondering what was about to happen.

Prince Frederick returned with his bow in one hand, that of the princess in the other, and two quivers slung over his shoulders.

The prince set the bow and quiver he had given the princess on the table, then stepped into the garden, and began launching arrows at the target before calling to her.

The prince said, "Ashley, hath it been near a fortnight since ye hath last set an arrow to thy bow. Come, shall we practice a bit then might it please thee, upon the early morn shall we hunt in the forest."

Princess Ashley looked over at Lady Victoria with a look of astonishment.

Smiling, Lady Victoria nodded her head. A gesture instructing her to join the prince. The princess hurried into the garden to stand beside the prince.

They, then stood together, launching arrows at the target

Sir Milford stepped out onto the terrace. He bowed to Lady Victoria, then stood silent for a few minutes watching the archers.

He said, "Me word, Lady Victoria! Hath been weeks since last viewed the princess wield a bow. Hath she become quite proficient."

She replied, "Sir Milford, when in the forest ensuring the wellbeing of the princess, hath ye not viewed the progress?"

Sir Milford chuckled and said, "Me Lady, must confess, upon deeming Leland a man of honor then bearing witness to the princess embracing him, thought to afford the two a bit of privacy. Solely then, I began to accompany the princess to the Tate cottage, permitting her to continue on to the forest without escort."

Lady Victoria said, "Sir Milford, the king and queen might well hath frowned upon the course ye chose. Yet, must admit, were it me in thy stead, would hath done the like. However, must ye agree 'twas a bit of folly placing thyself in such a position.

Thus, should me ere feel the need to recount our wee chat to another, shall it be to the wind."

Sir Milford said, "Me Lady, know well thy ability to be discrete. Were it otherwise, would hath not taken ye into me confidence,"

"Sir Knight, should we not soon succeed in finding the archer, me fear the princess shall begin to wither as me garden in the waning days of autumn," replied Lady Victoria.

Queen Margaret stepped out onto the terrace.

Sir Milford stood to bow.

The queen signed for the knight to sit then raised a finger to her lips. She stood watching the prince and princess for a few minutes, smiling. Pleased to see the riff between the two was on the mend, she retreated into the palace.

Chapter 56

Before first light the next morning, Prince Frederick came awake. For the first time in weeks, he awoke with a positive attitude. The anger Princess Ashley had harbored within her had begun to dissipate. Aware of her fragile state of mind, he would need to be overly cautious in what he said when in her presence.

Tom, awakened by the stirring below left his bed, dressed, and took the stairs to the chambers of the prince.

Tom said, "Good morn, me Prince; might ye be in need of me?"

The prince replied, "Aye, Tom, hurry to the kitchen. Mildred is to prepare hen fruit, bread with preserves, and a bit of tea for the princess and meself. Shall we take our meal in the kitchen. Must ye then awaken the princess for we art to hunt this morn. Shall await her in the kitchen."

The prince dressed for the hunt, fetched his bow and quiver, then went to the kitchen to wait for the princess.

Mildred was not in the kitchen when he entered. Bridget and Tom were about to prepare each other's breakfast.

Seeing the prince enter, Bridget curtsied then greeted him.

She said, "Good morn, me Prince; hath prepare thee a bite."

Tom, with a cup and a ewer of tea on a tray, went to wake the princess.

Minutes later, Princess Ashley entered the kitchen wearing a deerskin jacket, matching calf length skirt, and a feathered cap. She held her bow in one hand and her quiver slung over her shoulder.

Bridget curtsied and greeted her saying, "Good morn, Princess Ashley. Must say, 'tis comely attire hath ye donned for the hunt."

The princess said, "Good morn, Frederick, Bridget. Be famished."

Bridget set plates of eggs, bread, and preserves on the table for the prince and princess. Then she and Tom walked out of the kitchen into the courtyard, leaving them alone to have their breakfast.

A bit of light from the rising sun was visible atop the castle wall. Yet, the courtyard was still dimly lit when the prince and princess stepped out of the palace.

Robert, seeing the two approach, held open the gate; bowing as they passed through. Outside the gate, the princess sand prince stood to watch the light from the sun creep down the outer castle wall. Much of the hillside was still in darkness as they walked toward the forest.

Leland, sleeping beneath the willow, came awake to the sound of two people talking on the riverbank. He came quietly to his knees.

The clearing beyond the river was in partial sunlight. The two figures were but silhouettes.

Their conversation was muffled by the flowing river. They stood talking for a bit, then continued walking carefully down the deer run. By the way they chose their steps, Leland was certain they were hunting. Not knowing who they might be, he thought it better to remain concealed. He waited until they were out of sight, then climbed the willow to his stand. He had thought to hunt that morning, but with the two strangers on the deer run he would need to wait till sunset.

Their bows at the ready; the prince and princess had slowly walked quite a distance with no success. They decided to return to within sight of the clearing and wait for the deer to come to drink at the river.

Rays of sunlight pierced the forest canopy, lending partial light to them.

Nearing the fallen tree that lay across the river, the prince put his hand on the arm of the princess, holding her back and whispered to her.

He said, "Look ye there, Ashley, beyond the clearing in the thicket. See the rack of four protruding above the foliage? It be a young stag. Must we wait in silence unto he comes to take water."

The two hunters were not visible to Leland, but he had also seen the rack at the edge of the clearing. The archer could have easily downed the stag should it come to drink. Yet, then to retrieve the animal he would need to risk being seen.

He stood frustrated as the buck broke through the thicket and made his way to the water.

Having taken its fill, the stag turned from the river to retreat into the thicket. Leland saw two arrows strike the animal broadside and the buck staggered a bit, then fell to the ground.

From his stand, Leland heard two voices celebrating the kill. Minutes later, he saw the two hunters cross the fallen tree to stand beside the slain deer.

Only then did Leland recognize the two as the prince and princess.

A sense of pride overtook the archer, knowing he had tutored the two so well.

The hunters stood over the animal for several minutes, talking.

The prince said, "Ashley, shall we return to the palace. Tom, and his mates will be sent to fetch the animal and return it to the butchery."

Leland watched them cross the fallen tree onto the deer run, then moments later walk past the willow. He felt the need to let the princess know he had witnessed her kill yet did not dare.

He waited for them to be well out of earshot before leaving the stand and drawing his blade, crossing the river to gut the deer. Retrieving an arrow from his quiver, Leland laid it beside the animal.

The princess could hardly wait to tell everyone of her morning in the forest.

Returning to the palace, she went directly to her mother's chambers.

Entering without knocking, she began to speak before closing the door behind her.

Excitedly, she said, "Mother, hath it been a wondrous morn! At first light, in the forest with Frederick, we came upon a stag taking water at the river. We both let fly our arrows and downed the stag."

Surprised, her mother replied, "Indeed! Hath ye become quite accomplished in the use of the bow. Leland hath tutored thee well. Be quite pleased to see thee in such a festive state."

Meanwhile, entering the palace grounds the prince asked one of the sentries to fetch Tom to his chambers.

The prince, then went his chambers to change his garments.

Minutes later, Tom entered the room.

The prince said, "Tom, with Bryce, go to the forest. Follow the deer run to the stately oak by the water. In the clearing beyond the river, there be a fallen stag. Fetch it to the butchery."

At the lunch table, Princess Ashley related the excitement of her kill. The king smiled through the entire recounting of the event. He then addressed Sir Milford.

He said, "Milford, what say ye? Haps shall we entertain the thought of assigning Ashley to the military. Her skill with the bow shall serve me well."

The princess said, "Father, must ye not make light of me achievement. Hath labored long and hard to become an accomplished archer; not to mention the humiliation of laying in the mire at the river, smiting its waters with me hands."

The king replied, "Spoke but a bit of folly child. Art ye to be commended for enduring the pain and labor required to master the weaponry."

The conversation was interrupted by Godfrey entering the dining hall requesting to speak to the prince.

The king waved his hand as a sign of permission.

The butler said, "Prince Frederick, forgive me interruption. Tom hath returned from the forest expressing a desire to speak with thee."

"Fetch the lad to me, Godfrey," the prince replied.

The butler bowed, then hurried out of the dining hall.

Moments later, Tom entered, bowed, then waited for permission to speak.

Prince Frederick asked, "Well, Thomas; why the need for such urgency?"

He replied, "Me Prince, when at the clearing in the forest, found the stag hath already been gutted. Two arrows yet be imbedded in the carcass, and another lay beside the fallen deer. Here be the third."

"Come Thomas; bring the shaft to me," said the prince.

Tom walked across the room, handed the arrow to the prince, bowed, and left the room.

The prince looked at the arrow for but an instant.

He exclaimed, "Gad Zeus! Sir Milford, Ashley, 'tis one of Leland's!"

Princess Ashley jumped out of her seat and ran to take the arrow from the prince. She looked at it for a minute before speaking.

Excitedly, she said, "Indeed it be! Must he hath been quite near to witness the kill."

Addressing the king, the princess then said; "Father, Leland hath not fled, be he yet about."

The king said, "The sly fox! Yet, a man of honor. Hath he been something less, would he hath made off with the carcass, and no one would hath been the wiser. Haps the dressing of the stag be the archer's way of displaying atonement."

Turning to Sir Milford, the king said, "Milford, attempting to find Leland in the forest, be futile for 'tis the archer's domain. 'Tis best to seek information in the villages upon where he might be."

Chapter 57

The next morning, Sir Milford left his quarters to join Sir Cartwith for breakfast in the men's dining hall. The knight's intention was to brief his subordinate on the discussion he had with the king regarding the placards and to issue instructions as to how they intended to proceed.

Sir Milford greeted him saying, "Good morn, Sir Cartwith. We hath been assigned a task for this day. The same men of the cavalry who posted the placards t' other day art to return to see they art in place. The site of those which might hath been discarded, art to be made known to me."

Sir Cartwith replied, "Shall dispatch the men this very morn, Sir Milford. Hath thought Leland to be a man of honor. Yet, his Majesty be determined to find him. Hath he committed so heinous a deed as to warrant such an earnest pursuit?"

In reply, Sir Milford said, "To the contrary, Sir Cartwith. His Highness hath a need to speak with the archer in an attempt to a 'right a blunder made by the prince with good intent.

The archer thought the actions of the prince not to be an error, but an attempt by the prince and princess to play him the fool.

Leland in turn, displaying disrespect for the royal family, fled and the search for the archer began.

The archer, then perceived he hath been pursued to be punished for the contempt he displayed."

Sir Milford continued, saying, "This be known to me. The archer be in the forest as we speak. For the soldiers to continue searching for the man would be a waste in effort. For, Leland be quite skilled in the art of concealment. To this hath said will ye surely attest. Recall the night sought we the lad Jarin? The archer be so near as to hear the words spoken yet remained we unaware be he about."

"Recall it well, Sir Milford. As then and as this fortnight past, be we deceived by the crafty archer," replied Sir Cartwith.

Sir Milford said, "Well, Sir Knight, best me leave thee to assemble the cavalry and see to the task at hand. Return well a 'fore sunset and render me a report."

They left the dining hall together.

Sir Cartwith went to assemble the men while Sir Milford went to speak with the prince and princess in an attempt to learn more of what had taken place in the forest the previous morning.

Sir Milford finding the prince, princess, and Lady Victoria sitting on the terrace chatting, bowed and took a seat.

Princess Ashley seemed in a better frame of mind knowing the archer had not fled the area. The subject of conversation was how the prince and princess could entice Leland out of hiding.

The princess said, "Frederick, Monday morn we will return to the hunt. Shall we set by the great oak beside the river and speak kindly of Leland. Hearing our words, he will know we mean him no harm. Might he not then reveal hisself?"

The prince replied, "Ashley, in Leland's mind we art not worthy of his trust. Doth he yet think he hath been played the fool. Will he deem our words but a ruse to lure him from his lair. Shall we leave the pursuit to Sir Milford for the present."

The princess said, "Frederick, the 'morrow be the Sabbath. Might we ride with Victoria and Sir Milford at mid morn to set beside the river? Should Leland be nearby, haps in some manner will we be made aware of his presence."

The prince replied, "Might it please thee, Ashley, shall accompany thee willingly. Haps the archer may be about. Yet must ye not be displeased should he fail to reveal hisself."

"Frederick, 'tis not expected. 'Tis but a desire hath expressed," said the princess.

Sir Milford spoke, saying, "Me Princess, must ye forgive me absence upon the 'morrow. With Sir Cartwith, will begin inquiring in the villages as to where the archer might be and how to, then proceed."

Lady Victoria turned to the knight and said, "Sir Milford, 'tis known Leland be much revered by the people in the village wherein he resides for tending to those in need. Will they not remain silent should a knight of the king come inquiring as to where he might be?"

He replied, "Indeed, Lady Victoria. Shall we not enter the villages as a knight, but as a lowly roaming peasants; haps a bumbling sots as well. The villagers will not suspect the true purpose for our presence.

Shall we speak a bit more of this as we dine this night. At the present, beg thy leave for hath thought to go request a few tattered garments from the butcher, Martin, to don upon the 'morrow."

Sir Milford rose from his seat, bowed, bid the others farewell, then left the terrace to visit the butcher.

Entering the butchery, the knight found Martin sitting at a table with Mildred having a cup of tea.

On seeing the knight enter, Mildred came to her feet bearing a blush.

Sir Milford understood the cook's reaction to him finding her with the butcher at mid-morning yet chose not to inquire. He simply extended a greeting.

Sir Milford said, "Good morn, Martin, Mildred. Hath come to request a boon of thee, Martin. Be in need of a few of thy garments. The more unsightly the better."

The butcher replied, "Me word, Sir Milford. What need hath thee for tattered attire which hath been kept solely to scour the butchery?"

"Martin, will don them on the 'morrow to visit the villages as a peasant in an attempt to seek information as to where the archer might be. The villagers art more apt to speak freely in the presence of a pauper than one of the military," said Sir Milford.

"Mildred, might ye fetch the garments Sir Milford requires? Be they kept in a sack 'neath the cot in me sleeping quarters," said Martin.

Mildred went to get the clothing, leaving the men to continue talking.

Minutes later, she returned with the tattered clothing.

Sir Milford thanked the two, bid them a good day and left the butchery to stow the tattered clothes in his quarters.

After Sir Milford left the butchery, Mildred returned to sit beside Martin. She sat silent for a bit, sipping from her cup.

Snickering, she whispered to the butcher; "Martin, might the knight suspect be we mates?"

He replied, "Mildred, Sir Milford be not a fool. What purpose might ye be here about other than for a bit of foolery?"

The two laughed boisterously at the butcher's humorous reply.

Chapter 58

Sir Milford came awake early the next morning. He sat on the edge of his bed reviewing the report Sir Cartwith had given him upon returning late yesterday afternoon.

The men had found two placards missing: one in the village at Pategill, and the other in Penrith.

At the outset, Sir Milford needed to determine why and who had removed the postings.

Turning up the flame of the lantern beside his bed, he rose to don the garments given him by the butcher.

Minutes later, Bryce entered the room with a basin of water. Seeing Sir Milford wearing the tattered clothes, the paige began to laugh.

The lad said, "Good morn, Sir Milford, 'tis certain the ladies will swoon upon seeing thee in the garments ye hath chosen to don for this day."

Sir Milford replied, "Hold thy tongue, ye thankless lout. Fetch me steed from the stables and tether Titus to the hitching post at the entrance to the palace. Make haste lest me smite thee with the back of me hand."

Still laughing, the paige set the basin on the table beside the bed then quickly left the room to do his master's bidding.

The knight was certain, being the Sabbath, many of the villagers would not be about until late morning. Thus, there was no need to hurry.

From his quarters he could see the flicker of candles emitting through the portals of the kitchen.

The knight left his quarters to have a bit of breakfast.

Crossing the courtyard, Robert called out to him.

The sentry said, "Hold ye there! Who be ye, and what be ye about this morn?"

Sir Milford chuckled, and replied, "Good morn, Robert; be at ease. Be Sir Milford. Hath ye done well to be alarmed."

Startled, Robert replied, "Gad Zeus! Hath ye given me a start. Good morn, Sir Milford. Thought ye to be but an intruding beggar in those tattered garments."

The knight chuckled and continued on to the kitchen.

Upon entering, he found Mildred puttering about. She had already lit a fire in the hearth and the stone ovens.

Turning to greet him, she said; "Good morn, Sir Milford. Hath me not known of thy intent at a masquerade, would hath thought thee to be a lowly peasant."

He replied, "Good morn, Mildred. Pray the villagers deem me as one."

Sheepishly, she said, "Hath not thought to deceive thee the morn past, Sir Knight. Martin hath requested me hand in marriage. Shall we be wed soon after the festivities for Prince Frederick and Lady Rebecca hath been concluded."

The knight replied, "No need for thee to explain thy courtship with the butcher. Hath ye labored hard these many years alone to sustain thy brood."

"Me thank thee for those kindly words. Now then, might me prepare thee a portion of hen fruit, bacon, and a bit of tea?" Mildred asked.

Sir Milford replied, "Indeed, Mildred. Intend to visit the hamlet of Pategill this morn. Dare say, little fare will be afforded a lowly beggar this day in the hamlet."

The knight finished his breakfast, thanked Mildred, and bade her farewell.

The drawbridge had not yet been lowered so he led Titus through the gate being held open by Robert. Beyond the castle wall, he mounted his steed and rode to within walking distance of Pategill before tethering the horse out of sight of the road.

As expected, upon entering the hamlet, but a few of the townspeople were about.

Sir Milford, walking to the billboard where placards had been posted and gave it a passing glance.

Noting that the second posting of Leland by the men of the cavalry was yet in place. He sat beneath the postings, took out his flute, and began to play.

Children playing leapfrog, and another hitting an iron barrel ring on the road with a stick, stopped their play and approached.

Sir Milford played a bit longer, then stopped to speak with the children.

He asked, "Hath any of ye children been tutored to read? Haps so, what might these placards above me head be about?"

The children stood silent, looking at the postings, then at each other. Moments passed, then one of them spoke."

"Sir, oft when a 'bed, me mum, from out a book of scriptures will relate to me a tale of yore. Might it please thee, shall fetch her; haps might she be of aid to thee."

He said, "Go ye lad; shall await thy return."

Sir Milford returned to playing his flute.

The other children sat around him; some tapping their bare feet on the dusty road. Minutes later, the child returned, leading a woman by the hand.

Sir Milford stopped playing, came to his feet to greet her.

He said, "Good morn, dear Lady. Pray hath not taken thee from thy chores. Be a bit curious. What be writ here upon these placards?"

The woman gave the man in tattered garments standing before her a condescending stare for a moment, then spoke.

She said, "Very well; grant me a moment. One be of a flat to let, another seeking to purchase a plow horse, and yet another offering a reward for information leading to an archer."

Sir Milford asked, "Madam, upon that of the archer, doth it state a name? Haps so, might this man be known to thee?"

She replied, "Heard say he be the archer who emerged victorious in the tournament held by the king in Penrith. Thus, were he to reside in this village, would he for certain be known to me.

Well now, enough of this waddling; hath many chores yet to tend."

Without another word, the woman turned on her heels and hurried away.

Sir Milford returned to sit and play his flute.

The children remained to listen for a bit then one by one, returned to their games.

Sir Milford walked out of the hamlet to his mount and returned to Penrith.

Entering the palace courtyard, Sir Milford was greeted with a roar of laughter by the people seeing him in his tattered garments.

In a gesture of good fellowship, Sir Milford dismounted Titus, removed his cap, then bowed to his audience.

Gavin came to take his steed.

Sir Milford then retired into his quarters to change into proper attire.

Sir Milford's morning masquerade was the initial subject of humorous conversation at the dinner table that evening. The knight took the ribbing in good stride.

King Frederick then asked what he had learned in Pategill.

The knight sat silent for a moment before replying.

He, then said, "Your Majesty, the woman to whom me spoke this morn knew solely of the archer for his feat in the tournament. Thus, be certain Leland be not of that village. Must confess, even at the outset held little hope of finding him so far from Penrith.

As ye well know, Your Highness, 'tis quite a trek for a hunter a 'foot to access the king's forest from a distant hamlet. Would wager the archer resides much closer to the woodlands."

The king replied, "Well thought, Milford. Beknown the archer hunts to feed the needy of a village, thus the village must be near the forest. Me thinks thy days be better spent in the village closest to the forest."

"Agreed, Your Majesty, visiting the villages, be a task to be performed by another for be me known in Penrith. Must it be someone the townspeople would least suspect," said the knight.

Everyone at the table fell silent attempting to determine who in the palace might be best suited to be sent to spy in the village. Names were being tossed about, yet no one would agree on any of the names suggested.

Minutes passed. Prince Frederick jumped to his feet to speak.

He said, "Who would suspect a young maiden of Scottish descent? The lass Bridget be quick of wit, and an able servant.

Father, the maiden with ease will find a position in the village pub. Her ears will then gather the information we seek."

The king replied, "Splendid!"

Then addressing the knight, the king said; "Milford, as a courtesy, must ye inform Verna of our intent prior to speaking with the young maiden."

"Your Majesty, hath ye spoken words of wisdom. Dare me not slight Lady Verna lest she not be forgiving. Shall speak with her in the morn."

Queen Margaret asked the princess if anything unusual had happened on their ride to the forest that morning.

"Mother, 'twas without incident. Alas, found we no signs of Leland yet 'tis certain be he lurking about," replied the princess.

Chapter 59

Aware Lady Verna would be occupied, supervising the servants in their housekeeping of the palace until early Monday afternoon, Sir Milford waited until late afternoon to speak to her.

He found her sitting in the garden by the pool with Lady Victoria. He bowed to the ladies, then extended a greeting.

He said, "Good day, your Ladyships. Forgive me for the intrusion. Lady Verna, might we speak?

Lady Victoria, ye may remain seated for this am about to discuss with Lady Verna be not of a personal nature."

The ladies returned the knight's greeting then Lady Verna asked what it was he wished to discuss.

"Me Lady, request a boon of thee. Be in need of someone, not known in the village Penrith, to be me ears. Prince Frederick hath deemed the maiden Bridget well suited for the task. With thyne approval, shall speak to the lass. Must advise thee, however, might she be willing, will the lass be absent from her chores here at the palace for a fortnight at most," said the knight.

Lady Verna replied, "Sir Knight, might the lass be of aid to thee in the pursuit of the archer, shall not be a hindrance in this endeavor."

Lady Victoria said, "The entire affair hath been as a pall upon the palace. Pray will it soon be brought to a conclusion. Princess Ashley hath been in a sorry state of late. Solely the return of Leland will remedy the sadness within her."

Sir Milford replied, "Indeed, Lady Victoria. Yea too, should it be a time of jubilation for Prince Frederick; knowing will he soon be wed to the Lady Rebecca. Yet, aware his actions that dreadful day hath caused the princess so much misery. He, too, be in a state of discontent."

Lady Verna replied, "Would seem then, Sir Milford, the solution to this dilemma rests upon thy shoulders. Pray ye succeed, and in haste."

Sir Milford said, "Shall not rest unto me task hath been completed. Beg to leave thee, for must seek the maiden with whom must speak."

Lady Verna answered, "Go ye then, Sir Knight. Hath assigned Bridget the task of preparing the dining table for the evening meal. There will she be found."

The knight bowed and left the garden for the dining hall.

Bridget was setting dinnerware on the table when he entered. Not wanting to startle her, he waited for Bridget to look up from her task before speaking.

He said, "Good eve, Bridget; might we speak? Hath come to request assistance in a pressing matter of which ye yet be not aware."

"Good eve, Sir Knight. How come ye to seek the aid of a lowly servant?" she asked.

The knight answered, "Prince Frederick spoke of thy position at an inn from whence ye came. Be in need of a lass with the ability to pose as a servant in the Penrith village pub."

"Sir Knight, 'tis a task many of the servants could perform with ease. What need hath thee of one strange to the villagers?" she asked.

Sir Milford replied, "Bridget, for precisely that reason ye be chosen. The servants in the palace reside in the village. We seek an archer named Leland. Might he reside in Penrith, the servants will not speak of it for the archer be revered for tending to the needy."

The knight hesitated a bit, then said, "Must ye approach the proprietor of the pub, seeking a position as a servant then be me ears in the pub. No inquiries art to be made by thee of the archer. For, then will ye be held suspect.

Heed well the chatter of the patrons. Bryce, me paige will come by each night. What ere ye hear of the archer, relay to the lad.

Seek lodging in the village lest ye be seen walking to and fro. Will ye return to the palace when ye art informed thy task hath been completed."

Bridget said, "Sir Knight, hath been to the village with Thomas, and introduced by name to the wee lass, Tiffany. Thus, haps might it be prudent to render the proprietor a name not familiar to the lass."

He replied, "Prince Frederick hath said be ye bright of mind. This ye hath suggested doth bear witness to his statement. Be at ease in this. For, shall assign one of me men to protect thee."

Assuring him she was up to the task, she replied, "Shall not be in fear, Sir Knight. For as me mum's mum oft said, "Wit's for ye'll no go past thee. Meaning, what ere shall befall thee, shall befall thee."

Sir Milford chuckled, and said, "Aye, 'tis so lass. Blood of fearless Vikings coursed within thy grand mum, and thyne as well. Shall leave thee to thy chores. 'Tis near time for the evening meal. Be expected to dine with the royal family this night.

At sup's end, fetch Tom then come to me quarters. Will acquaint thee with the lads Bryce and Quinn."

Sir Milford left the dining hall to change into proper attire for supper.

Entering his bedroom, he found Bryce laying out his garments. Interrupting the paige at his task, the knight spoke.

He said, "Lad; shall sup, then return to me quarters. Will then assign thee and Quinn a task with instructions."

The paige replied, "Sir Knight, shall speak with Quinn in the men's dining hall. At sup's end will we await thy return here in chambers."

Bryce left the knight to his grooming to cross the courtyard to the men's dining hall.

Quinn was sitting with other men of the cavalry at a long table. Bryce went to tap him on the shoulder then spoke.

Bryce said, "Quinn, forgive me interruption. Be advised Sir Milford hath requested our presence in his quarters at sup's end. Will come fetch thee then."

Some minutes later, Sir Milford entered the palace dining hall, bowed, greeted the royal family, then took his seat beside Prince Frederick.

The tension between the prince and princess seemed to have ebbed. Everyone was exchanging pleasantries.

Sir Milford waited for the conversation to subside before speaking.

He said, "Your Majesty, earlier spoke with the Scot, Bridget. Expected a bit of opposition to me requesting she seek a position at the village pub to be me ears. To the contrary, the lass became elated. She deemed it an adventure to participate in our quest."

The king replied, "The lass doth indeed bear spirit, Milford. Will she not give ground to any man. Observed this upon our ride from Gretna. However, might she succeed in obtaining a position in the village, she must be protected from the ruffians who frequent the pub."

"Hath seen to it, Your Highness. Quinn, unobserved, shall be at hand to hold the sots at bay might an incident occur.

Bryce will ride to the village each night to obtain a report from the lass," replied the knight.

Content, the king said, "Ye hath thought it through, Milford. Now then, leave us see what comes of this bit of intrigue."

The remainder of the evening meal was spent discussing the arrival of Countess Sarah.

Princess Ashley voiced discontent over Edward's persistence in his courtship.

Queen Margaret suggested she, the princess and Lady Victoria get together to discuss a polite method of putting an end to the marquess' unwanted advances.

Godfrey entered the dining hall, bringing the conversation to an end.

The butler bowed, then asked to speak with Sir Milford.

With the flick of a hand, the king granted the butler permission.

Garfield crossed the room to whisper to the knight.

He said, "Sir Milford, Bryce requested ye be advised. Quinn, Tom and the lass to whom ye wish to speak, await thee in thy quarters."

Sir Milford thanked the butler.

Godfrey bowed to the group, then returned to the kitchen.

Turning to the king, Sir Milford said, "Your Highness, request permission to be excused. Must instruct the participants in this undertaking as to the role each will be required to play."

"Go ye then, Milford. Leave us pray this attempt to ferret out the archer will bear fruit and put an end to this discontent," the king replied.

Sir Milford bowed and left the dining hall to return to his quarters.

He entered to see a look of uneasiness among the waiting group. The knight told them to sit and relax, then addressed the manservant.

Sir Milford said, "Tom, hath ye been to the village with Bridget. Be told by the lass ye acquainted her with the wee tot Tiffany, and no other."

Tom replied, "Aye, Sir Knight. Come upon the child playing with her mates on the road. She came running to greet me. There be no one near."

"Well then, there be no need for concern. Bridget shall attempt to obtain a position at the pub to be me ears. Will she with ease avoid an encounter with the child," said Sir Milford.

He then turned to Quinn and said, "Now then, Quinn. Ye art to visit the pub each night to be Bridget's guardian. Should an incident occur, and the lass be in harm's way, ye art to intervene. Will ye not mingle with the patrons nor address the maiden other than to request a tankard of ale."

Addressing his page, the knight said, "Bryce, Bridget will attempt to learn if Leland resides in the village. If so, where he might be.

Ride to the pub each night. Must ye not approach the maiden. Will she come to thee might she bear any information. Ye art to report to me upon returning to the palace."

Speaking to the group, Sir Milford said, "Hath the roles assigned to each of thee been well explained? Haps not then let it be known. Shall instruct thee further."

Bridget spoke, saying, "Sir Knight, there be but one concern am about to voice. Pray ye shant interpret it as a lack of willingness to participate in this endeavor.

Me fear Lady Verna would be quite displeased with me absence."

Assuring her, he replied, "Lass, set thy mind at ease for spoke to the Lady prior to approaching thee. Will ye not be chastised. This shall pledge to thee."

Once more addressing the group, Sir Milford said, "Ye lads, I assume by thy silence there be no other matters to discuss. Thus, shall bid thee a good eve."

The group bid Sir Milford a good night, then left.

Tom and Bridget walked together out into the courtyard. Bridget took Tom by the hand to lead him into the shadows of the palace, then turned to him to whisper.

"Thomas, shall be away for at most a fortnight. In me absence must ye not stray. For to do so will lay waste to me love for thee."

Tom replied, "Dear Lass, shall count the moments unto ye return. Shall not betray thee. Bear in mind, me thoughts will be solely upon thee, and no other."

Tears falling to her cheeks, Bridget pulled him to her, kissing him passionately, then hand in hand they continued into the palace.

Chapter 60

Bridget came awake early the next morning. After grooming and dressing, she began packing a satchel. The clamor of her movements awakened Christy, who sat up in her bed and asked what she was doing.

Bridget replied, "Good morn, Christy; hath been given an assignment by Sir Milford. Shall remain in the village for haps a fortnight, haps less. Thomas will be about to tend to thee in me absence. Should ye not wish to remain in this room alone, then pass thy nights in the butchery with thy mother.

Must not tarry. Shall fetch a bite in the kitchen, bid Mildred a farewell, then be off to the village."

Bridget gave Christy a hug, kissed her on the forehead, then with satchel in hand, hurried to the kitchen.

Mildred, seeing the maiden with a satchel, expressed concern.

She asked, "Mercy, child, where be ye bound? Be ye not content here at the palace? Hath someone given thee cause to depart?"

"Mildred, be at ease. Be it not as it might seem. Hath been given a task by Sir Milford to aid in the search for the archer. Speak with Thomas, will he explain the role hath been given to play," Bridget replied.

Mildred said, "Heavens lass, hath ye given me a start. Thought to lose thee. Well then, come set. Shall fetch thee a bite."

The two sat talking while Bridget ate her breakfast.

Bridget having finished her breakfast, gave Mildred a hug, bid her farewell and left the kitchen.

At the palace gate, Robert stopped and began to question the maiden.

Through a portal in his quarters, Sir Milford saw the guard interrogating the girl. He stepped out onto the courtyard and signaled his permission for her to leave.

Robert opened the gate, allowing Bridget to pass. She thanked him, then continued to the village.

A robust fellow in his mid-fifties, still wearing a night cap, was sweeping the steps leading into the pub when Bridget walked up to greet him.

Bridget went to him, and said, "Good morn, Sir. Might the proprietor of this establishment be about? Wish a word with the gent."

He replied, "Good morn, lass. By thy greeting would suspect ye be a stranger in the village. The gent with whom ye desire to speak be a bit occupied at the moment. He be prancing about these steps with a broom. What be the nature of thy business?"

Bridget replied, "Sir, be from Scotland. Hath come seeking a position at the pub. Held the like in the village of Gretna to the north."

The proprietor of the pub said, "Be ye a comely wench. Me patrons become a bit unruly at times. Will ye bolt should some sot attempt to accost thee?"

She replied, "Sir, hath been there. Woe to he who would dare. For shall he be kissed in good measure with the back of me hand."

"A spirited lass ye be, indeed. At the outset must advise thee, however, there be little could afford in way of compensation," said the gent.

She answered, "Kind sir, but room and board would do me well."

The gent said, "The matter be settled then. There be a wee chamber beyond the kitchen with a cot upon which to slumber. When might ye begin?"

Bridget replied, "Surrender the maiden with whom ye dance, and will tutor her in the jig.

Oh Sir, be named Jinny. The pub bears the name Becket. Shall address thee as Sir Becket."

The two laughed. Becket handed Bridget the broom then entered the pub.

Bridget was quite pleased with herself for having easily completed the first part of her mission.

Completing the task at hand, she retrieved her satchel, took it to her sleeping quarters behind the kitchen, then returned to begin tidying up the pub.

Becket stood watching the maiden, thinking how fortunate he was to have the young lady in his employ. The winsome lass would bring many more young men to his pub.

The presence of her scurrying about that night serving the patrons lent a festive air to the pub.

Becket was quite pleased with her performance.

Chapter 61

Wednesday after midday, Queen Margaret sat in her chambers with Lady Verna discussing preparations for the impending arrival of Countess Sarah and the festivities preceding the wedding ceremony. The meeting was brief for she was well aware Lady Verna was quite capable of preparing for the many guests to be accommodated in the palace and in organizing social affairs.

In Sir Milford's quarters, Bryce was reporting to the commander on his visit to the pub the previous night.

He said, "Sir Milford, Bridget hath succeeded in acquiring a position at the pub. Upon me arrival, entered to set alone at a table. With the wave of me hand, signaled to the lass for a tankard of ale. No words passed 'tween us. Quinn, too, sat alone with a full view of the establishment. Late in the evening, one of the young gents who was permitted a bit much of the ale to pass his gullet lay hands upon the lass. Quinn came to his feet, about to intervene when Bridget cooled the sot's ardor, dousing him with a full tankard of brew, to the delight of the other patrons."

Laughing, Sir Milford replied, "Indeed! Would suspect then the lass will never give ground to anyone. Hath ye done well Bryce; leave us see what the 'morrow hath in store."

Meanwhile, Prince Frederick, the princess, and Lady Victoria had gone to sit out on the terrace after lunch. They were involved in a conversation concerning the relationship between Lady Juliana and the cavalryman, Donald, when Godfrey stepped out onto the terrace.

The butler bowed, then informed the princess the Marquess of Edenhall had come to call.

The princess, displaying a good portion of irritation, instructed the butler to wait a bit then escort the man to the terrace.

Princess Ashley, then voiced her discontent, saying, "Be damned! How much longer must this twit's vile advances be endured? One might expect by now; the ogre would come to learn his persistence in this courtship be but an effort in futility."

Lady Victoria said, "Calm thyself. Thy mother spoke of our coming together to discuss a proper manner in which to rid thyself of this misery. Haps 'tis time."

The sound of footsteps approaching put an end to the conversation.

Edward stepped out onto the terrace and bowed before speaking.

He said, "Good day, Prince Frederick, ladies. Hath come to the village to tend to a bit of business. Thought to stop by in passing."

The group returned the marquess' greeting.

Prince Frederick invited him to sit, then turned to Godfrey and asked him to fetch an ewer of wine and glasses.

The butler went to do his master's bidding.

Edward took a seat beside the prince, then spoke.

The marquess said, "Me Prince, riding to Penrith, observed placards affixed to trees beside the road bearing the name, Leland. Be he not the chap to best all the other archers in the tournament held by His Majesty, and that tutored Princess Ashley in the use of the bow? Must the offense the man hath committed been most severe to warrant such a handsome reward."

The prince replied, "Yea. 'Tis so Your Lordship. Yet, beg thy forgiveness, for at the moment be not at liberty to render thee any further information. Leave us state 'tis a matter solely of importance to the royal family."

The prince quickly changed the subject of conversation by inquiring as to the health of the marquess' father.

Godfrey aided the prince in his attempt by returning with the wine.

For the better part of an hour the group indulged in polite conversation yet guarded, avoiding any reference to the archer.

The conversation was interrupted once again by Tom stepping out onto the terrace, bowing before speaking.

"Me Prince, hath ye need of me? Haps ye not, thought to visit the village."

"Thomas, a 'fore ye ride off, speak to Sir Milford. Will ye abide by the instructions the knight renders thee."

Tom thanked the prince; bowed; then left the terrace.

Tom found Sir Milford fencing with Sir Cartwith. The manservant stood waiting for the men to disengage before speaking.

Tom said, "Sir Milford, forgive the intrusion. Hath thought to ride into the village. Be instructed by Prince Frederick to speak with thee a 'fore leaving."

Sir Milford asked, "Hath ye a desire to visit with the maiden, Bridget? Alas Thomas, me fear 'tis not permitted. Should ye two be seen together, the task assigned to her may be placed at risk. Hath ye an urgent message for the lass; scribe it, then present it to Bryce. Will he pass it to her."

"No need, Sir Milford. Be but a bit concerned for the lass. Shall leave thee and speak to Bryce as to her wellbeing upon the 'morrow," Tom replied.

Tom was a bit disappointed yet understood Sir Milford's reason for refusing him permission to visit with Bridget.

He left the knights, crossed the courtyard, and entered the palace.

Prince Frederick and the others with him on the terrace came walking down the corridor.

Tom bowed as they passed, then took the stairs to his room in the tower.

At the palace entrance, Lady Victoria turned to the prince asking why Tom was still about when he had expressed a desire to ride to the village.

The prince replied, "Victoria, would suspect Sir Milford refused the lad permission to leave. And for good reason."

The prince wisely did not offer any further explanation in the presence of the marquess. He turned, shook Edward's hand, and bade him farewell.

The marquess bowed to the ladies, descended the palace steps, mounted his steed, and rode out of the courtyard toward Edenhall.

Lady Victoria then turned to the prince with a question.

Lady Victoria asked, "Now then, me Prince; for what reason hath the lad been denied permission to go to the village?"

The prince replied, "Victoria, haps be ye not aware of the feelings hath Tom and the lass and she for Tom. The two be smitten with each other. Tom desired to visit with her at the pub."

The princess asked, "Frederick, thought the maiden to be a servant here in the palace! Hath she been dismissed?"

The prince answered, "Nay, Ashley; hath she been instructed by Sir Milford to procure a position at the village pub to be his ears. 'Tis a ruse created to obtain information as to where Leland might be. The knight spoke of it t' other night. Haps ye hath forgotten."

The princess speaking, said, "Victoria, on the 'morrow shall we speak with Mother of this ninny who hath plagued me these many months. Must this annoyance be brought to an end."

Chapter 62

At the breakfast table the next morning, Princess Ashley, still visibly upset over the visit of the marquess the day before, voiced her discontent.

She said, "Mother, something must be done for me to be rid of that Godless twit. The gall of this ogre! Come courting with words of flattery, pretending to be a righteous noble; when 'tis known the treachery within his heart."

The queen replied, "Ashley, calm thyself. Would not do for thee to become distempered oer the likes of this man. Shall we set and speak of it a bit later in me chambers."

Speaking to the prince, the king asked, "Frederick, for what reason might Milford be absent from this table? Hath thought to be given a report this morn."

He replied, "Father, Milford be occupied with Bryce at present. Upon hearing what the lad hath learned, will he come speak with thee."

The prince then turned to the ladies, and said, "Ashley, Victoria, on the 'morrow haps will we ride to the forest. Shall send Tom to the kitchen with instructions for Mildred to prepare a basket of food and drink.

We will take our midday meal by the river."

Elated, the princess replied, "A grand suggestion, Frederick. With a bit of good fortune might we come upon a trace of Leland. Haps a footprint; an arrow spent. Aye, haps 'tis folly yet one must be permitted to hope."

Minutes later Sir Milford entered the dining hall, bowed, extended a greeting to the group, then took a seat beside the prince.

The queen asked if he would like a bit of breakfast.

He replied, "Me thank thee for thy kindness, Your Highness. Hath eaten in the men's dining hall with Bryce.

Unfortunately, the lad hath naught to report. However, would seem the presence of the winsome maiden in the pub hath brought good fortune to the proprietor. Bryce be made to stand. For seats at the tables be occupied.

Bridget will surely be missed upon completing her task therein."

The queen said, "Ye men be engrossed in conversation. We ladies shall leave thee to think through, how to deal with the marquess.

Come Ashley, Victoria; will we retire to me chambers and attempt to resolve this situation involving the oaf."

The men came to their feet as the ladies left the dining hall.

Lady Winfred was tidying up the room when they entered.

Queen Margaret gave the lady-in-waiting a look.

Lady Winfred understood and quickly left the room, closing the door behind her.

The queen said, "Now then, what ere is to be done in this situation must be done discretely. Would not do to cause further hostilities 'tween the duke and the king.

Ashley, haps a note, scribed politely informing the marquess of thy lack of interest in the courtship."

The queen thought a bit, then said, "Ashley, take quill in hand, and scribe as we attempt to compose a proper letter affording the marquess a bit of dignity. Mercy, dignity be not a word, would in truth to be set forth to describe the man. However, when dealing with a fool void of scruples, one must be permitted to take exception."

The ladies laughed at the queen's derogatory remark, then composed themselves and began compiling the contents of the letter.

Lady Victoria said, "At the outset, haps the note should begin informing the marquess will he ere be made welcome at the palace, then an apology for holding him at bay for these many weeks."

The princess replied, "Aye, Victoria; well put. Will me then confess to the marquess me heart be no longer mine to give. For be it held by another. There be no need to inform the imp as to who this other might be."

Lady Victoria said, "Quite pointed, Ashley. In conclusion, ye might afford the marquess a bit of dignity by stating ye yet hold him in high regard. Will it then be complete."

The queen said, "Set ye ladies to compose it properly. Present it to thy sire for approval a 'fore dispatching it to Edenhall by one of the cavalry.

The messenger must be instructed to present the note directly to Edward and no other. Am certain the marquess will be left quite displeased upon perusing it. Yet, let the devil be damned."

The princess and Lady Victoria left the queen's chambers.

Lady Winfred was waiting in the hall to reenter.

The ladies continued on to the chambers of the princess to compose a proper letter for delivery to the marquess.

Chapter 63

Midmorning the next day, Howard, concerned for Leland's wellbeing, knowing the archer had been living solely on fish and game, thought to take him some fresh fruit, vegetables, and loaves of bread. He instructed his mate to fill a basket then a 'foot left for the forest. The smithy came upon Leland fishing on the riverbank. Leland was quite pleased to see his friend and greeted him warmly.

He said, "Good morn, Howard. Be ye missed. What hath brought thee to me stately manor in this enchanted forest? Come, set beside me."

The smithy replied, "Good day, ole friend. Hath ye made light of thy plight of late. Yet, be ye indeed in a wretched state. How long expect ye to survive in this dismal environment?"

"Howard, be me not concerned with meself but with the needy in the village who hath been made to suffer for me folly. Leave us no longer speak of this," replied Leland.

The smithy shook his head, and said, "Very well then, Leland. Hath not come to chastise thee, but to bring thee a bit of fresh fruit, greens, and loaves of bread. For certain hath ye wearied of but fish and game."

Leland said, "Me thank thee, Howard. Leave us pass the morn engaged in pleasant conversation."

Meanwhile after breakfast, Princess Ashley and Lady Victoria had gone to change into their riding attire.

Prince Frederick had sent Tom to have Gavin saddle the horses for the ride to the forest.

The basket of food Mildred had prepared for them, and a blanket were sitting on the landing at the palace entrance.

Some minutes later, Tom and Gavin came to tether the horses to the hitching post beside the palace entrance.

Gavin returned to the stables.

Tom went about fastening the basket and the blanket to Silvermane with strips of hide.

Prince Frederick stepped out onto the landing while Tom was completing his task.

The prince, calling to the manservant, said, "Tom, Shadowmere and Goldentrot bear side saddles. The ladies hath gone to don their riding garments. Quickly return the horses to the stables and instruct Gavin to fit them with Roman saddles."

Tom uttered a grunt as he untied the horses and ran with them in tow back to the stables.

Prince Frederick stood laughing at his manservant's vocal discontent.

Princess Ashley and Lady Victoria stepped out onto the landing, standing silent for a moment, both bearing a look of bewilderment.

The princess asked, "Frederick, what of our mounts? Art we expected to go to the forest a 'foot?"

The prince replied, "Must ye be patient Ashley. Will it be but a bit. Gavin, in error, hath fitted thy steeds with sidesaddles. Look ye. There be Tom with the horses."

The three stepped down onto the courtyard. Prince Frederick mounted Silvermane, and Tom held the reins of the other two horses until the ladies sat comfortably in their saddles.

Crossing the courtyard toward the drawbridge, the guards bowed to the royalty as they pass.

Meanwhile, Leland and Howard were still conversing when they heard hoofbeats on the path.

Leland scrambled for his fishing gear and the food basket and ran to conceal himself beneath the willow.

Howard sprang to his feet, threw his hood over his head, stepped onto the path. With his head lowered, he walked slowly toward the approaching horses.

The riders, upon seeing the man on the path, reined in their horses, and waited for the stranger to come near.

The prince asked, "Me good man, why be ye about in the king's forest this morn?"

Without looking up, the smithy addressed the prince.

He replied, "Sir, might ye hath observed, bear no arms. Thus, hath ye naught to fear of me. Will, however, grant thee a reply.

Hath been to Pategill returning a mare hath a 'fixed with shoes this day past. Thought to pass through the forest for 'tis a shorter route to Penrith than the road."

The smithy then reached up, threw back his hood, and looked up at the riders.

Lady Victoria, seeing the man's face, spoke.

She said, "Princess Ashley, know we this fellow. Be he the smithy hath ye engaged to forge the rings and stakes for the game of quoits."

The princess replied, "Aye, Victoria; be he indeed the kindly smithy in the village."

The princess hesitated, then said, "Sir, should me memory serve me well, recall bear ye the name, Howard. Be it not so?"

Howard replied, "Aye, your Ladyship. 'Tis a wonder ye remember the name of a lowly peasant. Beg forgiveness for me rudeness at the outset. 'Twas not known the gent who spoke be of royalty."

The princess said, "No need for forgiveness, good fellow. At the outset thought ye to be a poacher. Be on thy way. Be well."

Howard bowed as the riders passed him by. The smithy, then realized the princess was the maiden Leland had tutored and the prince had been the archer's hunting mate.

After taking a few steps Howard looked back to see the riders dismount by the huge oak tree. Amused, he chuckled to himself for little did they know Leland was within talking distance from where they stood.

Leland, sitting in his stand, had heard the entire conversation below yet he was not amused. Seeing the princess, he thought of what might have been had the princess been the peasant maiden he thought her to be.

Prince Frederick removed the basket and blanket from his steed, set the basket on the ground, then spread the blanket on the riverbank.

Sitting by the river, they engaged in conversation.

Lady Victoria, knowing Howard resided in Penrith, asked why no one asked the smithy if he knew Leland.

The prince replied, "Victoria, Leland's dedication to the needy in the village in which he resides hath created a bond 'tween him and the villagers. No villager would knowingly divulge any information to a stranger which would place Leland in jeopardy."

The princess said sadly, "Alas, in this very place those many hours with the man, now be left to wonder if haps I should hath been a bit more forward with Leland.

Might he be aware of how deeply he be in my heart, would he not run to me?"

Leland heard every word uttered by the princess and wondered if they were spoken solely with the intention of tempting him to reveal himself.

Chapter 64

Saturday morning, at the breakfast table during the conversation, Prince Frederick expressed a bit of concern for Bridget.

He asked, "Sir Milford, the 'morrow being the Sabbath, the village pub will not be oped. Must the maiden Bridget be made to pass the day in solitude? Surely there be some means for the lass to be permitted a bit of leisure. 'Tis a point to ponder."

The knight replied, "Me Prince, there be but one in the village to whom the lass be known. 'Tis the child, Tiffany; daughter to the widow, Whitney.

Should the child not be about for the day, then Bridget will be permitted to venture out.

Must she return to the pub prior to the other servants residing in the village being dismissed from the palace."

Sir Milford paused for a moment, then continued saying, "Christy and Tiffany be mates. Mildred resides in the butchery with Martin, leaving a vacant bed in Christy's room.

Shall speak to Sir Cartwith instructing him to fetch the tot to the palace to pass this night and the 'morrow with Christy. Will it be an arrangement pleasing to all."

Relieved, the prince said, "By George, Sir Milford; 'tis an excellent course hath ye set forth. Hath ye eased me concern. See to it."

After breakfast, Sir Milford went to speak to Sir Cartwith.

He found the knight watching some of the men at a table outside the barracks at a game of maw.

The commander tapped the knight on the shoulder, then spoke.

He said, "Sir Cartwith, might ye accompany me to me quarters? There be a matter of little consequence. Yet. it should be addressed."

Entering the commander's quarters, they sat to speak. Sir Milford explained the situation of Bridget not having any relief from her task at the pub to his subordinate then asked Sir Cartwith if he would mind bringing Tiffany to the palace to spend the night, and much of the Sabbath with Christy.

Sir Cartwith Replied, "Sir Milford, this ye request of me be not an imposition, but an opportunity to pass the 'morrow with me lady. Shall fetch me steed, ride to the village and return within the hour."

Sir Milford said, "Sir Cartwith, might ye come upon Bryce instruct him to come to me quarters for hath need of the lad."

The knight nodded, then left the room to go to the stables.

On his way to the stables, he found Bryce playing at a version of English football with his peers.

He gave Bryce the commander's message, then continued on to the stables.

The page immediately left the game, running to see to his master.

Entering Sir Milford's quarters, Bryce asked Sir Milford how he could be of service.

Sir Milford replied, "Bryce, when at the pub this night speak briefly to Bridget. Inform the maiden she will be permitted to mingle with the villagers on the 'morrow if she so chooses. Must she return to the pub prior to the dismissal of the palace servants."

Meanwhile, at the stables, one of the stable boys had saddled Sweet Sorrow.

Sir Cartwith mounted his steed and rode off to the village.

Howard was tinkering in his shop when Sir Milford rode up to the millinery. The smithy called a greeting to the knight.

Howard said, "Good morn, Sir Knight. Hath it been a bit since last we spoke."

The knight waved, dismounted, tethered his horse, then walked over to speak with the man.

Sir Cartwith replied, "Good day, Howard. How fair thee this morn? What be ye about of late?"

Howard replied, "Be in good stead, Sir Knight. This day past in the forest, come upon a young gent, Princess Ashley, and Lady Victoria. At the outset, they thought me to be a poacher.

'Twas fortunate Lady Victoria be present to intervene. She informed the gent, be me known to her as the village smithy. Otherwise me might not hath fared too well."

The knight laughed, and said, "Howard, the gent be Prince Frederick. Hath we been seeking the archer for weeks with no success, causing the prince and princess a bit of distress. Might ye hath noticed the placard posted in the village."

Howard a bit surprised said, "Mercy, the gent be the prince! Prey be he not offended, for paid him no mind."

The smithy then said, "Hath seen the posting in passing. Yet, paid it no mind for tend to be occupied with me own affairs."

Sir Cartwith replied, "Shall leave thee. Intend to fetch Tiffany to the palace to visit with her mate. Be well, good fellow."

Sir Cartwith left the smithy to take the stairs to the flat above the millinery.

His knock on the door was answered by Tiffany.

Seeing the knight, she smiled then jumped into his arms.

The knight carried the child into the flat.

Whitney was sitting at the table in the kitchen having a cup of tea with Eleanor.

Greeting them, he said, "Good morn, Eleanor, Whitney. Hath come for the little one."

Whitney, pretending to a little annoyed said, "Eleanor, who be this fellow? Might he be known to thee? Should we run him off or bade him welcome?"

Eleanor said, "Good morn, Sir Knight; must ye tread lightly, for me fear Whitney hath of late been plagued with neglect."

Sir Milford replied, "Eleanor, haps would me do well to summon a physician. Nay, hath a potion of me own to remedy her affliction. Must the lady wait, however for the potion to be administered. This day hath come for Tiffany. Should her mother permit, shall return with the lass to the palace. Will she pass this day, night, and the Sabbath with Christy."

Tiffany pleading, asked, "Mother, might it be permitted?"

Whitney replied, "Tiffany, shall consent solely upon thy pledge to behave. Must ye be courteous, and not go about the palace in soiled garments."

Tiffany said, "Mother, pledge not to dishonor thee. Shall be ere the lady."

"Very well then; come. Will we prepare a satchel with fresh garments for thee to don upon the Sabbath," Whitney replied.

Sir Cartwith set the child down.

Whitney rose from her seat, took Tiffany by the hand, and led her into the bedroom. The knight stood talking with Eleanor until the two returned.

He bade Eleanor a good day. Then, with Tiffany and Whitney, he stepped out of the flat.

On the landing Whitney told the child to go wait for the knight beside Sweet Sorrow. She waited for the child to be out of sight, then put her arms around the knight and kissed him before speaking.

Whitney asked, "Sir Knight, what might this potion be ye intend to minister to ease me neglect?"

He replied, "Prepare on the 'morrow, with a basket of food, shall come fetch thee. We will ride to Haweswater and partake of the food by the lake, then shall I ravage thee."

With a haughty attitude, she asked, "Indeed! Should me resist thee as punishment for thy neglect, what then Sir Knight?"

Laughing, Sir Milford replied, "Alas, me love; must ye not. For, there will,then be two bearing like maladies with no recourse but to suffer."

Chapter 65

Three days passed with nothing for Bryce to report to Sir Milford from Bridget at the pub, frustrating the commander.

Prince Frederick, in an attempt to prevent Princess Ashley from losing hope, had ridden with her and Lady Victoria to the forest Monday, and intended to take her again this morning.

Tom was in the kitchen speaking with Mildred. Lamenting over Bridget's absence from the palace.

He said, "Mother, be left quite displeased with this task assigned to Bridget. Be concerned for her wellbeing. Long for her return."

She replied, "Thomas, be she well protected by Quinn. No harm will befall the lass. Sir Milford hath stated would she be in the village at most a fortnight. Bear in mind, hath she been called upon to aid in restoring joy to our princess. Be patient."

Meanwhile in the forest, Leland had finished his breakfast of bread and cheese Howard had brought and was about to hunt when the sound of someone approaching drove him into his tree stand.

From his vantage point, he saw five men walking the deer run from the road. By their appearance, Leland ascertained they were not of the military nor were they from Penrith. None of them was familiar to him. Only one of the men was finely dressed.

As they drew near, the archer could hear the well-clothed man shouting orders.

The man shouted, "One of ye lads continue upon the path. At the entrance to the forest, stand and watch for anyone coming to the woodland from the castle. Ye others, scatter and look about with a keen eye. Should we find the archer, will me deal with the bastard properly."

The men drew their weapons and began thrusting their swords into the underbrush as they walked along the path.

Leland wondered what the men were doing in the forest. Then, realized the men were searching for him for the reward and they had no intention of bringing him to the king alive.

The archer stood up in his stand with his bow at the ready. Should anyone step beneath the branches of the willow, he was prepared to let fly his arrow. From his position of advantage, he could have easily slain the others before they were close enough to do him any harm.

The search had gone on for nearly an hour when the man who had been chosen to be the sentry at the forest entrance came running to tell the marquess that riders were approaching.

The marquess signaled to the others to leave the woodland.

Leland watched as they ran from the forest toward the road.

Some minutes later, Prince Frederick, the princess, and Lady Victoria rode onto the deer run and dismounted at the riverbank.

The prince looked around for a moment and walked along the path. He stopped to examine bushes and clumps of grass, then turned to speak.

He said, "Someone hath been about. 'Twas not one, but many. See there upon the path, bits of brush, trampled grasses, and footprints going to a. The underbrush be hacked with swords. Others hath come to search for Leland. Haps for the reward set forth by Father. Might they yet be about. Best we leave in haste."

The three quickly mounted their steeds and rode the path out of the forest.

As they rode the hill toward the palace Lady Victoria spoke.

She said, "Mercy! Leland may be in peril. Something must be done to protect Leland, and with haste."

The prince asked, "And what might ye suggest, Victoria? Art we to station soldiers about the forest? Would then, not Leland be led to believe the men stationed there to be an effort to restrict his movements?"

Princess Ashley was in tears. Lady Victoria's efforts to comfort the maiden fell on deaf ears.

Suddenly, the princess spurring her steed to a gallop toward the palace.

Prince Frederick and Lady Victoria quickly followed.

Meanwhile, Leland sat on the stand attempting to sort out what had just taken place. One thing was certain to him; the forest was no longer a safe place to hide. The men who had come looking for him this morning would certainly soon return.

Minutes later, Princess Ashley rode into the courtyard of the palace and dismounted Goldentrot. Leaving the horse unattended, she went directly to her chambers.

Prince Frederick and Lady Victoria, following close behind, rode up to the palace entrance and dismounted. The prince grasped the reins of the three horses and called for assistance, while Lady Victoria followed the princess to her chambers.

Stable boys came running to relieve the prince of the horses.

Prince Frederick went directly to speak with Sir Milford to recount the events of the morning. They passed the remaining part of the morning attempting to devise a method to insure the archer's safety, then went to lunch.

Entering the dining hall, Sir Milford bowed to the royalty.

Prince Frederick took his seat beside the king.

The knight sat beside the prince.

Princess Ashley and Lady Victoria were not present.

The queen quickly inquired, "What might be keeping those two? Shall instruct Godfrey to fetch them."

The prince quickly said, "Mother, refrain from doing so. Will they not be coming to the table. Ashley be in a sorry state oer what hath come to pass in the forest this morn. Might ye indulge me, shall relate to thee the incident in its entirety."

With a bit of concern, the prince continued saying, "Upon arriving at the river, 'twas apparent, others hath been there earlier.

Grasses be trampled and portions of the underbrush severed with swords lay upon the deer run. There be footprints all about. Someone other than our soldiers be seeking Leland.

Me fear the archer may be in danger. Might ye well imagine the thoughts coursing through Ashley's mind."

The queen, expressing concern, said, "Good Lord! Husband, something must be done. Should ill befall the archer, Ashley will be lost."

The prince said, "Mother, hath discussed with Sir Milford that very concern. Shall leave it for him to relate the course hath we thought to follow."

Sir Milford said, "Your Majesty's, must we assume Leland hath taken sanctuary in his beloved forest. Should this be so, soldiers roaming about will impede the man's ability to sustain hisself.

The presence of the soldiers would affirm what he hath thought since fleeing the castle, that be he pursued for lack of respect for the royal family. Thus, thought to station sentries at the forest entries from dawn unto dusk, one upon the hillside, and another upon the road.

The men art to challenge anyone attempting to enter the forest."

The queen said, "These men seeking Leland may well hath been doing so for the reward set forth by thee, Husband. Should they succeed in finding him, Leland will surely resist, and haps be slain. Mercy, the thought of it!"

The king said, "Milford, act quickly in the posting of sentries at the forest entrances. These rascals must not be permitted another opportunity to approach the archer."

"Will see to it immediately, Your Majesty," replied the knight.

Chapter 66

Bryce entered Sir Milford's quarters the next morning to wake him. The commander was in his bed, already awake. Bryce spoke quickly, certain the knight was about to reprimand him for not reporting to him the night before.

He said, "Forgive me, Sir Milford, for delaying in rendering thee a report from the maiden. Bridget came to me early on, whispering for me to wait for all the patrons to leave the pub.

"'Twas near midnight a 'fore she returned to speak.

Hath she heard men speak of the archer, and his ability to evade the soldiers. Leland doth indeed reside in the village. Might the maiden be told to return to the palace?"

Sir Milford replied, "Nay, not yet Bryce. Soldiers art to be deployed this morn to peruse the village for signs of the archer.

Should the lass suddenly vanish, might she become suspect."

Resuming, Sir Milford said, "This night must ye return to the pub. Approach the maiden with caution.

Instruct her to speak to the proprietor politely, informing the gent upon the morn of the Sabbath, that she hath procured a more favorable position.

She will then be permitted to return to the palace."

Upon completing this task hath assigned thee, there be no further need of thee at the pub. The presence of Quinn at the establishment to protect the lass will suffice."

The knight paused, then said, "Now then, Bryce, go to the palace and return to inform me when King Frederick and the queen hath entered the dining hall."

Bryce left the room to do his master's bidding.

Sir Milford dressed then went to Sir Cartwith's quarters.

Entering the room, he said, "Good day, Sir Cartwith; hath a task for thee to quickly perform this morn.

From early light unto sunset, soldiers art to stand guard at entrances to the forest, one upon the hillside, another upon the road to Clifton.

No one must be permitted to enter.

Two other men art to be sent to the village. They must not bear arms, nor must they question the villagers. They art to simply peruse the village for signs of the archer. Relieve the men at proper intervals. Shall advise thee when these assignments will no longer be required."

Sir Cartwith replied, "Shall see to it within the hour, Sir Milford."

They left the room together

Sir Cartwith went to carry out the commander's orders and Sir Milford returned to his quarters to wait for word from Bryce.

Minutes later, Bryce returned to tell Sir Milford that the king and queen had entered the dining hall.

The knight thanked him then left the room to join the royal couple at the table.

Upon entering, he bowed, then said; "Good morn, Your Majesties. Prince Frederick, Princess Ashley, and Lady Victoria hath not yet arrived. Art they expected?"

The queen replied, "Frederick will be a bit late. As to the others, with the frame of mind Ashley be in of late, one be left to wonder when they will be about."

Sir Milford said, "Me Queen, might the princess and the Lady be summoned? 'Tis certain the information given Bryce by Bridget this night past and reported to me this morn, will afford the princess a bit of encouragement."

The queen replied, "Indeed, Milford. Be she be in dire need of a bit of good news. Go ye then, speak with Godfrey. He will fetch the ladies."

The knight bowed and was about to leave when Prince Frederick entered. Sir Milford bowed, bade the prince a good morning, then left to speak with the butler. Returned minutes later, He bowed, and took his seat at the table beside the prince.

Princess Ashley and Lady Victoria entered the dining hall.

Sir Milford stood, bowed, then waited for them to sit before returning to his seat.

Princess Ashley spoke with a bit of annoyance.

She said, "One be not permitted a bit of solitude? Hath no desire to sit in idle chatter this morn. What matter of urgency requires me to come to this table?"

The queen replied sternly, saying, "Ashley, look ye about. Everyone at this table be committed to bring the matter at hand to a joyful conclusion and hath labored hard to that end. Solely ye hath conceded defeat. Milford hath a bit of news thought to be of interest to thee. Set ye. Heed well and display a bit of grit.

Proceed, Sir Milford."

Sir Milford spoke, saying, "At the outset, me Queen, leave me inform thee that Leland doth reside in Penrith.

In an effort to learn more about the archer's movements, two soldiers art being dispatched to the village. Will we maintain a presence, therein; from early dawn to dusk, unto 'tis no longer required."

Continuing to speak, Sir Milford said, "In an attempt to protect the bowman from harm while in the forest, sentries hath been posted upon the hillside and the road to Clifton. Hindering access to the woodland by anyone. They will remain at their post from early light unto the dark of night."

The king said, "Well done, Milford. As to another matter, hath received a message from Earl William this eve past.

Countess Sarah with Lord Morley and Lady Juliana will be arriving this week next. Earl William, Lady Rebecca, Lord Gaelan, and family will be arriving the week to follow."

He went on to say, "Milford, 'tis not known precisely when the countess nor the earl art to arrive. Thus, the sentry's art to keep a keen eye out for their approach. They art to be greeted properly."

He then added, "This matter of Leland must not be discussed in the presence of our guests.

Will we, however, continue upon our quest, and discuss our progress clandestinely. Heed well, this shall demand of thee. Ye will, despite thy feelings within, display a festive posture when in the midst of our guests."

The queen, addressing the king, said, "Husband, the countess will be occupied assisting me in the preparing a list of guests to be invited to the ceremonies."

The king replied, "Margaret, Lord Morley will be left to Lord Fendril, for hath they much to discuss. Now then, what of the Lady Juliana?"

The prince chuckled, and said, "Father, Lady Juliana be not one to sit and pass the day in idle chatter. The Lady's interests lie in much more physical activities."

King Frederick laughed boisterously.

The others at the table did not understand the humor in the statement made by the prince.

Chapter 67

Four days passed. Leland was constantly on the alert, expecting the men who had come searching for him to return. To his wonderment, he was left undisturbed. Perhaps the search had been abandoned. Yet, were that so, why had not Howard come to him? Reluctantly, he decided to investigate.

Cautiously, he walked the deer run toward the forest entrance on the hillside. Nearing the entrance, he saw the sentry standing guard. Retreating, Leland made his way to the entrance on the road to find the other entrance manned by a soldier as well.

Leland returned to sit beside the river and assess his situation. He then thought King Frederick was determined to find him, and the king was quite certain he had taken sanctuary in the forest. Thus, the sentries had been posted to restrict his movements.

Many of the residents in the villages surrounding the forest had been to the archery tournament and had seen Leland in the competition. Were he to leave the forest and be seen, surely someone would be tempted to inform the king and claim the reward. Only in the village Penrith would he not be betrayed.

Leland realized he was in dire need of information, were he to survive. The only one who would dare provide it was the smithy. The archer needed to slip past the sentry to get to the village.

The bowman waited until sunset to make his way to within sight of the sentry, then sat to wait.

When only rays of candlelight could be seen emitting through the windows of the cottages in the village did Leland begin to crawl cautiously toward the forest entrance. To his delight, he found the guard had abandoned his post.

Being the Sabbath and after dark, the village was quiet. Leland easily made his way to the smithy's to tap on the back door.

Howard asked who was calling.

The archer identified himself in a whisper; asking the smithy to lower his lantern. Leland waited for the light of the lantern to fade, then entered.

Leland said, "Good eve, Howard. Forgive me for disturbing thee at this late hour, yet hath no other recourse. For there be sentries posted at the forest entrances unto sunset."

The smithy replied, "Mercy, Leland; hath ye placed thyself in peril wandering about. Hath seen the soldiers at the forest. Hath they hindered thee from leaving, and permitted no one to enter, as well. For this reason, hath not come to thee.

There hath been soldiers about the village from early light unto twilight. Fear for thee, me friend."

Leland said, "Howard, 'tis for this information hath come to thee. Knew not what hath been a 'foot beyond the forest."

Howard turned to his wife, and said, "Woman, make haste. Prepare a bite to eat for Leland then a place for him to pass the night.

Leland expressing his gratitude said, "A bit of food will surely be welcome. Yet, dare not pass the night herein for would set thee in harm's way. Shall retire to me hut, then return to the forest a 'fore dawn."

Continuing he said "Howard, 'tis not right for the villagers to suffer for ills committed by another. Upon this, shall need to ponder for a time."

Leland sat to eat the food prepared for him, bid his friend, and mate a good night, then went to his hut.

Entering, he lit a single candle, gathered the remaining edible food in the hut into a blanket, and set the parcel by the door to take with him in the morning. He then lay on his cot deep in thought.

Knowing the soldiers were not allowing anyone access to the forest, permitting him to roam as he pleased was no consolation. Leland came to realize but a few courses remained for him to follow. He could sustain himself in the forest at least until winter and attempt to flee or surrender. None of the options appealed to the him.

Chapter 68

Well before sunrise the next morning and after a restless night, Leland, with his parcel of food left the hut for the forest. Although quite familiar with his surroundings, he chose to sit at the entrance to the forest and wait for some activity at the castle.

At first light, four soldiers stepped through the palace gate and marched down the hillside. At the fork in the road, two of the men broke formation and walked toward the village. The other two continued on toward the forest.

Leland came to his feet and took the deer run to the river. From the blanket he had taken with him, he took two boiled eggs and a bit of cheese to eat for breakfast.

Late in the morning he decided to hunt for his evening meal, but his heart was not in it. Preoccupied with his plight, he ignored a grouse he had flushed from a thicket.

Later in the day, he slew a rabbit to roast for his supper.

In the waning hours of the day, he again walked within sight of the soldier at the forest entrance and waited for him to leave before returning to his hut.

He had wearied of being hunted as a beast in the forest. Soon autumn would give way to winter, and he would need to brave the chilling wind and snow.

Leland sat in his hut that evening, agonizing over his situation. He had lost the maiden he had come to love, and the joy of the hunt. The inability to no longer provide for the needy in the village also weighed heavily on the archer. Not wanting to eventually be set upon by a host of ruffians bent on collecting the reward, he chose to accept whatever punishment he was to be given by the king. He decided to surrender himself to the knight who had relentlessly pursued him.

Owing an explanation of his decision to the smithy, he left his hut and walked to the blacksmith shop to speak with Howard who was at his forge.

Howard turned to him, then displayed a look of concern before speaking.

The smithy said, "Leland, 'tis madness for thee to be about when soldiers be yet in the village. Should ye be recognized, will it be the death of thee."

Leland replied, "Howard, 'tis no longer a concern. Hath come to inform thee of me intent. The king be determined to succeed in me apprehension. Soon, in desperation, will he send many soldiers to scour the village. The villagers will be made to suffer. There be others in me pursuit as well; some with intent to slay me. Hath been hunted as a beast in the forest. 'Tis time for this to end. For hath wearied of this chase.

A'fore sunrise, shall send a message to the king's commander, advising him of me decision to surrender. Will he be advised to come to the clearing beside the river at mid morn this day next. There, he will find me standing with me bow and quiver at me feet, offering no opposition."

The smithy said, "Leland, hath ye lost thy wits? Will it be the end of thee. Surely there be some other recourse to follow."

"Howard, hath pondered long upon this decision. Wish not to pass me days in flight. Hath ye been a good friend as be many of the villagers. Would lose all respect for meself, should any of thee be harmed for me indiscretions."

Leland went to hug his old friend, then turned and walked away.

The smithy called after him. The archer ignored him and continued on to sit in his hut and write his message to Sir Milford.

He attached the note to an arrow in his quiver then waited for the night to pass.

Chapter 69

Well before sunrise Tuesday morning, Leland left his bed, picked up his bow, quiver, and left his hut.

He walked to within range of the castle walls, launched the arrow bearing the note into the castle gate, then walked down the hillside into the forest.

Hearing the sound of the arrow strike, Robert opened the gate and saw the arrow with the note attached imbedded in the gate. He dislodged it and took it to a lantern hanging on the castle wall.

Seeing the note addressed to the commander, he ran to Sir Milford's quarters, and pounded on the door.

The knight, startled awake, came to his feet, turned up the flame on the lantern beside his bed, then opened the door to see Robert standing with the arrow in his hand.

The knight said, "Ye Gads, Robert! What hath ye found to be so pressing as to awaken me at such an ungodly hour?"

Quickly, Robert said, "Sir Milford, forgive me for the disturbance. Dared not wait unto the morn to wake thee. For thought it to be a matter of some importance. This arrow be launched to strike the gate but moments past. There be a message attached addressed to thee."

Sir Milford took the shaft from the guard into the light of the lantern. He recognized it immediately as being one of Leland's.

He thanked and dismissed the guard. The commander, then sat on his cot to read the note.

The battle-hardened warrior could only imagine what the archer was going through. Had Leland known the true reason for being pursued, he would have been spared weeks of torment.

The knight waited for the palace to come alive before leaving his quarters to go tap on the door to the king's chambers.

Lady Winfred opened the door for the knight to enter.

Sir Milford found King Frederick still in his nightshirt, sitting at a table and sipping a cup of tea.

The knight bowed and stood waiting for the king to speak as Lady Winfred returned to help the queen with her garments.

The king said, "Good morn, Milford; what hath brought ye to me chamber at this early hour? Come set ye beside me."

The queen addressed the lady-in-waiting saying, "Lady Winfred, might ye fetch Sir Milford a bit of tea from the kitchen?"

She replied, "Will see to it, me Queen; shall return shortly."

Lady Winfred bowed, left the room, closed the chamber door behind her, then stood in the hall listening to the conversation being held within the room.

Sir Milford said, "Your Majesty, hath received a note from Leland in the wee hours of the morn. The archer hath wearied of the chase. Will he be at the clearing in the forest at midday upon the 'morrow; waiting to surrender."

The queen, concerned, said, "Husband, haps would be best for no one beyond these walls to be made aware of this. Might it be best for thee and Milford to fetch Leland. Should no others be with thee.

The fewer approaching Leland, the less chance for a mishap, resulting in an injury to the archer.

Might something go awry, Frederick and Ashley will never forgive thee. For, the burden of blame will then be upon thee.

The king agreed, and replied, "So it shall be, Margaret; share thy concern for the bowman, thus will we proceed with caution."

Turning to the knight, the king said, "Milford, come the 'morrow will we proceed to the forest. We shall bear no arms.

Leland is to be certain we mean him no harm. The agony hath we inflicted upon this man will soon come to an end."

The queen said, "Husband, Sir Milford; speak kindly to the bowman. Must he be made at ease. Shall leave ye men to devise a plan to insure the archer's safety."

Sir Milford rose from his seat and bowed. He waited until the queen left the room before returning to his seat.

Minutes later, Lady Winfred returned with the knight's tea. King Frederick and the knight sat for a while in idle chatter before Sir Milford excused himself, bowed, and left the room.

Chapter 70

Early the next morning, the marquess, disguised as a monk, left Edenhall to ride to Penrith. He had received a message the previous night, informing him the archer who stood in the way of his winning the hand of the princess would be in the forest in the clearing beyond the river by the huge oak tree. The note also advised him there were sentries stationed at the forest entrances.

When at a distance, well out of sight of the castle and the sentry at the forest entrance, the marquess dismounted his steed, tucked his bow and quiver beneath his robe, then took the road toward Clifton and walked slowly past the sentry.

Out of sight of the sentry, he shed the robe then entered the forest through the underbrush and made his way to the deer run.

He followed the path to within range of the clearing, then concealed himself to wait for Leland.

The archer came to the forest at mid-morning. He crossed the river over the fallen tree and stood in the clearing to wait for Sir Milford. His bow and quiver lay at his feet, as his note to Sir Milford had stated.

Leland had resigned himself to his fate and intended to show no opposition to being apprehended.

Hearing hoof beats in the distance, the marquess came to his feet. He stepped out from behind a tree and let fly an arrow striking Leland in the upper thigh.

As the king and Sir Milford drew near, they saw the arrow strike the archer but could not see the assailant.

Leland fell to his knees.

The marquess, seeing he had only injured the archer, reached to his quiver for a second arrow. He set the arrow to his bow and was about to release it when he heard horses approaching.

Startled, the marquess hesitated for a few moments, fearing discovery. He thought it prudent to flee.

In the meantime, Leland had picked up his bow and an arrow; set the arrow to his bow, and let fly the shaft, striking the marquess in the chest. The marquess fell to the forest floor.

The king and Sir Milford reined in their steeds and dismounted to assess the scene. It was obvious to them that the assailant had intended to murder the archer, and that Leland had acted in self-defense.

The king quickly told Sir Milford to ride and order the sentry waiting on the hillside to hurry to the castle, and return with four men, a litter, and a cart.

Sir Milford quickly remounted and spurred his steed to a gallop as King Frederick crossed over the river on the fallen tree to kneel beside Leland.

Leland said, "Your Majesty, do with me as ye wish, for hath wearied of this game of fox and hound. Yet, in me defense, must say hath it been known to me at the outset that the lass encountered here in this forest be the princess, would hath shunned the maiden as the plague.

Be left bewildered as to why the princess continued to return to the forest, surely not out of interest for a peasant! Thus, upon entering the dining hall, and finding the maiden hath come to love be the princess.

Alas! To then learn the man hath befriended in the forest standing beside me, be the prince. I thought to be made the court jester. In ire, fled, insulting the royal family.

Seeing the soldiers, the next morn entering the forest, 'twas certain to me be hunted for me impudence toward thee and thyne.

When the prince and princess entered the forest a few days later and spoke kindly of me. Thought it to be but a ploy, tempting me to reveal meself."

The king said, "Leland, for a man so skilled and bright of mind, be ye a fool in matters of the heart. Will we speak on this a bit later.

Must commend thee, 'twas quite a feat to discharge an arrow as ye knelt wounded and down the lout attempting to slay thee. Will he be identified by Sir Milford upon his return, then the matter dealt with. Shall ye be taken to the palace and tended to by me physician."

The king hesitated, then said, "Hath but one question for thee at the present, which hath plagued me since the day of the tournament. Why chose ye to refuse the purse, then to request permission to hunt the forest in its stead?"

Leland replied, "Your Majesty, in the village Penrith, there be widows, orphans, and the infirmed in need of sustenance.

When yet a lad, be me too left to fend for meself. Be fortunate for me sire hath tutored me well in the use of the bow a 'fore passing. When a man, took it upon meself to render aid to those less fortunate. The king's forest be a means to that end."

Sir Milford returned with the foot soldiers and the litter. The cart and the other two soldiers remained at the entrance to the forest on the hillside.

The knight dismounted his steed and went to identify the assassin lying on the forest floor.

The knight exclaimed, "Damnation! Your Majesty, 'tis the marquess! Hath he expired. Thought to slay Leland to rid hisself of a rival. How be it known to him Leland would be at the clearing this very morn? Your Highness, hath we a conspirator in our midst."

The king replied, "Indeed Milford! Edward be deserving of his fate, and the one who rendered that bastard aid must be found."

The king then turned to the soldiers, and said, "Ye others, heed well this be about to state. Must ye dare not speak of this ye hath seen."

Continuing, the king said, "At the present must we tend to the archer. As to who rendered aid to the marquess in this treachery, shall it soon come to light.

One of ye men go, remove the arrow from the swine lest the corpse be found, and the arrow identified."

Speaking to the others, the king said, "Two of ye lads fetch the archer, and tote him to the cart. Leland must be taken to Sir Milford's quarters.

Ye men must then return to remain with the marquess. A 'fore sunset tote the cur to the hillside. The cart will be waiting. Place the marquess in the cart. Instruct the men in the cart to wait unto sunset, then under cover of darkness, go cast the coward into the waters at Pooley Bridge; never to be found. A fitting end to a tyrant's treachery."

The soldiers crossed over the river on the fallen tree with the litter. They placed Leland in it, then carried him out to the cart.

The king mounted Morgan, Sir Milford mounted Titus, and they rode toward the castle.

At the drawbridge they reined in their horses. The king told the guard to fetch the physician and bring him to Sir Milford's quarters.

The guard ran to do the king's bidding.

The king and the knight continued on to the stables. They handed the reins of their horse to Gavin, then went to talk in the knight's chambers while waiting for the soldiers to arrive with Leland.

The king said, "Milford, indeed there must be someone in the castle conspiring with the marquess. We must learn who hath rendered aid to Edward in his attempt to slay Leland."

The knight replied, "Aye, Your Majesty; will begin by discovering who delivered the message to the marquess. He may well be within our ranks. The messenger and the conspirator may be one in the same. Haps not, then the conspirator will be known to the messenger. Must speak to the sentry guarding the forest entrance at the road as to how the marquess passed unseen as well."

Sir Milford, hearing the rumbling of the cart's wheels in the courtyard, went to open the door.

The cart came to a standstill before him. The soldiers quickly took hold of the litter and carried it into knight's quarters. They removed Leland from it and set him on the cot.

The soldiers bowed to the king before leaving the commander's quarters.

Several minutes later, the physician arrived with the guard. King Frederick dismissed the guard.

The physician tended to Leland. The arrow had pierced Leland through the upper thigh.

Cutting through the arrow beyond the arrowhead, the physician removed the feathered end of the shaft from the wound. Saltwater was used to rinse the wound. A salve was applied, and the thigh bandaged with a cotton fabric.

Addressing the king, the physician said, "Your Majesty, the wound be not severe. A fortnight, haps less a 'bed will be required. Will return upon the 'morrow to inspect the wound and change the bandage."

The physician stood from Leland's side, bowed to the king, and left the room, closing the door behind him.

King Frederick and Sir Milford stood over Leland for a moment before the king spoke.

He said, "Well then, Leland, good fortune hath smiled upon thee. Within a fortnight will ye once more be a 'foot. Rest ye now."

The king turned to Sir Milford and said, "Milford, wait unto the palace be a 'bed, then Leland will be taken to a chamber on the second level of the palace. Naught is to be said of this unto the conspirator hath been identified.

Two trusted sentry's art to be posted at the chamber door at all times. No one, other than we two, the queen, Bryce, and the physician will be permitted entry."

Through all this activity, Leland could not yet understand why such a fuss was being made over him. He then posed a question to the king.

He asked, "Your Majesty, be left to wonder, all this intrigue be not a waste in effort? Shall me not be punished for me insults to the thee and thy family?"

The king replied, "Leland, shall enlighten thee. Hath it long been known the archer who launched the arrow sparing me son from the charging stag, and the man who aided in the capture of the lad Jarin, the horse thief, be one in the same.

'Twas then suspected the archer to be a poacher, hunting the forest with no regard for the king's law. Hath the savior of me son been a noble, would there be no reason for the man to avoid detection."

Puzzled, Leland asked, "Your Majesty, how be it known the two events be related? Be me not seen by anyone."

Chuckling, the king replied, "Indeed, be thee quite skilled in the art of concealment. Two stags be slain that day in the forest; one by Frederick, t' other by the archer.

Later that evening, men be dispatched to retrieve the felled stags. But one of the animals remained. Solely the one slain by the archer. Upon examination of the stag by Frederick and Ashley, the arrow found imbedded in the carcass be much longer than one used by the prince, and its feathers be that of a raven.

Days later, at the site where the horse thief be found bound to the birch, a broken arrow be found as well. Upon comparing the shaft to the one imbedded in the stag fetched from the forest, they be deemed alike.

With this evidence, Frederick thought to identify and reward thee for sparing him from the charging stag. 'Twas not known however yet, be ye a poacher with honorable intent, or haps but a poacher and a man without honor. Thus, he thought to befriend thee not as a prince, but as a fumbling son of a layman. Would ye never approach the lad hath he been garbed as a noble.

Leland, the tournament, though enjoyed by the participants and the observers, be held simply to entice thee to participate.

Sir Milford with Bryce manned the targets seeking an arrow with raven feathers. By these feathers be ye identified.

Unto that day, Ashley hath deemed thee but a poacher to be punished. 'Twas not unto she stood with Frederick at midafternoon upon the ramparts, observing the competition, ye be seen by her with the children. Ye then became a man of interest to her.

The prince upon befriending thee spoke of thee as a gentle, caring man. Hearing this, the princess too expressed a desire to befriend thee.

Garbed as a village maiden, Ashley came to the forest with that intent. Within those many days, she came to hold ye dear.

The prince erred in coming to the palace with thee that night for be ye not prepared to discover Ashley to be the princess. Should it hath been left for Ashley to reveal this to thee at the proper time. Thought ye then to be played the fool, thus in ire ye fled.

Will leave thee with Milford, for the present. On the 'morrow, shall come speak with thee once more."

Chapter 71

It was past noon when the king left Sir Milford's quarters. Leland lay on the cot with the knight sitting by his side.

Sir Milford was certain the archer was quite confused and had many questions in mind, wanting to be answered. The knight thought to give the archer some time to absorb all that had happened earlier.

He then said, "Leland, hath me not eaten since early morn; would do with a bite of food. Shall leave thee for a bit. Rest easy; will ye not be disturbed."

Sir Milford left the room to go to the kitchen.

The midday meal was being served in the dining hall. Mildred was standing at the sturdy table at center of the kitchen when he entered through the side door. The knight went to the cook and whispered to her.

He said, "G 'day, Mildred. Might ye prepare two plates, and a ewer of grog? Bryce will come by to fetch them."

Mildred replied, "Aye, Sir Milford; yet must ye forgive me, will it be a time for we all be occupied serving the royal family. There may be a need for Bryce to wait a bit."

The knight said, "Mildred, 'tis understood; there be no need for haste."

The knight quickly left the kitchen and walked across the courtyard with intentions of returning to his quarters.

He saw Bryce standing in front of the barracks, engaged in conversation with a group of soldiers.

Sir Milford went and told Bryce to wait a few minutes, then go to the kitchen and speak to Mildred.

The knight, then returned to his quarters to continue his conversation with Leland.

Entering, Sir Milford said, "Leland, must admit these months past, hath ye given me quite a task. Might ye not hath thought to surrender, me thinks ye would never hath been found."

"Sir Knight, 'twas not with ease. Yet oft when pursued, thy men be well within range of me arrows."

Curious, Sir Milford asked, "Pray tell, from whence come the arrow slaying the stag charging the prince?"

Leland laughed and said, "Recall ye the willow beside the river? Hath fashioned a stand within its branches. The stand afforded me a view of the deer run and the clearing beyond the river. Hath removed many of the branches hanging to the forest floor and left others for concealment. This permitted me to see out yet not to be seen.

'Twas from the stand me shaft be launched."

Leland continued, asking; "Sir Milford, this marquess of whom ye spoke. Why hath he sought me out to be slain? Be there some reason not known to me for the man to wish me harm?"

"Leland, the oaf hath wooed the princess for months with intent to wed, not for love of the lady, but for power. Upon learning the princess' heart belonged to another, he thought to rid hisself of his opponent. The tyrant be well deserving of his fate.

The marquess be not alone in this treachery. Hath he an accomplice who will soon be found and punished severely."

Leland said, "Sir Milford, speak ye of love. Love or no, a king would demand that his daughter be wed a man of royal lineage, surely not a peasant."

"Leland, this ye say be true. Yet a king hath the power to bestow a title upon any man be deemed worthy.

Would one expect an orphan to one day become commander of the king's forces? Here set me beside thee," Sir Milford replied.

Leland, curious, asked, "Sir Knight, there be many other matters be me left upon to wonder. What sort of man would permit a young maiden to wander about the forest alone, much less a princess?"

Sir Milford smiled, and replied, "Ah! Me friend, never be the princess alone with thee unto be ye deemed a man of honor.

Unbeknown to thee, stood me within view of all hath passed 'tween ye two. Prepared to defend the princess should she be in peril. Must pledge to thee, however, what ere hath seen shall never pass me lips."

Bryce came with their food, interrupting the conversation. He waited for them to finish then gathered up the dishes.

Sir Milford spoke as Bryce was leaving.

He said, "Bryce, this hath ye seen, herein, must be kept secret. Go ye now, there be no further need of thee. This man must be left to rest."

Chapter 72

Sir Milford had no intention of waiting to find the perpetrators of the conspiracy. He went to Sir Cartwith's quarters to speak to the knight.

He said, "Sir Cartwith, assemble the soldiers and the cavalry, leaving only the palace guards at their posts.

March the men to the flats and wait; will join thee shortly. Upon returning, might there be a need to replace the palace guards with other men. Will me address it in the flats, sending those now at their posts to the men's dining hall. Shall advise thee then, should the changing of the guards be needed."

Sir Cartwith hurried out of the room to do his commander's bidding without asking any questions.

Sir Milford returned to sit beside Leland, waiting to hear the troops leave the courtyard.

Minutes later, he went to the stables for Titus, mounted, and rode to the flats. He reined Titus to a stand before the assembled men and dismounted.

He walked slowly between the rows of troops and dismounted cavalry with his hands clenched behind his back.

Returning to stand before the men assembled, Sir Milford turned to face them before speaking.

He said, "Hath ye been assembled for me to impose a question upon thee. Shall there be no punishment for a reply.

Anyone who hath been given a message to be delivered these two days past, come forward."

Sir Milford waited a few minutes. Six of the cavalrymen broke ranks. The commander ordered the six to return to the palace and wait for him in the men's dining hall.

He then turned to Sir Cartwith and said, "Sir Cartwith, return the men to the palace, then come to the dining hall.

There be no need to replace the guards at present."

Mounting Titus, Sir Milford rode to the castle to wait in the men's dining hall for the six men and Sir Cartwith.

Returning, the men entered the dining hall, and stood at attention.

Sir Milford asked if any of them had delivered a message given them directly by the king, queen, prince, or princess. If anyone had, they were to step forward.

Four men broke ranks. They were dismissed.

The knight, then asked the remaining two men who they had been given a message by and to whom it had been delivered.

Asher stepped forward to say he had been given a message by Sir Cartwith for the widow Whitney at the millinery in the village.

Quinn then stated he had delivered a message to the minstrel, Rowan. Given to him by Lady Winfred.

Sir Milford asked, "Quinn, must ye know where the minstrel resides. Thus, ye with Asher, make haste. Go fetch this minstrel. Must ye not return lest ye hath the man in hand. Upon returning to the castle, cast the man into the dungeon. Advise the jailor the man must not be permitted to speak with anyone. Inform me upon thy return."

Addressing Sir Milford, Quinn said, "Sir Milford, the minstrel resides nearly a league from Penrith. Must we not be expected for a time."

Sir Milford replied, "I understand. Go ye, in haste."

Sir Milford asked Sir Cartwith to accompany him to his quarters.

On entering the room, Sir Cartwith stood a moment looking at the archer lying wounded on Sir Milford's cot with an expression of surprise.

Seeing Leland, Sir Cartwith exclaimed, "Mercy, Sir Milford; be this not the archer who emerged victorious in the tournament? Why be he concealed in thy quarters?"

Sir Milford replied, "Leave me acquaint thee with Leland. Aye; be he the victor in the competition. Too, be the archer who spared the prince from a charging stag and be he the captor of the horse thief as well."

Sir Cartwith greeted the archer saying, "G 'day, Leland. Must say, be ye a sly fox indeed. Go ye about the forest unseen as a spirit.

Sir Cartwith paused, then continued, asking; "Sir Milford, how come this archer by this injury?"

In a lengthy explanation, Sir Milford replied, "Sir Cartwith, this shall me hence reveal to thee be not for the ears of others.

Since the competition, hath we attempted to ferret out Leland at the request of the royal family. With no success.

But two days past, be informed by Leland his willingness to surrender to me in the forest. This be known to but a few.

This day, mid morn in the forest, an attempt be made to slay Leland. The assailant be slain.

Others art involved in this treachery. Shall they soon be known to me.

Of the six cavalrymen bearing messages these two days past, four be dispatched by the royal family. T' others carried messages from thee, and Lady Winfred.

Sir Cartwith, 'tis certain hath ye no reason to harm Leland. Thus, but one remains, Lady Winfred.

When apprehended, Rowan, the minstrel, will be questioned. Might there yet be others involved in this treachery, the fate of these conspirators will be decided by the king."

Permitting Sir Cartwith to absorb all that had been said, the commander paused for a moment, then continued.

Sir Milford said, "Late this night, Leland shall be moved to chambers in the palace. Two trusted soldiers and a litter will be needed to transport him. Not a word of Leland's presence in the palace must be spoken.

Shall wait in me quarters for Asher and Quinn to return with the minstrel."

Leland recognized the knight. He waited for Sir Milford to finish with his instructions to the man, then spoke.

Leland said, "Sir Cartwith, hath seen thee in the forest with Sir Milford one day at the hunt. Hath me, a bit earlier slain a buck. Hearing thee approach, thought to conceal meself.

Ye men went off with me kill. Must confess, be me not pleased with thee at that moment."

Sir Cartwith turned to his commander, and said, "Sir Milford, recall ye the stag we found slain when at the hunt? Be we left to wonder who hath slain such a fine beast, but to leave it.

Hath the stag been felled by Leland."

Sir Milford replied, "Aye, Sir Cartwith; recall it well. Leland, 'twas proper payment for thy poaching. Me men dined well that night."

The three men burst out laughing. They, then spent some time recounting the episode of Leland apprehending Jarin.

Sir Milford asked the archer how he had known that Jarin was being sought for a crime.

Leland replied, "Sir Milford, hath but moments earlier seen the rider being pursued upon the hillside by the cavalrymen. A bit later, come upon the same man in the forest. Found it quite humorous seeing ye men come upon the lad, bound to the birch."

Sir Cartwith said, "Leland, must ye hath been within viewing distance of the scene at the time."

Chuckling, Leland said, "Indeed, Sir Cartwith; be a few paces away. Concealed prone in the underbrush. Nearly be tread upon by ye gents!"

Once again, they burst out laughing.

Chapter 73

It was nearly midnight when Asher and Quinn arrived at the palace with the minstrel. Quinn took Rowan to the dungeon, while Asher went to the commander's quarters for Sir Milford who waited with Sir Cartwith.

They all walked to the dungeon.

Entering the dungeon, Sir Milford ordered the cavalryman to wait outside before speaking to Rowan.

Sir Milford, addressing Rowan, said, "Well Sir, haps be left to wonder why be ye brought to Penrith at this ungodly hour. Leave me enlighten thee.

Hath been informed ye hath been receiving information from someone residing within the palace.

Now then, take care to speak true for might ye be found to lie, will ye be punished severely. What be the nature of this information, and to whom be it relayed?"

A bit shaken, Rowan replied, "Sir Knight, be they writ and sealed. By whom they be writ be not known to me for be given to me by a cavalryman. Thought them to be letters 'tween two lovers.

Be compensated by the proprietor at the pub in Edenhall. And well deserving of it, for much of me time be passed in the to and fro."

Sir Milford asked, "Rowan, the proprietor at the pub. What name doth he bear? Yea too, broke he the seal to read the note?"

The minstrel replied, "Aye Sir, the seal be broken. Stood to wait for the man to peruse the notes and haps to response. The proprietor be named Floyd."

Sir Cartwith interrupted the conversation. He asked Sir Milford for a moment. Calling him aside, Sir Cartwith whispered to the commander.

He said, "Sir Milford, the minstrel be known to me. Hath seen him at the pub some time past when in Edenhall. He stood at a table with a chap identified by the barmaid as the proprietor. Suspect the minstrel speaks true."

Sir Milford nodded, then said, "Sir Cartwith, upon the 'morrow, ye with Asher, and Quinn art to play the role of peddlers.

In a cart, ride to Edenhall. Wait for the sun to set, then lure the proprietor from out the pub. Attempt to seize him without detection. Restrain the filthy cur, then return with him to the palace. The soldiers art to be told not to speak of this event."

Leaving the dungeon, Sir Milford returned to his quarters.

Sir Cartwith stopped to speak to Asher and Quinn.

He instructed them saying, "Ye two men art to stand guard at a chamber door in the palace this night. Speak to no one.

Asher, fetch a litter, then come to Sir Milford's quarters. Quinn, come with me."

Leland was taken to a vacant room on the second level of the palace. Asher and Quinn took their positions on either side of the chamber door.

Several minutes later Sir Milford entered and dismissed Sir Cartwith, then sat beside the archer through the night.

Well before sunrise, Sir Milford went to the barracks. The knight rousted two men from their cots, telling them to dress and replace the men at their post at the palace. He instructed the men not to permit anyone to enter and to speak to no one.

Sir Milford left the palace and walked to the dungeon.

Entering, Sir Milford said; "Mortimer, be ye me ears. Another is to be brought herein for thee to tend. Heed well all be said 'tween the minstrel, and the one yet to arrive. Shall ye then reveal to me all hath transpired 'tween the two. Remain alert."

The knight then entered Jarin's cell, woke him gently, and quietly instructed the lad to follow him.

Outside the dungeon, Sir Milford again addressed the lad.

He said, "Fear not lad, for be me not displeased with thee. T' other prisoner must remain alone for reasons need not be known to thee.

Aye; 'tis a bit early. Nonetheless, go ye to the stables, not to return unto the 'morrow. Hath ye been obedient, and hath labored hard in the stables. Art ye to be commended. Shall soon speak to the king upon thy behalf. Expect the king will agree to pardon thee."

Tears falling to his cheeks, Jarin thanked Sir Milford. He, then hurried off to the sables in obedience to the knight.

Sir Milford left the dungeon. He returned to sit beside Leland and rendered a more detailed account of why the marquess had attempted to slay him.

The knight remained at his side, thinking of the caliber of the man before him. Sir Milford fantasized as to what he could achieve if all his men were as skilled as the archer.

Chapter 74

That morning, Prince Frederick came awake to the stirring of people in the palace. He went to the privy, washed, then donned the clothes laid out for him by Tom.

Leaving his room, he saw the two guards standing in front of a room he thought to be vacant.

Approaching, he addressed the guards.

The prince asked, "Ye men, these chambers be not occupied. For what reason, be ye on guard before these doors?"

One of the men replied, "Forgive me, Prince Frederick; be commanded by Sir Milford to speak to no one, and to forbid entry to everyone. Haps Your Highness might best be served requesting an explanation from the commander."

The prince did not press the guards any further. He walked off wondering what Sir Milford was up to yet trusted the knight to have a valid reason for not wanting anyone to enter the chamber.

The conversation outside the room startled Leland awake who had been napping. He came to a sitting position in the bed, to see Sir Milford sitting beside him.

He said, "Sir Milford, Gad Zeus! Set ye beside me through the night and this morn as well. Hath me not slept in such comfort through all me days."

Sir Milford replied, "Good morn, Leland; remain at rest. Soon the physician shall be by to tend to thy injury. Will ye then be given a bit to eat."

Sir Milford went and open the door to inform the guards the physician would soon be by. They were to permit the man to enter.

Several minutes later, the physician entered the room. Sir Milford told him he was leaving, but someone would soon come with breakfast for Leland and would remain with the archer.

The knight left the room, telling the guards Bryce would be by with food. They were to permit him entry.

Leaving the palace, Sir Milford noticed the drawbridge had not yet been lowered and Sir Cartwith in the cart, waiting to leave the castle.

Instructing the guard, Sir Milford said, "Robert, lower the drawbridge. Men in a cart hath requested permission to leave the palace. Art they to fetch a parcel for the king. Shall they return well into the night. The drawbridge must be lowered permitting them entry."

Sir Milford then returned to his quarters.

Bryce was tidying up the room. The paige was told to go to the kitchen and ask Mildred to prepare a plate of food and a bit of tea. He was to wait, then take the food to the chambers on the second level with guards posted at the door. He was to sit with the occupant until relieved.

Sir Milford then went to speak to the king.

Lady Winfred was helping Queen Margaret dress for breakfast when the knight entered.

Sir Milford bowed asked for a word with the king.

The king held up his hand, instructing the knight to hold, then said, "Good morn, Milford; be me not fully clothed yet. Might ye wait in the garden? Shall join thee in a bit."

Sir Milford was pacing to and fro in the garden dreading to have to tell the king one of the ladies-in-waiting had played a major part in the attempt to slay the archer.

Several minutes later, the king came to the garden, and said, "Well then Milford, Leland be in good stead this morn? What news hath thee of the conspiracy?"

Sir Milford replied, "Aye, Your Majesty; the physician be with the archer as we speak.

Our suspicion of a conspiracy to slay Leland be valid. For some time, messages hath been dispatched from the palace to Edenhall by a lady in the palace. Cavalryman Quinn delivered them to the minstrel, Rowan.

They, then be taken by the minstrel to the landlord of a pub in Edenhall. Both Quinn and Rowan swear the messages be sealed when they be given to the proprietor. Thus, knew they naught of what be writ within.

The seal be broken and read by Floyd, the proprietor of the pub in Edenhall. Rowan stood waiting for haps the man might wish to reply. Never be one given."

The king said, "Milford, no one will be accused of any ill deed, lest one be found to bear witness to this Floyd breaking the seal and reading what be writ within.

Should what Quinn and Rowan had stated be true, then the information be given to the marquess by this Floyd."

The knight replied, "Your Highness, then Quinn and Rowan be but messengers. Playing no other part in this treachery.

Rowan be held in the dungeon. When he and Floyd speak together, desire to know what might be said 'tween the two.

Sir Cartwith with two men shall leave for Edenhall soon to apprehend and return with Floyd by midnight."

The king said, "Milford, hath ye not as yet divulged the name of the lady who hath dispatched these messages to Edenhall."

"Your Majesty, be me saddened to say, hath she been identified by Quinn as the Lady Winfred."

The king angered, replied, "Be damned! Lady Winfred! What must be done with the wench?"

A while later, King Frederick went to visit Leland.

Bryce quickly came to his feet when the king entered. He bowed to the king and wished him a good day.

The king instructed the lad to wait in the hall while he had a few words with the archer.

Bryce left the room, closing the door behind him.

The king said, "Good morn, Leland. Leave me speak a bit. Ye art to heed well me words.

Haps unbeknown to thee, the royal family hath held thee in high regard. Hath we erred grievously in many ways. Thus, be ye forced to live in misery. 'Tis time for amendment. Henceforth, shall ye bear the title of Lord Thomas, Keeper of the Loaf. Be ye charged with providing for the widowed, orphaned, and infirmed in the village Penrith, and hamlets throughout the realm.

Thy appointment to Lordship shall be announced at a feast in the great hall with another forthcoming event to soon be celebrated. However, will it be a bit. Shall ye remain within these quarters unto ye hath recovered a bit from thy injury. Sentries will remain on guard at the door, permitting but the chosen to enter.

Thy presence in the palace will be known to but a few. Should the Duke of Edenhall learn the marquess hath been slain by thee, he will seek vengeance.

This sordid conspiracy be yet investigated. Unto those involved hath been identified, and sent beyond the ears of the duke, be ye in mortal danger."

Leland replied, "Your Majesty, ye honor me. Words elude me. At present, might me request a boon of thee?

'Tis known to a dear friend in the village of me intent to surrender. Will he assume by me absence, hath been apprehended and cast in the dungeon. Might not the man be informed of me wellbeing?"

"Lord Leland Thomas, hath ye been quite secretive in the past. Thus, know not from whence ye came nor the name of thy mate," said the king.

Leland said, "Me King, hath a cottage in the village Penrith. The man of whom me speak be the smithy, Howard, residing therein."

"It shall be done. Rest ye now. What ere might ye be in need of or desire, Bryce shall fetch it for thee. We will speak on the 'morrow," replied the king.

King Frederick bade the archer a good day and left the room.

Leland was not happy about having to be confined to his room for so lengthy a time. Being a free spirit, he would soon be yearning for his days at the hunt.

He lay thinking. Had the king given him a title for some reason other than the deeds he had performed? To the archer the deeds surely were not worthy of a Lordship. Yet, when he lay in the clearing, wounded, with the king beside him, His Majesty spoke of the archer's lack of understanding in matters of the heart. What matters of the heart was the king referring to? Surely not the love he had for the forest maiden.

When in the forest with the princess, Ashley had declared her love for him. Had she been sincere?

Was the king then speaking of Princess Ashley? These many questions, with no answers, were then dismissed thinking them to be wishful thinking.

Bryce entered the room with a breakfast tray, interrupting Leland's thoughts. He asked Leland how he was feeling.

The archer replied, "Lad, hath lain upon this cot with visions of foppery, yet quite awake. Me thinks haps hath become a bit demented."

Bryce had no idea what the archer had just said to him. Thinking the archer might be a bit delirious from his injury, the paige offered no reply.

Bryce passed much of the day tending to Leland's needs.

Sir Milford came to relieve Bryce a bit after the knight had eaten his supper and stayed until Leland had fallen asleep.

Weary, Sir Milford, then returned to his quarters to nap until Sir Cartwith returned with Floyd.

It was well past midnight when Sir Milford was awakened by a tapping on the door.

With permission, Sir Cartwith entered, apologizing to the commander for the intrusion at such a late hour.

He said, "Sir Milford, hath but moments past returned from Edenhall with the proprietor of the pub. Be he taken to the dungeon by the soldiers. The man offered no resistance when taken in hand.

Hath attempted to ferret out a bit of information from the man of this conspiracy with no success. He chose to remain silent."

Sir Milford replied, "Well done, Sir Cartwith. Haps for good reason hath he refused to speak. Might he be burdened with guilt.

There be naught remaining to be done this night Sir Cartwith. Shall Floyd be pressed to speak on the 'morrow.

Chapter 75

Bryce entered Sir Milford's quarters early the next morning to wake him.

Coming awake, the commander instructed the paige to fetch Sir Cartwith to him. Minutes later, Sir Cartwith came as requested, accompanied by Bryce.

Sir Milford said, "Good morn, Sir Cartwith. Might ye summon one of the men to relieve Mortimer.

Return ye with the jailor. We will then hear what the minstrel and Floyd hath said, one to t' other. 'Tis certain words be exchanged 'tween the two this night past.

Turning to the paige, Sir Milford said; "Bryce, go ye, tend to Leland. He will be in need of a bite. Remain with the archer unto hath ye been relieved."

The two went off to do the commander's bidding.

Sir Milford washed and dressed, then sat to wait for Sir Cartwith to return.

Sir Cartwith returned with Mortimer some minutes later.

Sir Milford addressed the jailor saying, "Good morn, Mortimer. Hath requested for thee to be me ears this night past. Hath ye remained alert as to what transpired 'tween the two prisoners?"

Mortimer replied, "G 'day, Commander. Aye! Might the two hath been within reach of each other, one surely would not hath survived the night.

At the outset, both remained silent. The minstrel paced to and fro, then accused t' other of involving him in a conspiracy. The man brought to the dungeon by Sir Cartwith denied the minstrel's accusation. He, then stated hath he no knowledge of a conspiracy. Curses then passed 'tween the two most the night."

Sir Milford praised the jailor saying, "Well done, Mortimer. Go ye, fetch the minstrel to me. Art we to speak to him. There will then be no further need of thee. Ye art to return to thy post, relieving the soldier."

Sir Milford to the knight, and said, "Sir Cartwith, be ye certain the man ye hath seen at the pub in Edenhall waiting beside the owner, Floyd be the minstrel?"

Sir Cartwith replied, "Aye, Sir Milford; when first set eyes upon the man, thought him to be familiar. Yet then could not recall where be he seen a 'fore. In the dungeon, it came to mind. Be one of the musicians at the celebration of Earl William's return from Leeds."

The door to Sir Milford's quarters opened. The jailor nudged the minstrel into the room.

Mortimer leaving, closed the door behind him and returned to the dungeon.

Rowan stood visibly shaken, fearful of his fate.

Sir Milford looked at the man for a minute before speaking.

He said, "Rowan, would seem thy recount of these events doth bear a bit of consideration. Some doubt yet doth remain. Unto the investigation of this conspiracy be completed, art ye to remain incarcerated. Heed ye well these instructions shall now render thee.

Should Floyd press thee for information as to what hath transpired within these quarters, must ye dare not reply. 'Tis understood?"

The minstrel replied, "Indeed, Sir Knight; be a bit relieved. For in spite of what ere be said to thee by Floyd of me part in this, will ye soon deem me words to be true."

Sir Milford then spoke to his subordinate saying, "Sir Cartwith, return Rowan to the dungeon. The king awaits word of our progress in this investigation. Will be speaking to his Majesty readily."

Sir Cartwith left with the minstrel.

Minutes later, Bryce entered to tidy up the room, expecting the knight to be at breakfast.

The paige was about to retreat when Sir Milford said, "Good morn, Bryce; thought to take me morning meal in me quarters. Go ye to the kitchen, fetch me a bite, then go tend to Leland.

Remain with the archer unto ye be relieved. Thy chores may be left to wait."

The sentries at Leland's chamber door had surely been seen by one or more of the royal family. Thus, Sir Milford was not about to sit at breakfast in the dining hall dodging questions as to why the unoccupied chambers were being guarded.

Should the question be posed upon him, he would have no recourse but to lie. He thought to wait until after breakfast. He would, then speak to the king in private.

Bryce returned to Sir Milford's quarters with the commander's breakfast. Without hesitation, he left to tend to Leland.

The commander finished eating, then went to Sir Cartwith's quarters to have a word with him. The two exchanged greetings, then Sir Milford spoke.

He said, "Might ye be requested to appear in the throne room this morn. Should ye receive such a message, ye art to proceed in the following manner.

Send sentries to stand guard at each entrance to the throne room.

With Quinn, fetch the minstrel and Floyd. Floyd unshackled. Ye must, then proceed to the entrance to the throne room to wait.

When all the people involved in the conspiracy be present, His Majesty will enter.

Instruct the sentries at the entrance to permit no one to enter nor to leave, then enter the room with Floyd."

Sir Cartwith replied, "As ye wish, Sir Milford. Art we to put an end to this treachery this day?"

Sir Milford answered, "Haps this day, haps another. Will it be left for His Majesty to decide as to how we art to proceed. Shall present all be known to the king this morn."

Sir Milford left the knight's quarters to enter the palace.

He ran into the prince, princess and Lady Victoria leaving the dining hall. He bowed, then asked if the king was still at breakfast.

Prince Frederick replied, "Aye, Sir Milford; be they about to leave. Be ye missed at the table. Father inquired as to where ye might be."

Sir Milford said, "Must beg forgiveness of His Majesty for me absence. Hath been a bit occupied this morn. Must leave thee, me Prince, for there be a need to speak to thy sire."

The knight bowed, then hurried down the hallway to the dining hall.

The prince, princess, and Lady Victoria stood watching the knight leave, wondering what the reason for the urgency might be.

Sir Milford entered the dining hall. The king and queen sat alone. He bowed and requested a word with the king.

The king held up his hand, and said, "Milford, hold."

He then turned to the queen, and said, "Margaret, haps 'tis time for thee to learn what hath been a 'foot these days past.

Shall we retire to the garden. What is to be said must not be heard by others."

The three walked out of the dining hall to the far end of the garden. The king and queen sat on the stone bench. The knight stood before them.

King Frederick addressing the queen, said; "Margaret, as planned, two days past, rode to the forest accompanied by Milford to meet with the archer."

Excitedly the queen asked, "Husband, hath ye found the archer? Haps so, where might he be? Be he in good stead?"

He replied, "Margaret, be silent for a moment. Might ye recall, Milford received a note from Leland stating he hath wearied of the chase and desired not to pass his days being pursued. Thus, thought to surrender, and resigned hisself to accept what ere punishment might be bestowed upon him?"

The king paused, then said; "As we approached, an arrow be launched by an assailant then not known, striking the bowman in the thigh. Leland fell to his knees.

The assassin, seeing the archer be but wounded, thought to let fly another.

Leland's bow and quiver lay at his feet. The archer quickly fetched his bow, and an arrow. He let fly the shaft, mortally wounding the cur."

"Mercy, there be no end to the dear lad's suffering. And who might the tyrant be in this dastardly attempt to slay the archer? And for what purpose?" asked the queen.

The king replied, "Margaret, 'twas the Marquess of Edenhall. The swine intended to rid hisself of an opponent in the pursuit of Ashley's hand. However, be he not alone in this treachery. There be others involved as well. Milford at present be in pursuit of these others.

Margaret, it might be prudent for Frederick nor Ashley to know naught of this for a time."

Shocked, the queen said, "The marquess! Be we then rid of the bastard! Hath he been given a just reward for his treachery.

Husband, pray ye hath not left the archer wounded, alone in the forest. Where might he be at present?"

The king replied, "In chambers, upon the second level of the palace. Hath been tended to by me physician, Milford, and Bryce. Sentries be posted; permitting no one to enter. Be not concerned Margaret, the injury be not severe."

"Husband, Ashley hath not been herself since the night Leland fled the palace. Might she in the least be made aware of where the archer might be?" asked the queen.

The king sternly replied, "Nay, and for good reason. Knowing Edward hath been courting Ashley, 'tis certain his sire will soon be about. inquiring as to the disappearance of his son. The less be known to Ashley of it the better and Frederick as well."

The king, then turned to the knight, and said, "Now then, Milford, hath Sir Cartwith returned to the palace with the proprietor of the pub in Edenhall?"

Sir Milford replied, "Aye, Your Majesty; the man be held in the dungeon. Thus, all those who hath taken part in this conspiracy hath been identified. Await thy instructions as to how we art to proceed."

The king then spoke to the queen saying, "Margaret, one of the participants in this treachery be quite near to thee. Never would one suspect she be capable of involvement in such a foul deed. Doth pain me to inform thee, be the Lady Winfred."

Disbelieving, the queen said, "Frederick, this cannot be! Be ye certain of this? For what reason might Winfred collaborate with the likes of the marquess?"

The king hesitated, then said, "Know ye well the viper hath courted Ashley not for love, but to enhance his position. Haps the marquess hath pledged to grant the Lady Winfred favors should he succeed in his quest. No matter, the lady hoped to gain by her involvement with this caitiff imp. Thus, must she be made to suffer the consequences of her actions."

Then to the knight, he said, "Milford, all the parties in this plot and the witnesses to it, art to be taken to the throne room. Must ye take measures to insure the secrecy of this meeting."

Sir Milford replied, "Your Majesty, in anticipation of thy decision, took the liberty of instructing Sir Cartwith as to how to proceed. Will speak with him immediately. Shall we await Your Majesty in the throne room."

"Milford, hath been left quite disturbed by this occurrence. Wish not to be present at these proceedings. Might ye first inform the sentries on guard at the door to Leland's chambers, shall soon be by to visit with him?" asked the queen.

"As ye wish, me Queen. Shall see to it," replied Sir Milford.

Sir Milford bowed, then left the garden to go and give the sentries the instructions given him by the queen.

Entering the chambers in which Leland lay, the knight told the paige and Leland of the queen's intentions to visit.

Sir Milford asked Bryce to step into the hall when the queen arrived.

He then addressed the archer saying, "Leland, need ye not rise to bow to the queen. Hath Her Highness been made aware of thy injury. Thus, will she not deem it a sign of disrespect should ye fail to do so. Bryce will return upon the queen's departure. Be at ease."

The knight left the room and went looking for Godfrey. Finding the butler in the kitchen, he asked the butler to deliver a message to Lady Winfred requesting her presence in the throne room.

Leaving Godfrey, Sir Milford went to speak with Sir Cartwith.

Finding him in his quarters, he said, "Sir Cartwith, proceed as instructed. King Frederick will come to sort this matter out then render a decision.

Everyone must enter the throne room through the men's dining hall. The less seen, the better."

Sir Cartwith replied, "Shall it be seen to, precisely as hath been instructed, Sir Milford."

Sir Milford left Sir Cartwith to go and wait for everyone to assemble in the throne room.

Lady Winfred was the first to enter. She asked the commander why she had been summoned. The knight asked her to be patient.

Minutes later, the door to the throne room opened. Sir Cartwith entered with Quinn, Rowan, and Floyd.

Sir Milford stood watching Lady Winfred. He noticed the lady had become quite agitated.

Some minutes later, the king entered. The men bowed; Lady Winfred curtsied.

King Frederick paused to look at everyone present for a minute, then took his seat on the throne before speaking.

He then said, "There be the scent of a conspiracy within these walls. A few 'mongst ye gathered here stand accused of treachery. Hath learned messages be passed from the palace to a pub in Edenhall. Information in these messages be used in an attempt to slay a man of honor, two days past.

Be forewarned, should ye wish to speak in defense of these charges, choose well thy words. For, solely the truth shall gain thee mercy.

Now then, Quinn; what part played ye in this conspiracy?"

Quinn replied, "Your Majesty, be but the messenger. Knew naught of that be writ within the letters; solely the recipient, Rowan, the minstrel."

The king then speaking to the minstrel said, "Rowan, the letters be given thee by Quinn. Be the information within for thy own use? Haps not, then for what purpose be these letters passed to thee?"

He replied, "Your Highness, hath no knowledge of their contents for be they sealed. Be instructed upon receiving the notes they were to be taken to the pub in Edenhall."

"Rowan, from this be said thus far, these sealed messages be given to Quinn by one in the palace with knowledge of Princess Ashley's movements. Who pray tell might that be?" asked the king.

When Rowan and Floyd had entered the throne room, Lady Winfred realized the purpose of these proceedings. Were she to lie to the king, it would be the death of her. Aware of this she stepped forward.

She said, "Mercy! Your Majesty, never thought the information in the notes sent to the marquess be used in an attempt to slay another."

A bit angry, the king said, "Regardless Winfred, as lady-in-waiting to the queen, know ye well what ere be heard or seen within these walls must be kept in confidence. For what reason chose ye to betray that confidence be of no importance to me. Thy willingness to partake in this treachery hath led me to believe ye not to be loyal to those who feed and care for thee, but to a serpent.

Rowan, hath stated earlier these letters be delivered to a pub in Edenhall. The recipient of these messages be among those gathered here?"

Rowan replied, "Aye, Your Majesty, be he the proprietor of the pub, Floyd."

The king turned to the proprietor of the pub, and said, "Floyd, come forth. Hath Rowan spoken true? Hath these letters be delivered to thee? Haps so, when received, be they yet sealed or oped?"

"Be merciful, Your Highness, the minstrel hath spoken true. The letters be yet sealed upon their receipt," Floyd replied.

"What then be done with these messages, Floyd?" asked the king.

Floyd replied, "Your Majesty, they be read, then cast into the hearth at the pub."

The king asked, "The name of the villain who attempted to slay the archer in the forest be known to thee?"

He replied, "Your Highness, pledge to thee, be not certain who it might hath been. When the marquess come to the pub, that be scribed within the notes be related to him. Haps 'twas the marquess hisself."

With finality in his voice, the king said, "Floyd, pray hath ye been well compensated by the marquess for thy part in this treachery, and hath enjoyed the purse of silver for a bit. However, 'tis time for retribution."

The king turned to the minstrel, and said, "Quinn and Sir Milford hath spoken well of thee, Rowan. 'Tis apparent, hath ye no knowledge of the conspiracy under foot. Hath ye been exonerated. Be at ease. Yet, be ye aware ye may be in mortal danger, for soon there will be men sent to silence thee. Suggest ye make haste and leave this place for parts unknown; never to return."

The king instructed Quinn to escort the man out of the palace.

He then to the lady-in-waiting and the pub proprietor and said, "Now then, Lady Winfred, Floyd. I hath no desire for further bloodshed. However, ye two art to be punished severely for thy part in this treachery. Ye art to be escorted forthwith to the port of Silloth. There will ye be secured passage upon the next ship to set sail for the Americas. Dare ye never return to these lands. For were I to hear of it, shall ye then be seized and sent to the gallows.

Sir Milford, see to it!"

Without another word, King Frederick came to his feet and left the throne room.

Sir Milford turned to address Sir Cartwith.

He said, "Sir Cartwith, summon the sentries at the entrances. These two art to be taken to the dungeon for the present. Guards art to be posted at the entrance with instructions to permit no one to enter nor to leave. Preparations art to be made to escort the Lady Winfred and Floyd to the port of Silloth upon the 'morrow."

Chapter 76

Before King Frederick had left the queen prior to going to the throne room, the king told her he was going to bestow upon Leland, the title of Lord, Keeper of the Loaf, and would make it known on the day he announced the upcoming marriage of Prince Frederick to Lady Rebecca.

She stood, went to kiss him on the cheek, and said, "Frederick, hath ye pleased me with this disclosure. Leland be well deserving of a title. Shall it afford the man the opportunity to court Ashley with no fear of reprisal."

He replied, "Margaret, might he not be of royal blood, yet find him to be more honorable than many who now bear a title simply by birth.

Must leave thee, Love, for justice waits to be served."

The king left to go to the throne room.

Queen Margaret followed, taking the stairs to visit with Leland.

Seeing the queen approaching, one of the guards opened the door to Leland's room, permitting her to enter.

Bryce came to his feet, bowed, then left, closing the door behind him.

The queen addressed the archer, saying; "Good morn, Leland. Pray be thee in good stead.

Be told by the king several moments past, will he bestow upon thee the title of Lord, Keeper of the Loaf. Be ye well deserving of it, Leland."

She paused, then continued saying; "Hath ye been tended to properly?"

Leland replied, "G 'day, me Queen; forgive me for not rising. Be a bit hampered at the moment. Sir Milford and Bryce hath been most attentive. Be not deserving of this title ye speak."

She said, "Indeed, ye be. Shall we not speak of it further.

Unfortunately, Leland, the prince and princess will not be coming by to visit. Hath they no knowledge of what hath occurred these days past, and for good reason.

The absence of the marquess from Edenhall by now, must be of much concern to his sire. Soon, the duke will be sending men about attempting to discover the reason for his son's disappearance.

Ashley and Frederick hath no knowledge of what hath occurred in the forest. 'Tis best they be left with the ability to respond truthfully to any inquiries made of them by the duke's men."

He replied, "Understood, me Queen, yet quite arduous for me to comprehend. What possessed a man of stature to act with such evil intent upon a lowly commoner?"

The queen responded, "Must one assume the marquess thought thee to be a rival in his quest to wed the princess. Thus, sought to eliminate the competition. Hath he paid dearly for his treachery.

'Twas indeed fortunate hath ye the strength to slay the cur a 'fore the coward launched a second shaft in an attempt to complete his task."

Leland said, "Your Highness, never hath it been me intention to launch a shaft to slay another. Me arrows be meant for the hunt, and the hunt solely, to sustain the needy in the village. Launched me shaft to slay the assassin solely to defend meself.

His Majesty and Sir Milford be familiar to me. Seeing the two upon the deer run approaching, then to be struck by the arrow. I harbored no doubt, the attempt to slay me be not by order of the king. For, might His Majesty wished me slain, the deed surely would not hath been carried out in such a cowardly manner."

The queen smiled and said, "Leland, soon this horrid chain of events will be put to rest to one day be but a dimming memory. Thus, leave us henceforth speak of more pleasant matters.

At the outset, Ashley thought of thee as but a rogue poacher in need of punishment. She lay eyes upon thee at the tournament. Ye then became a man of interest.

The prince, in thy debt, thought to acquaint hisself with thee in an effort to measure thy character.

Upon the prince befriending thee, ye then became the subject of conversation at the dining table.

The more Ashley heard of thee, the more she desired to meet with thee.

Certain ye would wish to avoid an encounter with an approaching lady of royalty, she thought to present herself to thee as a village maiden. O'er the weeks passed with thee in the forest, ye became quite dear to her."

"Be this as ye say Your Highness, Then, be not fetched to the palace by the prince but to be played the fool?" asked Leland.

The queen replied, "Nay, Leland; hath Frederick taken thee to the palace to acquaint thee with the royal family.

Ashley became quite displeased with the prince when ye fled in anger. As yet be the prince not entirely forgiven.

For many days to follow, Sir Milford with soldiers came in search of thee. Frederick and Ashley passed days together in the forest attempting to find thee with no success."

Leland said, "Queen Margaret, hath born witness to this ye hath said, yet thought it a ruse to ferret me out,".

"Enough said for the present, Leland. Shall leave thee for be ye in need of rest. Will return another time to speak with thee," said the queen.

Later at the supper table, Prince Frederick asked his father why there were two sentries posted outside of empty chambers.

Not wanting to lie, the king replied, "Frederick the reason for the sentries at the chamber door be a matter of concern solely to me. 'Tis not a subject to be discussed at the table this night."

The king's abrupt reply to the prince's question resulted in utter silence at the table for the duration of the meal.

Later that evening, the king and queen sat chatting in their chambers. The queen asked her husband if he thought it wise to keep Leland's presence in the palace a secret for an entire week.

He replied, "Nay, Margaret; hath it already begun to arouse suspicion. Leland spoke of a friend named Howard, a blacksmith in the village. Upon the 'morrow shall send Sir Milford, garbed as a peasant, to speak with the man. He is to request shelter for Leland unto the night of the feast honoring Earl William's arrival in Penrith.

Should the smithy agree, upon the 'morrow 'neath the cover of darkness, Leland shall be taken to the village. Me physician will visit him daily to insure his recovery.

The village tailor shall be commissioned to fashion garments befitting a Lord, to be worn by the archer the evening of the festivities."

The queen said, "Husband, hath ye thought well upon this. No wonder the love I held within for thee since first lay eyes upon thee many years past hath not waned. Could me hardly wait to see Ashley's expression upon seeing the archer.

Frederick, 'tis indeed much too soon to speak of it, yet out of curiosity, must inquire, should they one day be wed, what will become of Ashley? Surely will she not be expected to reside in a wee cabin in the village!"

The king replied, "Nay, woman! Should it come to that, a manor shall be erected within the woodland; surroundings befitting two with a love for the forest and the hunt."

Chapter 77

Saturday morning, the king and queen sat in their chambers talking. Queen Margaret found herself without a lady-in-waiting.

Godfrey came tapping on the chamber door with the tea. The queen bade him enter. The butler bowed, set the tray on the bed stand then turned to leave.

The queen said, "Godfrey, hold. Lady Winfred hath contracted some sort of malady. Be in need of a lady-in-waiting. Might ye fetch Lady Gloriana to aid me with me garments? Oh, might ye summon Lady Verna to me chambers as well?"

The king then said to the butler, "Godfrey, a bit later will wish to speak with Sir Milford. Shall await the knight in the garden."

Godfrey replied, "Shall fetch the ladies for thee, me Queen; then speak to Sir Milford, Your Majesty."

Godfrey bowed, then left the room.

Minutes later, Lady Gloriana came to help the queen dress for breakfast. The queen was certain Lady Gloriana would be left to wonder why Lady Winfred was not about. To prevent the entire palace from learning what had happened the past few days. The queen chose to explain. Yet not truthfully.

She said, "Lady Gloriana, at present will ye assume the duties of the Lady Winfred. Be she plagued with a malady, yet unknown. Heaven knows when she shall be fit to return."

The lady replied, "Me Queen, 'tis an honor to serve thee. Will do me best to please thee. Shall pray for the quick recovery of Lady Winfred."

Lady Gloriana went about helping the queen dress for breakfast.

The king drank his tea, then left the room to meet Sir Milford in the garden.

Minutes later, Lady Verna tapped on the chamber door. Lady Gloriana hurried to open it.

Entering, Lady Verna curtsied to the queen, then asked why she was summoned.

The queen replied, "There be much to do Verna. Countess Sarah will be arriving soon, and Earl William with Lady Rebecca some days later.

A feast shall be held Saturday next. King Frederick will be announcing the wedding of the prince to Lady Rebecca, and another matter of importance. Hath prepared a list of guests to be notified. The palace is to be spotless. The grounds art to be tended. Know ye well, Verna, the many arrangements to be made.

Oh! A player of bagpipes must be included with the minstrels who art to entertain at the festivities.

A note must be sent to Cardinal Gregory by messenger, requesting His Eminence to come visit prior to the festivities."

Meanwhile, King Frederick went to the garden to speak with Sir Milford. The knight was already there waiting for him. He bowed as the king drew near, then greeted him.

"Good morn, Your Highness. Ye hath summoned me. How might me be of aid to thee?"

His Majesty replied, "G 'day, Milford. Hath thought long on what is to be done with Leland unto the night of the festivities. His presence in the palace might well be discovered, then made known to Frederick and Ashley.

Leland spoke of a friend in the village, a smithy named Howard. Haps he will shelter the archer unto the feast; Saturday next.

Ride to the blacksmith this morn. Speak with the smithy and seek his aid. Should he be a friend indeed, shall ye not be refused.

Must Howard be told the presence of the archer in his abode is to be kept in secret. However, me physician must be permitted to visit."

The knight said, "Your Majesty, shall see to it at once. Should the smithy be receptive to harboring the archer, Leland will be taken to the village this night 'neath the cover of darkness."

Sir Milford bowed, then went to change into garments of a commoner before going to the stables for Titus.

Mounting the steed, he rode to the smithy's.

Howard was shoeing a horse when the knight rode up to the shop. The knight dismounted, tethered his steed, then walked over to the smithy.

He said, "G 'day, Howard. Come to speak to thee of an acquaintance of thyne; an archer named Leland Thomas. Spoke of thee as a friend."

Suspicious, the smithy asked, "Sir, for what purpose come ye by me shop to speak of one haps be not known to me? How come ye by this name?"

Sir Milford said, "Howard, be at ease, the archer requested a message be given thee as to his wellbeing.

An attempt hath been made to slay him. Leland sustained an injury yet be in good stead. Be tended to by the king's physician in the palace."

Howard stopped his work. He stood a 'right with a look of suspicion on his face. He paused to think, then spoke.

He asked, "Why art ye to be trusted to speak true? Be ye not known to me. What position hold ye at the palace to speak for the king?"

Understanding the smithy's concern, Sir Milford replied, "Be commander of the king's forces. Me second in command be Sir Cartwith. The knight hath courted the lady Whitney for a time. Be she employed by Eleanor, the needlewoman here in the village. Whitney be widowed with a daughter, Tiffany. Leland be an avid hunter in the king's forest for many years. In weeks past, hath he tutored the maiden, Ashley, in the use of the bow. Be this all not so?"

Comforted, Howard replied, "Well then, Sir Milford, know ye much of me friend not known to others. Be aware hath he been pursued for his disrespect to the king. Leland spoke of surrendering, for hath wearied of the chase.

I went to his hut this night past to find him gone. Thought him to be cast into the dungeon. 'Tis a relief to hear be he yet in good stead."

Sir Milford said, "Howard, the king requests a boon of thee. The presence of Leland in the palace be known to but a few. For reasons be not permitted to reveal, the king desires his presence to not be detected. Request thyne aid in this.

With thy permission, Leland shall be brought to thy abode this night. The king's physician must be permitted to visit. No one must be aware of Leland's presence in the village.

Come Saturday next, shall come with garments befitting a nobleman for the archer to don. Shall we, then mount a coach and return to the palace.

At a feast in the great hall, King Frederick shall bestow upon the archer the title of Lord Thomas, Keeper of the Loaf.

This hath revealed to thee be said in confidence. Must it not leave thy lips unto it hath come to pass."

The smithy, hearing Leland was safe and was to be given a title, smiled, and said, "Sir Milford, 'tis welcomed news indeed!

His Majesty's request shall be adhered to as ye hath stated. Leland, a dear friend from early childhood, will be made welcome in me abode.

Pledge to thee Sir Knight, no word of this shall be spoken.

Me mate will prepare quarters for the archer."

Sir Milford thanked the smithy, bade him a good day, mounted Titus and returned to the palace to speak with Sir Cartwith.

Finding his subordinate, the commander said, "Sir Cartwith, two soldiers with a cart will be needed this night to bring Leland to the smithy's in the village.

Speak to Robert. He must be told to lower the drawbridge. The men involved in the transport of Leland art to be commanded to speak 'naught of these activities."

Sir Cartwith replied, "Shall see to it, Sir Milford. Will accompany the men to insure all doth go well.

Chapter 78

Sunday morning in chambers, King Frederick was in a discussion of the archer with the queen while she was being tended to by Lady Gloriana. The queen was expressing concern over the embarrassment Leland might be made to suffer; not being accustomed to mingling with royalty.

The queen said, "Frederick, Leland will be quite ill at ease come Saturday eve at the festivities 'mongst our guests."

Irritated, the king replied, "Mercy, Margaret, what might be done of it? The man be a hunter, not a pompous jay."

The queen remained silent for a few minutes, deep in thought, then spoke to her lady-in-waiting.

She said, "Gloriana, shall request a boon of thee. Ye will be permitted to refuse with no consequence. 'Tis understood?"

Lady Gloriana replied, "Yea, Your Highness; what ere it might be, shall not refuse thee."

The queen smiled and said, "Well then. In the village at the residence of the blacksmith, will ye find a man yet in recovery from an injury. His Majesty shall bestow a title upon this commoner at the festivities Saturday next.

Lacking in the social graces, he is to be tutored a bit.

Request thy assistance in this endeavor. Yea, 'tis but a week unto the festivities, yet he is solely to be made to feel at ease when in attendance."

"Shall do me best, Your Highness; and when art these lessons to begin?" asked Lady Gloriana.

"The presence of this man in the village must be kept secret. Thus, upon the 'morrow and each day to follow, will ye go to the village with a soldier as escort.

Must ye both be garbed in peasant attire to avoid suspicion.

Sir Cartwith will ride to the village this morn to advise the smithy of thy arrival and of the purpose for thy visit."

The queen paused, then continued, saying, "Gloriana, at the present, might ye dispense a servant to fetch Sir Cartwith here to me chambers?"

Lady Gloriana thanked the queen for the opportunity to be of service. She curtsied, then left the room.

Lady Gloriana quickly returned and resumed tending to the queen.

The queen felt ill at ease for speaking falsely when she had given Lady Gloriana the reason for Lady Winfred being absent. She thought the maiden deserved the truth.

She said, "Gloriana, this shall reveal to thee must be held in confidence. The reason given thee for Lady Winfred's absence be not true. Hath she been banished from the palace for her involvement in a conspiracy to slay the archer, Leland. The gent ye hath been requested to tutor be the archer."

Shocked, she asked, "Heavens, me Queen! What possessed Lady Winfred to participate in such treachery? 'Tis known be she set a 'back since the arrival of Lady Victoria."

A tapping on the chamber door brought an end to the conversation. Lady Gloriana opened the door, permitting Sir Cartwith to enter.

The knight bowed, greeted the royal couple, then stood waiting for someone to speak.

The queen said, "Good morn, Richard. Hath ye been summoned to be given a task. Lady Gloriana will be visiting with Leland upon the 'morrow, and daily unto next week's end, to tutor the archer a bit in the social graces.

She will be in need of escort. The soldier is to be garbed in peasant attire.

Must ye ride to the village. Speak to the blacksmith. Inform him of her arrival, and the reason for the visits."

"Shall see to it this very morn, Your Highness," replied Sir Cartwith.

The knight bowed, and quickly left the room to fetch his steed. At the knight's request, Gavin instructed one of the stable boys to saddle Sweet Sorrow.

Sir Cartwith thanked the stable boy, mounted the horse, and rode to the village.

Howard was in his shop making a crutch of oak for Leland when the knight rode up to greet him. The smithy returned his greeting.

Howard said, "Good morn, Sir Knight. What hath brought ye to the village? Haps ye come to visit with Whitney?"

Sir Cartwith replied, "Nay, Howard; hath come for a moment to speak with thee. 'Tis odd to see thee laboring upon the Sabbath. What be ye about?"

The smithy said, "Hath thought to fashion a crutch to aid me friend in going about. Hath he managed to hobble to the table this morn yet with much discomfort. Why come ye by?"

The knight replied, "Howard, be aware Leland be with thee here in the village. The Lady Gloriana will come with an escort to visit with Leland. Will they be garbed as villagers to avoid suspicion.

'Tis the desire of the queen for Leland to be tutored a bit in the social graces. The Lady Gloriana be given this task. Pray ye make her welcome."

Howard said, "Indeed, Sir Knight! Sir Milford hath expressed intent to garb me friend in baubles and lace. Will he now be made to prance about as a peacock?

Mercy, what is to become of the lad?

Alas, Sir Cartwith. 'Tis not me position to refuse Her Highness. Me door will be oped to the lady."

"Me thank thee, upon the queen's behalf. Must flee, for hath other matters to tend to. Farewell, good man," replied Sir Cartwith.

Sir Cartwith rode off, leaving the smithy standing with his hands on his hips, his head swiveling to and fro.

Later in the afternoon, Payton, standing watch in the west tower of the castle, shouted to the guards below.

"A coach of four with escort approaches."

Sir Milford, sitting in his room with his paige, heard the sentry. Certain it was the countess, he instructed Bryce to run to the stables and have Gavin saddle Sweet Sorrow and six other horses.

He, then left his quarters, shouting for Sir Cartwith.

The knight came running.

Sir Milford said, "Sir Cartwith, Countess Sarah approaches. Quickly, with six of the cavalry, ride to escort the countess to the palace."

Without replying, Sir Cartwith ran to the barracks.

Sir Milford hurried to inform the royal family sitting out on the terrace, of the approaching coach.

Passing the kitchen, the knight told Godfrey to assemble the staff in the courtyard.

He then continued out to the terrace.

Stepping out onto the terrace, the commander bowed, then spoke.

He said, "Your Highnesses, a coach draws near. Must it be Countess Sarah. Sir Cartwith and the cavalry hath been dispatched to escort Her Ladyship."

The entire group came to their feet. As they walked along the corridor, King Frederick instructed Sir Milford to dispatch a messenger to the residence of Lord Fendril, inviting the chancellor to dinner that night.

Passing the kitchen, the prince instructed Godfrey to set more chairs out on the terrace and prepare refreshments for their guests.

The king, queen and the others stepped out onto the landing at the palace entrance as Sir Cartwith galloped across the courtyard, over the drawbridge, with the six men of the cavalry following in formation.

Nearing the coach, Sir Cartwith broke from the formation to ride beside the coach to greet the passengers.

Sir Cartwith said, "Countess Sarah, Lord Reeves, Lady Juliana, bade thee welcome to Penrith. 'Tis a pleasure to see thee once more."

"Good eve, Sir Cartwith; be ye missed. Must we chat a bit in these days to follow," the countess replied.

"Would pleasure me to do so, dear Countess," said the knight.

By then the cavalrymen had turned their mounts and were leading the coach toward the castle.

Sir Cartwith spurred his steed to take his place at the head of the column.

Entering the castle grounds, Sir Cartwith dismounted and handed the reins of his horse to Gavin.

The cavalry continued on to the stables, followed by the earl's men.

The coach came to a stand at the palace entrance. Sir Cartwith hurried to hold open the door the door of the coach.

Lady Victoria stepped from the landing to greet the countess, then led the guests to the waiting royal family.

Greetings were exchanged.

As the group entered the palace, the queen said, "Should ye wish to refresh thy selves, the servants will escort thee to thy chambers. Might ye then come to the terrace for a bit of refreshment."

The king then spoke saying, "Lord Reeves, hath invited Lord Fendril to our table this night. Shall it afford thee an opportunity to acquaint thyself with the chancellor."

Lord Reeves replied, "Splendid, Your Majesty. There be much in need of discussion."

That evening in the dining hall, the servants came to serve dinner. They returned to the kitchen, snickering.

Mildred asked what had tickled them.

Millicent replied. "Mercy, Mildred. Lord Reeves be donned in a skirt."

Chapter 79

At midmorning the following day, Queen Margaret sat at her desk with Countess Sarah. They were addressing invitations for Saturday's festivities and the wedding to follow. The queen was quite pleased with the countess having already dispatched invitations to family and friends in Scotland.

The queen's list of names was compiled in groups of villages in the realm. Upon completing the notes for a villages, the queen's lady-in-waiting took them to one of the messengers for delivery.

By midday, the task complete, the ladies thought to go to lunch.

About to leave the room, the queen turned to speak to Lady Gloriana.

The queen asked, "Gloriana, hath ye not forgotten thyne appointment in the village?"

Lady Gloriana replied, "Nay, Your Highness. Thought to wait unto hath ye no further need of me then shall be on me way."

The queen and the countess then left the room for the dining hall.

Lady Gloriana went about organizing the chambers a bit before going to change into peasant garments.

After lunch, the diners went to sit on the terrace.

King Frederick and Lord Reeves were engaged in a conversation as to what the ambassador's role was to be at the palace.

Lady Juliana sat fidgeting with little interest for a while, then asked the prince to join her in a walk about the garden.

The prince obliged her.

They walked a bit, then went to sit by the pool. Lady Juliana turned to the prince to speak.

She said, "Might ye hath suspected, me Prince, affairs of state be of little interest to me. A romp about the countryside, however, would be quite entertaining."

The prince replied, "Should it please thee, me Lady, shall request the accompaniment of Ashley, Victoria, and Sir Milford."

Lady Juliana then said, "Splendid, Your Highness! Will there then be three ladies but two men. Might ye not provide me with an escort?"

The Prince replied, "Be ye indeed a vixen, me Lady. Shall speak to Sir Milford. Haps the cavalryman, Donald, will provide thee with a bit of entertainment. Come, shall we see to it."

Prince Frederick and Lady Juliana strolled around the garden for a bit longer, then returned to the terrace.

The prince waited awhile before speaking.

He then said, "Ashley, Victoria, Sir Milford, haps a ride about Penrith this afternoon would be entertaining for Lady Juliana. What say ye?"

The princess said, "A splendid suggestion, brother Frederick. Come ladies, leave us don our riding attire. Will we join ye men in the courtyard."

The ladies went to their quarters to change. The prince and the knight left the terrace to stand at the palace entrance. Prince Frederick turned to speak to the knight.

He said with a smile, "Sir Milford, a spirited steed for Lady Juliana. Hath she requested an escort. Shall it be the cavalryman, Donald. Will he entertain Lady Juliana properly. Oh! Donald must be told the name of the lady he will be escorting."

Sir Milford did not ask for an explanation. He bowed then went to speak to Gavin before going to the barracks to speak to the cavalryman.

The knight then returned to stand beside the prince and wait for the ladies, Donald, and the horses.

Prince Frederick, suspecting what Lady Juliana had in mind when suggesting a horseback ride, thought to alert sir Milford as to what might happen while on their ride.

The prince said, "Sir Milford, Lady Juliana be an excellent horsewoman as ye will soon discover. Donald and the lady be well acquainted for hath they ridden together when in Dumfries. The maiden hath a hearty appetite for male companionship. Thus, must ye not be concerned should the two suddenly bolt out of sight."

Sir Milford remained silent. He simply nodded, displaying a knowing grin.

Gavin, Donald, and a stable boy came from the stables Each with the horses in tow. They waited for the ladies to mount their horses, then handed them their reins.

The men mounted their steeds, then at a walk, the party rode out of the courtyard, down the hillside, onto the road toward Clifton.

As Prince Frederick expected. Upon reaching the bend at the bottom of the hill, Lady Juliana spurred her horse to a gallop.

Her Ladyship shouted to her escort. "Come ye, Donald; shall wager thee, will ye not remain a 'breast of me."

The cavalryman spurred his mount in pursuit of the maiden. Quickly they were out of sight of the others.

Sir Milford and the prince looked at each other, grinning.

Lady Victoria expressed concern.

She said, "Mercy, Lady Juliana be not familiar with the surroundings. Were she to outpace her escort, what will become of the lass?"

The prince replied, "Be at ease, Victoria. 'Tis certain Donald will not lose track of the lady.

Come, shall we continue on to the River Lowther. Will we rest the horses for a bit, then return. Surely will we encounter the two upon returning."

At the river, Sir Milford removed his cloak and spread it out on the bank for the ladies to sit. The knight stood with the prince a bit away, talking.

Sir Milford addressed the prince saying, "Your Highness, upon returning must we kept a keen eye upon the road for the hoof prints of the two steeds. Haps the two rode into the forest."

The prince laughed, and said, "Be not concerned, Sir Milford. Hath they gone to within sight of the huge oak.

Might Leland be at the hunt, he may well bear witness to a bit of foppery."

Sir Milford was amused yet not for what the prince had said, but because, unbeknown to the prince, the archer was safely tucked away in the village.

Later that night at the dinner table, Queen Margaret asked Lady Juliana if she had enjoyed her ride about the countryside.

The maiden replied politely, "Indeed, Your Highness; 'twas quite pleasant. Found meself a bit turned about in the woodland, to be rescued by me gallant escort."

Chapter 80

Tuesday after breakfast, King Frederick and Lord Reeves went to the cabinet room for a meeting with Lord Fendril. The chancellor had not yet arrived.

Prince Frederick left the dining hall to speak with Tom. He was about to take the stairs to his room when Lord Fendril entered the palace. Prince Frederick went to greet him.

The prince said, "Good morn, Lord Fendril; Father with Lord Reeves await thee in the cabinet room."

Lord Fendril replied, "G 'day, Prince Frederick. Pray hath not kept his Majesty waiting too long. Must confess, be me not as brisk a 'foot as in years past."

"Be not concerned, me Lord. 'Twas but moments past, Father and Lord Reeves left the dining hall," said the prince.

"Heavens, me Prince; the servants hurry about with urgency. Haps 'tis best for me to be on me way lest be under foot," said Lord Fendril.

The prince replied, "Must ye forgive the bedlam. The entire palace staff be quite occupied preparing for the festivities of the week's end."

The two men bade each other farewell.

The chancellor hurried down the corridor for his meeting with the king.

Prince Frederick took the stairs to his room in the tower.

Entering the room, he called to his manservant.

Tom came running down the stairs from the room above asking how he might be of service.

The prince replied, "Tom, a bit past midday, see to setting a target at the far end of the garden. For, with the princess thought to practice a bit with the bow."

Tom bowed and left the room. The prince followed close behind.

Nearing the kitchen, Tom ducked in, thinking to visit a bit with Bridget.

Hearing her son's voice, Mildred turned from her work to speak.

She said, "Thomas! Hath ye come for the lass. Leave Bridget be hath she chores yet to complete. Hath ye naught to do but pester the lass? Be gone! Lest me smite thee with me ladle."

Everyone in the room laughed as Tom hurried through the open side door of the kitchen into the courtyard.

Needing help retrieving the target from the arms room and setting it in the garden, Tom went looking for his servant friend, John.

Out on the terrace that afternoon, Queen Margaret sat with Countess Sarah, Lady Victoria, and Lady Juliana, watching the prince and princess launching arrows at the target.

Impressed, Countess Sarah said; "Your Highness, must say Princess Ashley be quite proficient with the bow. How come she by this skill?"

The queen gave her niece a look.

Lady Victoria understood. She knew the queen was not comfortable speaking of the relationship between the princess and the archer with Lady Juliana present.

Lady Victoria quickly volunteered to give Lady Juliana a tour of the palace and the castle grounds.

She and Lady Juliana came to their feet, curtsied, then left the terrace.

The queen and the countess then resumed their conversation.

The queen said, "Countess, Ashley be tutored by an archer from the village. In the process, the princess matured a bit. For, the bowman, a stern task master, demanded obedience.

Sir Milford who bore witness to the many lessons, reported seeing Ashley lying prostrate upon the riverbank, smiting the waters with her palms."

The countess surprised, said, "Heavens, Your Highness! How dared the archer subject the princess to such dastardly treatment. And Sir Milford standing by permitting it to occur?"

The queen replied, "Dear Countess, 'twas not known to the archer that Ashley be a princess. The lass chose to encounter the bowman in the forest garbed as a village maiden."

The countess said, "Your Highness, recall Rebecca spoke of an archer who felled a buck charging the prince. Might he, and this bowman of whom ye speak, be one and the same?"

The queen replied. "Yea, Countess. To then identify the man and draw him out became a tedious endeavor.

Days passed, attempting to arrive at a solution to the problem. With much difficulty, agony for Ashley and hardship for the archer, the situation finally be resolved.

The king and I hath deemed it wise for Frederick, Ashley, and Victoria not to be aware the archer hath now been found. Shall relate to thee the night of the festivities, the reasons for the secrecy."

Shaking her head, the countess responded, "Hath ye no mercy Your Highness? Be left in suspense.

Thought the princess to be a bit melancholy."

The countess hesitated, then continued, saying; "This ye hath revealed to me doth leave me with a bit of wonderment. Thus, shall pose a question to thee. Need ye not reply, might ye so choose.

Doth the princess harbor feelings for this archer?"

The queen smiled, and said, "Countess, be quite impressed with thy perception. Of this ye inquire, however, will be made known to thee at the festivities should ye be alert.

Countess, the night of the festivities, be alert to see Ashley's change in mood, the elation displayed by Frederick and Victoria as well, when Leland enters the great hall accompanied by Sir Milford."

The countess in reply, said; "Will there then be more than one cause for celebration come the week's end, Your Highness. Shall look forward to the night with much anticipation."

The queen asked, "Countess, speak ye of anticipation. How hath fared Rebecca these week's past?"

The countess replied, "Gracious, me Queen; the lass be out to high doh. One moment prancing about singing as a nightingale. T 'other, stomping to and fro, behaving akin to a shrew.

William hath instructed the stable master not to permit the lass to ride without escort for fear she might bolt for Penrith."

Chuckling, the queen said, "Countess, years hath passed, yet ye must too recall quite well those days of uncertainty, waiting to be wed."

The countess replied, "Indeed, Your Highness. Be assured, Rebecca will go sleepless this night for the group art to leave for Penrith in the early morn. Thus, would expect the party to arrive two days hence.

William and Rebecca will be accompanied by brother, Gaelan; Lady Marion, spouse to Lord Reeves; daughter, Lady Allison; and many of William's mates.

She continued saying, "Be forewarned, Your Majesty; William's mates be a spirited lot. Tranquility will not return to the palace unto hath they departed."

"Dear Lady, a bit of foolishness will be a welcomed change. There be little in the way of merriment about herein of late," the queen replied.

The countess said, "Your Highness, take heart for many of the issues which hath plagued thee and thyne of late, may well be resolved the night of the festivities."

Chapter 81

After breakfast the next morning, Queen Margaret and Countess Sarah retired to the sitting room. The queen asked the countess why she had asked for Sir Cartwith to accompany the king to Dumfries.

The countess replied, "Your Highness, when upon our journey to Leeds, William thought it prudent for me to remain in a wee hamlet away from the impending encounter with Oliver.

Me queen, 'twas Sir Cartwith who came to inform me the village of Leeds hath been secured. Passed the knight and I a time, chatting. Found the gent to be delightful, and quite well bred.

Spoke he of a widow woman hath encountered in the hamlet, Skeeby. Must he hath become quite taken with the woman for persuaded the lady to come with a wee one to Penrith. At present, be she in the employ of the seamstress in the village."

The queen said, "Indeed! Hath seen Sir Cartwith riding off with Christy, daughter to our cook, and a tot upon a wee Welch horse.

The lass be garbed in riding attire akin to those fashioned for Ashley, Victoria, and Rebecca by Eleanor, the village needlewoman."

Replying, the countess said, "Must confess, Your Highness, upon seeing Rebecca riding about bearing the garments, became quite envious.

Prince Frederick acquired a rendering of the pattern from the needlewoman and presented it to me upon arriving in Dumfries. With the pattern, a woman in Dumfries created the garments for me as well."

The queen asked, "Countess, upon donning the garments and riding about, hath the men not deemed it a mockery?"

The countess chuckled, and replied, "Dared they not lest they be made to suffer the wrath of their spouses. For, upon me being seen wearing the garments, the ladies hastened to the needlewoman in Dumfries to purchase the like for themselves."

She continued, saying, "Your Highness, might Sir Cartwith be not occupied, thought to ride with him this morn. Desire to see a bit of the village Penrith."

"Sir Cartwith would be honored to ride with thee. Come, shall instruct Godfrey to fetch him to the terrace," replied the queen.

The two ladies walked to the kitchen. Queen Margaret spoke to the butler, then they went to sit on the terrace to wait for the knight.

Minutes later, Sir Cartwith stepped onto the terrace. He bowed, bade the ladies a good morning, then asked the queen how he might be of service.

The queen replied, "Good morn, Sir Cartwith. Countess Sarah hath expressed a desire to ride with thee this morn. Might ye accommodate her?"

Sir Cartwith turned to the countess, and said, "Would be an honor to ride with thee, Countess Sarah. Shall see to the horses."

Speaking to the knight, the countess said, "Hold, Sir Knight. Please, a mild spirited mare; saddled for a man. Must rid meself of these burdensome garments and don me riding attire. Will me be a bit. Shall join thee in the courtyard."

Sir Cartwith bowed and left the terrace to see to the horses.

The two ladies followed: taking the stairs to their chambers.

The countess changed into her riding garments, then went to join Sir Cartwith, waiting in the courtyard.

He assisted the countess into her saddle, mounted Sweet Sorrow; then they left the courtyard at a walk down the hill to the village.

Men bowed and ladies curtsied to the countess as they rode slowly through the village. The countess acknowledged their courtesies with a nod.

At the far end of the village, the countess asked where Whitney might be found.

Sir Cartwith answered, "Your Ladyship, Whitney be employed by the needlewoman at the millinery. Might ye desire to become acquainted with the lady?"

She said, "Indeed, Sir Cartwith. Shall we pause and visit for a bit in passing. Wish to know the lady who may one day be thy spouse."

Tiffany was at the window in the flat above the millinery when the knight and Countess first rode by. Seeing the knight, she hurried out of the flat to stand and wait by the road for them to return.

The riders reined in their horses at the hitching post in front of the millinery.

Sir Cartwith dismounted Sweet Sorrow, tethered his horse, then assisted the countess off the mare.

Tiffany curtsied to the countess, then greeted the them.

She said, "Good morn, Sir Cartwith, your Ladyship. Hath ye come to visit with me mum?"

The knight and the countess returned the child's greeting. Tiffany took both their hands and led them into the millinery.

The ladies, at a table, came to their feet when the three entered. They curtsied to the countess, then waited to be introduced.

Sir Cartwith said, "Good morn, Eleanor, Whitney. Might me introduce to thee, Countess Sarah of Dumfries."

They all exchanged greetings, then Eleanor commented on the workmanship of Countess Sarah's riding garments.

The countess responded, "Eleanor, the woman needed but to follow the pattern ye hath created, set shears to the fabric, then sew the garments together. Ye art the one to be commended."

"Me thank thee, Countess, for thy kindly words. Hath the woman received requests from others for the garments?" Eleanor asked.

The countess said, "Mercy, dear Lady; the poor woman be overwhelmed with requests made by ladies clamoring at the door of her millinery."

Eleanor chuckled, and said, "And here in Penrith as well, Countess. Know not what might hath become of me were it not for Whitney."

The countess, addressing Whitney, said, "Whitney, within a fortnight me daughter, Rebecca shall wed Prince Frederick. Pray ye come join in the celebration as me guest. Haps escorted by Sir Cartwith?"

Whitney replied, "Would be honored, your Ladyship. Might Sir Knight not deem it an imposition to escort me to such a regal affair."

Sir Cartwith stepped in, and said, "Dear Whitney, would escort thee to the ends of the earth should ye so request."

The countess said, "Well then, Whitney, Sir Cartwith, there be no more to be said. Shall we take our leave. Farewell Tiffany, Whitney, Eleanor."

Leaving the village, Sir Cartwith noticed five men riding hard from the east. One with a horse in tow. Drawing near, the knight recognized one as the Duke of Edenhall. He spoke to the countess with urgency.

"Your Ladyship, haps something be a 'foot. Must we make haste. Upon entering the courtyard, dismount, then go directly to thy chambers."

Entering the courtyard, Sir Cartwith instructed one of the guards to assist the countess from her mount, then escort her to her chambers.

The knight then continued on to Sir Milford's quarters, calling out to the commander.

He shouted, "Sir Milford, hath seen the Duke of Edenhall riding upon the road to the castle with four men. Shall inform his Majesty of their approach."

Sir Milford came running out of his quarters fastening his sword about his waist to stand on the drawbridge.

The riders reined in their horses before the knight.

Sir Milford bowed then addressed the duke.

He said, "Good morn, Your Grace. Bade thee welcome. How might I serve thee?"

The old gent replied, "Hath come for a word with His Majesty. Might ye inform the king of me presence?"

Sir Milford turned and walked toward the palace entrance. The duke and his men followed close behind.

Sir Cartwith stepped out of the palace, bowed, then spoke.

He said, "Good morn, Your Grace. King Frederick awaits thee in the throne room."

The group dismounted, tethered their mounts, then followed Sir Milford and Sir Cartwith into the palace.

The king sat on the throne with four soldiers standing nearby.

Entering, the knights took a position in front of the king on either side of the main aisle. King Frederick remained seated.

The duke and his men came to stand before him.

The king addressed the duke saying, "G 'day, Your Grace; what hath brought ye to me door this morn?"

The old gent replied, "Your Majesty, me fear some ill hath befallen Edward. Hath he been absent from the manor since this Wednesday past.

Hath we scoured Edenhall and its surroundings with no success. We then thought to broaden the search. This morn come we upon Edward's steed tethered to a birch beside the road to Penrith. The beast be near death for lack of water."

The king asked, "Indeed! And what gave thee reason to suspect Edward might hath come so far from Edenhall?"

The duke replied, "Your Highness, in an attempt to discover some evidence as to where Edward might hath gone, come upon a letter in his chambers writ by the Princess Ashley. Edward might hath become quite disheartened by the note. Thought haps he rode to Penrith to speak with the princess."

The king recalling the prince speaking of having evidence of men scouring the forest, said, "The marquess hath not been to the palace of late. Haps he thought to visit with Ashley, as ye say, to be then set upon by brigands along the road.

Hath received reports of men roaming about in me forest. Might they well hath been poachers or haps scoundrels.

To avoid an incident, soldiers be dispatched to stand guard at the entrances to the forest. One might hath seen something of significance."

The king turned to the knight, and said, "Sir Cartwith, know ye the men assigned to stand guard at the forest. Fetch them here to the throne room. Shall we inquire."

Minutes later, Sir Cartwith returned with four soldiers. On entering, the men bowed, then stood at attention.

The king addressed them, saying; "Now then ye lads, when at thy posts at the forest, might any of ye seen anyone suspicious passing? Haps so, come forth."

Many moments passed, then one of the soldiers broke ranks to speak.

He said, "Your Highness, haps 'tis of no consequence, yet thought it a bit odd. Quite early one morn a hooded monk a 'foot alone passed. Bade the holy man a good morn. Received no reply.

Me post be, then upon the road to Clifton. Be relieved at midday. The monk be not seen returning unto then."

King Frederick remained silent for several moments before speaking to the soldiers.

He said, "None of ye other men hath come forth to speak, thus would assume the monk be not seen returning."

To the duke, the king said; "Your Grace, a discourteous holy man would well be suspect. Haps this hooded man be a brigand posing as a monk. The horse found tethered to the birch might hath been ridden to Penrith by this fellow. Then seeing the sentry upon the road, he abandoned the horse, and proceeded a 'foot; knowing a monk upon such a fine steed would surely draw suspicion."

The king continuing said "Should this monk be found, haps might he shed some light upon this mystery.

Your Grace, might this well be the course for thee to follow. Be ye in need of assistance in this endeavor, it shall be readily provided. Other than that, know not what more ye might request of me."

The duke thought for a moment, then said, "Your Highness, me thank thee for thy kindly assistance in this matter. Haps it might be best to return to Edenhall and attempt to sort it out. As to the monk, seen a week past, but the Lord may know who and where he might be."

The duke bid the king a farewell, then he and his men left the throne room.

King Frederick ordered the soldiers not to speak of what had transpired within the room then dismissed them; leaving Sir Milford and Sir Cartwith to discuss the matter further.

Sir Milford waited for the soldiers to leave then addressed the king.

"Your Majesty, know ye well who the monk might hath been. The marquess came to Penrith in disguise."

The king replied, "Aye, Milford; yet no robe be found beside the assassin. Must he hath removed it prior to entering the forest.

Sir Cartwith, wait a bit unto 'tis certain the duke and his men hath left the area, then see to dispatching soldiers to search the edges of the forest along the road to Clifton for the robe. Must it be found and destroyed a 'fore 'tis come upon by others then per chance finds its way into the hands of the duke.

Without the robe, the duke will soon reason the monk be the key to the marquess' absence, and 'twas the monk who rode the steed to Penrith."

Sir Cartwith then remembered Master Eldridge, the farmer in Edenhall from whom he had purchased the pony for Tiffany, not speaking well of the marquess.

He thought to bring the ill treatment of the villagers by Edward to the attention of the king.

He said, "Your Highness, when in Edenhall upon an errand some weeks past. Hath occasion to speak with a kindly ole farmer. The gent spoke of the marquess and his henchmen demanding coin for protection from the merchants in the village."

The king replied, "Indeed, Sir Cartwith! 'Tis certain then the Duke be aware of these unlawful activities conducted by his son.

Might it not yet be known to the duke that Floyd, the proprietor at the pub, hath vanished from the village as well. Upon learning of it, he will then conclude Edward hath been pressing Floyd for goodly sums of tribute as well and the man hath wearied of it. Will the Duke surely assume the culprit to be Floyd, disguised as a monk, and leagues away.

Might he well, then abandon the search for his son.

Alas, the duke, long in years, unable to sire another, will be left with no heir to assume the dukedom. One might say 'tis a fitting end for a man who harbored naught but his own interests at heart."

Godfrey entered the throne room and bowed to the king, announcing lunch was about to be served in the dining hall. The king dismissed the butler, then spoke.

The king said, "Ye lads, come join me at the table. Be advised, however, should anyone in the dining hall inquire as to the nature of our meeting with the duke, leave the response to me."

Everyone in the dining hall stood when the king entered with the knights. Sir Milford and Sir Cartwith bowed to the royalty, then waited for the king to take his place at the table before taking their seats.

In the course of conversation at the table, Countess Sarah asked Sir Cartwith why, upon returning to the palace, he had ordered the sentry to spirit her to her chamber. The king responded to the countess.

He said, "Countess, Sir Cartwith exercised a bit of caution, and rightly so. The riders, not immediately known to the knight, became a concern for thy safety.

Fortunately, 'twas the Duke of Edenhall and his men come to visit upon a matter of little consequence.

Upon another matter, Countess, when might we expect the arrival of Earl William?"

The countess replied, "Your Majesty, William thought to leave Dumfries this morn. Should all go well, expect William will arrive in Penrith well past midafternoon upon the 'morrow."

Chapter 82

Prince Frederick did not sleep well that night; anticipating the arrival of Lady Rebecca had left him restless.

At early light, he left his bed, donned a robe and slippers, then called to Tom to draw a bath.

The manservant came scrambling down the stairs from above to do his master's bidding.

Prince Frederick left the room to stroll about the garden. The morning dew wet his slippers, yet he paid it no mind. It was to be a long day for him.

The sun was above the tree line when Tom stepped onto the terrace to inform the prince his bath was ready.

The prince instructed Tom to have Mildred fetch a pot of tea to the terrace, then left the garden to bathe.

After bathing, he donned the garments Tom had laid out for him, then returned to the terrace to sit alone wondering how he was to pass this day.

Minutes later, Christy stepped out onto the terrace, curtsied, asking if the prince would like a bit of sweets with his tea.

The prince replied, "Me thank thee Christy. Nay. Ye may, however inform me when the morning meal is to be served."

Christy curtsied, then went skipping off into the palace to the kitchen.

The prince shook his head smiling; thinking how simple life had been when he was Christy's age.

Some minutes later, Lady Victoria stepped out onto the terrace with a pair of shears in hand. She curtsied, bade him a good morning, then asked what he was doing on the terrace alone.

He replied, "Good morn, Lady Victoria. Alas, hath it been a wretched night. The hours passed slowly. Lay sleepless unto early light. Thus, thought to leave me bed and stroll about the garden for a bit. What be ye about bearing shears so early in the morn?"

Lady Victoria responded, "Thought to fetch a few flowers for a bouquet to present to Lady Rebecca upon her arrival. Would please me for thee to be of aid. Might it serve thee as a distraction for a time."

The prince came to his feet and the two went walking the garden path. Lady Victoria went along cutting the flowers and handing them to the prince to hold.

Having picked enough for a bouquet, she and the prince went to sit beside the pool to chat.

Several minutes later, Godfrey came out to the garden announcing breakfast was about to be served.

Lady Victoria handed Godfrey the bouquet, instructing him to have Mildred put them in water, then she and the prince followed the butler into the palace.

Entering the dining hall, Lady Victoria curtsied to the king, and queen, then she and the prince took their seats at the table.

King Frederick was speaking to Sir Milford.

He was saying, "Milford, Earl William must be greeted properly upon arriving. Six of the cavalry art to be dispatched to meet and escort Earl William and his party to the palace."

"Your Majesty, the sentry's in the towers hath been instructed to sound an alert upon seeing the coach at the bottom of the hill. Will we then dispatch the cavalry, and inform thee of the earl's arrival," replied the knight.

The prince sat silent thinking of how he might quickly pass this day. He was oblivious to the conversation between the king and the knight.

The queen, aware of her son's distraction, waited for the two men to end their conversation then turned to speak to the prince.

She asked, "Frederick, in body be ye here, yet suspect in mind be ye far removed from this table. Pray tell, what might it be doth trouble thee?"

The prince replied, "Mother, hath grown impatient with this waiting. Haps after our meal at midday shall ride north to greet Earl William. Must ye not fret for 'tis me intent to instruct Sir Milford to provide two cavalrymen and Father's standard bearer as escorts."

Countess Sarah, quite aware of the reason for the prince's restlessness, spoke.

She said, "Prince Frederick, suspect 'tis not me husband at the root of thyne anxiety, but another. Doth hearten me however to know ye hold Rebecca so near to thy heart."

"Countess Sarah, the absence of Lady Rebecca hath plagued me since leaving Dumfries. Solely her arrival in Penrith will cure this malady," replied the prince.

Speaking to his father, he then said, "Thus Father, request permission to be excused, for wish to prepare for me ride."

His mother replied in the king's stead, saying, "Frederick, hath ye not yet eaten."

He replied, "Mother, be not concerned. Doth not yet hunger."

With the wave of a hand, the king gave his permission to the prince to leave the table. The prince hurried out of the dining hall to find his manservant.

Princess Ashley bolted from her seat at the table and ran from the dining hall.

Lady Victoria, concerned for the princess, asked to be excused; then followed the princess out of the room.

Countess Sarah, aware of the reason for the discontent of the princess, asked why she had not yet been told the archer had been found and was safe in the village.

The queen replied. "Countess, at present 'tis best for Ashley and Frederick to know naught of it. The night of the festivities will be soon enough. Ashley's tears of sadness will then turn to those of joy."

The countess said, "Hath noted, Lady Victoria be quite attentive to the princess. Would seem hath they a bond expected 'tween siblings rather than mere cousins."

"Yea, Countess. Victoria coming to reside here at the palace hath been a comfort to me. Ashley holds Victoria in her confidence, oft seeking counsel from her in matters of concern. Be they so loving of each other; ye never hear an unkind word pass 'tween the two," the queen replied.

Meanwhile in the kitchen, Tom was helping his mother with the morning meal. He turned to see the prince beckoning to him from the doorway.

Tom left the task at hand to speak to the prince.

Tom asked, "Me Prince, hath ye summoned me. Hath ye an errand wish me to fulfill?"

The prince responded, "Aye, Tom. At midafternoon, go to the stables. Speak to Gavin. Instruct the stable master to saddle Silvermane, and a gentle mare for Lady Rebecca. The mare must bear a sidesaddle.

Bring and tether the two steeds to the hitching post at the palace entrance then come fetch me.

At present, go ye to Sir Milford. Inform the knight hath a need to speak with him. Shall be in wait of him upon the terrace."

Tom bowed to the prince, then quickly went off to fulfill the instructions he had been given.

Prince Frederick then beckoned to Mildred. She came, curtsied and asking how she might be of service.

The prince said, "Mildred, be on me way to the terrace. Might someone come to me with a bit of tea? Sir Milford will soon be joining me. Haps another cup for the knight."

"As ye wish, me Prince. Shall see to it," she replied.

The prince sat alone on the terrace waiting for Sir Milford and the tea. He felt much better than he had earlier, knowing he would not be passing the entire day idlily waiting for Lady Rebecca to arrive.

Godfrey stepped out onto the terrace carrying a tray holding two cups, a pot of tea, and a plate of fresh fruit and tarts. He bowed to the prince, set the tray on the table, then spoke.

He said, "Good morn, Prince Frederick. Upon tidying up the table in the dining hall, noticed ye hath not eaten. Thus, thought ye might desire a bite."

The prince replied, "Good morn, Godfrey. 'Tis very thoughtful of thee. Haps shall partake of it. Might ye thank Mildred for me as well."

The butler bowed, then retreated into the palace.

The prince heard Godfrey and Sir Milford exchange greetings as they passed each other in the corridor.

Moments later, Sir Milford stepped out of the palace, bowed, then greeted the prince.

The knight said, "Good morn, me Prince. Tom came to inform me ye hath a desire to speak with me. How might me be of aid?"

"Sir Milford, come set ye. Hath thought to ride north this afternoon to greet Earl William's party. Be in need of escort. Might ye assign two of the cavalry and the standard bearer to the task?" asked the prince.

Sir Milford replied, "Shall see to it, me Prince. Might Tom advise me when ye art about to depart. The men will await thee in the courtyard."

Chapter 83

At midafternoon, Prince Frederick went to change into more regal attire. Satisfied with his appearance, he called to Tom.

The manservant hurried down the stairs and spoke.

Tom said, "Me Prince, would seem be ye prepared to depart. Shall see to the horses and await thee in the courtyard."

The prince said, "Tom, Sir Milford awaits word of me departure. Speak to him."

Several minutes later, Prince Frederick left his room for the courtyard. The standard bearer and the men of the cavalry stood waiting.

Tom held the reins of the horses. Prince Frederick mounted Silvermane and took the reins of the mare from Tom and joined the waiting cavalrymen and the standard bearer, the prince shouted to the sentry in the tower.

"Peyton, a keen eye upon the road for the king's standard. When in sight, inform Sir Milford of Earl William's arrival."

The sentry waved, acknowledging the prince's command as the group rode out of the courtyard down the hill to the road heading north.

Prince Frederick and the others rode for the better part of an hour before stopping. An open stretch of road lay before them. The prince thought it an excellent place to watch for Earl William and his entourage.

He ordered the men to dismount, and rest at ease. The standard bearer drove the staff of the king's pendant into the ground beside the road; then took a deck of cards from his saddlebag and the men sat to play a game of maw.

The prince stood pacing to and fro, impatiently, as the hours grew late. He began to wonder perhaps the earl had not left Dumfries as planned, when suddenly, in the distance, he heard the rumbling of wheels on the rutted road.

The men came to their feet to stand beside the prince and wait for the coach to come into view.

Sir Cadwalter, riding at the head of the column of cavalry and the four coaches, saw the men standing in the middle of the road. Not certain as to who they might be, he called the column to a halt.

Prince Frederick recognized the leading coach as that of Earl William. He quickly took hold of the mare's reins, mounted Silvermane, and spurred his steed to a gallop.

Sir Cadwalter, seeing the rider coming near, shouted; "Be alert, ye lads; a rider approaches. Hold! Gads Zeus, 'tis Prince Frederick with a spare mount in tow."

The door of Earl William's coach flew open. Lady Rebecca did not wait for assistance. She jumped from the coach, running toward the approaching rider.

Prince Frederick reined his steed to a halt beside Lady Rebecca. He vaulted onto the road and took Lady Rebecca in his arms to greet her with a kiss.

The prince's escort and the earl's cavalry, seeing the show of affection, cheered boisterously.

The prince then spoke to the Lady.

He said, "Love, would seem a year hath passed since last held thee thus. Come; ride with me. Must greet thy sire and thyne Uncle Gaelan properly."

Prince Frederick helped Lady Rebecca onto the mare, mounted his steed, and they rode, side by side, back to the earl's coach.

The prince extended his greetings to the earl, Lord Gaelan, and the children before riding with Lady Rebecca to join Sir Cadwalter at the head of the column.

Prince Frederick exchanged greetings with the knight.

Sir Cadwalter motioned for the column to continue on.

The cavalrymen escorting the prince joined the column as it passed. The king's standard bearer took the lead.

The sun had fallen to the tree line, casting a shadow across much of the hill below the castle, when Peyton, standing guard on the ramparts, saw the column coming from the north.

He turned and shouted, "Hear ye, a column and coaches approach, led by the king's standard bearer. Inform Sir Milford."

Sir Milford, sitting with Sir Cartwith in his quarters, heard the sentry cry out.

He quickly instructed Sir Cartwith to assemble six of the cavalry to ride and escort the column to the palace.

Sir Cartwith hurried from the room, followed by Sir Milford, going to inform King Frederick of Earl William's arrival.

Prince Frederick, aware time would be needed for everyone to assemble in the courtyard to greet the earl and his party, asked Sir Cadwalter to bring the column to a halt and wait to be escorted to the castle.

Sir Cadwalter complied.

Family and friends in the three coaches behind that of the earl's were already in a festive mood. They were laughing at remarks being passed to and fro.

Three of the male passengers wearing kilts, bolted from the coaches and began doing the jig, to the delight of the others.

Lady Rebecca displayed a bit of embarrassment; attempting to apologize for her kin, and friends of the earl.

She said, "Me Prince, must ye forgive the lot for their rowdy behavior. Hath they wearied, and must admit, hath they consumed a goodly portion of grog."

The prince replied, "No need, Rebecca. A bit of foppery by thy sire's mates will ensure the festivities shall long be a memorable occasion."

Meanwhile, the members of the cavalry, led by Sir Cartwith, had ridden out of the palace grounds toward the waiting column below.

After arriving, and exchanging greetings, the king's escort led the column up the hill toward the palace.

At the moat, the king's cavalry, and that of the earl, fell to either side of the road; permitting the standard bearer, followed by Sir Cartwith, Sir

Cadwalter, Prince Frederick with Lady Rebecca, and finally the coaches, to pass into the courtyard.

The standard bearer and the knights reined in their steeds a bit beyond the palace entrance, as did the prince, Lady Rebecca, and the coaches.

Prince Frederick dismounted and helped Lady Rebecca from the mare as Lady Victoria stepped down from the palace entrance to greet Lady Rebecca and present her with the flowers.

Earl William stepped from the coach, as did all the occupants of the coaches, which led to bedlam for several minutes as loved ones reunited.

Introductions and greetings were exchanged.

The guests were, then escorted to their quarters by servants, to freshen up a bit before reuniting again in the great hall to chat before the evening meal.

Chapter 84

Lady Rebecca was in her room the next morning, dressing for breakfast. Lady Juliana was in attendance. She asked her cousin if she had been behaving these days past.

Lady Juliana replied a bit sheepishly, "Rebecca, here at the palace, hath been quite the Lady. However, t 'other day when upon a ride with others and Donald along as escort, spurred me steed to a gallop, leaving the others behind, soon to lose meself in the woodland. 'Twas fortunate Donald gave pursuit to find me. The others continued on. We two thought to remain and await their return."

Lady Rebecca shook her head, and said, "Juliana, might ye one day be the death of me. Doth me not expect thee to pass thy days in Penrith as a nun in a cloister. Yet, bear in mind thyne actions reflect heavily upon me."

Her cousin replied, "Be at ease, Rebecca. Shall be mindful of thy position, and the consequences of me ill behavior. Thus, pledge to thee, when arranging an encounter with a man, caution shall prevail."

Lady Rebecca emitted a deep breath and said, "Pray, dear cousin, will ye one day soon be courted by a proper suitor, and wed, setting aside these mischievous activities."

Meanwhile, in his tower room, Prince Frederick had already dressed and was waiting to go to breakfast. Tom went about his chores.

The prince asked him to go below and listen at Lady Rebecca's door for stirring.

Tom left the room, to soon return; informing the prince he had heard two ladies engaged in conversation.

The prince waited a few minutes before leaving the room to tap on Lady Rebecca's chamber door.

Lady Juliana opened the door and curtsied to the prince. She, then wished him a good morning.

The prince replied, "Good morn, Lady Juliana. Might ye inform Lady Rebecca shall await her in the sitting room below?"

Lady Rebecca, hearing the voice of the prince, quickly called out to him.

"Me Prince, might ye linger a bit? Shall be but a few moments. Need but to don me slippers."

The prince did not reply but stood waiting as the Lady had requested. True to her word, seconds later, she stepped out of the room into the hall closing the door behind her.

Lady Rebecca came against the prince, pushed him to the wall, put her arms around his waist, pressed herself to him, and kissed him passionately. The prince returned her kiss. Breathing heavily, the prince then whispered in her ear.

He said, "Rebecca, be ye truly a temptress, arousing me with thy passion. These seven nights to pass unto we be as one, will seem an eternity."

Still clinging to him, she replied, "Indeed, me love; be forewarned. Shall not leave thee be this week hence. 'Tis me intent for our first night together to be one shall we long remember."

"Enough, Rebecca; for 'tis an effort to retain me sanity. Come, will we descend the stairs to the sitting room and wait for the others," said the prince.

The two sat chatting; soon to be joined by Lady Victoria. They bade the lady a good morning.

Lady Rebecca asked about Princess Ashley.

Lady Victoria replied. "The princess be a bit disturbed this morn. Will be taking her morning meal in chambers. Haps we might devise an activity for after midday to distract her from her melancholia."

The prince said, "A ride about the countryside might entice her. Lady Victoria, after breakfast speak to her. If need be, insist."

"A splendid suggestion, me Prince. Will see to it," Lady Victoria replied.

Chapter 85

Well into the afternoon, King Frederick sat with Earl William out on the terrace, chatting over a ewer of wine. The earl asked the king where the young ones had gone. The king replied. "Frederick and Milford hath accompanied the ladies upon a ride about the countryside. Thought they to afford Ashley a bit of pleasure. Hath she been a bit out of sorts of late."

"Your Majesty, when in Dumfries spoke ye of Princess Ashley and her involvement with an archer. What hath become of it?" asked the earl.

The king replied, "Alas, there be much confusion, and much in the way of treachery involved in setting it a 'right.

An attempt be made by a vindictive noble to slay the archer. Dare say, the bastard be no longer 'mongst the living.

In the encounter, Leland sustained an injury. This shall relate to thee bore witness to meself. The archer with the arrow firmly lodged in his thigh, managed to retrieve his bow, and let fly a shaft of his own; slaying the assailant."

The earl said, "Your Majesty, 'tis a grizzly tale indeed. Yet surely the slain noble be missed.

Were he me kin, would scour the forests and the villages for the man. And what hath become of the archer?"

The king replied, "The noble indeed be sought as we speak. Yet, 'tis certain will he never be found.

In the village from whence he came be he known for his treachery, thus the townspeople surely hath refused to aid in the search.

As to Leland, be he well-tended to by a trusted friend in the village. Ashley nor Frederick be not yet aware the archer be at rest in the village; and for good reason.

Two days past, the noble's sire came to the palace inquiring of his son. Might he hath requested to speak to Frederick or Ashley. Knowing naught of where the man might be they would hath replied with honesty."

"Your Highness, for what reason might the man expect Princess Ashley or Prince Frederick to know the whereabouts of his son?" asked the earl.

The king replied, "The noble's sire be aware his son pursued Ashley with a passion; with intent to win her hand. Might he suspect ill befell the man while on a visit to Penrith."

The earl said, "Your Majesty, when on the road to Penrith, Rebecca spoke of Princess Ashley being quite displeased with Prince Frederick for a misdeed which caused the archer to flee the palace quite distempered, for thought he hath been played the fool."

The king nodded his head and said, "Indeed! 'Twas a mishap of grave proportions. Unto that night Leland thought Ashley to be a village maiden. For, when with Leland in the forest, she and Frederick be garbed as peasants.

Upon the archer being escorted into the dining hall by Frederick, all went awry.

Leland, seeing Ashley at the table with Margaret, thought the entire occurrence to be but a pretense. Ired, Leland then fled in a most discourteous manner.

In an attempt to correct the error made by Frederick, come morn, ordered Milford to assemble a party to search for the archer.

Leland then thought he be pursued and to be punished for his insult to the crown.

Leland be not a fool. Being an accomplished hunter, and quite clever in the art of concealment, he managed to evade the soldiers for weeks.

He then dispatched a note to Milford, stating he hath wearied of the chase and would surrender in a clearing by the river in the forest at mid morn, the day next.

Rode to the forest with Milford, determined to convince the archer we meant him no harm.

'Twas then, bore we witness, to the noble's dastardly attempt to slay the bowman."

The earl now aware of the feelings the king had for the archer, said, "Your Highness, suspect ye hold this young man in high regard. Yet, what might become of this hath passed 'tween the bowman and Princess Ashley?"

The king replied, "Earl William, Ashley would welcome being courted by the archer, in the wink of an eye. 'Tis Leland who must be assured the feelings Ashley hath for him be sincere."

The earl asked, "When might me be afforded the pleasure of being acquainted with this archer?"

His Majesty replied, "Being a villager, 'twas certain be he a bit lacking in propriety. Thus, Lady Gloriana, Margaret's lady-in-waiting, hath been with Leland these days past, tutoring him in the social graces.

Upon the 'morrow, Milford will fetch Leland from the village and escort him to the palace. Leland shall be introduced to thee in the great hall at the festivities.

Prior to announcing the nuptials of Frederick to Rebecca, shall bestow the title of Lord, Keeper of the Loaf, upon Leland.

Earl William, at the festivities, be attentive. For, by Ashley's expression upon seeing Leland entering the great hall, will ye be aware of the depth of her feelings for the man.

The king paused, then said, "Ole friend, shed ye no tears for the Duke's loss of his son; for be not deserving.

Recall when ye dispatched a message to me requesting aid in thy campaign against a common foe?

I went immediately to the Duke of Edenhall to solicit his involvement. The noble refused, stating he could foresee no profit in the venture. As be the father; so be the son. The Duke of Edenhall and the marquess be the two of whom hath spoken."

The earl said, "Your Majesty, surely would ye not hath permitted the princess to wed such a scoundrel. Yet ye chose not to object to the marquess courting the princess."

The king replied, "Aye, 'twas but a means to avoid a confrontation with the duke. Indeed, a viper slithering about me palace would never hath been permitted."

Chapter 86

Early the morning of the festival, carts came to the palace delivering fresh fruit, produce, assorted meats, and fowl.

Immediately after breakfast, the kitchen staff began baking breads and creating fancy pastry for the evening feast. Servants and gardeners went about grooming the palace grounds and gardens. Tables and seating for guests were arranged in the great hall. The hall itself was being decorated in regal splendor. An air of excitement grew throughout the palace as the day progressed in anticipation of the evening's event.

Late in the afternoon, Sir Milford, with Bryce in attendance, donned his finest attire. Satisfied with his appearance, he sent his paige to the stables with instructions to have a coach brought to his quarters. The knight followed Bryce out the door to sit and wait for the coach.

Some twenty minutes later, the coach came to a stand at the knight's quarters. Sir Milford mounted the coach and instructed the coachman to take him to the smithy's in the village.

Howard, hearing the coach approach, hurried to open his cabin door, and stood to wait for the knight on the landing.

Seeing the coach come to a stand at the blacksmith's, some of the villagers in the street came to gather around the coach in wonderment.

Sir Milford stepped from the coach to be greeted by the smithy.

The knight extended his hand to the blacksmith and returned his greeting.

He said, "Good eve, Howard. Hath come to fetch Leland to the palace. Pray the gent be in good stead."

The Smithy replied, "Bade thee enter, Sir Knight. Hath Leland been well tended to by the king's physician. However, doth he yet bear a bit of a limp.

Lady Gloriana hath been about these days past, tutoring Leland in a bit of propriety. However, Leland doth yet express concern, fearing be he ill prepared for this night's festivities.

As to the lad's appearance, be he groomed handsomely; akin to royalty."

Leland stepped out of his room bearing a sheepish grin, feeling uncomfortable in his well-tailored garments.

Greeting the knight, Leland said;. "Good eve, Sir Milford. Must confess to thee, harbor a bit of discomfort bearing this finery. Yea too, fear me lack proper manners will make me out the fool this night."

Sir Milford chuckled, and said, "Good eve, Leland. Must say, present ye a stately figure. The nobles will not be certain whether to extend hands to thee or bow.

As to when be ye 'mongst the Lords, Ladies, and dignitaries, hath found it prudent to but smile, nod me head in agreement, and speak solely when required.

Fear not, Leland, will ye fare well. Come, leave us return to the palace. Shall we set in me quarters at leisure to await the commencement of the festivities."

The two men bid Howard a farewell and stepped out to the waiting coach. The villagers who had gathered began to cheer as Sir Milford helped Leland into the coach. The cheering continued as the coach made its way back to the palace.

A bit later, many other coaches began arriving bearing nobles and dignitaries. Villagers stood along the roadway, waving to the occupants as they passed.

Lords and Ladies, dressed in their most elegant attire, began trickling down from their chambers above.

Over the sound of music being played by the minstrels, the nobles gathered in groups and engaged in conversation.

Ladies-in-waiting, having attended to their mistresses, were free to join the king's knights waiting in the great hall.

At the appointed hour, guards at the entrance to the great hall threw open the doors.

Lady Verna, standing to the side of the main aisle, began hammering her staff to the floor, announcing the titles and names of the guests as they entered.

When all the guests had entered and were seated, Lady Verna left her position and walked the corridor to the king's entrance to stand and wait.

Bryce waited attentively at the front entrance of the palace. Seeing Lady Verna pass, he ran to Sir Milford's quarters.

Bryce, tapping on the commander's door and given permission, entered to see Leland sittin on the knight's cot.

Bryce said, "Sir Milford, King Frederick and his party will soon be entering the great hall."

The knight thanked Bryce and dismissed him.

Sir Milford, assisting Leland, left his quarters and walked the archer to enter the palace and sat on the bench beside the entrance.

The minstrels continued playing their instruments while the guests engaged in polite conversation.

Lady Verna entered the hall through the king's entrance, leading King Frederick with the queen on his arm, followed by Prince Frederick with Princess Ashley, then Earl William, Countess Sarah, and Lady Rebecca.

Lady Verna paused at the entrance and hammered her staff to the floor, calling for silence; then announced the arrival of the royal family, and their honored guests.

She then walked the main aisle to take a position beside the main entrance to the hall.

Those in attendance cheered as the royalty filed into the great hall.

The king took his seat at the head of the table; the queen beside him. Prince Frederick sat beside the king, Princess Ashley beside her mother. The others in the king's party waited for the royal family to be seated before they took their assigned places at the table.

Princess Ashley was not a willing participant in the festivities. Earlier she had voiced objection to attending, still a bit at odds with brother Frederick, and still melancholy over the shattered relationship with her beloved archer. She had only relented after being commanded to do so by her father.

Minutes later, King Frederick came to his feet, signaling to Lady Verna.

The Mistress of Revels stepped out from her position beside the entrance into the center aisle of the great hall.

Hammering the staff, she held firmly in her hand to the floor, she stood waiting for the hall to grow silent before speaking loudly.

She shouted, "Your Majesties, Lords, Ladies, invited dignitaries; present to thee Sir Milford, commander of the king's forces, and Master Leland Thomas."

The two men left the bench and stepped through the main entrance to the great hall, then walked together down the aisle to kneel before the king.

King Frederick came from behind the table to stand between the two kneeling men. He lay one hand on Leland's shoulder, and the other on Sir Milford's.

Princess Ashley could not believe her eyes. She had all she could do to contain herself.

Queen Margaret quickly took her hand, fearing her daughter might bolt and run to the archer, interrupting her father.

The princess turned to hug her mother with tears falling to her cheeks.

The prince stood bewildered; unable to utter a word.

King Frederick waited a moment, then spoke.

He said, "Lords, Ladies, Dignitaries, invited guests! Here before thee art two gallant men. Sir Milford, Captain of the king's forces. A man of courage who once took an arrow to spare me life.

Sir Milford, thy devotion in service to the crown hath afforded thee a boon. Speak, Sir Knight. What hath thee in mind that would please thee?"

The knight, speaking humbly, said, "Your Majesty, all that I desire, doth ye provide. However, there be another to whom shall request this boon be given.

Mother Tate and daughter hath served Princess Ashley well these weeks past. Sadly, the woman's son, Jarin be yet imprisoned. The family be deserving of the king's mercy. Request the lad be permitted to return to his kin."

Without hesitation, the king replied, "Granted, Sir Milford; and to prevent the lad from once more being tempted to lay hands upon a steed of another, shall he be given one of his own."

The great hall came alive with the clapping of hands and cheers. The king raised his hand calling for silence, then continued speaking.

He said, "Now then, as to this other good fellow. This man of righteousness once placed hisself in grave peril, stepping forth to spare Prince Frederick from a charging stag.

Leland Thomas, for this deed, and others ye hath rendered to the crown, shall this night bestow upon thee the title of Lord Thomas, Keeper of the Loaf.

Ere be in thy debt, lads. Rise, Sir Milford, Lord Thomas; to be honored."

The occupants in the great hall once again came alive with the clapping of hands, and cheers.

King Frederick waited several minutes for the revelry to subside before he raised his arms, once more calling for silence.

The king said, "Yet another cause for jubilation be forthcoming here in the palace. There shall be a celebration of a great event in Penrith upon the coming of this next week's end.

Frederick, Lady Rebecca, come stand before our guests."

Sir Milford and Leland came to their feet, and stepped to either side of the center aisle, leaving a place between them for the prince and Lady Rebecca.

King Frederick waited for the prince and his lady to stand before him, then continued speaking.

"With me blessing, and that of Earl William of Dumfries, Cardinal Gregory shall perform a ceremony joining Prince Frederick and Lady Rebecca, daughter to Earl William, in Holy Wedlock. Come, leave us rejoice!"

Once again, the guests clapped and cheered. Queen Margaret let loose of Princess Ashley's hand.

The princess hurried from behind the table to stand beside her beloved Leland.

Taking his hand in hers, she whispered to him with much emotion.

"Me beloved, hath thought ye lost to me, forever. These many weeks hath been in agony! This moment hath turned to joy. Might ye love me but a portion of the love me bear for thee, shall be content."

Leland replied, "Confess to thee, dear one, hath ye endeared thyself to me as no other. Might ye hath been gone from me forever, fear me days could not endure."

With a bit of concern, the princess said, "Leland, upon entering the hall with Sir Milford, noted thy steps not to be firm. Suspect hath ye sustained some sort of injury."

"Me love, shall we speak of it another day. Must we dwell upon the present, and pass this night in merriment," Leland replied.

Lady Rebecca, seeing the princess rush to stand beside Lord Thomas, found herself quite confused. She requested an explanation from the prince in a whisper.

"Me Prince, be left quite bewildered. Recall when in Dumfries spoke thee of Princess Ashley's discontent oer the loss of her beloved archer. Yet, here she be, this night, beside another, bearing an expression of great joy."

The prince laughed, and replied, "Dear Rebecca, Lord Thomas standing beside Ashley, and Leland, the archer who spared me from the charging stag, be one, and the same. Would seem me love, me sire hath seen fit to bestow a title upon me dear friend."

Lady Rebecca said, "Thy sire must be commended. Leland be well deserving of a title for aiding thee in thy moment of peril.

Me Prince, be aware, me fondest dreams will soon be a reality, and Princess Ashley, being reunited with the archer, hath heightened me elation two-fold this wondrous night."

Needless to say, Edward, the Marquess of Edenhall; and Lady Winfred, the former lady-in-waiting to Queen Margaret; were not in attendance that festive night nor would they be present at the wedding ceremony.

Princess Ashley was left to wonder what lie ahead.

Printed in the United States
By Bookmasters